R. Barri Flowers is an a
crime, thriller, mystery and r
three-dimensional protagonists, ~~~~~~ piots, unexpected
twists and turns, and heart-pounding climaxes. With an
expertise in true crime, serial killers and characterising
dangerous offenders, he is perfectly suited for the Heroes
line. Chemistry and conflict between the hero and heroine,
attention to detail and incorporating the very latest
advances in criminal investigations are the cornerstones
of his romantic suspense fiction. Discover more on popular
social networks and Wikipedia.

New York Times and *USA Today* bestselling, award-winning
author **Lisa Childs** has written more than eighty-five
novels. Published in twenty countries, she's also appeared
on the *Publishers Weekly*, Barnes & Noble and Nielsen
Top 100 bestseller lists. Lisa writes contemporary romance,
romantic suspense, and paranormal and women's fiction.
She's a wife, mum, bonus mum, avid reader and less avid
runner. Readers can reach her through Facebook or her
website, lisachilds.com

MISSISSIPPI MANHUNT

R. BARRI FLOWERS

LAST MISSION

LISA CHILDS

MILLS & BOON

First Published in Great Britain 2024
by Mills & Boon, an imprint of HarperCollins*Publishers* Ltd
1 London Bridge Street, London, SE1 9GF

www.harpercollins.co.uk

HarperCollins*Publishers*
Macken House, 39/40 Mayor Street Upper,
Dublin 1, D01 C9W8, Ireland

Mississippi Manhunt © 2024 R. Barri Flowers
Last Mission © 2024 Lisa Childs

ISBN: 978-0-263-32243-9

0824

MISSISSIPPI MANHUNT

R. BARRI FLOWERS

In memory of my cherished mother, Marjah Aljean, a devoted lifelong fan of Mills & Boon romance novels, who inspired me to excel in my personal and professional lives. To H. Loraine, the true love of my life and best friend, whose support has been unwavering through the many terrific years together; and Carole Ann Jones, who left an impact on me with her incredible talents on the screen; as well as the loyal fans of my romance, mystery, suspense and thriller fiction published over the years. Lastly, a nod goes out to my amazing editors, Allison Lyons and Denise Zaza, for the wonderful opportunity to lend my literary voice and creative spirit to the Heroes line.

Prologue

Nikki Sullivan was admittedly bored to death on this summertime Saturday night as she paced lazily around her cozy, minimally furnished third-story apartment in Gulfport, Mississippi. An artist, one year removed from receiving a Bachelor of Arts degree from the University of Mississippi, she wasn't especially in the mood to do any canvases. She was single again after kicking her cheating and financially strapped boyfriend, Felix Kovell, to the curb two weeks earlier and was the better for it. She debated whether or not to call her best friend, Brigette Fontana, to see if she wanted to hang out or something. Brigette was currently in a relationship with Gavin Lynley, whom Nikki found to be incredibly good-looking and otherwise drenched in masculinity, while ever attentive to his girlfriend. But one would never know these admirable qualities in the man, based on Brigette—who was stunning herself—seemingly taking him for granted while having a roving eye on other guys, believing there was more than enough of her to go around. And around again whenever Gavin wasn't looking. Or was otherwise preoccupied. Though Nikki felt bad for him, she thought it wasn't her place to come between them and expose Brigette. Much less suggest to him that he could do better than her in a partner. Even if he could.

He'll find out sooner or later and then can decide for himself, Nikki told herself, fantasizing that maybe they could even wind up together someday—assuming things didn't work out between him and Brigette. Before she could call her friend, having lifted the cell phone from the back pocket of her midrise skinny jeans, Nikki received a call from Brigette instead.

"I was just thinking about you," Nikki confessed truthfully, feeling a tad guilty as well in thinking about Gavin in romantic terms.

"Hopefully, good thoughts," Brigette joked, none the wiser.

"Of course," Nikki claimed, sitting on her leather sofa, folding her legs beneath her.

"So, what are you up to?"

"Not much. You?"

"I was supposed to go out with Gavin, but something came up and he canceled." She muttered an expletive in displeasure.

"Sorry to hear that," Nikki said, and truly meant it. But she knew that Gavin worked in corrections and sometimes, maybe more often than not, duty called. Even when he might have wished otherwise.

"Doesn't mean I need to sit here and mope about it," Brigette grumbled. "Let's go out and have some fun."

"What did you have in mind?" Nikki switched the phone to her other ear deliberately. "We could hang out here and watch some TV," she suggested. Or not.

"I'd rather do a few shots and some dancing," her friend countered. "Are you game?"

Nikki considered it for a moment or two before realizing how persuasive Brigette could be. Not to mention feeling antsy herself in wanting to get out of the stuffy apartment. Both were twenty-three, with Nikki having reached that age exactly two weeks ago. "Count me in," she agreed.

"Cool. I can be at your place in ten minutes or less."

"I'll be ready," Nikki promised and disconnected. She stood and shut her blue eyes for a moment as Nikki pulled her long light blond hair out of the low ponytail it was in, before changing into what she believed to be more suitable clothes for going out.

When Brigette arrived in her white Audi A3—recently purchased after the Arkansas State University graduate landed a job as an event coordinator with a prestigious public relations agency—Nikki hopped in. Taking one look at her gorgeous friend, who had bold apple-green eyes, mounds of wavy raven hair and a stunning body to kill for, Nikki found herself somewhat envious and sad at the same time that Brigette never seemed to appreciate what she brought to the table as a person, and could lose if she wasn't careful.

"So, where are we going?" Nikki asked coolly.

"I know the perfect place," Brigette answered evasively, and took off.

Nikki chuckled, ill at ease. "You're scaring me." She wasn't sure if it was from the speed at which her friend was driving, the mystery of where they were headed, or both.

"Really?" Brigette laughed and seemed to go even faster down the narrow street. "Where's your sense of adventure, girl?"

"Guess I'm about to find out," she relented, sucking in a calming breath.

They drove to a nightclub on Pickford Street called Johnnie's Shack in a seedy part of town, again giving Nikki some fresh concern. "You sure about this?"

"It'll be fine," Brigette promised. "Relax. I've been here a couple of times. We won't stay long."

"Okay." Nikki followed her friend's lead this time and went inside, where they did some tequila shots and then stepped onto a small dance floor and danced together to an upbeat song, before a tall, muscular man joined them and danced with them. He was in his early thirties and not too hard on the eyes, with defined features, dark eyes, medium-length brown hair in a windblown pompadour and an aquiline nose. He wore a multicolored plaid shirt and black distressed jeans.

He flashed a crooked smile and said affably, "I'm Perry."

Brigette smiled back flirtatiously. "I'm Brigette and this is my friend Nikki."

"Nice to meet you ladies." He grinned again and continued to move his Chukka boots to the music. "Hope you don't mind if I dance with you?"

Though Nikki's radar suddenly went up that he was being a bit too friendly and getting in their space—or putting it simply, he was bad news—Brigette apparently felt just the opposite, seemingly forgetting all about the fact that she had a boyfriend in Gavin, and told Perry enthusiastically, "Why not?"

After leaving the dance floor ten minutes later, he joined them at their table for more drinks, but didn't try to put the moves on either of them. Nikki still felt that something was off with the man, even if she couldn't quite put a finger on it in so many words, and convinced a reluctant Brigette that it was time to go. With no invitation for Perry to join them. When he thankfully put up no argument, remaining at the table as they left, Nikki thought they were home free of the potential threat. It was only when she began to feel light-headed in the dimly lit parking lot, and noticed the same with Brigette, that it became painfully obvious they had been drugged.

By who? Perry?

Nikki had her answer, as she watched the man in question picking Brigette up off the ground, where she had collapsed, and tossing her like a sack of potatoes in the back of a black Ford E-250 Super Duty cargo van. Then he did the same to her as, barely able to stand on wobbly legs, Nikki was unable to resist him before she passed out in his muscular arms. The last thing to enter her mind was whether or not she or Brigette would survive the night and the monster who had taken them against their will in a manner reminiscent of the serial killer who had been on the prowl in town.

PERRY EVIGAN COULDN'T help but chuckle with delight as he drove his latest captives back to the house he lived in on Robinson Road. Sitting on two acres of grassy land, it was far enough away from neighbors to allow him to come and go freely without attracting too much attention. He'd been planning on drugging and bringing back a single person for his trouble. He hadn't counted on two women for the price of one for him to have his way with before killing them and disposing of them as he had his other victims. But there they were, ripe for the taking like apples off the tree—for which he was only too happy to oblige.

Admittedly, he could tell that the one calling herself Nikki was suspicious of him from the start. For a minute there, he thought with her watching him like a hawk, he'd never get the chance to spike their drinks with gamma-hydroxybutyrate. Thankfully, her attractive friend Brigette was more amenable to them hanging out together—even to the point of allowing him to buy the next round of drinks and pick them up—which, unfortunately, would prove to be a big error in judgment, as both women would soon regret having ever laid their pretty eyes on him once he was done with them. Something told him they were already regretting this, as he glanced at the two still-unconscious women lying in the back of the van. It had been almost too easy to slip the GHB into the drinks and then watch coolly as they sipped innocently on them while laughing at his stale jokes to keep them occupied. All he needed to do was let the two leave of their own accord for all to see and then pretend to leave casually on his own afterward and abduct them as they passed out, with no one being the wiser. He would come back later for the vehicle they drove in to the bar.

Arriving at the two-story, two-bedroom Greek Revival-style house with a shed and woods out back, he carried the women, one by one, inside the residence, where he lived alone but always welcomed the right company. Soon, the fun would begin. At least for him. For them, he had to admit with a laugh within, not so much.

THE NIGHTTIME RAID by heavily armed FBI agents and Gulfport Police Department detectives and SWAT Team, supported by Harrison County Sheriff's Office investigators from the Criminal Investigation Division and K-9 Patrol dogs, on the house on Robinson Road, led to the arrest of suspected serial killer Perry Evigan. The nude body of a woman identified as twenty-three-year-old Brigette Fontana was discovered in a bedroom. She had been sexually assaulted and strangled to death, barehanded, by Evigan, according to the autopsy report two days later.

Another woman, Nikki Sullivan, who had been abducted by Evigan at the same time outside Johnnie's Shack nightclub, and was described as a good friend of Ms. Fontana's, survived the vicious attack. Upon her full recovery, Ms. Sullivan was expected to testify against her attacker, dubbed the "Gulfport Nightmare Killer," who was believed to have strangled to death at least ten women over an eight-month span within the city of Gulfport, Mississippi, Harrison County's co-county seat.

Chapter One

During a violent nighttime uprising at the Mississippi State Penitentiary in Sunflower County, Mississippi, three hard-core inmates seized on the opportune distraction to stage a dramatic getaway. After quickly overwhelming prison guards, the trio made a daring escape from Area I of the maximum-security prison on Parchman Road known as Parchman Farm.

The leader of the escapees, a convicted murderer, spotted a red GMC Sierra 1500 parked not far from the prison. Its driver, a lanky, thirtysomething, baldheaded male, was talking on a cell phone, seemingly oblivious to his surroundings. Or the potential peril present. Once the inmates had his attention, it was too late for him to deny them what they wanted: his vehicle and the phone. Unfortunately, leaving behind a witness to their car theft wasn't in the cards. Strangling the man to death with his own leather belt was easy for the ringleader. After all, he'd had lots of experience using this method to kill others. And if things went as planned, he fully intended to pick up where he left off years ago.

Starting with the pretty one who escaped death before he could squeeze the life out of her.

The prisoners climbed into the pickup truck and headed

west on Highway 32 toward the city of Ruleville, Mississippi. There, they would get a change of clothing, food, money and maybe switch cars, before fleeing the area entirely, ahead of the correctional authorities and other law enforcement personnel's determined efforts to recapture them. Or do whatever it took to prevent the dangerous fugitives from living in the free world again.

SPECIAL AGENT GAVIN LYNLEY of the Mississippi Department of Corrections, Corrections Investigation Division's Special Operations Unit, removed the FN 509 MRD-LE 9mm semiautomatic pistol from the tactical thigh holster as he cautiously approached the black Hyundai Sonata. It was parked outside a ranch-style home on Frinton Street in Vicksburg, Mississippi. A run on the license plate confirmed that the vehicle belonged to Titus Malfoy, a probation officer for the MDOC, who was wanted for embezzling money from probationers. The victims were working to pay off their debts to the court as required in the terms for regaining freedom. Instead, an internal investigation revealed that Malfoy pocketed what wasn't his to have at their expense, resulting in longer sentences for those victimized unsuspectingly.

Gavin glanced at the other side of the vehicle, where Special Agent Jean O'Reilly, her gun drawn, was also prepared to act should the suspect behind the steering wheel make the wrong move. Peering at the probation officer, who was talking on his cell phone, recognizing him, Gavin said with an edge to his voice, "Step out of the car and keep your hands where I can see them."

Looking surprised, Titus Malfoy cut the call short and complied with the order. He opened the door carefully and climbed out. "What's this all about?" he demanded as his brow creased in three irregular lines as though totally perplexed.

Gavin noted that they were about the same height of six feet and three inches. But he was in better shape than Malfoy, who was African American, a year younger at thirty-five than the man, had darker and shorter hair than the probation officer, who had a bleached high top and textured dreads, and was gray-eyed compared to the brown color of the suspect's eyes, which were shifting nervously. "Titus Malfoy, you're under arrest for embezzlement and abusing your position as a probation officer."

"What?" Malfoy cocked a thick brow of denial. "This has to be some kind of mistake."

"I don't think so." Gavin was confident that the monthslong investigation of his crimes was spot-on. He frisked the man and found that he didn't have a firearm or other weapon on him. "You messed up big time, Malfoy," he told him bluntly. "Now you'll have to answer for it."

Agent O'Reilly, slender and thirtysomething with long crimson hair in a tight bun, big blue eyes and fresh off a divorce, handcuffed the suspect behind his back and said skeptically, "If you're really innocent, you'll have ample opportunity to prove it. If not, you could be looking at decades behind bars. Sorry." Her tone indicated the apology was sarcastic rather than sincere.

As Malfoy muttered an expletive in response, Gavin told him tersely, "Let's go." He wondered just how many more bad apples they would discover in the probe of corruption within the ranks of the Mississippi Department of Corrections. It was troubling, to say the least, as he wanted to believe that this was just an isolated problem and not broad in scope for an organization that Gavin had been employed with for more than a decade. Or ever since shortly after he had received his undergraduate degree in Criminology from Mississippi State University, and followed the long tradition of family members who made careers for themselves in law enforcement.

Gavin led the suspect to the official CID vehicle they had driven to the scene, a dark ash metallic Chevrolet Tahoe SUV. Malfoy was put in the back seat, then Gavin sat in the front passenger seat, while Jean got behind the wheel and drove to the Vicksburg Police Department on Veto Street, where the suspect was turned over for processing.

Afterward, they took a mostly silent forty-five-mile drive to the Mississippi Department of Corrections Central Office headquarters on North Lamar Street in Jackson, where the report was filed on the arrest of Titus Malfoy, and Gavin settled into his office for some follow-up work. He was at a height-adjustable standing desk, glancing at his laptop, when the Director of Investigations at MDOC, Marvin Whitfield, strode in. He had an iPad in his hands.

Whitfield, African American, was in his forties, medium height and solidly built, with a short and tapered black Afro and sable eyes. "Good job, Lynley, with Agent O'Reilly, in taking Malfoy into custody without incident," he said, squaring his shoulders inside the jacket of his crisp navy suit worn with black plain leather Derbys.

"I wish it hadn't come down to that," Gavin said, twisting his lips in despair. He knew that the arrest indicated that one of their own had crossed the line, implicating the entire department to one degree or another by association. If not guilt.

"Yeah, I know what you mean." Whitfield pinched his

broad nose. "But it is what it is... Unfortunately, we've got other problems to deal with." He paused, ill at ease. "Last night there was a riot at the Mississippi State Penitentiary."

"Yeah, I heard about it." Gavin recalled the news about an uprising at the prison related to conditions that had been described by some as deplorable. From what limited information he gathered, at least one inmate had been killed and several injured, before guards were able to bring things under control.

"While conducting an emergency head count at five this morning, it was discovered that three inmates were missing." Whitfield sighed noisily. "They took advantage of the melee and killed one guard—Stan MacGregor, age thirty-nine, who was married with four kids—while seriously wounding another, before the trio managed to flee the prison grounds. Along the way, the escapees stole a pickup truck after killing the driver, thirty-four-year-old Jason Ollero."

"Wow." Gavin felt terrible for the guards attacked, as well as the pickup driver, who was obviously in the worst place at the worst time. He hoped the injured guard pulled through.

"It gets worse," the longtime director muttered. "One of the escaped inmates is Perry Evigan..."

"What?" Gavin's heart sank into his stomach, even as Whitfield reiterated this disturbing news, and showed him Evigan's mug shot on the tablet. Seeing his chiseled face and foreboding hazel eyes, along with closely cropped brown-gray hair, gave Gavin the creeps.

"Yeah, freaks me out too," Whitfield muttered. He identified the other escapees as Craig Schneider and Aaron Machado, pulling their images up on the tablet.

Gavin glanced at Schneider, who was white, round-faced and blue-eyed, with a black crew cut and anchor beard.

Machado was Latino, baldheaded, smooth-shaven, triangular-faced and had dark brown eyes. While noting their appearances, Gavin's focus was squarely on Perry Evigan. Ten years ago, Evigan raped and murdered Gavin's then-girlfriend, Brigette Fontana. She was strangled to death by him. Known as the Gulfport Nightmare Killer, Evigan had killed a total of ten young women by ligature strangulation in and around Gulfport. Brigette was his last homicide victim, who was abducted by the killer along with Brigette's best friend, Nikki Sullivan. Though she survived the kidnapping and attempted rape, Nikki was left with a broken jaw, busted lower lip, seriously sprained ankle and a concussion—along with the psychological wounds she sustained during her victimization—before being rescued by the authorities from Evigan's house.

Perry Evigan himself—a then-thirty-four-year-old divorcé and journeyman, with a dark fixation on such serial killers as the so-called Boston Strangler, believed by many to be serial rapist Albert DeSalvo, and cousins Kenneth Bianchi and Angelo Buono Jr., known as the Hillside Stranglers—was taken into custody, in spite of Evigan's resisting arrest. He would eventually be convicted for his crimes and sentenced to spend the rest of his life in prison. Until now.

"Do we know where they are?" Gavin asked the director tartly, hating the thought that Evigan was tasting freedom for even a second, after what he'd done.

"Unfortunately, not at the moment." Whitfield furrowed his forehead. "They made their way to Ruleville and ditched the pickup. We're not sure what they're driving now. We have the department's Fugitive Apprehension Strike Team and K-9 unit trying to track them down, with assistance from the FBI and US Marshals Service, along with the Jackson Police Department, Sunflower County Sheriff's Office and surrounding law enforcement agencies on full alert. We'll get them back," he said confidently. "But until such time, we need to protect the one woman who miraculously managed to survive Perry Evigan's attempt to sexually assault and murder her from being added to his list of fatalities. That's where you come in, Lynley—"

Putting aside his conflicting thoughts at the moment, Gavin met the director's eyes sharply. "You want me to be a bodyguard?" Even when questioning him, Gavin knew it was not nearly that simple.

"I want you to keep the person alive whose critical testimony helped put Evigan away, ensuring that he would spend the rest of his miserable life behind bars." Whitfield drew a breath. "At least that was our intention. Now he's out there somewhere, free as a bird, and just might try to track down Nikki Sullivan, insane as that sounds. But we can't put anything past Evigan, who, as I recall, singled out Ms. Sullivan as his one regret—not killing her when he had the chance."

"I remember," Gavin muttered painfully, knowing it was hard to forget, all things considered.

"Maybe he wants a redo." Whitfield jutted his chin. "We can't let that happen. As a member of the Special Operations Unit, Lynley, we need to be able to occasionally provide protection, when warranted. This seems to be one of those times, with the prisoners' escape under our jurisdiction. As you and Ms. Sullivan share a common bond with Evigan's last murder victim, Brigette Fontana, this assignment should be right up your alley. Am I right?"

Gavin hesitated in his response. Normally, he would have agreed with this assessment. How could he not, given the situation as it were? But in this instance, he had an undeniable large chip on his shoulder where it concerned Nikki Sullivan. He blamed her for placating Brigette's reckless desire to go out that night, leading her right into the crosshairs of Perry Evigan. Though Gavin admittedly blamed himself just as much, considering he had to work the night in question, preventing him from being with Brigette and presumably saving her life—he was certainly glad that Nikki had come out on the other side and been given the opportunity to move on with her life. This notwithstanding, being around her right now would only remind him of what he lost in Brigette and any future they might have had. And everything that could have come with that package—like a family and home together. Wasn't that where they were headed? But that wasn't exactly an acceptable excuse for not being able to do his job effectively. Was it? Even if that job meant reuniting with Brigette's best friend, in order to keep her safe from the same serial killer who put Brigette in the grave at the young age of twenty-three.

Gavin nodded at the director, maintaining his cool in the process. "Of course, I'll do my best to keep Ms. Sullivan out of harm's way while Evigan is still at large." *Hopefully, that will be of short duration, or Evigan could be apprehended even before I have to come face-to-face with Nikki for the first time in years*, Gavin told himself, knowing that the sooner they located the three escapees, the sooner they could wipe the proverbial egg off their faces in having to account for the escape in the first place on their watch.

"Good." Whitfield flashed him a satisfied look. "Of course, we'll need to locate Nikki Sullivan first—assuming she hasn't remained in the same place—wherever she might be if she's still in Mississippi after a decade, before Evigan can, and warn her about the possible danger to her life."

"I understand." Gavin had not kept track of Nikki's whereabouts after Evigan's trial and conviction. There had been no need to with neither on particularly good terms with the blame game. Both had gone their separate ways. But he had heard through the grapevine that Brigette's gorgeous, as he recalled, and talented artist friend had smartly moved from Gulfport and the dark memories left behind. Now he just had to find out where she was and make sure she remained safe till the escaped serial killer was back in custody where he belonged.

An hour later, after making a few phone calls and doing some double-checking, Gavin had his answer. Nikki Sullivan had relocated to Owl's Bay, a town in Yaeden County, about thirty miles down the coast from Gulfport and approximately one hundred and seventy miles from Jackson. Moreover, Owl's Bay was around three hundred miles from Ruleville, where Perry Evigan and the other escapees were last spotted. Though it seemed like a stretch that Evigan would try to make his way back to the area where he perpetrated his serial murders, if this were the case, he'd had a head start.

Gavin alerted authorities along US 49 South and I-55 South, leading into Owl's Bay from Ruleville, to be on the lookout, or BOLO, for the fugitives, who could be driving any type of vehicle while on the run. And that was under the assumption that they hadn't split up. For the moment, Gavin was more focused on Evigan, in particular, with his mug shot sent to the local law enforcement agencies. Should he be foolish enough to go after Nikki.

Against his better judgment, Gavin decided not to call Nikki, sure she'd hang up on his face. Freaking her out by leaving a disturbing message probably wasn't a good idea either. He assumed that she had heard about Evigan's escape and was taking precautions accordingly. *I don't want to spook her by leaving a text that her life could be in danger*, Gavin told himself, trusting that he could get to her in time to protect her. In the meantime, he would give the locals a heads-up on the situation as it related to Nikki Sullivan.

Gavin left the MDOC Central Office headquarters and climbed back into the Chevrolet Tahoe he had arrived in, then swung by his Louisiana-style house on a cul-de-sac on Heritage Hill Drive. He lived alone in the spacious two-story home that sat on two acres of land with mature landscaping and tall oak trees, but would gladly share it with the right person, were she to come into his life. He once thought that might be Brigette, but they were never allowed to put it to the test, before her life ended.

Stepping through the front door, Gavin headed across the vinyl plank flooring and up the straight staircase. He grabbed a few extra clothing items and toiletries, in case this assignment turned out to be longer than a day or two—stuffing them into a black leather tote bag—then headed back downstairs and out the door.

With any luck, Perry Evigan and the other escapees would be back in custody and a prison cell before Gavin ever arrived in Owl's Bay. He only wished he could take luck to the bank, where it concerned a ruthless serial killer on the loose and a woman from Gavin's past who potentially had a target on her back.

NIKKI SULLIVAN SAT in a club chair in the circle of a support group for survivors of traumatic events in the large backyard of the vintage home in the small Mississippi coastal town of Owl's Bay. She had participated off and on ever since relocating there from Gulfport eight years ago. She considered it a security blanket of sorts to be around others who had been left with permanent scars on their psyche—and in some cases, the accompanying physical scars—as a result of experiences they could never forget. Even if they tried. This was certainly true for her, even as she tried to distance herself by moving away from the scene of the crime and the man who unfairly blamed her for it.

Nikki trained her ocean-blue eyes on Blair Roxburgh, a trained psychologist and the homeowner who started the group, which currently consisted of six women and two men. She and Blair were both the same age of thirty-three and similarly slender in build, but Blair was a couple of inches shorter than Nikki's five-foot-seven-and-a-half height, and had a darker shade of blond in her short shag than Nikki's long and layered yellow locks that were fashioned in a blunt U-shaped cut. She listened as Blair retold her terrifying tale for the benefit of those new to the group.

"I was sexually assaulted as an eighteen-year-old college freshman," she said, her hazel eyes dampening as though thrust back in time to the moment the attack occurred. "My attacker was someone I thought I knew. Till he turned out to be someone entirely different—a monster hidden behind a handsome face. For the longest time, I blamed myself as many victims do when missing the warning signs that place you in danger, before gaining the courage to affix blame where it was due—squarely on the rapist himself." Blair took a moment to regain her composure. "We're all here today because of what we've been put through and are now survivors with a greater sense of self-worth and solace in knowing that we're not alone." She gazed warmly at Nikki and said even-toned, "Tell us your story, if you feel comfortable doing so."

Nikki smiled softly at her, having established a rapport that helped her feel at ease. "I'm Nikki Sullivan," she told the group in a well-practiced and affable tone. "Ten years ago, I was the victim of a brutal attack by a serial killer named Perry Evigan. He sexually assaulted and then strangled to death ten women, including my best friend, Brigette, after he drugged us. I was supposed to die too, but the FBI and local authorities miraculously came to my rescue before he could finish the job. I got lucky—if you could call it that—ending up with a broken jaw in two places, that still aches on occasion, a concussion, badly sprained ankle and a bloodied lower lip." She winced at the thought. "In spite of my best efforts to the contrary, the regrets about what happened and what I might have done differently if I could go back in time have never gone away. Or the nightmares." She sucked in a deep breath as Nikki mused about Perry Evigan, hating that he still had a hold on her somewhat as a sexual predator, even after all these years, and knowing he was safely put away in prison for the rest of his life. "Anyway, that's my story," she said, lifting her chin defiantly, "and, like everyone here, I'm a survivor and proud of it."

With that, there was applause and Nikki smiled, while knowing that the strength in numbers was what kept each of them going when left to themselves. And that the ebb and flow between sadness and empowerment would continue as each person recounted his or her experience. The last to speak was one of the male survivors, Harry Rosen, a forty-three-year-old US Air Force veteran, traumatized from his experiences when serving in Afghanistan. It cost him one of his legs. He finished by saying courageously,

"It's been tough some days, for sure. But right here, right now, I can tell you that I'd enlist all over again in representing my country in the military."

More applause came before it swung back to Blair. After the group meeting was over and they were alone in the backyard, Nikki was approached by the counseling psychologist, who had become a trusted friend. Blair said to her, "Are you free for lunch?"

Nikki shook her head. "I can't," she responded reluctantly. "My latest artwork won't paint itself, if I'm going to have it ready for the showing on Saturday."

"Understood," Blair said. "Not a problem."

"Rain check?"

"You've got it."

Nikki smiled gratefully. "See you at the next meeting."

Blair patted her hand. "Wouldn't miss it," she joked.

Nikki laughed. "Didn't imagine you would."

"If I ever did, you could always fill in for me."

"You think?"

"Absolutely." Blair nodded. "Everyone likes you and feels comfortable with you, which encourages them to talk about their ordeals."

"Hmm." Nikki flushed. "I'll keep that in mind."

She left the four-sided brick home on Aplen Avenue and headed for her car on this early afternoon with the sun shining brightly to remind her it was mid-July. She climbed inside the red Subaru Crosstrek and headed home, where she had her studio. Art had been her passion for as long as she could remember and Nikki had managed to turn it into a successful career over the years, specializing in landscape, still life and portrait oil paintings—with showings across the state and occasionally elsewhere.

She hadn't been nearly as successful with her love life. The few times she had dated someone over the years, Nikki had come up empty. That included a guy she had gone out on a date with exactly one time recently—a personal trainer named Kenan Fernández—only to find there was absolutely no chemistry whatsoever. He seemed to feel otherwise, but she had not seen him since, ignoring his phone and text messages.

The reality was that she had yet to find the right person to have a serious romance with. It left Nikki wondering if her standards were too high. Had her brush with death left her emotionally damaged? Or was it more about her unwillingness to take a chance on someone, only to fail and have her heart broken? Would that be more than she could take in only wanting a happy ending, after losing a friend to a serial killer?

Nikki's thoughts drifted away as her attention turned to the news brief on the radio. "According to the Mississippi Department of Corrections," the female broadcaster reported tensely, "in the midst of unrest at the Mississippi State Penitentiary, three inmates managed a brazen escape in the wee hours of the morning, killing a guard and the driver of a pickup truck along the way. The escapees, all lifers for serious crimes of violence, have been identified as forty-four-year-old Perry Evigan, thirty-six-year-old Aaron Machado and Craig Schneider, age twenty-seven."

Nikki's heart skipped a beat at the mention of Perry Evigan's name, even as she heard the newscaster say in dramatic fashion, "Evigan, once dubbed the Gulfport Nightmare Killer, strangled to death ten women—sexually assaulting them beforehand—before being captured a decade ago. One woman was able to survive an attack by the serial

killer and testified at his trial nearly nine years ago, resulting in a conviction and life sentence. The escapees are described as armed and extremely dangerous..."

What? Evigan is out of prison and on the loose, Nikki
thought, the very notion shaking her to the core as her fingers trembled around the steering wheel. How could that
have happened? He was supposed to be locked away forever in a maximum-security facility. With no escape possible. She shuddered in recalling Perry Evigan's haunting
last words to her during his trial.

*I'll see you again someday, Nikki, and finish what I
started. Trust me.*

She had totally rejected his threat as the ravings of a defeated and defiant man on his way back to prison. Was he
now in a position to make good on that threat? she had to
wonder. *Am I in danger*? Nikki asked herself, worried. Did
she need to go into hiding while that bastard remained free?
Or would the authorities, who, according to the news report,
had intensified their search for the escaped convicts, have
them back in custody long before Evigan could seriously
entertain tracking her down nine years later?

Nikki mulled over this troubling development and the
potentially high stakes for her own life, security and future, as she pulled into the driveway of her custom-built,
three-bedroom Creole cottage-style home on Waconia Way,
outside the garage. With a stunning backside view of the
nearby Jourdan River, the property was bordered by sugar
maple trees, giving her some privacy. Only when she got
out of the car, did Nikki notice the dark-colored Chevrolet
Tahoe parked across the street. Had it been there before?
Did it belong to her neighbor?

A spasm of fear ripped through her, as the vehicle's

driver-side door opened. Could Perry Evigan have already found her? Not that it would have been too difficult as she hadn't exactly tried to hide from him, per se, not believing she needed to. Picturing the smug face of the man who tried to kill her, Nikki's first instinct was to bolt for her front door, where she had a good security system inside that would protect her and alert the police. Short of that, she had a stun gun in her leather hobo bag to defend herself with. If that failed, she could always make use of the skills she'd learned in the self-defense courses she'd taken after her attack and refreshed herself with periodically.

When a tall and very fit male stepped out of the car, Nikki spied the somewhat familiar devilishly handsome face of a biracial man. One she never expected to see again, even if not necessarily her preference. Or maybe she had felt it was for the best, when considering the bad blood that had existed between them in the wake of Brigette's death. Now in his midthirties, he still had the taut oblong face, piercing gray eyes and slightly crooked mouth she had last seen right after Perry Evigan's trial ended. New was the five o'clock shadow beard and trendy style of his short raven hair in a midrazor fade. She stood there flatfooted as he quickly closed the distance between them in his boat shoes, to go with a light blue polo shirt and dark chinos. Her instinct to run away from him was stilled by curiosity, if nothing else.

"Nikki," he said tonelessly and paused. "It's been a minute."

"More like nine years," she said wryly to her late friend Brigette's former boyfriend, Gavin Lynley. Nikki fluttered her lashes. "What are you doing here?"

Gavin pinched his Roman nose and said without preface, "Perry Evigan has escaped from prison."

"I just heard it on the radio." Nikki's brow furrowed as she fought to maintain her composure. She was admittedly still piqued as to why Gavin needed—or even wanted, after the way they left things—to convey the news in person. Peering at him, she asked pointedly, "So, did you come to tell me that he's been recaptured?"

"I'm here to say I hope that will be a done deal shortly." Gavin glanced down at his shoes and then lifted his eyes to meet hers fixedly. "Until such time, I've been assigned to make sure Perry Evigan doesn't come anywhere near you."

Chapter Two

Gavin could tell that Nikki saw him as almost as much her enemy as Perry Evigan. Not that he could blame her any. The last time he had laid eyes upon her, they had parted as nothing but two people who had lost someone each cared about. They certainly hadn't moved in opposite directions on a positive note. Much less, as friends. Whether he cared to admit it or not, Gavin knew that he had to bear much of the blame for that. He had pushed Nikki away as the only person he knew with a direct line to Brigette when she was alive and, in theory, could have been a shoulder for Gavin to lean on. And vice versa.

But he had been too wounded at the time to think in those terms. All he wanted to do was try to put the past behind him—including Brigette's best friend, whom he'd been attracted to since the day they first met, but never acted on out of respect for Brigette in not wanting to cross any lines—and move on with his life. Clearly, this had been Nikki's intent too.

Till he unceremoniously reentered the picture. Thanks to their mutual foe: Perry Evigan.

Gavin studied her now, as Nikki glared at him with those enchanting royal blue eyes. They were beautiful, along with a delicate nose and generous mouth on a heart-shaped face, which had only gotten more attractive with time. The blunt cut of Nikki's long blond locks agreed with her. She was still appealingly slender and the perfect height in relation to his own, while wearing a peach-colored smocked-trim top, navy trouser pants and moccasin flats.

Now came the hard part. He needed to break the ice that had formed a thick barrier between them over the past nine years and at least try to remain cordial while keeping her out of harm's way.

"You're joking, right?" Nikki's eyes flashed hotly at him. "You've shown up out of nowhere to be my bodyguard? Maybe I'd be better off taking my chances with Perry Evigan. At least I know who I'm dealing with in him. As opposed to you, who outright accused me of being responsible for Brigette's death. My best friend. And never seemed to back down, as I recall. Now this?" Her lashes curled whimsically. "How did you expect me to react?"

Oh boy, this is going to be harder than I'd imagined, Gavin told himself, as he eyed her resting a hand on a slender hip. "Just the way you have," he had to confess. Or at the very least, he hadn't exactly expected a welcoming committee. He glanced about to assess the surroundings. Seemed pleasant enough, with mature cypress trees lining the streets and an otherwise peacefulness in the atmosphere. Unfortunately, this did little to make him feel at ease, fully aware that the facade would be perfect cover for a ruthless serial killer to go on the attack. Gavin turned back to Nikki and asked in a pleading tone, "Do you mind if we go inside and talk about this?" He looked over her head at the two-story cottage she called home.

Without uttering another word, Nikki turned and headed

up the walkway, inviting him with her silence to follow, which he did. On the front porch, there were two black wicker chairs that they bypassed.

Walking through the door, Gavin stepped onto the travertine floor and took in the Spanish Cedar millwork and open concept with a high ceiling, cottage-style ceiling fan and symmetrical windows with vinyl Venetian blinds. There was a good-size living and dining area, wicker furnishings, floating staircase and gourmet kitchen with a marble countertop and breakfast nook. He took note of the security system, as well as the double-cylinder dead-bolt front door lock.

He gazed at Nikki and said sheepishly, "Nice place."

"Thanks," she responded tonelessly, her arms folded while waiting anxiously to hear more from him on the situation they found themselves in.

"Look, I know I'm probably the last person you expected to see show up at your house," Gavin conceded, "short of Perry Evigan. Truthfully, I wasn't expecting it either. But due to the circumstances…" He paused. "So, here's the deal…" Gavin knew there would be no sugarcoating this. So why try? "As a special agent with the Mississippi Department of Corrections, protecting crime victims and witnesses is part of my duties. Given that Perry Evigan was one of the escapees from our prison system and swore vengeance against you—and also happened to be responsible for the death of Brigette Fontana, my then-girlfriend—I suppose I was the obvious choice of my boss to keep you safe in the remote chance that Evigan manages to evade recapture and tries to make good on his threat."

"Obvious choice. Really?" Nikki pursed her lips skeptically. "Maybe not the best choice, given our strained history. To say the least."

Gavin found that hard to argue with on its merits. "I wanted to call to see if you were okay with this, but figured my best bet was to do it face-to-face," he said.

She reacted with a sneer. "I'm not so sure about that."

"Look, if having me around, even for a short while, really makes you uncomfortable, I can get the locals to assign an officer to protect you." Gavin met her eyes. "Until such time, I can wait outside till the officer arrives…"

Nikki seemed to weigh her options, before saying tentatively, "That won't be necessary. If this is your job, I suppose I can handle it, if you can."

He nodded in agreement. "I'm sure I'll be out of your hair in no time flat." Even in uttering the words, Gavin couldn't help but wonder what it would be like to run his fingers through that long luscious hair of hers.

"Fine." She took a breath. "Do you really think that Perry Evigan would risk his newfound freedom to try and find me after all these years?" she questioned.

It was something that Gavin had already asked himself more than once. Assuming Evigan still had a little common sense and even a little intelligence, it would seem improbable that he would roll the dice in coming for Nikki when he had to know that the risk would not likely justify the means. As it pertained to his staying on the lam successfully, it was a tough task under the best of circumstances. But something told Gavin that the psychopath in Evigan might well be driven by impulses beyond his own best interests. Or normal behavior.

Trying to keep it as diplomatic as possible, Gavin responded evenly, "Probably not. But the man is a serial killer and knows that with the high probability that he'll be caught sooner rather than later—he may feel he has nothing to lose and everything to gain, in trying to finish what he started ten years ago." Gavin reached out and touched her shoulder. He ignored the powerful sensation that this small gesture brought about, while telling her in earnest, "I won't let that happen."

Nikki gave a slow and grateful nod. "Thank you."

"Not a problem." Even if it had been, he wouldn't have admitted to this. He was on an assignment and owed it to her—and the shared memory of Brigette—to see it through, with minimal disruption of Nikki's life before walking away from her. Again. "So, are you still an artist?" The question was more conversational than anything. In the course of establishing her whereabouts and out of curiosity, Gavin had discovered that she had, in fact, made a name for herself in the local art world with prominent showings and paintings in high demand. Nikki had not used a pseudonym when relocating from Gulfport to Owl's Bay. Meaning that Evigan would likely have little trouble using social media or online news sources to discover her location, which concerned Gavin.

"Yes," she answered matter-of-factly. "Mostly landscape and still life, with some portraits."

"Nice." Gavin grinned, recalling how he had seen and admired some of her paintings back in the day when Brigette had insisted that he come along to check out a few that Nikki had laid out in her apartment. He imagined her work would be even more compelling today.

"Speaking of which—" Nikki broke into his thoughts "—I do need to get to my studio, down the hall, for some work. It will also keep my mind occupied on something other than Perry Evigan possibly trying to kill me…and—" she made an uncomfortable expression on her face "—sexually assaulting me beforehand, per his MO." She looked away. "Since you'll probably be here for a little while, I guess you can make yourself at home, Gavin. There are drinks and half an apple pie in the fridge, if you get thirsty or hungry. And the first-floor bathroom is just off the kitchen."

"Thanks." He appreciated the hospitality, even if Gavin didn't feel particularly welcomed and rightfully so. They'd had their differences and they wouldn't be resolved overnight. But that didn't mean they couldn't be nice to each other while occupying the same house. As soon as he got word that Evigan had been arrested and was no longer a threat to Nikki or anyone else, Gavin would get out of her life and they could each go about their business.

Or was this a good time to address the past and losing Brigette to senseless violence, once and for all?

He watched as Nikki walked away, before Gavin took out his cell phone and rang Marvin Whitfield. "I'm with her now," he told the director equably.

"No trouble?"

"Not yet," Gavin responded.

"Good. How's she doing with the news that Perry Evigan is out?" Whitfield asked.

"Probably as well as could be expected." Gavin glanced down the hall and saw that Nikki had gone into her studio. "Honestly, though she's put on a brave face, Nikki's spooked, and with good reason. Any word yet on the whereabouts of Evigan and the other escapees?"

"Reports have come in that the trio may have been spotted in Tennessee," Whitfield indicated. "But others claimed to have seen them in Alabama." The director sighed. "Right now, we don't have a solid fix on their whereabouts. With the head start the inmates had before we realized they were missing, Evigan, Machado and Schneider could be anywhere, frankly. They are believed to be driving a black Chrysler Pacifica that was stolen in Boyle. According to the elderly owner, Donald Takeuchi, who wasn't home at the time, the trio also broke into his house and stole two legally purchased firearms—a Glock G43X subcompact semiauto pistol and a SIG Sauer P365 9mm pistol, along with ammo."

"That's not very comforting," Gavin told him bluntly, though hardly surprised that the escapees would arm themselves while on the run. "Evigan and his killer pals are not likely to turn themselves in peacefully and miss out on their one big opportunity to escape to greener pastures. They could've left the state—which would have been the smartest move—or chosen to lay low in Mississippi, traveling the back roads while trying to bypass roadblocks they would have to get past in whatever stolen vehicle they were driving."

"Yeah, desperate as they are, there's no telling what their mindset is while trying to avoid capture," Whitfield voiced. "All we know for certain is that they're still on the loose, armed and extremely dangerous."

Gavin muttered words in agreement. "Which makes the situation all the more aggravating and frightening."

"Just keep Ms. Sullivan safe," the director ordered, "till we can bring in Evigan, in particular, as well as Machado and Schneider."

"Will do," Gavin promised. Even if Nikki would probably still prefer another person to be her protector. Or had she begun to let her guard down a bit with him—and vice versa—in spite of the animosity between them spanning a decade, which he now regretted?

APART FROM FEELING most like herself in the studio, Nikki admittedly used it as a way to mask the strong physical awareness she unexpectedly had for Gavin Lynley's presence. Was it wrong to have romantic vibes for someone who hated her for allowing Brigette to talk her into going out that fateful night ten years ago? Was it just as wrong for Gavin to believe that Brigette walked on water as the love of his life—when in reality, she was anything but the faithful girlfriend with eyes only for him?

Telling him now would only make it seem like I'm rewriting history in knocking Brigette off her pedestal when she's no longer alive to defend herself, Nikki mused sadly as she glanced about the art studio. With natural light coming in from a large picture window, there were canvases in various stages of completion on long wooden tables and lining the walls on the floor, along with pencils, brushes and multiple colors of paint ready to use. She liked to move back and forth between projects, tackling one or another whenever the spirit moved her. Aside from when she needed to prioritize for commissioned artworks. Or showings. She imagined painting Gavin, seeing him as the perfect human subject with his handsome, defined features and strong jawline. But his assignment would likely be over practically before it started—ending that fantasy where it probably belonged. In her head and now her heart.

The fact that she'd secretly had feelings for Brigette's boyfriend years ago but had wisely kept them to herself, not wanting to betray her best friend, did not change the reality that there was little chance that anything could happen now between Nikki and Gavin. Apart from the strained relations between them, she had no reason to believe he would ever be interested in her romantically. For all she knew, he was in a serious relationship—if not a marriage—with someone else, now that Brigette, his presumably first true love, was no longer around to give him the family Brigette had indicated he wanted someday. Never mind that Brigette didn't necessarily share his vision for her own future.

I won't open up a can of worms for someone who is merely here on assignment as a special agent, Nikki told herself as she headed to a canvas on an easel that she had started working on. It was a painting of Mississippi wildflowers. It was best not to go there and allow Brigette to rest in peace and Gavin to keep her memory in any way he saw fit. Just as Nikki chose to do, knowing that Brigette would always hold a special place in her heart, flaws and all.

Not to mention that no matter who was responsible for their going out that night, it was Brigette who made the ultimate sacrifice. Even if that was never her intention. While Nikki had somehow managed to escape her own date with death, though not for lack of Perry Evigan's wanting to see her suffer too, through a sexual violation, followed by ligature strangulation.

And now, she feared, he may still come after her, just as he promised, to deal her the same fatal blow he dealt Brigette and nine other women—all with the better part of their lives still ahead of them. Until that was no longer the case.

Nikki could only hope that Gavin was as committed to preventing this as he appeared to be, their issues notwithstanding. Or that Perry Evigan was captured and put back behind bars, long before he could ever make his way to Owl's Bay.

GAVIN POKED HIS head into the art studio, where he had given Nikki a few uninterrupted hours to work and process the circumstances that brought them together again so suddenly. She was standing before a canvas, painting, and seemingly totally in focus. That didn't mean she had all but forgotten he was there. He was certain that she was just as ill at ease about it as he was. But no matter the second-guessing about the events that led to Brigette's death, it was necessary for him to occupy Nikki's space, as her safety was front and center. Not only as a matter of his directive as a special agent of the Mississippi Department of Corrections CID, but also on a personal level. Gavin hadn't been able to save Brigette from that monster. He would be damned if he allowed Evigan to harm her best friend as well.

He stepped inside the studio and said, to catch her attention, "Hey."

Nikki stopped painting the still life of wildflowers and turned to face him. "Hey." She flashed a tentative expression. "Any news on Perry Evigan?"

Gavin only wished he could tell her that Evigan and his fellow prison escapees had been recaptured and were no longer a danger to the public. Or her, in particular, where it concerned the serial killer. "I'm afraid that Evigan is still on the loose," he told her frustratingly.

She wrinkled her nose. "How have they been able to avoid capture? I assume law enforcement is on full alert on the prison escape?"

"They are," Gavin assured her. "Trust me, we're doing everything we can to find the escapees. How have they avoided capture?" He waited a beat while moving closer to her. "We're talking about hardened criminals here. They may well have planned their escape long before it actually happened and developed a strategy for staying hidden or otherwise circumventing the law. On the other hand, Evigan and his cronies may simply have gotten lucky, thus far, in evading the authorities. Either way, a BOLO has been issued for the trio, who are believed to still be together, along with the stolen vehicle they may be driving. It's only a matter of time before they're apprehended."

Nikki rolled her eyes. "Why doesn't that give me much comfort?"

"Probably for the same reason it doesn't me," Gavin told her in all honesty. "With Evigan's murderous track record—and Aaron Machado and Craig Schneider aren't any better, as they're also convicted murderers—we can't afford to let our guard down till Evigan's back behind bars."

"No, we definitely can't." A look of apprehension flashed across her face. "So, what now?"

"I stick around for as long as it takes while the man who attacked you and Brigette remains a fugitive." Gavin jutted his chin. "If that's all right with you—?"

Nikki nodded thoughtfully. "It has to be," she said in no uncertain terms. "I just want this over so I can get on with my life without needing to look over my shoulder."

Or having to deal with me and our shared and tragic history, Gavin mused. "I understand." He resisted the urge to touch Nikki's face, imagining how soft it would feel to his fingertips. "If you're hungry, how about we do takeout? It's probably best not to go to a restaurant at night right now," he indicated, knowing that exposing themselves under the cover of darkness could well be playing right into Evigan's hands, assuming he was able to continue to dodge the dragnet.

"Actually, I'm starving," Nikki said. "And, yes, takeout is good. And quicker than cooking something, as I wasn't, umm…prepared for a guest. Short of day-old apple pie."

Gavin grinned sideways. "I had a piece," he told her. "It was tasty."

"Glad you liked it." She showed her teeth, which brightened her good looks that much more. "Brigette taught me how to make one. Before then, I was pretty useless when it came to desserts."

He remembered Brigette being good with apple, cherry and pecan pies—and even chocolate and caramel cake— having been taught the art of making delicious desserts from her own mother. It was one of the things that attracted Gavin to Brigette, given his sweet tooth and all. If only he didn't have to work that fateful night, forcing him to cancel their date. Then Brigette would still be alive and neither she nor Nikki would have ever been victimized by the likes of Perry Evigan.

This was something Gavin would have to live with. Even if he wished Nikki had been stronger in pushing back against Brigette's greater risk-taking ventures.

THE ESCAPED CONS traveled down the back road in the stolen Chrysler Pacifica. They were armed, antsy, hungry and looking for a way to keep the journey to freedom going for as long as possible. In fact, none of them relished the thought of going back to prison. On the contrary, each was willing to do whatever was necessary to avoid doing just that. Having managed to circumvent their pursuers only emboldened them to continue fleeing from them and let the chips fall where they may.

If that meant taking out anyone who stood in their way, then so be it. With nothing to lose, all options were on the table. That included taking hostages and making sure that any and all of their demands were met. Or else.

At least one of the escapees thought that Mexico might be a good option. It would be relatively easy to disappear once there and start over in some small town where each person's business was his own.

Another saw that as a stupid idea, knowing from experience that living south of the border with the authorities in full pursuit would be no walk in the park. Just the opposite. For his part, he would rather remain on the lam in the United States, moving from state to state if necessary. There were plenty of places to hide where one might never be found. Staying one step or two ahead of the law might be challenging, but possible with determination and ingenuity.

The other escapee and self-appointed leader of the group, Perry Evigan, had his own agenda, but kept it to himself. No need to ruffle any feathers at this point when not in a position to speak his mind in a way that would not potentially blow up in his face.

Sitting in the front passenger seat, he gripped tightly the Glock G43X subcompact semiauto pistol in his hands. He saw it as not only protection, but also a means to an end for his desire to achieve his objectives in picking up right where he left off a decade ago as the Gulfport Nightmare Killer.

The one who got away had haunted his dreams, and only she could allow him to be himself again. He wanted that—*her*—more than anything. But before he could even seriously begin to think in those terms, Perry knew he had to figure out a way to survive, with the walls closing in on them, he sensed.

He hadn't come this far in his quest only to be denied. Not when his quarry was out there, waiting for him, more or less.

The pretty face of Nikki Sullivan filled his head. He couldn't help but crack a grin at the thought of her. If he had his way, Perry was sure they would meet again. But the forces working against him could prevent that from ever happening.

Or not.

Chapter Three

In the dining area, Gavin sat in an upholstered side chair across a pedestal table from Nikki and decided it was time to address the elephant in the room. At least this was what he sensed during the mostly quiet and clearly strained eating of their take-out dinner consisting of country-fried steak, mashed potatoes and garden salad, along with coffee. Gazing at her, he said in an earnest tone, "Look, I think we need to clear the air…"

Nikki stopped eating, staring back at him. "The air in here is pretty clear, last time I checked," she spoke wryly.

"I'm sure you know what I mean." Or was this trip down memory lane only one-sided?

She dabbed a paper napkin to her mouth and said thoughtfully, "Well, go on, say what's on your mind."

Gavin took a breath and put down his fork, before responding apologetically, "I shouldn't have taken my frustrations about what happened to Brigette out on you."

"But you did," Nikki said with an edge to her tone. "For the past ten years, you gave me a guilt complex—made me believe that I somehow should've stopped Brigette from wanting to go out. As if." Nikki rolled her eyes at the absurdity of it, with them both knowing just how headstrong

Brigette could be when she made up her mind to do something. "And that I was responsible for putting us in harm's way—or the crosshairs of a serial killer—by not insisting that she stay put on a Saturday night after you bailed on her. So, why the change of heart now?" she challenged him.

His shoulders slumped as Gavin was forced to look squarely at his own culpability in not only Brigette's death, but Nikki's suffering at the hands of Perry Evigan. Not to mention being present when he killed her best friend. "You're not going to make this easy for me, are you?"

"Nope." Nikki gave him a firm expression. "Did you want me to?"

"I guess not," he answered, knowing full well that going light on him would only be a cop-out. Which he didn't deserve. Gavin collected his thoughts and said, "The truth of the matter is, on some level—actually, more than that—I've always known that you weren't to blame for what happened to you and Brigette. You were twenty-three-year-olds, just wanting to do what most young people liked to do on a Saturday night—go out and have fun. Neither of you could have anticipated that you would run into Evigan at a club. Or that he would spike your drinks and victimize you further."

Gavin picked up his fork and moved the salad around, as his own guilt took center stage. "If anyone deserves blame for what you were put through—besides the creep who perpetrated the attack—it's me. I've kicked myself more than once over the years, wishing I'd not canceled the date with Brigette. At the time, I was still getting my feet wet on the job and didn't feel I could afford to slack off when duty called. Had I stuck with getting together with Brigette, it probably would've saved her life and spared you what Evigan put you through."

"You can't know that for sure," Nikki countered and lifted her mug of coffee. "Even if Brigette and I hadn't gone out that night, we could have still ended up being targeted by Perry Evigan another night. Maybe that's how the universe works. Fate. Or whatever. Point is, there may have been nothing you or I could have done to prevent what happened—no matter how many times we replayed the what-ifs to try and rewrite history. Or at least reimagined it."

"You're right," Gavin said, somewhat surprised that she had come to his defense, after he had wanted to assuage his own feelings of guilt by putting it on her, to one degree or another. He could only wonder how their friendship would have evolved had they been on the same page years ago in putting the tragedy behind them. "It does no good to rehash everything that went wrong that night. But I'm still sorry that it took me so long to come to this place."

"Me too." She favored him with a tender smile, sipping the coffee. "I know that Brigette—as the person who brought us together—would have wanted us to at least remain friends over the years. So, better late than never, I suppose."

"Yeah, agreed." He grinned at her, believing that having Nikki in his life, even from a distance, was something he needed. The fact that she seemed to feel the same was just as pleasing.

They resumed eating and Gavin considered that the one positive that came from the ordeal was that Evigan was stopped in his tracks—preventing him from victimizing others down the line. That was something to take solace in.

Except for the fact that the serial killer had escaped from prison. And was still on the loose. Meaning that Nikki was in danger for as long as Evigan remained free.

NIKKI COULD HARDLY believe that she and Gavin had just had a heart-to-heart discussion in confronting the albatross that seemed to hang around their necks for the better part of a decade. She could only imagine Brigette scolding them both for taking so long to bridge the gap as two people important in her life, to one degree or another.

In the process, Nikki realized she'd had to come to terms with the fact that, on some level, she had blamed Gavin for her own victimization. Had he chosen Brigette instead of his job that night, Nikki would have likely stayed home, even if bored out of her mind—thereby sparing her from being almost raped and strangled to death by Perry Evigan. She realized now how foolish that was to think. Gavin had a right to reschedule his date with Brigette to work, not knowing what would go down by virtue of this. He was no more guilty of being responsible for what happened than Nikki was in not trying to talk Brigette out of going out on the town for drinking and dancing.

Agreeing on this was definitely a good thing, Nikki told herself, as she cleared the table with Gavin's help. She welcomed the opportunity to come away as friends, after the dust resettled with Perry Evigan once again behind bars. Or dead, if he resisted arrest.

They sat back at the table with a slice of apple pie for dessert and a glass of red wine. After a few minutes of keeping things light, Nikki decided to be brave and asked Gavin out of curiosity, "So, are you seeing anyone these days?" She hoped she wasn't being too forward, prying into his personal life. But they were on friendly terms again, right?

"No," he responded over his wineglass and without prelude. "I've dated off and on over the years, but nothing stuck."

"I guess Brigette was a hard act to follow, huh?" Nikki

said, a twinge of envy coursing through her, knowing that her late friend's feelings weren't entirely reciprocated toward him.

Gavin kept a straight face as he sipped wine and answered coolly, "I did care about Brigette a lot, but I moved on, having no choice but to do so. As for her being a hard act to follow, she was certainly a handful at times as a girlfriend. The truth is, I'm not sure where things were headed between us. Maybe nowhere over the course of time. Regarding being single right now, I guess I'm still waiting for the right person to come along and see what happens—"

"I see." She tasted the wine, while wondering just how long it would take for that right person to come along. Or was he just as picky as she was?

"What about you?" Gavin caught her attention. "Anyone in your life these days?"

"Can't say there is," she told him honestly. "Like you, I've dated people from time to time since moving to Owl's Bay—including, most recently, a guy named Kenan Fernández, a personal trainer—and struck out, unfortunately, insofar as finding my soul mate, if you believe in that type of thing."

"Actually, I do believe it to be true," Gavin surprised her by saying. "When it happens, you just know it."

"Perhaps you're right." She wondered if he thought of Brigette as his soul mate when they were together. And, if so, would any other woman ever measure up?

He used his fork to cut into the slice of apple pie and said, "So, do you have family? I seem to recall from Brigette that you grew up in what, Clarksdale?"

"Yes, I did." Nikki smiled. "My mother and stepdad still live there. I lost my dad when I was five. I'm an only child.

How about you?" Didn't Brigette once mention to her that he had a younger sister?

"I have a sister, Lauren, two years my junior," Gavin confirmed. "She and her husband, Rory, live with their two cute little girls, Ellen and Miley, in Cape Cod. My parents passed away a few years ago, though separately," he said sadly.

"Sorry to hear that." Nikki considered Gavin's pain with having to deal with their losses coming after Brigette's death. Had that also destroyed any plans to have children of his own someday?

"Both had been dealing with some health issues off and on," he noted, "and went pretty quickly at the end. Apart from Lauren and Rory, I had a lot of support in dealing with it from cousins that I'm close to. They all happen to also be gainfully employed in law enforcement careers."

"I remember Brigette mentioning something about that." Nikki tasted the pie thoughtfully. "I'm sure they probably have something to say about the brazen prison escape by Perry Evigan and the others."

"Yeah, whether I want to hear it or not," Gavin quipped. "Seriously, they've got my back and definitely want to see Evigan behind bars again where he belongs."

She sipped her wine musingly. "Where do you think he is right now?"

Gavin put the wineglass to his mouth and then said bluntly, "Running scared and wondering just how much time he has left before his taste of freedom comes crashing down like a house of cards—one way or another..."

Nikki took solace in that assessment, while feeling even greater comfort in Gavin's presence as the last line of defense should Perry Evigan someway, somehow, still show up at her door. Only to have a second crack at her.

BRUSHING SHOULDERS AS they removed the dessert dishes and wineglasses, Gavin once again felt a spark when touching Nikki. Surely, she felt it too? Was there something between them that he had missed a decade ago? Had he hedged his bet wrong when turning his attention to Brigette, when Nikki was just as attractive? And perhaps a better fit for him, character-wise?

"If it's okay with you," Gavin asked Nikki evenly, "I'd like to camp out on your living room sofa for the night—while Evigan is still at large. Or, if that's cramping your style too much, I can sleep out in my car. Not a problem."

"Don't be silly." She dismissed that last notion with a wave of her hand. "No need to spend the night in your vehicle, Special Agent Lynley, in keeping me safe from a dangerous man. Or, for that matter, sleeping on my sofa. It's comfortable, but only to a point." Nikki smiled at him. "As it is, I have a guest room upstairs that you're welcome to stay in, as long as needed. It has an en suite as well, if you want to shower or anything."

"Thanks. I'll take you up on that." Gavin grinned while also feeling an underpinning of desire as he imagined her in bed in another room not far from the spare bedroom—and him in it with her. "I'll just step outside to get my bag."

As he did just that, Gavin scanned the perimeter, looking for any sign of Evigan, while keeping a hand close to the 9mm semiautomatic pistol in his holster. He saw nothing out of the ordinary or otherwise suspicious and so Gavin continued on to his Chevrolet Tahoe. *If Evigan dares to show up here, I'll arrest him and he'll be back in prison where he belongs in no time flat*, Gavin told himself, while grabbing his tote bag and heading back inside the house.

"I set some fresh towels on the bed," Nikki told him.

"Appreciate that." He smiled and they both climbed the stairwell and Gavin was led to the guest room.

"Here you go," she pointed out.

Gavin glanced inside the room and saw rustic furniture, including a log bed. He thanked her again for the hospitality. "This will do just fine," he said nicely.

Nikki gave a nod. "If you need anything, let me know."

"Will do."

"Good night."

"Good night," he told her, watching briefly as she walked away, while wondering how he could have wasted a decade blaming her for something that was entirely on Perry Evigan. And no one else. At least Nikki didn't seem to hold it against him after they had talked this through. Gavin saw that as a positive step forward for both of them.

After closing the door, he removed his firearm, setting it on the wicker nightstand, along with his holster. Then Gavin pulled out his cell phone and fell onto a rattan armchair, where he reached out to the Owl's Bay Police Department to make sure they were on the same page in terms of the BOLO for Perry Evigan and the other escapees. That seemed to be the case, which gave Gavin comfort, wanting there to be as many sets of eyes keeping watch in town for the prisoners as possible. Even if it appeared to be a long shot at face value that the trio would show up in Owl's Bay as a group. Gavin only wished he could feel as confident where it concerned Evigan operating alone, still envisioning the serial killer's smug face after his arrest, during the trial and upon his conviction. It was obvious that Nikki remembered this too.

Gavin called his cousin, Scott Lynley, returning a voice mail he'd left earlier. An FBI special agent and cold case specialist, working at the field office in Louisville, Kentucky, he and Scott, who was a few years older, were always cool and supportive of each other's careers and personal trials and tribulations.

Scott answered the video chat request, his oblong face appearing on the screen. "Hey."

Gavin gazed at Scott, who had gray eyes and thick black hair in a comb-over pomp, low-fade style. "Hey."

"I heard about Perry Evigan's daring escape from prison."

"Who hasn't by now?" Gavin pursed his lips.

Scott furrowed his brow. "Are they any closer to catching him?"

"I'd sure as hell like to think so," he told him. "But as of now, Evigan and his prison buddies, Aaron Machado and Craig Schneider, are still roaming free."

"That's too bad."

"Tell me about it." Gavin sighed, jutting his chin.

"No doubt your old girlfriend, Brigette, and the other women Evigan murdered are spinning in their graves, wondering how this could have happened."

"They seized on the distraction from the uprising," Gavin muttered. "Which shows there's still a major flaw in the system that the three were able to pull it off."

"They won't get very far," Scott said. "The FBI is doing its part to help track them down as soon as possible."

Gavin nodded. "I know and am grateful for the support."

Scott paused. "Have you contacted the surviving victim of Evigan? I know you had your differences…"

"Nikki's been alerted about the escape and is safe," Gavin reported. "I've been assigned to stick with her till Evigan is back in custody."

"Really?" Scott cocked a brow. "How's that working out?"

"Better than expected." He sat back thoughtfully. "We're good," he told him. "Or at least have found a better way to deal with Brigette's death without pointing fingers."

"That's good to hear."

"Yeah." Gavin listened as Scott briefly talked about his own latest investigation and recent second marriage, before they disconnected.

After taking a shower, Gavin hit the sack, falling asleep, while thinking about Nikki.

An hour later, he awakened to the sound of a woman screaming.

Nikki. She was in danger.

Jumping out of bed, wearing only knit pajama shorts, Gavin sprang into action. He grabbed his pistol off the nightstand and ran out of the room and down the hall toward Nikki's bedroom.

Stepping inside, Gavin expected to see Perry Evigan looming over Nikki, in the process of trying to strangle her. At which point, he would stop the serial killer escapee by any means necessary.

Instead, Gavin was quickly able to establish that Nikki was in the room by herself, restless on the platform bed from what appeared to be a bad dream. Evigan had not managed to disengage the security system and enter the house with murder on his mind.

Moving past traditional furnishings to the bed, where Nikki was squirming and moaning beneath a patchwork bedspread, Gavin sat on it and grabbed her gently by the shoulders and jostled her awake as he called out her name.

"Get off me!" Nikki shrieked, as she flailed at him as if he was attacking her. She half sat up and out of the bedding, wearing a red chemise lingerie nightgown.

"Nikki, it's Gavin," he said gently, blocking her attempts to strike him in the face.

"Gavin?" Nikki opened her eyes and settled down upon gazing at him. "What are you doing in my bedroom?"

"I heard you scream," Gavin explained, releasing her. "I thought you were in serious trouble. But it looks like you were just having a bad dream."

"Oh." Her tone quieted.

"You're safe."

"I remember now," she said, ill at ease. "I was dreaming that Perry Evigan was trying to…well, do everything he wanted to do before—" She drew a breath. "Thank goodness it was all in my head."

"Do you often have nightmares about him?" Gavin wondered, feeling bad that she'd even had one.

"I used to. Especially in the years right after it happened. Not so much lately." Nikki looked up at him. "Guess the fact that Evigan escaped triggered a return to the nightmares. Sorry if I woke you up."

"No apologies necessary," Gavin stressed. "I'm sorry that Evigan being on the loose triggered the bad dream. Hopefully, the dream and his freedom will be short-lived."

"I hope so too."

"Try to go back to sleep." Gavin felt a strong need to protect her at all costs. "I'll be just down the hall, if you need me."

"All right." Nikki touched his hand. "Thank you for coming to my rescue. Even if it turned out that I didn't really need rescuing in this instance."

"Actually, I think you did," he begged to differ. "Nightmares can be just as frightening as real life. I wouldn't have sat back and allowed you to be victimized again by Evigan, even within your subconscious mind."

Against his desire of wanting to stay the night in her room to make Nikki feel more secure, Gavin left and went back to his own room, knowing that the longer Evigan remained out of prison, the more he would be able to wreak havoc on Nikki's psyche, along with his own.

Chapter Four

"Were you able to get back to sleep last night?" Gavin asked as they ate breakfast the following morning.

"Yes, surprisingly," Nikki told him across the table, where she spooned cereal, to go with toast and coffee, while fully dressed. She had figured that, after the nightmare, she would stay awake all night, freaking out over the likes of Perry Evigan. But perhaps knowing that Gavin was just down the hall and committed to keeping her from harm made the difference. "How about you?" She hoped he said yes, hating to think that his guard duty included pulling all-nighters.

"Yeah, I pretty much slept like a baby," he claimed with a straight face. He added, "But kept one eye open, just in case."

She chuckled. "That must have been challenging."

"Not so much." He grinned. "Comes with the territory sometimes."

Nikki colored. "You mean you jar awake other witnesses or victims having nightmares, as a routine thing?"

"Not really." Gavin laughed and bit into a piece of toast. "But in this business, you have to be ready for everything. Including needing to get out of bed at a moment's notice in the wee hours of the morning."

She tasted the coffee and, eyeing him, asked curiously, "So, where do you live when you're not on bodyguard duty?"

"I'm based in Jackson," he said matter-of-factly.

"I see." She lifted her spoon. "I've visited Jackson a few times. There's a thriving art scene there."

"Really?" Gavin titled his face as though totally shocked. "Can't say I've been much into the art world—I'm more of a college-football-and spy-novels–type guy—but after seeing some of what you bring to the table, I'm becoming a true fan of your works."

Nikki blushed. "That's sweet of you to say." She would gladly invite him to her showing next week, but assumed he would be long gone by then. The notion of such was already depressing, even though it would also mean, presumably, that Perry Evigan had been captured. But then again, wasn't that why Gavin showed up at her house in the first place? No one said anything about him extending his time there. Much less moving beyond that by getting to know one another better. "Speaking of art," she said, shifting thoughts, "I need to step out for some supplies this morning." She assumed she wouldn't need to put her entire life on hold while Evigan was out there somewhere as a free man.

"No problem," Gavin spoke smoothly. He sipped coffee. "I'll drive you."

"Okay," she agreed, and bit into a piece of toast.

Shortly, they were in his vehicle and Nikki was still trying to come to grips with the fact that they were sharing the same space and no longer at each other's throats. She could only imagine what Brigette might think if she could see them now. Would she encourage them to cultivate their newfound camaraderie after years of animosity that centered squarely around her? Be jealous that there seemed to be a romantic connection of sorts forming between them? Or might Brigette have actually felt relieved that she could be single again and pursue someone other than Gavin, who might be more suited for her style and character?

"Have you always known you wanted to be an artist?" He intruded upon Nikki's thoughts.

"I suppose I have," she admitted, "ever since I was a little girl and spent much of my spare time with crayons and coloring books with all types of interesting pictures that I envisioned drawing or painting from scratch."

"Looks as though your instincts and talents have paid off for you."

"I do all right for myself," Nikki uttered modestly.

Gavin grinned. "Yeah, I think you have, and more."

"How did you end up working for the Mississippi Department of Corrections anyway?" She looked at him curiously. "As opposed to the FBI, DEA, Homeland Security, or a local police department?"

"It's a good question," he said, switching lanes as they approached an intersection. "Well, while I was a senior majoring in criminology at Mississippi State, their Career Center helped me land a job with the MDOC. I went with it—in separating myself from an uncle and cousins in law enforcement—and have been at this ever since. Overall, it's been worthwhile helping to deal with inmate issues inside and outside the penitentiary, as well as investigations involving corrections personnel who cross the line. Then there's special assignments, such as protecting crime victims or witnesses."

"Like me?" Nikki smiled at him.

"Yeah, exactly." Gavin glanced at her. "In this instance,

there was the added incentive of not wanting to see history repeat itself."

"Definitely wouldn't want that," she had to agree, while feeling maudlin thinking about what happened to Brigette— even more than what Nikki went through herself—in destroying her friend's life. And any chance she might have had of happiness, with or without Gavin.

GAVIN PULLED INTO the parking lot of the Owl's Bay Art Shop on Quail Street. As they got out of the car and headed for the store, he was keen on checking out the surroundings. There had been no sightings this morning, thus far, of the escapees. Least of all, Perry Evigan. Gavin had no reason to believe he had come to town, but kept a lookout for him nonetheless and remained armed to that effect.

Once inside, he took a sweeping glance at the main area with art supplies, then looked into two aisles with various arts and crafts, before deciding it was safe for Nikki to go about her business. Gavin watched as she grabbed a basket and said to him, "This shouldn't take long."

"Take your time," he said evenly, knowing he was committed to her well-being, wherever she happened to be while Evigan continued to circumvent the authorities. When his cell phone rang, Gavin removed it from the back pocket of his twill pants and saw that the caller was Special Agent Jean O'Reilly. Probably miffed that he left her hanging. Or appeared to. "I need to get this," he told Nikki.

"Please do." She offered him a grin. "I think I can manage on my own for a while."

He smiled. "All right."

Walking away, Gavin stepped outside, passing a shorter, solid-in-build Hispanic male in his forties, with shoulder-length brown hair parted on the side, who was entering the art shop. He was wearing workout clothes and white sneakers. His dark eyes met briefly with Gavin's, before looking away.

Gavin waited until the man had gone into the building before taking a few steps and accepting the video chat request. He watched Agent O'Reilly's face appear on the screen. "Hey."

"You might have given me a heads-up that you'd been reassigned, Lynley," she snapped.

"I had to leave on short notice," he said by way of apology. "Besides, technically speaking, I haven't exactly been reassigned, per se." He glanced at the art store window. "I'm sure you've heard about the prison break?"

"Of course. And Director Whitfield filled me in on your assignment of protecting serial killer escapee, Perry Evigan's former victim, while he remains on the prowl. I just don't get why it had to be you—with the FBI and US Marshals fully capable of keeping her safe."

"Maybe the director failed to mention that the victim, Nikki Sullivan, was the best friend of my then-girlfriend, Brigette Fontana—who was one of the ten women murdered by Evigan." Gavin wrinkled his nose, still feeling guilty for not being around to protect Brigette from him. Or Nikki, for that matter. "Nikki barely survived the ordeal herself. Anyway, between the two, it gave me added incentive to accept the assignment, along with the fact that it will be of short duration, in all likelihood—meaning that I should be back in Jackson in no time flat to continue mop-up work on the Titus Malfoy investigation."

"I didn't realize you had a personal connection to Evi-

gan's crimes." Jean's face reddened. "Sorry about your ex—
and for coming down on you."

"Don't give it a second thought," Gavin said. "I should
have called you and explained why I had to leave town
abruptly."

"So, how's Ms. Sullivan holding up?"

"Not that well, considering," he responded in all honesty. "Last night, she woke up screaming from a bad dream
about Evigan."

Jean frowned. "That's understandable, given what he
put her through."

"True." Gavin gazed again at the store, while wondering
just how many supplies Nikki needed to buy. "She's better today. But of course, until we can get Perry Evigan and
the other escapees back into custody, Nikki's likely to have
more restless days and nights."

"Their taste of freedom won't last long," she reassured
him. "We've got people searching everywhere and anywhere the prisoners were allegedly spotted—or may have
gone or be en route toward. Needless to say, the Mississippi
Department of Corrections has some major egg on its face
for allowing this escape to take place. As such, we're pulling out all the stops to make up for it—hopefully, before
the inmates can hurt anyone else."

"Good to know," Gavin told her, still feeling anxious till
it was a done deal.

"If you need any backup there, let me know," Jean said.
"I'm sure the case against Titus Malfoy can wait, especially
now that he's been arrested."

"I've got it covered, for now, with the locals on full alert."

"All right."

"I have to go," he told her, wanting to get back inside,

in case Nikki needed help carrying out her supplies. "See you when I see you."

"Ditto," she said.

Gavin closed down the conversation and glanced around, before heading toward the door of the art store.

"WHAT ARE YOU doing here?" Nikki asked, wide-eyed, as she stared Kenan Fernández in the face.

The personal trainer, whom she had made the mistake of going out to lunch with a week and a half ago, after meeting at an Owl's Bay fitness club, narrowed his eyes and said in a perturbed tone of voice, "Why haven't you returned my calls and text messages?"

She shuddered, sensing the hostility in him as someone who apparently didn't take rejection very well. "I thought I'd made it perfectly clear that I wasn't interested in anything further with you, Kenan," she spoke sharply, glancing over his shoulder for any sign of Gavin. "Responding to the calls and texts would only have encouraged—or upset—you. I didn't want either."

He lowered his chin. "Maybe if you just give us another chance, it can work out between us," he pleaded.

"I don't think so." She regarded him warily. "How did you know I was here?"

"I didn't," Kenan claimed, peering back at her. "I just happened to see you through the window when passing by."

"I don't believe you," Nikki said straightforwardly, switching the basket she was carrying from one hand to the other. She didn't believe in these types of random encounters. Not even in a relatively small town.

"It's the truth." Then, abruptly, he reversed the denial. "Okay, so I followed you from your place."

"You what?" She flashed him a hot stare while contemplating his chilling words. How did he know where she lived? "You're stalking me?"

"Not exactly." Kenan shuffled his feet. "When you never answered my calls or texts, I had my ways of discovering where you stayed and went there this morning—hoping we could talk. Then I saw you leaving with some dude. Who the hell is he to you...?"

As Nikki fumbled with a response, while considering the question at face value, recognizing the metamorphosis of her relationship to Gavin, she read the irrational jealousy in Kenan's glare. What gave him the right to pry into her personal life after one meaningless date?

Before an answer to his demand escaped her lips, Gavin walked up to them and looked from one to the other, then asked in a commanding voice, "Is there a problem?"

"Not unless he chooses to make it one," she answered tensely, and faced her stalker. "I think Kenan was just leaving. Isn't that right?" Nikki challenged him to say otherwise as he and Gavin stood toe to toe.

Gavin, taller and clearly the more intimidating of the two men, added more fuel to the fire in putting Kenan on notice, by saying boldly, "She's with me. Or I'm with her, whichever you prefer. I'd leave it at that, if I were you."

While Kenan seemed to be considering his options, Nikki was struck by Gavin's characterization of their *being together*. Though she was sure that it was meant more to send Kenan a message that she was unavailable in romantic terms than in Gavin's official capacity as her protector from Perry Evigan—Nikki almost found herself wishing that the former was true. Even if it may have been unreasonable to wish for, given their stressed history and association with Brigette.

Abruptly, Kenan made a noise that sounded like growling, eyeing Nikki sharply once more, and walking off like a defeated man.

She and Gavin waited till he was out of listening distance, after which Gavin said observantly, "So, what was that all about? I only caught enough of the conversation to gather that the man wasn't welcome company."

"He definitely was not," Nikki confirmed without prelude, as she suddenly felt the weight of her loaded basket. "That was Kenan Fernández, the personal trainer I mentioned going out with once. He followed us here from my house, wherever he got the address from. Looks like he doesn't know how to take no for an answer, even when calls and texts have gone unanswered."

Gavin frowned. "Sounds like the classic stalker. If you think he failed to get the message loud and clear, I can have a talk with him. Or make a call to local law enforcement about him…"

"Thanks, but neither should be necessary at the moment," she told him, though Nikki welcomed Gavin's coming to her aid outside his mandate. "I don't want to blow this out of proportion. Whatever his problem is, I doubt that he wants the police on his case," she stressed. "Hopefully, this will be the last I'll ever hear from him."

"Hopefully. But should that change while I'm still around, let me know," Gavin told her, an edge to his tone. "In my experience of dealing with inmates who were involved in intimate violence that included stalking and worse, this oftentimes escalated into more stalking and other criminal behavior."

"Hmm…" Nikki furrowed her brow, clearly uncomfortable. "Not exactly what I need at this time in my life—with Perry Evigan still on the loose," she admitted.

"I know. Just keep your guard up," Gavin cautioned, running a hand along his firm jawline. "Everything will be fine."

She nodded, taking him at his word. "If you say so."

"Why don't I grab that basket for you," he said, removing it from her hand before she could object, "and we can get out of here—if you have everything you need?"

"I do," she told him, offering a grateful smile. Other than perhaps peace of mind that was certainly reduced when having to deal with a potential stalker and a definite serial killer.

Chapter Five

Nikki was back in her art studio, putting away supplies, feeling like she was in her comfort zone. At least to the extent possible, with a ruthless serial killer potentially targeting her again—Gavin's strong presence in the other room notwithstanding. Beyond that disturbing reality of Perry Evigan still very much on the loose, it really irked her that Kenan Fernández knew where she lived, further encroaching upon the safety net she had established since moving to Owl's Bay. Perhaps she hadn't moved far enough away from Gulfport and the dark memories that had hung over her there like a cumulus cloud.

Could she have ever run far enough away from something that was bound to stay with her for the rest of her life, to one degree or another? Maybe not. But the fortitude that had empowered her over time would need to carry her through the present danger. And even afterward, when Gavin Lynley was no longer around to protect her from the bad guys. As much as Nikki had quickly gotten used to having him around, the man had a life of his own that didn't include her. Or Brigette, for that matter, as Gavin had obviously moved on from their short romance.

It was only brought back to the forefront with the prison

escape of Perry Evigan. Would Gavin just as easily be able to put the genie back in the bottle—and Nikki with it—once the serial killer was safely back behind bars? As if their bonding on one or more levels since Gavin had come to town had never occurred?

Being on her own these days had suddenly no longer seemed like the way to go. Nikki truly did want someone in her life. Could Gavin fill that void? Or was the specter of what happened to Brigette anything but water under the bridge?

"Hey," Gavin's voice penetrated her reverie.

Nikki turned to see him standing there, close enough to touch. She had to fight herself not to do that very thing. "Hey."

"Are you all right?"

"I'm fine," she told him with a straight face.

He smiled at her. "We'll get through this—together."

Nikki liked the sound of that: together. "Okay."

"So, what are you working on right now?" Gavin gazed over her shoulder at the painting covered by a sheet and over a canvas drop cloth on the floor. "Or is that a trade secret in your world, till your latest masterpiece is finished?"

"No trade secrets, I'm afraid." She laughed. "Not sure I would call the oil painting a masterpiece, but here it is..." Nikki lifted the sheet to reveal a landscape that showed off Owl's Bay, complete with open land, loblolly pine trees, housing and a snippet of the Jourdan River for good measure. "It's still a work in progress, but I'm just about there, as part of my showing on Saturday." She looked up at him with a curious slant of her eyes. "So, what do you think?"

"I think it's amazing," he responded without preface.

"You really know what you're doing in giving art lovers something to work with."

She blushed. "Is that so?"

"Yes, most definitely." He paused, rubbing his chin. "Brigette was always gung-ho on your talent—maybe even jealous in a way. I think she'd be applauding you now."

"Hopefully, she would be applauding us both," Nikki put forth contemplatively. "And we'd be applauding her in return, knowing that, as a go-getter, she would be a big success in whatever she chose to do."

Gavin gave her a thoughtful look. "I agree."

Nikki couldn't help but wonder if the two of them would have ended up together—no matter Brigette's preference for playing the field without Gavin being the wiser. Or would he have realized that they weren't right for each other at the end of the day and given someone else a chance to make him happy?

Nikki regarded Gavin keenly and gave an honest assessment when she put it out there by saying, "It would be great if I could paint you someday." She was sure this was an implausible scenario, given the time limit of his presence in town.

"Me?" Gavin cocked a brow. "Not sure I'd make a very good subject."

"Are you kidding? With your classic features and good looks, you'd make an excellent subject for a portrait."

"Thanks for saying that," he uttered. "I'm flattered."

Nikki toned down her enthusiasm. "Of course, I realize that you won't be around much longer, once Evigan is tracked down and sent back to prison."

"That's true," Gavin admitted. "But that doesn't mean I couldn't come back…to sit for the painting, that is…"

"That would be nice." She smiled at him, while trying hard not to read anything else into the suggestion. Such as wishing to do a return visit to spend more time with her as someone he was interested in seeing again.

I won't put unspoken thoughts into his head, Nikki told herself, even if she found appeal in the notion of extending this new comradery between them beyond his role as her special agent bodyguard.

Gavin's cell phone rang. He lifted it from the back pocket of his pants, gazed at it and said, "I better get this—"

Nikki nodded and watched as he turned away and took the call. "Lynley," he spoke routinely into the phone. His body language and tone of voice while responding to the caller told Nikki that something was up regarding the status of the escaped convicts.

GAVIN WAS TENSE as he listened to the MDOC Director of Investigations, Marvin Whitfield, who said in a heated voice, "There's been a major break in the investigation… We think that Evigan, Machado and Schneider are holed up inside an abandoned farmhouse in St. Clair County, Alabama—"

"Really?" Gavin glanced at Nikki, who was watching him intently, undoubtedly sensing that the call pertained to the prison escapees.

"Yeah, deputies from the St. Clair County Sheriff's Office spotted a black Chrysler Pacifica matching the one the prisoners stole in Boyle, Mississippi," the director said. "They changed the plates, but a neighbor reported seeing three men matching the physical descriptions of the escaped cons running from the car and inside the farmhouse. We were able to determine through the VIN and DMV that the vehicle in question was, in fact, the one belonging to and stolen from Donald Takeuchi, in Boyle."

"So where do things stand now?" Gavin asked anxiously.

"The farmhouse is surrounded by our Fugitive Apprehension Strike Team, US Marshals, FBI agents and the St. Clair County Sheriff's Office's SWAT Team," Whitfield reported. "We also have on hand a Mississippi Department of Public Safety crisis negotiator—with the aim of getting the escapees to give up and end this thing peacefully."

"Any indication that they have hostages inside?" Gavin wondered.

"Not at this time. If that is the case, we'll deal with it."

"Keep me posted on how this goes down," Gavin told him after being briefed a bit more on the logistics of the operation underway.

Once he was off the phone, Nikki moved closer to him and, with eyes narrowed, asked eagerly, "What's happening?"

"It appears that Perry Evigan and the other two escapees are surrounded inside a rural farmhouse in Alabama. They're trying to get them to surrender. That hasn't happened yet."

Nikki breathed a sigh of relief. "As long as the escapees are at least contained, it means Evigan can't get away to come after me—or anyone else," she stressed boldly.

"True." Gavin could see how much the prospect of the serial killer who victimized her being apprehended took a giant load off Nikki's shoulders. He suddenly found himself taking her into his arms for comfort. "It'll be okay," he maintained, feeling her heart beating fast, along with maybe his own. "Evigan is far away from here and has his hands full. He can't hurt you. I'll see to that."

When Nikki lifted her chin and peered into his eyes, Gavin sensed that she wanted him to kiss her as much as he wanted to do just that. He hesitated for a moment, questioning if it was wise to give in to desire, given their history—before tossing caution to the wind for what felt right. He lowered his head and claimed her mouth. The kiss was slow and steady, soft and hard, sizzling with intensity, rattling his bones while they held on to one another.

Gavin caught his breath after pulling back. He didn't want to ruin a good thing. Mislead. Or be misled. "Do you want to go grab a bite to eat?" he asked her. "With the threat of Evigan as a fugitive apparently being neutralized even as we speak, it shouldn't pose much of a risk to dine in a public place."

Nikki nodded as she touched her swollen lips. "All right."

He resisted the urge to touch her while offering a soft smile, even as Gavin wondered where things were headed— or not—for them, when he no longer had an excuse for being in her world once Perry Evigan was again out of the picture.

MARVIN WHITFIELD SAT edgily at his walnut L-shaped corner desk at the Mississippi Department of Corrections Central Office headquarters. His raven eyes flashed between the laptop before him and a picture window that provided a respite from the pressure he felt. As the Director of Investigations in the Corrections Investigation Division, it ultimately fell on him to spearhead the recapture of the escaped prisoners from the Mississippi State Penitentiary. Beyond that, he needed to learn what weaknesses in the system allowed Perry Evigan, Craig Schneider and Aaron Machado to exploit the prison riot to successfully engineer their escape.

Frankly, it drew the ire of Whitfield that this had happened under his watch. It wasn't exactly what he wanted on his résumé when the opportunity to move up the ladder of the MDOC presented itself. He would make damn sure to hold the MSP superintendent, Crystal Rawlings, and warden, Zachary Livingston, accountable for the melee and escape. Including, as a result, the death of correctional officer Stan MacGregor, with another guard, Stewart Siegfried, still listed in critical condition.

Right now, Whitfield was most interested in getting the inmates back behind bars where they belonged. Particularly Perry Evigan. He had been following the investigation into the serial killer's strangulation murders, and Whitfield was elated when they were able to apprehend, convict and incarcerate Evigan. The fact that Gavin Lynley had been involved with Evigan's last homicide victim, Brigette Fontana, and was acquainted with a surviving victim, Nikki Sullivan, made it all the more urgent that they recapture Evigan. Then both Gavin and Nikki could try to put this behind them again and get on with their lives.

At least that was the plan as Whitfield saw it. With Evigan and the other fugitives cornered in the farmhouse, it now seemed only a matter of time before their violent escape came to an end—through one means or another. The director grabbed his cell phone off the desk and called the leader of the FAST at the scene and crisis negotiator for an update.

NIKKI FELT NERVOUS excitement over the prospect of Perry Evigan being arrested again and put back in prison for the rest of his life—facing charges on at least two more homicides to add to his killings. *Who knows how many others he might have strangled to death or otherwise murdered the longer he had remained a free man?* she thought. Still, she was so glad that he and the other fugitives were nowhere near Owl's Bay, forcing her to have to relive a nightmare. Not that she didn't have help warding off danger in Gavin, who was just as affected by the serial killer's being a free man as she was. They both needed this to be over so Brigette could once again be able to rest in peace.

She glanced across the wooden table at the Owl's Bay Country Restaurant on Talridge Avenue, where Gavin was eating pan-seared Atlantic salmon with collard greens, as she had a tuna and butter bean salad. In the moment, Nikki couldn't help but think about kissing him. Or was it the other way around? Whichever—apart from the tickle she felt from her face touching the hair on his chin—the kiss had sent lightning shooting throughout her body like nothing she'd ever felt before. Then, just like that, it was over. Neither of them said a word afterward, as if to do so would imply that it meant something. Or not. She felt confused and had some clarity at the same time, knowing that she was beginning to develop feelings for the man. Even if it was one-sided and destined to go nowhere, all things being equal with their history and separate lives and locations presently.

"About the kiss…" they both voiced at the same time.

"Yeah, that…" Nikki colored, deciding to protect herself by taking the lead. "It was nothing," she suggested. "We were both just caught up in the moment. No worries."

"I was thinking the same thing," Gavin contended, dabbing a paper napkin to a corner of his mouth. "You're a great kisser though," he threw out, as though to lessen the awkwardness of the moment.

"So are you," she had to admit, and forked her salad musingly.

"We're good, then?" He met her eyes coolly, his face tilted to one side.

"We're good." Nikki was happy to leave it at that. Or maybe not, but felt it was for the best. Nothing to be gained by getting in over her head for the special agent whose mission and presence in her life were just about up.

As though to relieve the tenseness of the moment, Gavin asked her, "Aside from being an artist, which obviously can be time-consuming, what else do you like to do for fun or whatever?"

"Well, I teach an art class once a week at the local community college," she told him. "I wouldn't necessarily call it fun, but it's certainly rewarding in helping others learn the proper techniques in their own artistic pursuits." Nikki didn't need to give it much thought beyond that as she said, "On the fun front, I like to go to the gym, play tennis, swim, dance—though no style in particular—and read romance and thriller novels."

"Sounds pretty well-rounded to me."

"I suppose. And how about you?" she asked, lifting her glass of water. "What do you do for fun outside of working as a special agent for the Mississippi Department of Corrections?" Given what great shape he was in, Nikki could already imagine some pastimes.

"I like to work out," he confirmed evenly. "I jog, bicycle, listen to jazz and what else—oh, sing in the shower when no one else is listening." He laughed. "I'm not very good at it."

"Do you still go dancing?" She gazed at him thoughtfully. "I seem to recall that you and Brigette loved to hang out at dance clubs." Nikki tried to put out of her mind that Brigette was just as content to dance with any other guy who asked her when Gavin wasn't around.

"Every now and then," he responded. "Maybe if I had the right dance partner these days…"

Nikki refused to draw anything from that, though she too felt the same way, as she imagined them ballroom dancing together. Or slow dancing, cheek to cheek.

Gavin broke into her reverie when he asked, "Do you like to travel?"

"Yes," she said. "I've been to Mexico, England and Italy, along with typical hot spots in the US, like Las Vegas, Los Angeles, Miami and New York City—all with booming art scenes. I'd love to go on a cruise someday."

"Yeah, a cruise does sound like it could be fun." He sat back, thoughtful. "Can't say I can match that as far as overseas travel, but I have been to a law enforcement conference in Singapore, visited the Bahamas and a couple of places in Canada. Like you, I've made my way around the country, here and there, for both business and leisure—but always find myself back at home in Mississippi."

"Me too." Nikki smiled. Honestly, she had pondered moving elsewhere once or twice. Especially right after the ordeal with Perry Evigan. But she refused to allow him to drive her away from her home state, giving that monster more power over her life.

Gavin's cell phone rang. He met Nikki's eyes and her heart skipped a beat as she sensed that there was news on the standoff between the escaped cons and the authorities surrounding them.

Chapter Six

"Hey," Special Agent Jean O'Reilly spoke to him over the phone. "Just got word that the standoff is over."

"Really?" Gavin perked up as he gazed across the table to Nikki, who had an equally vested interest in this. He put it on speakerphone. "Tell me more…"

"Well, according to Matt Baccarin from the Fugitive Apprehension Strike Team, there was a shootout between the escaped convicts and our side," she said. "Whether something ignited accidentally or was started deliberately, the farmhouse caught on fire, trapping those inside. They were apparently determined to fight it out till the end—refusing to surrender."

Gavin shifted on the seat and asked, "So, they're all dead…?"

"Yeah, I'm afraid so," Jean confirmed. "Once the fire was put out by members of the St. Clair County Fire and EMS Association, three bodies were removed by the St. Clair County Medical Examiner and Coroner's Office."

"Have they been able to confirm that Perry Evigan is, in fact, one of the deceased individuals?" Gavin had to ask, eyeing Nikki again, knowing this was important for her peace of mind too.

"Not yet," the special agent told him. "The victims of the fire were burned beyond recognition. Dental records for Evigan, Machado and Schneider will be examined by forensic dentists to positively identify the deceased. Shouldn't take too long to confirm the identities, but all signs point to the dead being the three fugitives—Perry Evigan included."

"Okay," Gavin told her. He added, though knowing that Director Whitfield would fill him in on further details of the investigation, "Thanks for the update and keep me posted on any new developments."

"Will do." Jean sighed. "For what it's worth, if it turns out that Evigan is dead, both you and Nikki Sullivan should be able to breathe a little easier in knowing that the Gulfport Nightmare Killer will no longer be around to terrorize anyone he decides to target or who gets in his way."

"It's worth a lot, Jean," he assured her, and hung up, then identified her to Nikki for the record as Special Agent Jean O'Reilly of the MDOC.

Nodding, Nikki wasted no time in saying with a catch to her voice, "So, it looks like Evigan's evil deeds have finally caught up with him."

"Yeah, looks that way." Gavin gave her a little grin, then turned serious. "We'll know soon enough."

"For all his faults—and they seemed to be endless—Perry Evigan is still human," she stressed. "If he was truly inside the farmhouse, I'm pretty sure that he didn't develop wings and somehow fly away to evade capture and continue his evil ways."

"I agree. Evigan's definitely not superhuman. Or an invincible extraterrestrial." Gavin chuckled and ran a fork haphazardly through what was left of his collard greens. "Still, until we get the official word that he truly is dead, if it's all the same to you, I'd like to stick around." Gavin wasn't quite ready to return to Jackson and his own life full-time. Not with the passionate kiss they shared that still resonated with him, in spite of going along with the notion that it was merely a moment of weakness and nothing more. For his part, he wanted to put that theory to the test. If the kiss did mean something, didn't they owe it to themselves to explore this further? Or was his point of view entirely different from hers?

"I would like that," Nikki told him, flashing a nice smile. "What's that old saying about never counting the chickens before the eggs hatch? I think we should continue hanging out till Perry Evigan's death has been verified through forensic dentistry and the coroner, or any other means..."

Gavin grinned. "Then it's settled."

Even as he said the words, though happy to extend his stay at least a little while longer, per his assignment, internally, Gavin wasn't quite sure that was true where it pertained to his growing attraction to Nikki and where it could possibly lead down the road.

"HEY," NIKKI SAID to her mother and stepdad on a laptop video chat, while she sat in an Adirondack chair on the rear deck of her cottage. She had delayed phoning them as long as possible, knowing how freaked out they would be in learning that the man who tried to rape and murder her had broken out of prison and would possibly come after her again. Normally, Nikki might have assumed they had already heard the news. But she knew that the prison escape coincided with their long-awaited vacation to the Cayman Islands in the Caribbean. It was highly unlikely that the news would have traveled there, nor would she have wanted this to cast a shadow on their holiday. But now it didn't have to, with what she could tell them.

"Hi, honey," Nikki's mother said, a bright smile lighting up her pretty face. A retired middle school teacher, Dorothy McElligott was in her sixties, slender, blue-eyed behind horn-shaped glasses, and had blondish-silver hair worn in a pixie cut.

"Hey, there," William McElligott said, sitting beside her on a black leather sofa in their hotel room. Also in his sixties, big and strong, with slicked-back salt-and-pepper short hair, a hipster beard and gray-brown eyes, Nikki had always considered the pharmacist her mother married more than two decades ago to be her father, while barely remembering her real dad.

"How are you enjoying the Cayman Islands?" she asked them cheerfully.

"It's everything we thought it would be—and so much more," her mother gushed.

"Wish you could have joined us," William pitched in.

"Me too," Nikki said sincerely. "Maybe next time." She waited a beat before saying, "I have to tell you something—"

Dorothy's brows lowered, showing concern. "What is it?"

Nikki drew a breath and said, "Two days ago, Perry Evigan broke out of prison…"

"What?" Her mother cringed. "How?"

"He and two other violent prisoners managed to escape during a prison riot," she reported to them.

"And we're just finding out about this now?" William's thick brows knitted.

"I didn't want to worry you guys," Nikki explained, "putting a damper on your trip."

"We're your parents," Dorothy snapped. "It's our job to worry—no matter how old you are."

"She speaks for me too," her stepdad said earnestly.

"I'm sorry." Nikki almost felt as though she were living back at home under their protective thumbs again, but understood why they would be upset. "Anyway, the good news is that it appears Evigan and the other escapees were trapped in an Alabama farmhouse that caught on fire—killing all three."

"Well, that's a relief," her mother said, her features relaxing a bit, "even if you never want anyone to die that way."

William wasn't quite as magnanimous when he said bluntly, "When you break out of a penitentiary, whatever happens afterward is on you."

"Dental records will be used to positively identify the remains," Nikki told them. "But the authorities believe it's merely a formality at this point."

Dorothy said feelingly, "I'm so sorry this happened, Nikki, dredging up painful memories for you."

"I know." Nikki agreed wholeheartedly, but was forever grateful she'd had their unwavering support throughout the ordeal. She was reluctant to tell them about the recent nightmare she had that forced her to relive the victimization in much too vivid detail for her comfort. But Gavin had brought her out of it and she hoped there would not be a repeat performance now that the threat Evigan presented seemed to be over. "Something positive has come out of it though," she indicated.

"Oh…?" Her mother favored her with a curious look.

Nikki told them about her protector during the crisis being none other than Brigette's former boyfriend, Gavin Lynley, now a special agent with the Mississippi Department of Corrections. They had been made aware of the acrimony at the time between Nikki and Gavin surrounding Brigette's death. Nikki would never have imagined that they would ever break the ice—and more...

"Really?" Dorothy touched her glasses. "Who would've thought?"

"How's that worked out?" William asked cautiously.

"You mentioned positive...?" her mother questioned.

"Yeah, we've made peace with the past," Nikki was happy to report, offering them a genuine smile. "Turns out that all we needed was a face-to-face to air out our grievances surrounding Brigette's death and find a way to work around them."

Dorothy smiled. "I'm so happy to hear that. You both lost someone you loved. Nothing can bring her back, but the fact that you and Gavin are on speaking terms now is a good thing in moving forward."

"I agree," her stepdad said.

"Thanks, guys," Nikki told them, and couldn't agree more herself. She thought about the kiss she and Gavin shared and couldn't help but wonder if there was more of their story to be told, in spite of the very real possibility that they were living together on borrowed time.

KNOWING THAT NIKKI was on the back deck speaking with her parents, Gavin thought it might be a good time to step out on the front porch and catch up with his ecologist sister, Lauren Nolden. Though they lived in different parts of the country and didn't get together as often as he would have liked, he still felt close to her and loved his nieces, Miley and Ellen, like they were his own children. He hoped one day to start a family, believing he had what it took to be a great father. The trick was bonding with a person who could be good marriage and mother material. He once thought that Brigette might fill those shoes, in spite of wondering if this was truly something she was made of. The fact that Nikki came to mind in that moment left Gavin wondering if it was possible that what he had been looking for had been staring him in the face all along, minus nearly a decade of time apart.

"What's up?" he said casually with a grin when his sister appeared on the screen of Gavin's cell phone for a video chat.

At thirty-three, Lauren was attractive with voluminous black hair in a Rezo cut and their mother's brown eyes. "I'm good," she said, smiling. "How about you?"

"Well," he began thoughtfully, "the man who murdered Brigette broke out of prison recently." Gavin recalled how Lauren had been there to help him pick up the pieces when he was still trying to make sense of it all.

"You're kidding?" Lauren's mouth hung wide in disbelief in what was obviously news to her. "How did I miss that?"

"With all the info on cable and social media on violent crime and violent criminals across the country these days, it wouldn't have been all that hard," he told her in all honesty. "But the good news is that it seems as though Perry Evigan is dead, having been located hiding at a farmhouse in Alabama, along with two other inmates who escaped."

"That is good to hear." Lauren's features softened. "Having him on the loose, even for a day, must have had you climbing the walls," she voiced.

"Yeah, that about sums it up." Gavin furrowed his brow pensively. "There's more…"

"What?" his sister asked nervously.

He hesitated before replying, "I've gotten back in touch with Brigette's best friend, Nikki Sullivan." Gavin had shared his feelings at the time with Lauren on Nikki, in finding fault with her regarding Brigette's death. He knew now that this had been a big mistake and only wished he could take it back. But Nikki had forgiven him, more or less. Now he just needed to forgive himself.

"Oh, really?" Lauren gave him a long look. She had firmly rejected his position at the time, calling him misguided and unreasonable. "You're finally ready to bury the hatchet and acknowledge that Nikki was no more to blame as a crime victim than you were that Brigette fell prey to a callous serial killer?"

"Yeah, it's been buried," he told her happily. "Or at least we're getting there." Gavin glanced at the cottage, expecting Nikki to step outside. "I actually had my hand forced, so to speak, to make peace, in being assigned by the MDOC to protect Nikki while Evigan was still at large."

"I see." Lauren tilted her face to one side. "And now that the coast is clear…?"

He thought about the kiss they shared and general feeling of closeness developing between them. "We're going to keep in touch," he said sincerely, while thinking that could be an understatement when all was said and done.

"Good to hear. Something tells me that Brigette would believe it's the right way to go."

"I think so too." Even then, Gavin wondered if his former girlfriend would be on board as well were anything to develop with Nikki that moved more deeply into the romantic realm. Or would Brigette somehow view it as a betrayal from her boyfriend and best friend, even from beyond the grave? "Say hi to Miley and Ellen and Rory," Gavin said before disconnecting, only to find Nikki standing there. He wondered how much she had heard and what it might mean, if anything, moving forward.

NIKKI HAD OVERHEARD Gavin talking on the phone to his sister, Lauren. Though they had never met, Nikki sensed that they might have become friends had the opportunity presented itself back in the day—before disaster struck with Brigette's murder and Nikki's own brush with death. Along with Gavin's hostility toward her, lessening only slightly during her gut-wrenching testimony during Perry Evigan's trial, only to resume afterward. But things had taken a dramatic turn between her and Gavin since they got beyond their differences with his bodyguard duties. Didn't hurt matters any that they'd kissed. Or that he had been there when she'd had a recurrence of a nightmare involving Evigan trying to kill her.

Now, from what Nikki gathered, it appeared as though Lauren was in her corner—and had been all along—in believing that bygones should be bygones and Gavin and Nikki should have a camaraderie in modern times. At the very least.

"Hey," Nikki said evenly.

Gavin grinned easily at her. "Hey."

"Was that your sister?" she asked innocently.

"Yeah. Between work, marriage and two young kids, Lauren has her hands full these days."

"I'm sure." Nikki admired his sister for being able to juggle work and home life, as so many women did these days. She hoped to emulate this by becoming a wife and mother someday.

Gavin was thoughtful. "How are your parents doing?"

"Great! They're having the time of their lives in the Cayman Islands."

"How did they take the news about Perry Evigan?"

Nikki wrinkled her nose. "They were shocked to learn he had escaped from prison," she told him. "But were annoyed even more that I hadn't shared this with them sooner."

"Parents will be parents," he remarked understandably. "I'm sure they were relieved to know that the indications are that Evigan will no longer pose a threat to you or others."

"They were," Nikki conceded, just as his sister was. "Actually, on that note, I belong to a support group for survivors of disturbing events. We have a meeting this evening. In light of the recent events, I'd like to go as planned."

"Of course." Gavin stepped closer, meeting her eyes. "Mind if I tag along?" He paused. "Might do me some good to hear, outside of law enforcement, from others who have survived tragedies."

She nodded. "You're welcome to attend, Gavin." Nikki wondered if he might even wish to talk about what he went through with Brigette's murder, knowing that their perspectives were slightly different. Even if both arrived in the same place and suffered the same sense of loss.

He smiled. "Great. Hopefully, we'll both soon have closure with the official confirmation of Perry Evigan's death that you can share with the group at the next meeting as part of coming to terms with what happened to you."

"I hope so too." But for now, Nikki took solace in coming out on the other side of their shared experience and finding constructive ways of dealing with it.

Chapter Seven

Gavin was admittedly a little uneasy about attending the support group meeting, as he sat in the circle in the backyard surrounded by Japanese maple trees. Outside of family and a few friends, he had chosen to deal with his grief on his own. On the other hand, now seemed like a good time to, at the very least, show his support for Nikki as the group had obviously helped her deal with the victimization she'd gone through and also with what Brigette had experienced, paying the ultimate price by falling into the cross-hairs of Perry Evigan.

After listening to Air Force vet Harry Rosen recount the horrors of war that resulted in the loss of a leg, Gavin watched as the host, Blair Roxburgh, went through her trauma, followed by a slender woman in her late twenties named Miriam Broderick. Running thin fingers nervously through her short, choppy brown hair with blond highlights, she blinked her green-brown eyes and recounted how her year older brother, Quint, had been the pedestrian victim of a hit-and-run driver a year ago. The driver had been under the influence of alcohol and antidepressants.

"Seeing Quint's life and bright future taken away in such a senseless fashion by an out-of-control driver who should never have been behind the wheel, shook up my whole world," Miriam expressed painfully. She wiped away tears and said, "Being in a support group like this has helped me to better process my loss and focus more on the good memories I have of my brother rather than the end of his journey."

Nikki, who sat next to her and sought to comfort her, then picked up where Miriam left off. She seemed to go back in time as Nikki's lower lip quivered when summarizing her ordeal at the hands of Perry Evigan, which included his brutal attack on Brigette.

While avoiding eye contact with Gavin in the chair next to her, Nikki uttered solemnly, "Honestly, I wasn't sure I'd ever make it out of Perry Evigan's house alive. Quite the opposite. When he murdered my best friend, I felt I was sure to follow." She sucked in a deep breath and now regarded Gavin feelingly. "But somehow, someway, I must have had an angel on my shoulder, as rescuers came before Evigan could make me another victim of a sexual assault and homicide by strangulation." Another deep sigh. "And here I am, able to tell my story. Including the fact that my attacker escaped from prison two days ago, before apparently meeting his fate in a fiery death. Karma can work for you and against you. This time, it seemed to have worked out right for society itself, by and large."

Though resisting any show of affection, Gavin was deeply moved by her heartfelt trip down memory lane, bringing him back to his own perspective of that fateful day a decade ago. He wished he had been there for Nikki when she needed him most as someone who could relate to what she was going through. Now, as fortune would have it, he was given a second chance to make up for lost time, if she let him.

Blair, who sat across the circle, leaned back in her chair and said, "Gavin, why don't you tell us a little about yourself—and anything else you feel comfortable sharing regarding what you've gone through..."

Feeling put on the spot, Gavin felt ready nonetheless to get off his chest something he probably should have a long time ago. He eyed Nikki, whose expression was one of encouragement, and said equably, "My name's Gavin Lynley. I currently work as a special agent for the Mississippi Department of Corrections, Special Operations Unit. And, no," he joked to lighten the mood, "I'm not here to haul anyone off to jail." He got a chuckle or two in response, including one from Nikki. "Ten years ago, I was still a correctional employee, but also the boyfriend of someone who was a victim of a sexual assault before being murdered." He choked back the words, as the image of her final moments was hard to digest. "I was supposed to hang out with Brigette that night, but had to go into work at the last moment and, as such, was forced to cancel the date..."

Gavin paused and felt the empathetic hand of Nikki's on his. "Needless to say, it's haunted me ever since, to one degree or another, knowing that if I had only made different choices back then, Brigette would almost certainly be alive today—" He favored Nikki with an emotional gaze and said, squeezing her hand, "But through some means, Brigette's best friend—Nikki—was able to survive being a victim of the same psychopath and serial killer." He took a breath, looked away and then back at her. "I admit that there was a time when I tried to blame Nikki for something that obviously wasn't her fault. I deeply regret that now. The fault for what happened to her and Brigette lies entirely with the man who drugged and attacked them. I can't express enough how glad I am that Nikki didn't suffer the same fate as Brigette—and has found a way to get past that time in her life and make something out of it."

"Thank you for saying that," she whispered to him, her eyes watering.

"It's been long overdue," he returned with sincerity.

Blair smiled at him and said, "Owning up to past mistakes, while sharing your own story of loss, regrets and moving forward, is commendable, Gavin."

He grinned sideways. "It's a step or two in the right direction anyway," he allowed, knowing it would take more to make things right with Nikki—and himself, for that matter.

The host then invited another survivor to speak as Gavin listened, while focusing largely on Nikki and wanting to see her gain greater closure once they knew that Perry Evigan was indeed dead and soon to be buried.

After the session was over, Blair pulled Nikki to the side and said, "It was good of you to bring Gavin along, seeing that you two have so much in common with the ordeal you both went through."

"I'm glad he came too," Nikki admitted, not at all sure that would happen. She supposed he needed to let out what was bottled up in him all these years to a wider audience.

"Having your tormentor escape and then be stopped in his tracks must have sent you on a roller coaster of emotions."

"Yes." Nikki made a face. "I'm afraid my stomach is still tied up in knots as I process everything."

"I'm sure." Blair put a hand on her arm. "Staying in touch with Gavin should do wonders to get you over the hump."

Nikki glanced at Gavin, who was chatting with Harry Rosen. "That's the plan," she told her. Even if she was un-

sure to what extent. "Hope you can make it to my art exhibit tomorrow?"

Blair flashed her teeth. "You couldn't keep me away if
you tried."

Nikki laughed, happy to have her busy friend in atten-
dance. "I was hoping you'd say that."

They joined others and made small talk, before Gavin
asked Nikki, holding her elbow, "Are you ready to head
out?"

She felt his touch and warmed to a grin playing askew on
his lips, responding accordingly, "Yes, I think so."

The drive back to the cottage was mostly quiet. Nikki was
sure that Gavin was getting back in touch with his feelings
for Brigette, now that he had bared his soul in talking about
the crime and losing his girlfriend. For her part, Nikki felt
grateful that Gavin had gotten past accusing her of not doing
enough to keep Brigette from going out that fateful night,
as he seemed to acknowledge that Brigette was old enough
to make her own choices in deciding what she wanted to
do in her life from one day to the next.

The same had been true for Nikki. She had been restless
that Saturday night and relished the opportunity to have
some fun with her best friend. Especially when not that far
removed from having ended things with her disastrous boyfriend at the time, Felix Kovell. How could she or Brigette
have known that they were headed into a hornet's nest when
they went to Johnnie's Shack nightclub, where Perry Evigan
lay in wait like the evil vulture he was, lulling them into a
false sense of security?

Obviously, she should have relied on her instincts that
told Nikki that Evigan was very bad news and they should
never have invited him back to their table for another round

of drinks. But she rejected this in favor of trying to make her best friend happy—at least for the moment—in the absence of Gavin, whom Brigette didn't seem the least bit put off about that he'd left her hanging.

I can't change history, Nikki told herself candidly. She glanced over at Gavin behind the wheel and wondered if it was possible to change the future. Or their future, by taking a step back to the past. Or would they do more harm than good were she to spill the beans about Brigette to the man who clearly had never gotten over her? Spoiling his fantasy, perhaps, about the one whom he missed his chance with by virtue of a serial killer.

After having a nightcap, during which they spoke mainly about the near certainty of Perry Evigan's timely demise and the weight that would be lifted off their collective shoulders, Nikki and Gavin went to their separate rooms with just a simple good-night.

To Nikki, this was the best way to go. Even if she was undeniably interested in Gavin—whether it was wise or not—a one-night stand with someone soon on his way out the door was simply not in the cards. She doubted it was something he wanted either. And since a steady relationship seemed unlikely, why do anything they both would likely regret?

That night, Nikki tossed and turned in bed. Only this time, she wasn't having a nightmare about Perry Evigan, the Gulfport Nightmare Killer. Instead, she found herself dreaming about Brigette and the different faces of guys other than Gavin that she was cozying up to. Seemed as though her best friend had made a habit of two-timing Gavin right under his nose. That was so not cool, Nikki knew. But it wasn't her place to expose Brigette then.

And what about now?

That last thought was enough to wake Nikki from the deep sleep and disturbing dream. Though she felt her heart racing and was perspiring, she must not have made any sounds that resonated, as Gavin never showed up in her room to snap her out of it. She was glad, as Nikki wasn't sure how she would have responded had he asked about the dream. How might she have come across to him, in tarnishing what was obviously someone he had placed on a pedestal?

Climbing out of bed, Nikki went downstairs barefoot for a glass of water. Part of her wished Gavin would come down too, if only to talk. But he never did. She drank the water and went back to bed. It took a while, but she finally fell back to sleep. In the process, she'd debated whether or not to be honest with Gavin, as she would have wanted him to do with her had the shoe been on the other foot, before an answer came as clear as day.

WHEN GAVIN CAME down in the morning, he saw that Nikki had made breakfast. He noted that her hair was in a high ponytail and she had on jogging clothes and running shoes. Unlike last night, when she was probably wearing something similar to the red chemise lingerie nightgown she'd had on the previous night, conjuring up intimate images in his head. He'd heard her come downstairs and actually considered joining her for perhaps a nightcap, but decided against it. He'd invaded her space enough by his very presence, which, for better or worse, was close to running its course.

"Hey." He gave her a grin.

"Good morning." She returned the smile. "Hope you're in the mood for blueberry waffles with orange juice and coffee?"

"Sounds great," he said, stepping closer in his bare feet, while wearing tapered jeans and a casual shirt. "Can I help?"

"Feel free to take your plate to the table," she said, handing it to him with the steaming waffle.

Gavin did just that as he studied her. Seemed like there was something on her mind. He'd picked up on this ever since the support group gathering. Or, more specifically, ever since he had chosen to speak about his own ordeal ten years ago. So what was it? Had the trip down memory lane, mixed with the fall of their nemesis, Perry Evigan, messed with her head? Or was bringing Brigette back to the forefront a bad idea?

He waited till they were both seated across the black-and-pecan wooden corner breakfast nook table, before Gavin asked Nikki straightforwardly over his coffee mug, "Is there something you want to talk about...?"

She sliced the knife perfectly into her waffle, stuck the fork in and held it there, and gazed at him for a long moment, then said tentatively, "I've been debating whether or not to say anything..."

He cocked his brow curiously. "Regarding?"

"Brigette." Nikki set her fork down and tasted the orange juice.

"What about Brigette?" Gavin asked, but had a feeling he knew where this was going.

Hesitating again, Nikki responded, "First, let me just say I loved her like the sister I never had, in spite of our differences in personalities and styles..." She swallowed thickly and looked him in the eye. "I know you loved Brigette too, which makes this all the harder to say."

"Just get it out, Nikki," he pressed, resting his arms on the table in wait.

"All right." She sighed. "I hate to speak ill of the dead, especially after your impassioned thoughts about Brigette and how her life ended. But now that we've gotten to know each other better—along with the fact that I might not get another chance to be perfectly honest with you once you leave Owl's Bay—I think it's only fair you know that Brigette was not the loyal girlfriend you may have believed she was in plotting a future with her at the time..."

Gavin knitted his brows and raised a hand to stop Nikki from going further. "I know that," he said flatly.

Her eyes widened. "You do?"

"Yeah, of course." Whether he wanted to face up to the truth or not, Gavin knew it was high time he did just that. Especially if he had any hope at all of beginning something with Nikki without the specter of Brigette coming between them. Holding Nikki's intent gaze, he continued thoughtfully, "I caught her once making out with another guy. I knew then that she'd likely gone even further with him or others. On some level, I think I always knew she wasn't faithful to the relationship or took it as seriously as I did—but I chose to ignore this, believing I had what it took to make her see things my way." Gavin sat back, ruminating. "Guess it was just an ego thing. No one ever wants to accept defeat in a romance, no matter how challenging. When Brigette was murdered, I was at the point of ending things with her, realizing that we just weren't right for each other. But I never got that chance. Feeling guilty that I hadn't been there for her at the end, I chose instead to blame you for what happened. Along the way, I managed to push out of my mind the reality that Brigette and I were through, for all intents and purposes. Perry Evigan—that bastard—deprived me of the opportunity to ever tell Brigette."

"I'm sorry," Nikki expressed sincerely. "Sorry I ever brought this up."

"Don't be," he argued in earnest, forking a slice of waffle and coating it with maple syrup off the plate. "It needed to be said. If you hadn't done so, I would have, sooner rather than later. We both cared for Brigette and that can never die. But we also owe it to ourselves to put those feelings and the times that they represented to rest properly—especially since it appears that Evigan is no longer around to keep the dark memories alive and poisoning the atmosphere."

"You're right. It still feels a little weird though."

"For me too." He met her eyes musingly. "But it feels more right to get it out in the open and recalibrate our lives beyond Brigette—wherever that takes us—accordingly."

Nikki showed her teeth, indicating they were on the same page in that respect. "Okay."

He smiled back, feeling as though they had turned a corner, no matter what might be around it. "Good."

They finished eating and then she told him nonchalantly, "I'm going out for a run."

"I'll go with you," he said, knowing that until it became official that Evigan was no longer a threat, Gavin wasn't about to take any chances in making her a target of the serial killer.

"Think you can keep up?" Nikki challenged him.

"I can try." He expected he would do more than that, in spite of jogging not being his forte, per se, as an exercise option. "Let me get into my running shoes."

NIKKI FELT A huge sigh of relief that Gavin hadn't thought she was overstepping by spilling the beans about Brigette. Not only did he believe it was the right thing to do, but he'd

also already known that Brigette was not as into the relationship as he was. Gavin had planned to break up with her,
but had been deprived of this by Perry Evigan.

So where does that leave us? Nikki asked herself bewil-
deringly as she ran in front of Gavin down the tree-lined
sidewalk, with him keeping pace like running was as natural
for him as it was for her. She wouldn't deny having feelings
for the good-looking special agent. She sensed it was more
than a one-way street. Might they be able to turn it into a
real romance, now that everything was out in the open?
Or would their shared past continue to stand in the way of
any type of future—with Evigan seemingly now out of the
picture and Gavin no longer having a legitimate excuse for
remaining in town much longer?

"Remind me why I agreed to this?" he quipped, catching up to her and breaking the reverie.

"Because you're in great shape and working those long
legs comes with the territory in your business. Piece of
cake," Nikki added with a smile.

Gavin breathed out of his nose. "Then it's a good thing I
have a sweet tooth for tasty desserts, including caramel cake
and lemon cake—or need I remind you of that?"

"How can I forget?" She faced him while recalling how
he went to town on her leftover apple pie. "As for those
cakes, I'll have to look into that." Nikki wondered if he
planned to stick around long enough to give her a reason
to accept his kitchen challenge.

"Fair enough." He brushed shoulders and asked, "Is that
a hill I see up ahead?"

"Afraid so." She chuckled as they approached it. "Is that
going to be a problem?"

"I think I can manage," Gavin told her with a laugh. "I'll

wait for you up there." He suddenly took off, leaving her in the dust.

It took Nikki only a moment to recover before she went after him, while feeling she could get used to these mini challenges. And more, should it come to that.

When she got to the top of the hill, Nikki saw that Gavin was on his cell phone. From the gist of it, she gathered that he was talking to his boss. Between Gavin's disturbed expression and switching the phone to his other ear, she knew it was not good news.

But just how bad it truly was registered when Nikki heard him voice sourly, "You mean Perry Evigan is still alive—?"

Chapter Eight

"It sure as hell looks that way," Director Whitfield stated on the cell phone, as Gavin listened while eyeing Nikki, who had clearly picked up on the conversation once she caught up to him on the hill.

As it was, Gavin saw no benefit in keeping the disturbing news from Nikki that Perry Evigan was not in the farmhouse when it caught on fire, leaving three bodies charred. But he could at least delay this till they got back to her cottage. He asked Whitfield to hold that thought.

After surveying the area and seeing no signs of trouble, Gavin led the way in a quick and steady dash down the hill, while both he and Nikki stayed close to each other, a tense silence between them. For his part, Gavin was still caught up in seeing Brigette's betrayal in a new light, his growing feelings toward Nikki and how Perry Evigan's being seemingly still on the loose might impact their ability to move forward.

At the cottage, Gavin got Whitfield back on the phone, letting his boss know he was on speaker, and after meeting Nikki's keen gaze he said to the director in a straightforward tone of voice, "You were saying about Evigan and the farmhouse fire—"

"As you know, we pulled out three bodies—or what was left of them—from the burned-out location," Whitfield said intently. "Working with the St. Clair County Medical Examiner and Coroner's Office, a forensic dentist, Dr. Allie Tagomori, compared the dental records of the three escapees to the teeth belonging to the charred corpses. Well, two of the victims were officially identified as Aaron Machado and Craig Schneider. The third victim's teeth were not a match for Perry Evigan's dental records," the director lamented.

"How is that even possible?" Gavin furrowed his forehead, but he knew the answer, in spite of the improbability of the decedent being someone other than Evigan.

Whitfield responded knowingly, "Well, it looks like Perry Evigan was never even at the farmhouse, as shocking and disappointing as that is. He must have decided at some point to separate himself from the other escaped cons. Turns out to have been a good move on his part," the director admitted. "As arson investigators sifted through the charred wreckage, indications are that the fire was set deliberately by someone inside the farmhouse. Apparently, one or all of the fugitives had no intention of going back to prison alive."

The fiery ending at the farmhouse notwithstanding, to Gavin, it was less about Evigan making a good move or being smarter, per se, than the other fugitives from justice, and more a matter of being much luckier than them when he needed this most.

"So, who was the other victim of the fire?" Gavin asked, gazing at Nikki, who was undoubtedly just as curious as him.

"Turns out, it was an ex-con named Merrill Carlyle," Whitfield said. "Dr. Tagomori was able to create a DNA profile from the decedent's teeth that was entered into CODIS and came back with a hit on Carlyle. He was the cellmate of Aaron Machado. Carlyle was serving time for armed robbery before being released four months ago. Apparently, he and Machado kept in touch and rendezvoused at some point during the escapees' journey, and Carlyle chose to stay with them."

Gavin set his jaw, again turning to Nikki and her stunned reaction. "Any clue on the whereabouts of Perry Evigan?"

Whitfield made a sighing sound, then replied without elaboration, "We have reason to believe that Evigan may be attempting to evade capture by heading to Mexico. Information was found in his cell about Guadalajara. He could be driving a white Chevrolet Malibu. Someone matching Evigan's description was reported stealing such a vehicle from a shopping center parking lot in Blytheville, Arkansas. We're looking into it."

"With all due respect, that's not very reassuring as to Evigan's whereabouts," Gavin offered candidly, believing there was still a good chance that the escaped serial killer had no intention of leaving the country. "I'm still worried that Evigan may try to come after Nikki Sullivan." Gavin met her unreadable eyes. "For that reason—" and others he chose to keep to himself, such as wanting to remain in Nikki's company while they sorted out their feelings for one another "—if it's all the same to you, Director Whitfield, I'd rather stay with her as long as Evigan remains on the loose." *And who knows how long that could be?* Gavin told himself, seeing how resourceful the fugitive had proven to be at eluding capture, thus far.

Without prelude, Whitfield was in agreement. "Yeah, that's probably a good idea. You can stay with Ms. Sullivan for now." The director waited a beat, then warned,

"Just don't get too comfortable with this arrangement, Lynley. You do have other assignments," Gavin was reminded. "Wherever he's holed up, Perry Evigan has probably heard by now about his fellow escapees' fiery demise. Not to mention having every law enforcement officer in the country on the lookout for him. As such, he's likely not to want to go anywhere near her while on the lam with the authorities in hot pursuit. If it becomes necessary, we'll see to it that Ms. Sullivan has a personal protection detail to keep her safe."

"That's good enough for me," Gavin told him, sure that he was skating on thin ice in wanting to continue as Nikki's primary bodyguard while Evigan remained at large. But he would take whatever the director was giving him in allowing Gavin to use their time together to protect her and bond with her further.

"ARE YOU KIDDING ME?" Nikki's eyes narrowed at Gavin as they stood in the living room, where he had just ended his phone conversation with Marvin Whitfield. "I can't believe that Perry Evigan has managed to remain free while the two other convicts he escaped from prison with are dead—"

"I know." Gavin turned to her sympathetically. "It's just one of those things. He played his cards right this time. The next time, he might not be so lucky."

"And I'm supposed to put my life on hold till Evigan runs out of luck?" she complained, arms crossed petulantly, even as Nikki knew that the chances the serial killer would actually get his bloody hands on her again were nil at best. Particularly when Gavin had talked his boss into allowing him to stick around as her armed, much of the time, protector. She certainly wasn't complaining. Quite the opposite, in fact. Having him around for a while longer was just what Nikki needed to see what flames might erupt from the smoke that seemed to be swirling around them at every turn and was given room to grow now that the air had been cleared regarding Brigette.

In her reverie, Nikki barely realized that Gavin had drawn her very near to his body as he said attentively, "You should definitely keep your life going as normal as possible, with only some minor adjustments temporarily. Such as sharing your lovely cottage with me. And, of course, being aware of your surroundings and who might be lurking about. Or not." She felt his warm breath on her cheek as Gavin added, "Of course, I'll be around to make sure Perry Evigan doesn't get any wild ideas and try to act upon them in targeting you again for his sick impulses."

"That's nice to know," she had to admit, even if just how long it would last was unsettling, to say the least. She regarded him. "So, do you really think Evigan could show up here, even with all the heat he's facing, constantly needing to look over both shoulders and then some?"

"You never know," Gavin said with a straight face, still with his hands at her waist. "I gave up trying to figure out serial killers with a pathologically warped mind a long time ago. What I can tell you though, is that I don't want you to spend too much time worrying about the likes of Perry Evigan. Though he's still on the loose, the man is basically yesterday's news where we're concerned."

Nikki wasn't sure he truly believed that, considering Gavin's very—and strong—presence in her life. But she was happy to go along with it on both fronts. "In that case," she told him casually, "I suppose I can feel free to stick with the exhibition I have for this evening at an art gallery downtown?"

"Absolutely!" Gavin said smoothly. "No reason to cancel what you've been planning in showcasing your amazing talents," he insisted. "I'd love to see your art on display—and maybe I'll even buy a piece to put on the wall in my great room that's pretty barren."

"Hmm…" She smiled, trying to imagine the layout of his house. Would he ever invite her there, once his time in Owl's Bay was up? "In that case, I'd better head to my studio to put the finishing touches on one more painting to be in the exhibit."

"All right. And one more thing…" He cast his eyes upon hers, tilted his face, and Gavin moved slowly toward her lips as though to give Nikki an out in case he was overstepping his bounds. But she had no desire to do such a thing, and raised her chin just enough to accept the kiss.

Shutting her eyes, Nikki took in his hard mouth, opening her own slightly to perfectly contour with his, as she clung to him like he was all hers—at least while they kissed. But as her senses came back and Nikki realized she needed to restrain her desire for the man, she pulled their lips apart and, meeting his gaze, asked, "Is this another caught-up-in-the-moment show of weakness…?"

He held her stare and, tasting his lips, said frankly, "I think we both know it goes beyond that."

"Just checking." She grinned at him while acknowledging, "I think so too. But I still needed to hear you say it."

"I'm saying it," he affirmed solidly.

"Good." Nikki left it there, knowing she still had some work to do before the showing. And she also wanted to give them time to assess where this could lead and just how far and wide, once a serial killer was truly left in the rearview mirror once and for all.

ON A DIRT ROAD, Perry Evigan was driving a stolen gray
Buick Encore, having ditched the Chevrolet Malibu he had
stolen earlier in Blytheville, Arkansas, after making his way
back to Mississippi. With unfinished business, a decade in
the making, he was on a mission and would not be denied.

He considered the unfortunate deaths of his fellow escapees, Craig Schneider and Aaron Machado, along with
Aaron's former cellmate, Merrill Carlyle. Perry couldn't
honestly say that he was surprised. He knew that the authorities were gunning for them. He also knew that none
of the fugitives—himself included—had any intention of
going back to prison. Which was precisely why he separated himself from the others, as Perry believed his will to
survive was far stronger than theirs.

As was his determination to get the one who managed
to survive the power of his hands meant to strangle her to
death. Just like her friend, Brigette. And his other conquests.

Nikki Sullivan.

Perry thought back to when he first spotted the news
about the object of his desire to kill while accessing the
prison's library services. The piece was entitled, "Prominent
Local Artist to Showcase Work at Owl's Bay Art Gallery."

That artist was none other than Nikki Sullivan, the near
victim he could never quite get out of his system. Now he
was free and had another chance to go after her, to do with
as he pleased. Before strangling her to death like the others. The mere thought excited him no end.

The exhibition was tonight in Owl's Bay.

If lucky, maybe he could make it on time to rain down
on her parade.

Perry laughed at the thought, but then turned dead serious, knowing that it was anything but a laughing matter. At least not until the deed was done.

WHILE NIKKI WAS upstairs getting ready for her big art exhibit, Gavin took a video call from his cousin, Russell Lynley. He watched as Russell's square face appeared on the cell phone screen. Gray-eyed and black-haired, in a high, tight cut style, they were the same age. Like Russell's brother, Scott, he was an FBI special agent, working out of the field office in Houston, Texas, while specializing in serial killer and domestic terrorist cases.

"Hey," Gavin said evenly.

"Hey." Russell gave a little grin before turning serious. "Heard that Perry Evigan has somehow managed to dodge the fate of his fellow escapees."

"Yeah, looks that way." Gavin leaned back as he sat on a wicker accent armchair in the living room. "The man seems to have nine lives—as if to add up to the number of women he murdered plus one."

"He only has one life," Russell said firmly. "And its shelf life is hardly inexhaustible. FBI agents are working overtime with your guys to nab him, or otherwise stop him in his tracks."

"I know and I'm sure it's only a matter of time before we get him. But it's the wait that's driving me crazy—not knowing where he is at the moment and what he's up to..." Gavin drew a breath as he pictured the creep killing Brigette and damned near ending Nikki's life as well.

"I hear you," Russell put forth, his thick brows knitting. "I know you're concerned that Evigan might try to come after the surviving witness, Nikki Sullivan—"

"The thought has crossed my mind," he responded wryly.

"Which is why I'm doing guard duty as long as Evigan stays a fugitive." Gavin knew that his interest in Nikki had moved well beyond a professional obligation, but there was no reason to go there just yet. So long as the threat remained for her safety, first and foremost.

"It won't be long." Russell narrowed his eyes thoughtfully. "Have you two been able to reconcile with everything that went down with Brigette?"

"Yeah." Gavin nodded. "Nikki was every bit as much a victim of Evigan as Brigette," he acknowledged. "I get that now and only want to make sure she gets to live the life she's entitled to and that was taken away from Brigette."

"She will," Russell sought to reassure him, before they spoke briefly about a case he was working on as part of a task force that included Russell's wife, Rosamund, a Homeland Security Investigations special agent.

When Gavin got off the line, he spotted Nikki coming down the stairs. Taking one look at her in a figure-flattering, floral surplice jersey dress, worn with strappy black sandals and her long hair in a plaited bun, made his jaw drop. "Wow! You look amazing," he told her, getting to his feet.

Nikki blushed. "Why, thank you." She eyed him. "You're not so bad yourself, mister."

He grinned at the compliment but downplayed it nonetheless. "Guess it was a smart idea to bring along a set of nicer clothing," he said, wearing a crisp lilac dress shirt, navy slacks and black loafers. "Anyway, this evening is all about you, Nikki. I'm only along for the ride." *And to keep my eyes open for any signs of Perry Evigan*, Gavin told himself.

"I'm glad you could come," she told him, meeting his steady gaze. "That's good enough for me."

"Same here."

Both ignored mentioning the part where an escaped serial killer threatened to cast a dark shadow over the art exhibition.

Chapter Nine

At the Owl's Bay Art Gallery on Fellows Street, Nikki was ecstatic over having her art works on display. Though this wasn't her first merry-go-round, she did feel a little extra burst of adrenaline in having Gavin there to see what she brought to the table. It was also comforting to know that the special agent for the Mississippi Department of Corrections had her back, just in case Perry Evigan did decide to make an appearance.

Even if a part of her felt this was unlikely, given that the search was on to recapture the escaped con, Nikki wasn't about to let her guard down as long as he was still out there somewhere. *I can't let him get to me*, she told herself with determination, while surveying her portrait, landscape and still-life oil paintings with Gavin.

"So, what do you think?" she asked, gazing up at him as they both held flutes of champagne.

"I think you're incredible," he told her. His eyes lit up as he peered at a landscape work of art and then shifted his focus to look at a painting of a bowl of red and green apples.

Nikki laughed. "I bet you say that to all the girls." One she knew for a fact he did once upon a time.

Gavin chuckled. "Trust me, I don't. I know talent when I

see it—and so much more." He met her gaze and she could tell that the compliment went beyond her artistic skills.

"That's nice to know." She flushed and tasted the champagne. "Hopefully, there will still come a time when I can paint you," she threw out, already imagining the thrill of getting him on canvas.

"Count on it," he said confidently as Gavin sipped his own champagne.

They moved on and were joined by Blair Roxburgh and her boyfriend, Oliver Pascal, a tall, fifty-something chiropractor with shoulder-length, swept-back salt-and-pepper hair and a matching egg-shaped full beard. He touched his octagon glasses while turning blue eyes on Nikki, and said, "Your paintings are stunning."

"I told you they were out of this world," Blair marveled, holding a flute of champagne.

"We're all in agreement there," Gavin pitched in.

"Thank you all," Nikki said, grinning from ear to ear. Getting praise from people she knew gave Nikki all the validation she needed that this was what she was meant to do with her life. She told them humbly, "I'm still forever a work in progress as an artist, but I'm honing my craft with each painting."

"That you are, indeed." Blair smiled at her and raised her flute glass in toast, with everyone joining in.

"So this is where you've been hiding in plain view…"

Nikki heard the lyrical voice and turned to see the gallery owner, Jillian Yamaguchi. In her late sixties and a great artist in her own right, she was frail and had fine white hair in a chignon bun. "You found me," Nikki joked, and introduced her to everyone.

"Good." Jillian's brown eyes crinkled. She cupped an arm

beneath Nikki's and said, "Hope you don't mind if I steal her away for a bit? I have some people I want to introduce Nikki to, while playing up her exhibition."

Nikki looked to Gavin, in particular, for his approval and he nodded. "Please, go mingle with your audience. I'll try to stay out of your way."

She knew that meant he wouldn't go too far, in case she needed him. "Okay."

"We'll just check out more of your works," Blair told her, holding hands with Oliver.

"I'll find you later," Nikki told them, and headed off with Jillian.

GAVIN WATCHED NIKKI walk away with the gallery owner before he began wandering around, looking this way and that for any indication that Perry Evigan had made his way to the art gallery. Admittedly, it seemed like a giant leap to believe that the fugitive serial killer would actually have the wherewithal to track Nikki down in this location, at this time. But Gavin had been in law enforcement and corrections long enough to know that hardened and tenacious criminals could never be underestimated. That was certainly true for Evigan, who had managed to strangle to death ten women without being caught, before he finally had the hammer dropped on him.

The man had walked away from a maximum-security prison farm and remained on the loose for days, while his fellow escapees had perished in a fire. That alone told Gavin that Evigan was not one to be taken lightly, no matter the odds against his taking another shot at Nikki.

As a result, Gavin found himself checking out anyone and everyone who was anywhere near Nikki, while maintaining a good enough distance to allow her to bask in her success as a local artist. *I don't want to see Evigan spoil her showing by trying to take Nikki out*, Gavin told himself. She'd paid a high enough price for her earlier victimization by him. Not to mention, witnessing the sexual assault and murder of her best friend. Gavin would not allow Nikki to go through that again—so long as he was able to stick around and protect her while her attacker was out there.

He moved beyond the perimeter to see if anyone else matching the serial killer's general description came into view. Nothing. Breathing a sigh of relief, Gavin continued to walk around and took out his cell phone. He called Special Agent Jean O'Reilly. She picked up immediately. "Hey," he told her. "Any news on Perry Evigan and his whereabouts…?"

"The assumption is still that he's headed for Mexico," she reported. "But I'm not so sure about that. Evigan, who thinks he's smarter than everyone else—and seemed to spend much of his time in prison educating himself even more—doesn't strike me as someone who would be happy spending the rest of his life south of the border."

Gavin had the same thought, but asked, "What about the material on Guadalajara found in Evigan's cell?"

"From what I understand, it belonged to his cellmate, José Contreras, another convicted murderer, who came to this country as an illegal immigrant sex trafficker, by way of Guadalajara."

"Hmm…" Gavin muttered. "So, Evigan could pretty much be headed or hiding anywhere." *Even in Owl's Bay*, Gavin thought, but tried to push that notion away.

"True," Jean said, "but it appears that he might be moving toward the Midwest, or farther away from Mississippi.

The white Chevrolet Malibu Evigan was believed to have been driving was found abandoned in Arkansas. Someone matching his description was reportedly spotted in Indiana."

Maybe he isn't anywhere near Owl's Bay, Gavin thought, glancing about at the art lovers who showed up. Could be that he was giving Evigan far more credit than he deserved. Or maybe there was good reason to feel uneasy for as long as the escaped killer was not back behind bars.

"Keep me in the loop for anything else you find out," Gavin told her, knowing that he was just a bit preoccupied to be in the midst of the hunt for the Gulfport Nightmare Killer.

"You've got it," Jean promised, and Gavin hung up, realizing he'd managed to lose sight of Nikki and needed to find her in a hurry, to make sure she was all right.

"THIS IS KENAN FERNÁNDEZ." Jillian introduced the man she had described as an art lover.

Nikki cocked a brow with dismay as she stared at the personal trainer she thought she had seen the last of. "Kenan..." she gasped.

Jillian looked from one to the other. "Do you two know each other...?"

"We've crossed paths," Kenan responded, a smug grin on his lips.

"Something like that." Nikki peered at him, then told Jillian, "Can you give us a moment...?"

"Of course." Jillian flashed her a mildly concerned look. "Find me when you're through."

"I will." Nikki offered her a gentle smile and watched Jillian walk away; then Nikki scanned the room for Gavin, who seemed to have disappeared. But something told her that it wouldn't be for long. She glared at Kenan and snapped, "You shouldn't be here."

His brows joined. "Why shouldn't I? You invited me to your showing, don't you remember?"

Nikki had forgotten this and wished she could take it back. "That was before I realized that we weren't right for each other," she told him candidly. "You know it, I know it." She had blocked him on her cell phone. "Now I'd like you to leave, Kenan."

He scowled at her. "You can't get rid of me that easily," he spat. "I think there's still something between us. If you'd only get off your high horse and let it happen."

She shot him an icy stare. "Are we really going to do this—here? I have an art exhibition underway with lots of people around. Be smart, Kenan. Stalking is a crime, whether you want to believe it or not."

"Believe it!" Gavin's voice boomed as he came up from behind her. He got in Kenan's face and said, "I thought we understood each other?"

Kenan held his ground as best he could. "You thought wrong."

Gavin pulled out and flashed his identification. "I'm a special agent with the Mississippi Department of Corrections. One phone call and I'll have you arrested and charged with aggravated stalking," he asserted. "If convicted, you could serve five years in prison. Believe me, you don't want to end up there." Gavin allowed that to sink in and asked toughly, "So, what's it going to be? Will you leave Nikki alone?"

Kenan set his jaw. He eyed Nikki like a man who seemed still obsessed with her, but appeared to know when he was outnumbered and backed into a corner. Throwing his hands up, he muttered, "Yeah, whatever."

Nikki watched him storm off and said under her breath, "Hope he's finally gotten the message this time."

"So do I." Gavin frowned. "But in case he's still bent on harassing you, I think you need to take out a protective order against the man. If Fernández tries to circumvent it, he'll get himself further into hot water that won't end well for him."

"I'll do it," Nikki was quick to agree. "I've about had it up to here—" she raised her hand to her chin "—with him. If it takes a restraining order for him to back off, so be it." *And having you around as my bodyguard is certainly an extra deterrent*, Nikki told herself thankfully.

"Good." Gavin smiled at her warmly. "Anything else interesting happen since I left…?"

"Only that everyone seems to love my artwork," she answered, but sensed that he was referring to any sign that Perry Evigan had decided to pay her an unwelcome visit too. "No sighting of Evigan, thus far, knock on wood."

"I doubt that he'll show his face around here," Gavin spoke confidently. "He's got too much to lose by coming after the one living—and protected—witness to his serial crimes. Besides, Evigan's allegedly been seen in Indiana in his quest to evade recapture."

Though feeling relieved to hear this, Nikki still had to ask, "Do you think that's true?"

He hesitated before responding. "Perhaps. But we won't really know till Evigan's back in custody and we can interrogate him and see exactly what path he took to avoid capture."

"Well, that time can't come soon enough," she declared anxiously.

Gavin nodded. "I'm with you there."

"How's everything going?" Jillian asked when joining them.

"We're good," Nikki told her, glancing at Gavin.

"Yeah, she's all yours." He grinned as he looked at the
art gallery owner.

Jillian smiled. "Actually, this evening, Nikki is not just
mine, but everyone's artist extraordinaire."

"I couldn't agree more." Gavin flashed Nikki a devas-
tating smile and she took it in, while masking her growing
desire to be with him in ways that had nothing to do with
his safeguarding role in her life.

WHEN THEY GOT back to the cottage, Gavin double-checked
the perimeter for his own peace of mind that there was no
indication it had been broken into, that they had been followed, or otherwise suggested that Perry Evigan had been
there. Or even Kenan Fernández, for that matter. Though
both men had more reasons for staying away than coming
there, at risk to their freedom, Gavin wasn't convinced that
common sense and logic would overcome obsession, irra-
tionality and stupidity, where it concerned the two men.

*I have no problem going the extra mile to protect Nikki
from any potential predators*, Gavin thought, knowing full
well that this had become personal, as much as his duty for
the MDOC. He needed Nikki to stay alive and well, so they
had the opportunity to take what had been given them in
each other and run with it.

They entered the house and Nikki punched in the code to
the security system, after which Gavin took a quick walk-
through with Nikki close by, before he told her levelly when
they were back downstairs, "Looks like the coast is clear."

"That's nice to know," she said. "I would hate to think of

this cottage as ground zero for a serial killer on the prowl. But thanks for checking."

"Not a problem." *Not yet anyway*, he thought, and wanted to keep it that way. Gavin turned his attention away from threats to her big art exhibit. "It was fun seeing you in your element this evening. Your paintings, on full display, were incredible. And so are you."

Nikki blushed. "I try my best. Sometimes even that falls short, but what can you say?"

He grinned. "Not everything needs to be said. There are things that speak for themselves."

"You're quite the philosopher," she said with an amused chuckle. "So, I guess I'll allow my artwork to do the talking for me—and add my two cents every now and then."

Gavin laughed. "Seems like a pretty good plan of action."

She smiled and headed into the kitchen. "Would you like a glass of wine?"

"Sure, that sounds good."

He followed her and watched as she took the bottle of white wine from the stainless-steel fridge and removed two wineglasses from a cabinet. After filling each halfway, she handed him a glass and, after sipping from her own, said, "It's been nice having you here and getting reacquainted."

"I feel the same way," he made clear, putting the glass to his lips. "I wish it had been sooner to reach this point in time, but getting to know you now has been well worth the wait."

"I agree wholeheartedly." She beamed. "That is, getting to know the man you are today."

Gavin stared into her entrancing blue eyes and knew instinctively that this was the right moment to kiss her again. He cupped her chin and went for it, pressing their lips together for a stirring kiss that upped his desire for her a few notches.

As though she were reading his mind and matching it with her own, Nikki met his eyes and cooed sotto voce, "I want to get you into bed."

His libido soared even more. "I'd like nothing more than to make love to you, Nikki," he told her with a sense of urgency.

"Then what are you waiting for?" she challenged him. "Make love to me—now…"

In his head, Gavin imagined ripping her clothes off, lifting her onto the countertop and engaging in primordial sexual relations. But as he imagined that might be a bit uncomfortable for her, he showed restraint and uttered, "Let's go to your bedroom."

"Yes, let's…" she agreed, taking him by the hand and leading the way, as they brought the glasses of wine with them.

KENAN FERNÁNDEZ FINALLY decided to drag himself from the Hawthorne Bar and Grill on Burnsten Street before they kicked him out. He finished off the Alabama slammer whiskey shot and headed for the door, still miffed that Nikki Sullivan had decided he wasn't worth her time. Without even giving him a chance to show what he was truly made of, she'd essentially kicked him to the curb. That included blocking his calls and texts, adding insult to injury. She had apparently taken up with this other dude—a special agent—who had threatened to have him charged with aggravated stalking if he didn't back off his pursuit of Nikki.

Kenan muttered an expletive as he stumbled across the small parking lot toward his red BMW 228i Gran Coupe.

He had admittedly never taken rejection well. And he wasn't quite ready to start now. But how could he compete in a fair fight against someone who seemed equally determined to keep him away from the gorgeous woman Kenan had a thing for?

He climbed into the vehicle, buckled up and headed home to the nearby beachfront condominium he owned.

Caught up in his thoughts, Kenan was oblivious to the fact that he was being followed. It was only when another vehicle—a gray Buick Encore—pulled up alongside his on the driver's side with the passenger window rolled down, that he took notice. But by the time Kenan became aware that someone was pointing a gun at him through his own open window, it was too late to do anything about it, as a shot rang out, hitting Kenan squarely in the face.

His world had already gone dark by the time a second shot hit the mark, for good measure. Kenan Fernández's car veered out of control, crashing into a light pole.

The Buick continued on down the street as if nothing tragic had happened.

Chapter Ten

"Do you happen to have any condoms?" Gavin thought to ask Nikki as they stood in her primary bedroom, still fully clothed while they were between hot kisses. She had let down her hair.

She was happy that he was responsible in wanting to protect them from an unplanned pregnancy, but told him to ease his concerns, "I'm on birth control." Nikki added, "But if you'd feel more comfortable using a condom—"

"I'm good," he told her in a relaxed manner, indicating that Gavin was confident that neither of them had any sexually transmitted diseases and was ready to carry on.

"So am I," she let him know coolly, eager to be with him in intimate relations.

"Then let's do this." Gavin put his hands on her cheeks and they started kissing again.

Nikki felt as light as a feather as she inhaled his manly scent and fantasized about what was to come, a decade after her earlier fantasies about him. They pulled apart and stripped off their clothing. It took her only an instant to realize that Gavin's firm body in the nude and rock-hard abs were everything she had imagined and then some.

"You're perfect," she gushed, unable to resist saying it, even while he was perusing her admiringly.

He laughed. "Not sure about that, but I am sure where it concerns just how gorgeous you are from head to toe…and everything in between…"

"Hmm…" Nikki basked in the words every woman wanted to hear before making love. "Come here, handsome—"

Gavin obeyed, gave her a mouthwatering kiss, then scooped her up in his arms and carried her to the bed. Just as Nikki sought to take the lead in their foreplay, he told her smoothly, "Relax. And enjoy this…"

She did as she was told, closing her eyes, when Gavin used his mouth and masterful fingers over the expanse of her entire body to whip Nikki up into a frenzy. Unable to take it anymore, needing him as she had never needed anyone like this, she uttered demandingly, "I want you inside me—now!" She sighed and softened her tone, but not the fervent desire she had. "Please, make love to me, Gavin."

"I'm more than willing to do as you ask," he responded, his voice lowered an octave to reflect his own overpowering needs. "I want you too—more than you could ever know…"

He climbed atop her and Nikki lurched as Gavin plunged deep inside her. She wrapped her long legs around his hard back and moaned as the feeling of sexual satisfaction gripped her like a fever. The instantaneous nature of the climax shocked Nikki in a way, but was quite expected in another, as the pent-up needs were brought to the surface by Gavin and his determination to please.

It was only after this that she gave him the go-ahead to complete their lovemaking by reaching his own apex of fulfillment. Their slickened bodies clung together like second skins as Nikki had a second orgasm and cherished it, before things settled down and they lay side by side on the satin sheet, catching their breaths.

"Did we really just do that?" she had to ask with a nervous laugh while regaining her equilibrium.

He raised a brow. "Uh, if you mean red-hot sex, then the answer is yes, we did."

"Okay." Nikki colored. "I know what transpired—and I agree, it was mind-blowing—but was it because you truly wanted me or someone you could no longer have?" she questioned openly, as Brigette entered her head, perhaps unwisely.

"Definitely you," Gavin made clear, seemingly picking up on the insinuation. "What I had with Brigette was then—painful as it was to deal with her murder while knowing the escaped killer is still on the loose—and this is now and all about us as two people attracted to each other, who needed what happened between us and acted upon it."

She smiled, feeling relieved. "Good answer."

"I meant every word," he assured her. "I'm not looking to go backward in time—only forward to wherever that leads us."

"Me too." Nikki wondered just where that might be. She vowed not to overthink things, such as what would happen after the Perry Evigan episode had ended, and let it play out in real time.

Gavin cozied up to her. "Good. Now that we settled that, might a second round be in the cards?"

She chuckled. "Are you sure you have the energy?"

He laughed. "I think I can manage when I'm with someone who is a total turn-on."

Nikki felt him caressing her, causing her own need for

him to be reinvigorated. "Works both ways," she promised, then upturned her mouth to meet with his in a passionate kiss.

GAVIN TRIED TO sit still on the wooden stool in Nikki's studio the following morning. He had let her talk him into posing for an oil painting. As she had been persistent enough, the least he could do was capitulate and let her go to work, even if he didn't necessarily see himself as worthy of being the subject to be shown in a future art exhibit. Or even hanging on the wall surrounded by an expensive frame. But if Nikki felt otherwise, who was he to argue? Not to mention, he was flattered to be seen in a way beyond his professional life in corrections, zeroing in on his physical appearance that he had grown to take for granted through the years.

His mind shifted to making love to Nikki well into the wee hours of the morning. Gavin knew that she saw him as well in a more carnal sense that delved into both their basic instincts and natural attraction toward one another. He pictured her small but full breasts, taut body and perfect streamlined figure—even her small feet and cute toes did it for him. As did her pleasing scent and the way she laughed and blushed.

It made Gavin imagine what it would have been like had he connected with Nikki on this level a decade ago—instead of Brigette—and been allowed to build a relationship over the years. Maybe they would be married today, with children. How had he missed the boat then in not clearly recognizing what was staring him right in the face?

I was too blinded by my stubbornness to look past Brigette's unwillingness to commit to a serious relationship and my foolish attempts to get her to see things my way, to end things between us and look elsewhere for hap-piness, Gavin chided himself. But it was well past time to move on from past mistakes, and he had, with Nikki, who had come back into his life and helped him to see the light. Much of which shone all around her.

"You're not too deep in thought over there, are you?" She caught his attention as Nikki stood before the canvas, paintbrush in hand, a little paint having found its way on to her white bib apron.

Snapping to attention, Gavin gave a chuckle, realizing he had been caught in reverie. "You got me," he confessed.

She regarded him curiously. "Care to share?"

"I was just thinking that I'm so glad you reappeared in my life."

"Uh, I think it's the other way around," she said wryly.

"How about both?"

"Deal." Nikki studied her subject. "Any complaints?"

"None whatsoever," he promised her. *Both in and out of bed*, Gavin thought truthfully.

"Me neither." Nikki drew a breath. "Can you turn your head just slightly to the right for me?"

Gavin obeyed, then quipped, "Well, now that you men-tion it regarding complaints, it's anything but easy trying to stay still or keep the smile off my face when I'm desper-ate to do just the opposite."

She chuckled. "You're doing just fine. I promise, it won't be too much longer."

"Isn't that what all artists tell their subjects?" he ques-tioned.

"Only the ones who whine too much," she tossed back, causing them both to laugh.

"Point well taken." Gavin made a straight face. "No more whining, I promise."

It was this easygoing banter between them, among other things, such as her beauty and their intimate connection, that told him he wanted her in his life well beyond the time when Gavin's special agent duties had come to an end. Were they on the same wavelength here?

When Nikki's cell phone rang, she took the call and listened in, before her expression changed as she blurted out, "What?" Gavin tried to read between the lines, but waited till Nikki's next words were uttered forlornly. "Thanks for letting me know. Bye, Blair."

"What's up?" Gavin asked immediately, detecting the tension in her posture.

Nikki approached him, looking as if she had seen a ghost, and said tonelessly, "My friend Blair just told me that Kenan Fernández is dead."

"Dead?" Gavin got to his feet, meeting her gaze. "How?"

"He was shot to death while driving in his car," she said, a catch to her voice. "The killer is still at large—"

By the uncertain look in Nikki's eyes, Gavin knew that the murder of Kenan Fernández was for her, just as much as for him, a cause for concern. On its face, this may have been entirely coincidental as it related to Nikki. Or could this be connected in any way to the escaped con who was still on the loose as far as Gavin was aware, and potentially targeting Nikki?

HONESTLY, NIKKI WASN'T quite sure what to think as she sat beside Gavin while he drove them to the Owl's Bay Police Department. Had Kenan, whom she barely knew, been involved with some bad people? Was he targeted accidentally?

Or could Perry Evigan have somehow come after him in some sick form of revenge against her? This admittedly seemed like a hard pill to swallow. After all, how would Evigan have known about her one date with Kenan? Never mind the fact that she had absolutely no interest in the personal trainer. But stranger things had happened, hadn't they?

Of course, to believe any of this would mean that Perry Evigan was actually in Owl's Bay. And not in Indiana. Or wherever.

"You all right over there?" Gavin asked, breaking the silence between them.

"I will be, once we can get to the bottom of Kenan Fernández's murder," Nikki responded forthrightly. "Not that I have any vested interest in his death, per se," she pointed out. "Seriously, I never wanted to see him again—"

"But you didn't want to see him dead either, especially as a homicide victim." Gavin turned onto Vandeer Street. "I get that."

"Do you?" She eyed him, but knew they were very much in tune with one another in terms of the possible nature of the murder that neither could ignore.

"Of course." He drew a breath. "Let's not jump the gun though, in making any assumptions that may fall flat, till we see what the police have to say about Fernández's death."

"All right." Nikki yielded to his rational sense of logic. She glanced out the passenger-side window. Getting flustered over what-ifs would do her no good. And only feed into the paranoia she once had regarding Evigan. She couldn't allow him to play with her psyche again. Not unless there was good cause.

INSIDE THE POLICE STATION, Gavin and Nikki met with the homicide investigator assigned to the case, Brooke Reidel.

The fiftysomething, slender detective was blue-eyed and had layered strawberry blond hair in a medium cut.

"Nice to meet you, Agent Lynley, Ms. Sullivan," Brooke told them, as she shook their hands in her corner office and then offered a seat in two faux leather guest chairs next to her L-shaped wood desk. She leaned against it and asked, "You wanted info on the Kenan Fernández case?"

Gavin looked up at her from the chair and replied candidly, "Whatever you can share." Knowing it was an ongoing investigation, he added, "Nikki had a run-in with Fernández yesterday at her art exhibition."

Brooke gazed at her intently. "Did you know the victim?"

"We went out once," Nikki said tartly, fidgeting in the chair. "It was a dead end, as far as I was concerned. But Kenan seemed to believe otherwise. He showed up at my showing at the Owl's Bay Art Gallery."

"So, you're saying Fernández was stalking you?"

Nikki glanced at Gavin and back. "Yes, it seemed that way."

"I confronted Fernández at the exhibit and told him to lay off—threatening to have him charged with aggravated stalking," Gavin told her. "Fernández left at that point."

"And you never saw him again?" the detective asked, shifting her eyes from one to the other.

"No, and we were together till this morning." Gavin was more than willing to acknowledge their involvement with one another as their alibi, realizing that the encounter with Fernández technically made them suspects in his murder.

"Okay." Brooke took a breath. "From what we know thus far, last night, Kenan Fernández was at the Hawthorne Bar and Grill on Burnsten Street, before leaving at approximately ten p.m. Shortly thereafter, he was shot to death in his BMW by someone in another vehicle on Shaw Boulevard. We currently have a BOLO alert out for that vehicle, which is believed to be a gray Buick Encore, that was picked up on surveillance video around the estimated time the incident occurred."

"What can you tell us about the weapon used to kill Fernández?" Gavin asked her with interest.

"According to the medical examiner and ballistics, the victim was shot twice with 9mm Luger ammo that came from a SIG Sauer P365 9mm pistol," the detective said. She added, "Our Crime Scene Investigations Unit was able to collect the shell casings near the crime scene to corroborate this finding." She gazed at Gavin. "Why do you ask?"

"Nikki was a witness and the victim of an escaped serial killer, Perry Evigan," Gavin told her, glancing at Nikki, whose shoulders slumped understandably. "One of the weapons Evigan and his fellow escapees stole was a SIG Sauer P365 9mm handgun," he recalled, making him fearful that Evigan could be in Owl's Bay.

Brooke reacted to this revelation by creasing her brow. "Yeah, I heard about Evigan's escape and the farmhouse fire that took the lives of the other two fugitives and another ex-con." She eyed Nikki. "Sorry you were put through that. It must have been awful."

"It was," she confessed. "But that was a long time ago. I'm over it." Nikki sighed. "Or at least I was, before Evigan broke out of prison—"

"I get that," Brooke said sympathetically. "But from what I've gathered, Perry Evigan has gotten out of Mississippi."

"We'd like to believe that," Gavin said musingly. "However, given that Fernández was shot with the same type of pistol that Evigan may have in his possession, along with his unnatural desire to go after the only victim to survive his serial murders, I'm not prepared to leave anything off the table where Evigan is concerned."

Nikki's voice shook when she uttered, "I'm a bit spooked as well with the prospect that he might have murdered Kenan as some sort of psycho calling card to let me know he's back and coming for me…"

"I understand both of your concerns," Brooke told them. "It's certainly worth checking out. But we think that Fernández's death may be related to a drug deal gone bad."

Gavin cocked a brow. "Really?"

"Yes. The Hawthorne Bar and Grill has been a hot bed for drug use and trafficking in recent years," the detective said, leaning forward. "Moreover, a witness reported seeing Fernández having a heated exchange with an African American male, described as being in his mid-to late-twenties, shortly before Fernández left the bar. For now, this unidentified male is our primary person of interest."

"All right." Gavin had heard enough. He looked at Nikki and could see her strained features relax with the prospect that Fernández had been murdered by someone other than Perry Evigan. This too gave Gavin comfort, as the last thing he wanted was for the serial killer fugitive to have tracked Nikki down, with sure intent to do her bodily harm. He stood, prompting her to do so as well. "Thanks for your time," he told the detective.

Brooke nodded. "I know the BOLO for Perry Evigan is still in effect, as long as he remains free. If we get any credible information that suggests he has come to this town, you can be sure that the Mississippi Department of Corrections will be informed, Agent Lynley."

Gavin offered her a small grin. "Fair enough."

They walked out of the Owl's Bay Police Department with a renewed sense of safety. But in the back of his mind, Gavin still had an uneasy feeling that danger could well lurk around one corner or another as he knew there would be no rest as long as the Gulfport Nightmare Killer remained on the loose somewhere.

Chapter Eleven

Nikki was happy to resume the portrait of Gavin, if for no other reason than to take her mind off the unexpected death of Kenan Fernández. It may have been a big mistake when she agreed to go out with him, and he could be a real jerk in his persistence, but he certainly didn't deserve to die. Even if he was into drug dealing, as the police suspected, which she still found hard to believe. It seemed to her that, as a personal trainer, he prided himself on staying healthy and fit. Neither went well with drug use, which often accompanied those who were in the business of trafficking drugs. But what did she know?

"Now, if you could just bend your head ever so slightly to the left, that would be perfect," she told Gavin, who complied with a handsome grin playing on his nice lips. He was not only an excellent subject, with great bone structure and a flawless complexion, but he also didn't complain like some of her other subjects. Come to think of it, he checked a lot of the boxes for her—not only as ideal for painting, but as great relationship material as well. Not to mention, he was a good lover whom she could never imagine tiring of.

"If there's anything else I can do to make your job easier, just say the word," Gavin told her smoothly.

"Hmm…" Nikki flashed her teeth with a naughty thought. *Be careful what you agree to*, she mused. "I'll certainly keep that in mind." She worked on his gray eyes with her brush, feeling that they were something she could drown in, so enchanting they were. Her thoughts turned back to the murder of Kenan and how relieved she was that apparently this was not the work of Perry Evigan. So why did she still feel uneasy? As if his presence still loomed large? *Get your mind off this and focus*, she admonished herself, peering at Gavin, not wanting to allow her victimizer to ruin a good thing they had going. For however long it lasted.

"So, how are we looking over there?" Gavin asked patiently, his hands resting on his lap.

"Just about done," Nikki told him as she applied the finishing touches around the eyes, before changing brushes to work a bit more on his chiseled chin. "Hope you like it…"

"How can I not?" he expressed confidently. "I've seen your artwork. I'm more than honored to become a permanent part of it."

She blushed. "I'm equally honored that you agreed to sit for me." Not to mention break the ice in coming to her rescue with an escaped killer on the loose. "There," she voiced. "Done, save for a few touch-ups here and there once it dries. Come have a look."

"All right." Gavin got up, stretched his long legs and came over to her.

Nikki waited with bated breath to see what he thought, as he stared at the painting in utter silence. "Well… What do you think?" she asked nervously.

"I love it!" he declared. "You've done an incredible job in capturing the best parts of me."

"You think?" She smiled.

"Unquestionably. I never thought I could look so good on canvas. But you've made a believer out of me, Nikki."

She flushed. "Glad you approve."

He grinned at her. "Oh, I approve of a lot of things about you, Ms. Sullivan."

Her lashes fluttered coquettishly. "Is that so?"

"Yeah." Gavin wrapped his arms around her waist and drew her close. "Such as the sweet taste of your lips."

"Hmm…"

"Mind if I try them on for size?"

"Be my guest." She happily gave in to him.

They kissed for what seemed like a few minutes that definitely left Nikki all hot and bothered, before coming up for air. "I'd better get cleaned up," she told him, knowing she had managed to get paint on her face and hands.

"Okay, if you insist." He favored her with a sexy grin. "But just for the record, even with a few smudges, you still look great."

She laughed. "I'll take your word for that." Along with reading between the lines, which Nikki admittedly felt gave her hope for bigger and better things with him down the line. She headed upstairs to wash her face.

GAVIN WATCHED HER leave the studio, then he turned back to the portrait of himself. He really did appreciate it and wondered if it would find its way into her next art exhibition, before he could take it home. Actually, truth be told, he would rather bring Nikki back to his place, see how comfortable she felt there and see which way the wind blew in enabling them to seize this point in time for establishing a real romance. *Let's see if she's amenable to that when this*

Evigan business is behind us, Gavin told himself with optimism, before removing the cell phone from his khaki pants.

He checked his messages and saw a text from Marvin Whitfield, who was following up on their earlier conversation regarding the current whereabouts of Perry Evigan, which made Gavin nervous. He called the director with a video request and asked tentatively after Whitfield accepted it, "So, where do things stand with Evigan?"

Whitfield's brow furrowed. "We seem to have lost track of his possible whereabouts at the moment," he said disappointedly. "There've been a few sightings here and there, but nothing that has been substantiated."

"What about the last known vehicle Evigan was believed to be driving?" Gavin thought about the gray Buick Encore that the unsub in Kenan Fernández's murder may have been driving.

"That's just it," the director said, "we don't have a credible lead on that right now. Could be that he's driving around in a stolen car that had already been stolen by someone else. Hence, no report of it. If I had to make a guess, I'd say that Evigan is probably changing vehicles every chance he gets—trying to remain one step ahead of the law."

Gavin didn't disagree with that assessment. It still left open the door that Evigan could have shown up in Owl's Bay and was able to locate Nikki, while waiting for the right time and place to strike. He brought up the SIG Sauer P365 9mm pistol that was used to pump two rounds into Fernández's head. "Could be the same SIG Sauer firearm Evigan stole in Boyle from Donald Takeuchi," Gavin pointed out.

"Yeah, we're checking into that," Whitfield told him. "We've asked the Owl's Bay Police Department to submit the firearm casings to the National Integrated Ballistic

Information Network to see if any matching bullets have been used and, if so, where. Of course, getting ahold of the murder weapon would be very helpful if we're to link the homicide to Evigan."

"I know." Gavin resigned himself to the fact that without possession of the SIG Sauer P365 9mm pistol—in the absence of a positive identification of Perry Evigan in Owl's Bay—he couldn't know for sure if Evigan was the shooter. Or if, in fact, it was a drug-related hit and a local unsub actually carried it out.

"Is she doing okay?" the director asked.

"Nikki's holding up fine," Gavin said, but knew there were limits as to how long that would last. He was glad that Nikki had her art to keep her preoccupied while Evigan continued to elude authorities.

After ending the video chat, in which Whitfield made no mention of withdrawing him from the assignment for now, Gavin gazed again at his oil portrait. He used the cell phone to take a picture of it and then sent it to his sister, followed by his cousins, knowing that they would all enjoy seeing it. If he had his way, Gavin hoped that someday they would all be able to sit for their own portraits. This, of course, would mean that he and Nikki's relationship had become just that—evolving into something that would warrant get-togethers both ways with his family. As well as hers.

ON MONDAY AFTERNOON, Nikki drove to teach her art class at Owl's Bay Community College. Gavin came along for the ride, sitting in the passenger seat, looking at his cell phone. Neither had brought up Perry Evigan today, but she was certain that Gavin was mindful that the serial killer had still not been brought to justice and, consequently, they would remain on edge till such time.

She glanced at Gavin and couldn't help but wonder what his thoughts were for their future. Or had he given much thought at all to whether or not what they had between them was lasting? As opposed to taking a wait-and-see attitude? She wouldn't push him one way or the other—even if in her heart, Nikki knew that what she was starting to feel for Gavin was very real. And not at all subject to misconception. Or time-limited. But that was just her. He would need to decide for himself if he wanted a life with her firmly planted in it or not.

She pulled off Praceson Road and into the parking lot, where Nikki found a spot right in front of the Department of Fine Arts and Design. "Here we are," she told Gavin with a smile.

He looked at her and grinned. "Let's go."

They went inside the building, where Nikki's class was on the first floor. "You're welcome to come in, if you like," she invited Gavin, though suspecting he would decline.

"Thanks, but I'll wait out in the hall," he said. "I need to make some calls and give you your space at the same time. At least in the classroom."

Nikki would have been just as comfortable to have him in her space, but understood that he needed his own, while remembering that he was still on duty as a special agent and surveillance was part of that. So long as Evigan remained even the slightest threat.

"All right." Nikki smiled again at Gavin. "See you in a bit." Carrying a black leather satchel with art materials, she headed inside where students awaited her. She greeted them, including her newest student, Miriam Broderick, who walked up to her, and also happened to be a member of Nikki's support group. It was there that Miriam expressed a strong interest in developing her art skills and working her way past the tragic death of her brother a year ago.

"Hey, Nikki." She flashed a generous smile. "Thanks so much for inviting me."

Nikki's eyes lit up. "Thank you for wanting to come. Hopefully, you'll get what you need to improve your craft and I'll be here to help in any way I can."

"I appreciate that and I'm excited about the opportunity."

"Me too." Nikki grinned and walked toward a kidney-shaped laminate table, where she set the satchel and eyed various works of art lining the walls, and imagined others yet to come, before turning to the students to begin the class.

"I HAVE NEWS…" Jean O'Reilly told Gavin over the phone.

"Hopefully, it's good news," he said, while moving farther down the hall, away from Nikki's classroom.

"I wish," she moaned. "Two days ago, there was an unauthorized use of an ATM card in a town about a hundred and fifty miles from Owl's Bay. This led to a welfare check of the card owner, a fifty-five-year-old male veterinarian named Richard Pelayo. He'd been stabbed to death in his garage. The medical examiner believes Pelayo was killed at least twenty-four hours before his body was discovered."

"And this relates to Evigan how?" Gavin asked tensely.

"A man fitting his general description, and wearing a hoodie, was picked up on surveillance video outside the house," Jean replied matter-of-factly. "We're still trying to determine if it was Evigan or not by finding his DNA or fingerprints at the crime scene, or other means of identification."

Gavin swallowed thickly, switching the phone to his other ear. "Do you happen to know if Pelayo owned a car?"

"A Buick Encore was registered in his name," she responded. "We think it was stolen by whoever killed Pelayo—"

Gavin frowned. "It's the same make and model as a car involved in the shooting death of a man named Kenan Fernández here in Owl's Bay," he told her bleakly. "If Evigan is the man in the surveillance video footage, then he's likely responsible for both deaths."

"Hmm…" Jean hummed. "I can understand killing Pelayo in the course of a home invasion, but why Fernández?"

"It may have something to do with his interest in Nikki," Gavin said, and explained the convoluted scenario.

"Wow," she voiced afterward. "Seems like a stretch, insofar as motivation. Not to mention the high risk versus uncertain reward for Evigan, should he have been able to fit these pieces together in Nikki's life and times."

"I agree," Gavin told her, when it was put that way. "Maybe I have it all wrong about Perry Evigan. But my gut instincts tell me that I can't rule out anything in regard to what the escaped serial killer may be capable of. Which is why we need to find him ASAP."

"We're doing everything in our power to do just that," Jean assured him. "The Fugitive Apprehension Strike Team and our partners in law enforcement are all over this, looking at every lead regarding Evigan, whether he's still in the state or elsewhere."

"All right." Gavin took a breath. "Let me know what forensics comes up with on the Pelayo murder crime scene or otherwise."

"I will." She paused. "You'll get through this. So will Nikki Sullivan."

"Yeah. I hope you're right." After disconnecting, Gavin walked back toward Nikki's art class and peeked in the door window. He could see her. The need to protect her from the likes of Perry Evigan was stronger than ever. As were the feelings for Nikki that had begun to fill Gavin's heart in ways he couldn't have imagined just a few short days ago. Now it was something he would never want to turn his back on, no matter where things went with them.

He stepped away from the door and called Detective Brooke Reidel, informing her about the possible connection between the murders of Kenan Fernández and Richard Pelayo, with the potential common denominator being wanted fugitive, Perry Evigan.

PERRY HAD ADMITTEDLY grown restless in his intense desire to pick up where he left off as a heartless strangulation serial killer. Time had only increased his appetite for death of those deserving. Though he knew without question that the big prize would be Nikki Sullivan, he had been unable to get to her just yet, thanks to the presence of her bodyguard. Perry assumed he was law enforcement in some capacity, determined to keep Nikki alive.

This was the polar opposite of Perry's own quest and desire. He had waited this long; he could wait a little longer to achieve his ultimate objective. In the meantime, he needed a warm-up to get him back in the game in a way that could get him excited. And he had already latched on to the perfect target for his deadly craving. Now it was just a matter of luring her into his trap, for which there would be no escape.

Tilting the brim of the beige bucket hat he was wearing to help disguise his identity, along with dark cat-eye sunglasses and the stubble he'd allowed to grow on his face and neck, and a fresh set of clothing and boots, Perry walked inconspicuously away from the Owl's Bay Community College's Department of Fine Arts and Design building. Shortly, he arrived at the latest vehicle he had stolen—a blue Toyota Corolla Cross—having believed that the Buick Encore had become too hot now.

Climbing inside, he drummed his fingers on the steering wheel fretfully and waited.

Chapter Twelve

"Mom, Dad, this is Gavin Lynley," Nikki introduced him to her mother and stepfather, Dorothy and William McElligott, via a video chat while holding a tablet in the living room. They were back in Clarksdale after their visit to the Cayman Islands. Now seemed as good a time as any to have them meet Gavin, knowing the bad blood that had once existed between her and Brigette's former boyfriend. So much had changed since then—as it related to Nikki's evolving relationship with the handsome special agent—that it was incumbent upon her to share this with those she was closest to.

"Hi, Gavin," her parents spoke in unison in friendly voices.

"Hey." He looked over Nikki's shoulder. "Good to meet you both."

"You too," her mother said, smiling.

"Same here," her stepdad added, and after a beat, asked, "So, where do things stand on Perry Evigan? I've heard conflicting stories on his whereabouts and even whether or not he's still alive—"

So have I, Nikki thought unnervingly, while considering the latest news that the escaped serial killer may have been involved in an identity theft and home invasion turned deadly in a town a hundred and fifty miles away. The suspect's head was covered with a hood, but he seemed to match Evigan's description and apparently stole the victim's Buick Encore—the same type of vehicle believed to have been used by someone in the murder of Kenan Fernández. Were the culprits truly one and the same? Had her tormentor finally found her?

Gavin, who had managed to keep her grounded while doing his best to downplay the threat, even while being much more guarded against being confronted by the fugitive, responded candidly, "I believe Evigan is still alive. As to his whereabouts, we haven't been able to pinpoint this definitively as yet, but we're working night and day to apprehend him."

Dorothy frowned. "After what that man put my daughter through, I worry that the longer he remains on the loose, the greater the chance that he will find his way back to her for more terrorizing...and worse..."

"I will not let Evigan hurt your daughter," Gavin said firmly, trying to reassure her. "I'm not letting Nikki out of my sight till Evigan is back in custody. Or dead, so he can't ever come after her again."

"Listen to Special Agent Lynley," William said comfortingly to his wife. "Nikki's in good hands. He won't let anything bad happen to her."

"I do feel safe with Gavin nearby," Nikki pitched in, flashing him a smile of support, while knowing that the nature of their involvement had gone well beyond potential victim and protector. "Wherever Perry Evigan is, he's running out of time to remain free. We're okay here."

Her mother's blue eyes crinkled. "I'm happy to know that."

"Love you both," Nikki uttered sweetly, promising to

keep them abreast of anything new to report about the wanted escapee. Beyond that, she was eager to apprise them of where things were headed between her and Gavin, once Nikki knew herself in no uncertain terms.

After ending the video conversation, she gazed at Gavin, who grinned back and said thoughtfully, "Hope I made a good impression on your folks."

"You did," she said knowingly. "I'm sure they approve of you being here."

"Yeah?"

"Of course." She smiled, reflective. "If you get to meet them in person, they will surely fall head over heels for you." *Just as I have*, Nikki told herself.

Gavin blushed. "In that case, I look forward to getting together with your mom and stepdad. And for what it's worth, if my parents were still alive, they definitely would have been happy to meet you and get to know you as someone who's in my life. I'm sure Lauren and her family will be quite taken with you when they get to meet you."

"It's nice to know you feel that way." Even more comforting to Nikki was hearing him say that she was in his life—and wanted to extend that to those he was closest to—giving them both something to build upon.

The trick though, was to not allow Perry Evigan to find a way to come between them as someone who still wanted to see her dead.

AFTER HER OFFICIAL shift had ended on Monday evening, Detective Brooke Reidel received the call that an adult female had been found deceased under highly suspicious circumstances at a residence on Willow Lane. Knowing that her job for the Owl's Bay PD didn't give her the luxury of picking and choosing hours that worked best, Brooke grabbed her Glock 26 Gen5, holstered it and left her dog, an Irish Setter named Mandy, in their Craftsman bungalow, and hopped into her white Ford Explorer to head to the scene.

En route, Brooke got more info on what she was coming upon. According to a first responder, the dead female had been identified by her townhouse neighbor as Miriam Broderick, a twenty-seven-year-old product line supervisor for a trucking company and divorcée who lived alone. Brooke couldn't help but wonder about the other aspects of the victim's life that led up to it ending prematurely. Was it a happenstance victimization? Wrong place, wrong time-type circumstance? Or a terrible situation she put herself in by bad choices or a misguided association?

Truth was that Brooke had seen them all. Even in a relatively small town like Owl's Bay, where she had put in more than twenty years as a detective and more than a decade in homicide. Take, for instance, the death of Kenan Fernández two nights ago. It had all the earmarks of a drug hit. Except for the fact that Fernández was not a known player in the drug use and drug dealing sphere. Nor did he have a criminal record to suggest he was involved in this illicit activity.

On the other hand, Fernández had been accused of stalking. Had that been a factor in his death, as the search continued for the gray Buick Encore believed to have been used in his execution, as well as trying to track down the current person of interest in the case?

Complicating matters was the possibility that the vehicle was stolen and Fernández's killer might be responsible for the murder of another man a hundred and fifty miles away. Brooke considered that the unsub could well be fugitive serial killer Perry Evigan. Nikki Sullivan had managed to come away alive from her ordeal with him, after being drugged and kidnapped by Evigan. Had he shown up in Owl's Bay to take another crack at her?

Brooke left that one to ponder as she pulled up to the Cetona Townhomes complex on Willow Lane. After getting out of her car and bypassing onlookers, in what had clearly become a crime scene, she ducked under the yellow tape and made her way up the stairs to the victim's townhouse, where Brooke was greeted in the foyer by Officer Lester Hu. She flashed her identification at the twentysomething, slender Asian man, who was brown-eyed and had black hair in a faux hawk style, and asked him routinely, "What do we have?"

Lester furrowed his brow. "It looks to be a homicide," he spoke bluntly. "It's not pretty. See for yourself." He turned away from her.

Brooke stepped inside the contemporarily furnished great room and saw that it had been ransacked. Lying face up on the bamboo floor behind a coffee-colored love seat with flared arms was the nude body of an adult female with short, choppy brown hair with blond streaks. Her green-brown eyes, wide-open, were devoid of any signs of life. A scarf was wrapped tightly around her neck in a way that made it clear that this was no fashion statement.

A chill ran through Brooke as her mind went straight to the so-called Gulfport Nightmare Killer—whose calling card in a series of ligature strangulations included a scarf asphyxiation. Was he back in business—only now as the Owl's Bay Nightmare Killer?

GAVIN GOT A phone call from Detective Brooke Reidel. He assumed she had an update on the unsub and/or vehicle believed to have been used in the deadly attack on Kenan Fernández. Knowing that Nikki would want to hear this too, and feeling a need to keep her informed, he put it on speakerphone—even if he would rather shield her from any unsettling news pertaining to Perry Evigan. Especially with the promise made to her mom and stepdad about protecting their daughter at all costs. It was something Gavin stood by, as much for his own desire for a long-term future with Nikki in it, as doing right by Nikki and her folks.

"Detective Reidel," Gavin said apprehensively. "What do you have for me—or us?" he amended as he let her know she was on speaker, and gazed at Nikki, as they stood inside her art studio.

"I'm afraid it's not good…" Brooke sighed. "I'm at the scene of a homicide. The white female victim, age twenty-seven, was found by a neighbor. In a preliminary examination, the Yaeden County medical examiner believes that the decedent, Miriam Broderick, was strangled to death with the scarf wrapped around her neck…"

"Did you say Miriam Broderick?" Gavin asked, recognizing the name.

"Yes—do you know her?"

He turned to Nikki, whose expression dampened as she responded solemnly, "Miriam was in my support group for trauma survivors. She also attended an art class I taught today at Owl's Bay Community College." Nikki's voice shook as she asked the detective timorously, "Do you think this was the work of Perry Evigan?"

Brooke wasted no time in replying straightforwardly, "It fits the MO of Evigan's previous strangulation murders. Of course, we won't know for certain till we see if his DNA or fingerprints were left at the crime scene," she emphasized. "We're looking at surveillance video as well."

Nikki's eyes narrowed. "If it was Evigan, then he knows where I am and will try to come after me," she argued.

"If Evigan wanted to announce his presence, all he's done was bring more heat on him," Gavin stressed, placing his hand on the small of her back supportively.

"Agent Lynley is right," Brooke said firmly. "We'll be working overtime to solve Ms. Broderick's murder—whoever the perp is..."

"Anything more on the gray Buick Encore?" Gavin asked the detective. With its possible connection to the murders of Kenan Fernández and Richard Pelayo, there was also good reason to link the vehicle to Perry Evigan, now the chief suspect in yet another homicide.

"We're still trying to locate the vehicle," she told him, sounding irritated. "It's only a matter of time before we do, then we'll have a better idea of where we stand on the multiple investigations."

Gavin gritted his teeth. "Keep me posted."

"Of course," she promised. "In the meantime, we can put patrols around Ms. Sullivan's house, if you like?"

"Sounds like a great idea," he responded, but knew that this might still not be sufficient, if Evigan was intent on coming after her.

Once Gavin was off the phone, he faced Nikki, who uttered with watery eyes, "If Miriam was killed because of me—"

"You weren't responsible for her death, no matter who the killer was," he wanted to make clear, even if Gavin knew how easy it was for Nikki to blame herself, were Evigan behind it. "There was no way for you to know that Evigan would break out of prison and find a way to remain on the loose for days—killing anyone who stood in his path. Or otherwise, was ripe for the picking."

"You're right." She twisted her lips acquiescently. "But that doesn't make me feel a whole lot better."

"Come here." He brought her up to his chest, wrapping his arms around her. "You'll get past this, Nikki," he promised. "We both will."

In that instant, Gavin couldn't help but think about Brigette and how—through fate, by design, or whatever— her tragic death had brought him and Nikki together and given them a chance to come to terms with the past and see the light that a future could bring them. So long as the darkness of an escaped serial killer didn't snuff it out.

IN SPITE OF a mostly restless night's sleep, for all the wrong reasons, Nikki was up bright and early the next morning. She was still trying to square with the reality that her fellow survivor of a traumatic time and art student, Miriam Broderick, was a victim of a homicide. What was that all about? *Was she targeted because of me?* Nikki had to wonder, even when she knew that things did happen in life or the universe itself happenstance, with no one at fault, per se.

On the other hand, she knew that someone was most definitely at fault for Miriam's death. Was it Perry Evigan? Or someone else as perhaps payback for a drug deal gone bad?

As she wrestled with these thoughts, Nikki found Gavin sitting at the breakfast nook table, gazing at his computer. Beside him was a mug of hot coffee. He looked up at her and grinned, giving her the once-over, as she'd thrown on one of his button-down shirts—it was light green and oversize on her, but surprisingly comfortable. "Hey," he said.

"Hi." She blushed under his perusal.

"I don't imagine you slept much better than I did."

"I think you're right."

"Sorry about that." Gavin furrowed his brow. "Coffee's ready."

"Thanks." Nikki was happy that he seemed to have made himself quite at home in her kitchen and elsewhere. Sign of the times? Or future? She poured herself a cup of coffee and studied him, fully dressed for the day. "What are you doing?" Her voice rang with curiosity, knowing the uneasiness in the air with the latest revelations.

He hesitated. "I was just taking a look at the autopsy report on Miriam Broderick."

Nikki cringed while imagining her horrific death. "What were the results?" she asked, taking a seat across the table on the side bench.

"I'll spare you the details," he said protectively.

"Don't." She peered at him. "I'm a big girl, Gavin. I also witnessed firsthand someone being strangled." Brigette's once beautiful face appeared in Nikki's head, before it was forever tarnished by that maniac. "If this is the work of Perry Evigan, I need to know what he's up to, no matter the chilling nature of it…"

"All right." Gavin nodded understandingly. He took a breath, glanced at the screen and stated, "According to the Yaeden County Medical Examiner Flora Ueoka, Miriam was the victim of ligature strangulation, with the actual cause of death being asphyxia. She was also sexually assaulted by her killer…" Gavin paused and gazed at Nikki. "Do I need to go on…?"

"No." She'd heard enough and did not need more explicit information from the report on the suffering Miriam had been put through, before death came mercifully. Nikki sighed and asked pointedly, "Do you think it was him?"

Gavin tasted his coffee musingly and responded with candidness, "We need to be prepared for that distinct possibility."

Her eyes grew wide and her mouth hung open distraughtly. "How does one prepare for the reality that a monster is out there—back in force in picking and choosing which women to rape and strangle to death next?"

Reaching out and taking her hand, Gavin said composedly, "By steeling ourselves against falling into his trap of feeling helpless. Or a bad sense of inevitability. Wherever this thing goes, we control our own destiny. I'll be damned if I allow Evigan to dictate that for you or me. And I won't let you feel that way either."

Nikki wrapped her fingers around his large hand, with her pulse racing, but her heart telling her that having him on her side was more than she could ask for against a common enemy. Even if Perry Evigan was not the one responsible for Miriam's death, his sheer presence as an escaped serial murderer could not be dismissed. So long as the menace of him remained a serious thorn in Nikki's side for her health, well-being and longevity.

Chapter Thirteen

Gavin watched as Nikki headed upstairs to get dressed. If he had his way, he'd love to see her completely undressed and spend as much time as possible with her in bed. She had that kind of effect on him these days. Probably would have a decade ago as well, had he given her half a chance instead of his misguided belief that Brigette was *the one*. Clearly, she was not. He had already come to that painful realization, more or less, when she was killed. But by then, it was too late in the game to see if he and Nikki might have made a connection before someone else won her heart.

This is a whole new beginning for us, Gavin thought, tasting his second cup of coffee. He could live with that and see where it went. All that mattered for the time being was that they couldn't allow Perry Evigan to put a halt to their progress by victimizing Nikki as he wanted to do, in following what he did to Brigette.

Gavin phoned Brooke Reidel for a video chat as he paced around between the living and dining areas, returning her call from a couple of minutes earlier. When her face appeared on the cell phone screen, he said cautiously, "Hey. What's up?"

"We located the gray Buick Encore linked to the murder

of Kenan Fernández," Brooke said, running a finger across a thin brow. "It was abandoned behind a vacant building on Tuffas Road. We dusted it for prints and were able to retrieve some that belonged to Evigan. He was definitely in that car at some point," she stated matter-of-factly. "And he has to be considered the number one person of interest in the murder of Kenan Fernández."

Gavin jutted his chin and, before she could continue, asked her, "What about the Buick itself—was it...?"

"Yes, the car belonged to Richard Pelayo," Brooke confirmed. "As such, there's every reason to believe that Evigan killed him too, before taking his car and driving it a hundred and fifty miles to Owl's Bay to continue the murder spree..."

As Gavin digested this, it left the obvious question in his head and the anticipated answer. "Are you saying what I think you are regarding the death of Miriam Broderick?"

Brooke furrowed her brow and nodded affirmatively. "DNA removed from the victim as a result of being sexually assaulted was sent to CODIS. It came back with a match of Perry Evigan's DNA. Moreover, his fingerprints were also left at the scene of the homicide, leaving little doubt that he murdered Ms. Broderick and is still at large."

"And coming after Nikki." Gavin uttered what the detective was surely thinking.

"We've alerted the relevant authorities about this and Owl's Bay is now front and center in the search for the escaped con," Brooke said with concern in her voice. "In the meantime, the police department will assist in any way we can to keep Ms. Sullivan—Nikki—safe."

"All right." After he ended the call, while considering his options and waiting for Nikki to come down, Gavin wasted little time in phoning Marvin Whitfield to confer on the news that Perry Evigan was almost certainly still in Owl's Bay and, as such, a clear and present danger to Nikki.

Whitfield muttered an expletive and snorted, "How this bastard has managed to evade the law while resuming his murderous ways is beyond me."

"I'm in total agreement," Gavin told the director respectfully, in assessing Evigan's amazing ability to dodge recapture and add more notches to his belt as a serial killer and sociopath, "but that doesn't change the fact that by his mere presence in town, Evigan is threatening the very person you assigned me to protect. That's problematic, to say the least."

"I hear you." Whitfield took a breath. "So, what do you suggest?"

"I need to move Nikki out of Owl's Bay, to be on the safe side." Gavin took nothing away from the ability of the MDOC's Fugitive Apprehension Strike Team and other law enforcement agencies involved in the hunt for Evigan. Or, for that matter, the benefits of sheltering in place at the cottage with a good security system and him being armed. With the Owl's Bay PD providing adequate backup. But honestly, none of that gave Gavin comfort right now that the escaped killer might not still find a way to breach that safety net and place Nikki in harm's way.

I couldn't live with myself if I let Evigan have a repeat performance in victimizing Nikki again, Gavin thought, determined not to let that happen. He hoped the director was on board with this.

"Where to?" Whitfield asked.

"A lakefront cabin in the woods just outside of Gulfport," he said to him. "A friend of mine named Jake Kendrick owns it. I've spent time there. It's secluded and has plenty of windows to give me a 360-degree view of who's coming and going. I'm sure he won't mind letting us borrow it for a day or two, if necessary, while Evigan is being tracked down and ultimately taken into custody."

"Okay, then go for it," the director said. "If you're sure about this?"

"I'm just going with my gut here," Gavin told him frankly. "I think it's better to err on the side of caution by temporarily relocating Nikki." The thought had crossed his mind about taking her back to his house in Jackson as a safe refuge. But given the distance and high likelihood that Evigan would be recaptured shortly, Gavin opted against making a move that might seem a bit premature and presumptuous as it related to things evolving in their personal relationship sooner than Nikki might have desired. The last thing he wanted was to rush her. Or otherwise mess things up between them by jumping the gun. "Having lost someone to Perry Evigan ten years ago, I don't want to give him even the slightest opportunity to come for Nikki again—in a place that he may well have already sized up."

"I understand. Get her out of there, then, Lynley. We'll do everything in our power to recapture Evigan and put him back where he belongs. Hopefully, that will come sooner rather than later. Until then, Nikki Sullivan—and you— deserve some peace of mind while the serial killer remains on the loose."

"Thanks, Director Whitfield." Gavin took a calming breath, but knew there would be no comfort as long as the threat to Nikki's life remained real.

"As an added measure of security, we'll send along a US marshal to escort you and provide an extra set of eyes for your destination," Whitfield said.

Gavin thanked him again and disconnected, only to find Nikki standing there with a hand on her hip and a scowl on her face.

NIKKI HAD OVERHEARD some of Gavin's conversation with the Director of Investigations at MDOC. They were talking about moving her out of Owl's Bay, to a cabin in the woods, while Evigan remained free and a threat to her life. She cringed at the implications, but needed to get the scoop from Gavin on exactly why she needed to leave the cottage.

"Hey," Gavin said evenly, though his hardened expression gave away the uneasiness he felt about the current situation.

"What is going on?" she asked straightforwardly, peering at him. "Why the need to relocate me...?"

He drew a breath and, meeting her gaze directly, replied in an acerbic tone of voice, "It's been confirmed that Perry Evigan is in Owl's Bay. His DNA was found on Miriam Broderick and his prints were also found at the crime scene..."

Nikki gasped and put a hand to her mouth as the gravity of Evigan doing to Miriam what he did to Brigette hit her like a ton of bricks. Suspecting something was bad enough. Having it verified was so much worse and left Nikki speechless.

Gavin placed his hands on her shoulders and said knowledgeably, "Beyond that, Evigan's prints were also found in a stolen vehicle believed to have been used by the shooter in the death of Kenan Fernández and another man. Why Evigan would go after Fernández is anyone's guess. But I do know that while Evigan is still on the loose, you're not safe here, Nikki." Gavin's warm breath fell onto her face. "I want to take you to a friend's log cabin, where I can put some distance between here and Evigan's reach. Now that his location has been pinpointed, I expect our Fugitive Apprehension Strike Team and supporting law enforcement to close in on him at any time. But even that's not soon enough to want to wait around and give him a target—you."

"I don't want that either," Nikki said in a hushed voice. "I'll go pack some things."

"Good." Gavin flashed her a sideways grin. "Make it quick. We don't want Evigan to have any time to make his move."

She nodded. "Right."

Having Gavin at this cabin with her would certainly make it easier for Nikki to temporarily relocate from what was supposed to be her comfort zone, after leaving Gulfport eight years ago. Now Perry Evigan had managed to turn her world upside down. And make her cottage a place she could not feel safe in while he was on the prowl, having already murdered two people she was acquainted with in Miriam and Kenan.

The last thing Nikki wanted was to join them—and Brigette—in an early grave. But was there truly anywhere that she could escape the serial killer's wrath against her as the sole survivor of his onslaught?

HALF AN HOUR LATER, Nikki was meeting with her friend, Blair Roxburgh, at Calyne's Coffee Café on Foulter Way. She didn't dare go to Blair's house, potentially placing her in danger. But given the murder of Miriam Broderick, Nikki felt a need to reach out to the support group founder before she left town temporarily. A café in a public space made it unlikely that a wanted fugitive would show his face there. If he were to, Gavin, who was seated at another table to give them a little space and trying to keep a low profile while on the lookout for the serial killer, would nab Evigan in a hurry, as per his role as her protector.

Nikki waved Blair over as she spotted her entering the café. The two women hugged and Nikki cried, "I'm so sorry about Miriam."

"So am I," Blair uttered. "She didn't deserve to go that way."

"I know." Nikki pulled away, wiped her eyes and they sat at a square wooden table away from the window, where she had taken the liberty of ordering them both iced lattes and cinnamon rolls. "Perry Evigan killed her."

Blair lifted a brow. "Are you sure about that?"

"I only wish I weren't." Nikki frowned. "It gets worse. The police believe that Evigan killed Kenan Fernández too."

Blair's eyelids fluttered wildly. "What?"

Nikki told her what she knew about the crimes and the massive search for Perry Evigan underway in Owl's Bay. "Seems like he's been fixated on me ever since he escaped from prison, along with anyone I'm associated with…" She glanced over at Gavin, who was shifting his gaze this way and that for any sign of trouble, and turned back to her friend. "I never imagined that—"

"Stop it." Blair leaned forward, touching her hand. "You're in no way to blame for someone else's actions, Nikki. Least of all an escaped serial killer's. The fact that Perry Evigan has somehow been able to carry out more crimes while on the run is not your fault. You're as much a victim as anyone. But you're also a survivor—and don't ever let him or anyone else take that away from you."

Nikki grabbed a cinnamon roll, nibbled off a piece defiantly and then declared, "I won't." She couldn't give in to

Evigan's tactics, even if from a distance. Hadn't the years since the attack made her strong enough to withstand the psychological manipulation? She would not backtrack on that now. Especially with Gavin supporting her. And Blair too. "You're right," she told her. "I can't control what a fugitive serial killer chooses to do, no matter how vile."

"Exactly." Blair favored her with a tiny smile and picked up the latte, taking a sip. She glanced over at Gavin. "Does he want to come and join us?"

"Probably not," Nikki said. "He's fine keeping watch over me while trying not to crowd me. I'm good with that." Not that she had a problem with their spending lots of time together, as they had. The bigger issue still was how they fared once the threat to her life was over, one way or the other.

"Well, I'm glad he's got your back," Blair said. "And I'm sensing it's even more than that."

Nikki blushed. "Let's just say we're in a good place right now."

"Sounds like a nice place to be in."

"It is." She eyed him, and Gavin grinned and lifted his mug of coffee in an approving toast. "But right now, his focus and mine is on averting a confrontation with Perry Evigan. Which is why I'll be leaving town temporarily with Gavin, as the authorities try to close in on Evigan."

"I see." Blair sipped her latte. "I'm sure you feel it's better that I don't know where you're going?"

"Correct—for your own safety," Nikki pointed out, biting off a chunk of the cinnamon roll.

Blair's mouth tightened. "I can take care of myself, always have, ever since the attack back in college," she spoke bravely.

"I know." Nikki understood that, like her, Blair had taken

self-defense classes to better protect herself from villains. But even that could only go so far, should the perp catch them off guard. Or otherwise be relentless and lethal in an attack. She smiled at her. "If all goes right, I'll be back before you even start to miss me."

"I'll hold you to that." Blair chuckled, grabbing her cinnamon roll. "In the meantime, let's keep our fingers crossed that the man who ended Miriam's life will be brought to justice in no time flat and you can get back to your life."

Nikki nodded, while crossing her fingers on that thought and hoping for the best, even as something inside her still feared the worst when it came to the maniacal serial killer.

GAVIN LIFTED HIS mug of flat white coffee and took a sip, as he turned his eyes to Nikki and Blair at their table. He was sure that they were commiserating over the senseless loss of their survivor support group member, Miriam Broderick. Gavin knew that the only way the pain would be eased was with the capture or elimination of the person responsible for her death. Though he was certain that was imminent, and he would like nothing better than to slap the cuffs on Brigette's murderer himself, Gavin's number-one priority had to be protecting Nikki at all costs. He would defer dealing with Perry Evigan to his colleagues.

I need to get her out of here to a safe place where he can't find her, Gavin told himself, assuming Evigan, against all odds, managed to slip past the tracking operation well underway in town. He owed it to her to not give the escaped con an opportunity to replay the terror he'd instilled upon her a decade ago.

Lifting his cell phone, Gavin called his friend, Jake Kendrick. The two had known each other since they attended

Mississippi State University and lived in the same residence hall. Jake now lived in Winnipeg, Manitoba, in Canada, where he owned an upscale restaurant and was happily divorced. He kept his cabin as an investment property and for occasional getaways.

Jake accepted the video chat request. Thirty-six, with a medium build and dark hair in a sideswept undercut, and bearing a crooked grin on his round face, he said, "Special Agent Gavin Lynley. What's up, dude?"

Gavin grinned. "I'm good. How about you?"

"Busy as ever. That's the restaurant business for you. No rest for the weary, but I can't complain."

"Then you're in better shape than I am," Gavin said wryly.

"I seriously doubt that," Jake countered. "At least physically speaking."

Not going there, Gavin got to the point. "Say, I have a big favor to ask of you...?"

"Name it."

"I need to borrow your cabin for a day or two—it's important," he emphasized without going into the details. Jake had been there for him during his darkest hours, but now was not the time to relive the past or address the future. "I promise to leave it the way I find it."

"No problem," Jake said without prelude. "It yours for as long as you want. I don't expect to be back in Mississippi for the foreseeable future."

"Thanks. I owe you one," Gavin told him.

"And I won't let you forget it." Jake laughed. "There's some beer in the fridge, but not much else."

"That's a pretty good start," Gavin quipped. "I'll take it from there."

"Cool. And in case you've forgotten, the key is still under the mat."

"I remember."

"Have fun or whatever. Or with whomever."

Gavin smiled, looking at Nikki. He disconnected and briefly thought about Brigette and how the two women were so different. If only he had been able to better read the tea leaves back in the day, he might have been able to save Brigette and build something much sooner with Nikki. But he had now to turn the page and welcomed the opportunity to do so.

He stood and went over to Nikki's table. After acknowledging Blair, he asked Nikki, "Are you ready to go?"

"Yes." She smiled at him and rose. "All set."

Blair got up as well. Putting her hand on Gavin's elbow, she looked him in the eye and said sharply, "Take care of her."

"I will," he promised, while knowing it was something he didn't take lightly. Not by a long shot.

Chapter Fourteen

As Nikki waited in his car for the drive to the cabin, Gavin conferred outside it with the MDOC's Fugitive Apprehension Strike Team Commander, Eddie Prescott, telling him calculatingly, "Evigan's here, lurking in the shadows, daring us to find him and take him down."

Prescott, fortysomething, built like a brick, with graying hair in a buzz cut and a dimpled chin, narrowed his brown eyes and declared decisively, "If he's still in Owl's Bay, we'll find him—one way or the other. You can be sure of that."

Gavin only wished he could be. As it was, the fact that Evigan had skillfully eluded capture thus far, made the escaped serial killer that much more formidable an opponent. "I want to believe you can track him down, once and for all," Gavin told his friend. "With all the manpower we have in the pursuit, along with any help from the public, it should be a given that Evigan's days as a free man are numbered. But if it's all the same to you, I need to put some distance between Evigan and Nikki Sullivan, the one person who came out alive after crossing paths with that monster."

Prescott glanced at Nikki in the Chevy Tahoe and said understandingly, "Do what you need to do. Keep her safe till this is over."

"I intend to." Gavin shook his hand. "If this goes sour, don't hesitate to reach out to me."

"I won't," Prescott promised. "Now, get out of here."

"Okay."

Gavin walked away and over to the gray Chevrolet Blazer that belonged to US Marshal Everett Ulbricht, who was in the driver's seat. The marshal, who was in his midthirties, was assigned to follow them to the cabin and make sure they weren't being followed or threatened in any other way. He had on a black cap over curly brown hair and wore dark shades.

"Ready to hit the road?" Gavin asked him.

Ulbricht nodded, touching his sunglasses. "Yeah, let's do it."

"Okay," Gavin said, and glanced around before returning his gaze to Ulbricht. "If you see any sign of Evigan—"

"I'll let you know," the marshal told him in earnest.

"All right." Gavin went to his own car and got behind the wheel. He smiled at Nikki, trying to make this seem like a vacation getaway, rather than running and hiding from an escaped convict who had her in his crosshairs. "I think we're good to go now."

"Great." She smiled back, putting up a brave front, masking what Gavin was certain was an uncomfortableness in having her life put on hold. And all because Perry Evigan had not been taken into custody—keeping the danger he presented alive and well.

If there was a silver lining to the dark cloud the serial killer represented, Gavin saw it as another opportunity to bond more with Nikki in a neutral and relaxed woodsy environment. Even if short-lived, it could be just enough to make a difference in what they were starting to feel for one another.

AFTER A LARGELY silent ride down US Route 49 North, Gavin turned onto Blane Lake Street, an unpaved road in Osweka County. He waved at US Marshal Everett Ulbricht, indicating that the marshal was no longer needed as an escort the rest of the way. Nikki watched him give Gavin the thumbs-up and continue down the highway. She felt somewhat relieved that there had been no indication from Marshal Ulbricht that they had been followed from Owl's Bay, suggesting that Perry Evigan had no idea where she'd gone, as the authorities closed in on him.

Driving a short distance past groves of broadleaf and conifer trees, Gavin pulled up to the red log cabin. Nikki took one look at the two-level lakefront property and couldn't help but utter in awe, "When you said your friend had a cabin in the woods, I was just assuming it was a typical campground-type cabin—not this!"

"Yeah, it is pretty cool." Gavin chuckled. "Jake got a good deal on it, borrowing money from his folks to pay for it. Though he's living in Canada now, he wisely decided to hang on to the place, which is a perfect hideaway for us to lay low for a little while. Why don't we go take a look inside?"

"Okay."

Nikki wanted to forget about this being more about Perry Evigan threatening her life than building a future life with Gavin. Or were the two inexorably linked? How could they not be? Hadn't her shared experience with Gavin led to this point in time, with Brigette's killer still able to effectively mess with their heads?

But the unintended tugging at their heartstrings and what it might foretell was something that Nikki clung to as what she hoped to be the most important thing to come out of this ordeal, whenever it was over.

Upon grabbing their bags, they headed down the stone walkway and onto the wraparound deck, where Nikki watched as Gavin dug the key out from beneath a white-and-black-striped welcome mat and unlocked the door. "Here it is," he said, as they stepped inside.

Setting her things down, Nikki took a sweeping glance of the first level. It had a cathedral ceiling with exposed beams, laminate wood flooring, floor-to-ceiling windows throughout, offering breathtaking views of the lake from different angles, and rustic pine wood furniture. There was a full-size chef's kitchen with granite countertops. And a security system.

"Nice," Nikki had to say, admitting that if she had to relocate temporarily with barely a moment's notice, this might have been the place she would have chosen to be sheltered with Gavin. "Very nice."

"Yeah." He grinned at her. "Want to see the rest?"

"Sure." She followed him up the wooden U-shaped staircase to the second floor and took in the well-appointed main bedroom, with barn-wood furniture and a built-in sunroom. The thought of them making good use later of the rustic king bed excited her. Or did Gavin not have that in mind in his capacity as Special Agent Lynley? "I like the way your friend has decorated the place," she said, sending her thoughts in a different direction.

"Me too."

They finished the tour, which included an upstairs deck with more magnificent views, for which Nikki was glad she had brought along her sketch pad to draw for a future painting, before heading back down to the first level.

Gavin drew her near to him and said, "Sorry to have to pull you away from Owl's Bay and your life, but I prefer to go with the better safe than sorry philosophy than not."

"It's fine," she told him, smiling. "There are worse things in life than having to be tucked away in a lovely cabin by the lake with a wonderful man."

He gazed longingly into her eyes. "I feel the same way—only turning that around to being here with a gorgeous and sexy woman."

"Hmm…" Nikki felt a flutter of desire, but kept it in check. "So, we're even, then?"

"Yeah, you could say that." Gavin flashed her an askew grin. "Better yet, we're compatible in every way that counts, making what we have that much more compelling."

Her lashes fluttered. "You think?"

"Don't you?"

She answered without preface, "Yes, I believe we are very compatible."

"That really seems to fit when it comes to kissing," he told her.

"Oh…?"

"Yeah." He cupped her cheeks and laid one on her lips, as though to prove the point.

Nikki lost herself in the kiss for a long moment, taking her away from the peril that Perry Evigan had brought upon them in forcing them to escape to a place beyond his reach. When Gavin pulled back, he grinned and said lightheartedly, "Proves my point."

She touched her stinging mouth. "Guess it does."

They went into the kitchen, where Gavin opened up the refrigerator and Nikki saw that it was empty, aside from a bottle of ketchup and three bottles of beer.

"Jake wasn't kidding when he said there was nothing here," Gavin remarked musingly. "Even though we're likely only going to be here for a short while, I suppose we should've stopped at what was probably the only grocery store in town that we passed along the way to pick up a few items."

"There was a pizza place across the street from it," Nikki remembered, feeling her stomach start to growl.

"Why don't we head over there now and get what we need to wait this out," Gavin said, closing the refrigerator, "till the threat that Evigan poses has been brought to a close."

"All right." She wondered just how long that would take, wanting this to be over for good, even while she was happy to make the most of the time away with Gavin.

NIKKI WONDERED IF it was her imagination running wild. She could've sworn she saw Perry Evigan peering at her down the aisle at the supermarket. Or at least someone who resembled him. Granted, she hadn't seen Evigan face-to-face in nearly a decade and only had a mug shot and a photograph shown on television that was taken of him from a court hearing a few years ago when he'd gotten into trouble after a prison fight. But the way the man seemed to be looking at her made Nikki uncomfortable, caught her attention and left her shaking.

She turned to Gavin, who was grabbing a bag of potato chips from the shelf to put in the cart, and said almost in a whisper, "I think Perry Evigan has found us—"

"What?" Gavin tensed and she could see him nearly go for the firearm that was inside his concealed carry holster, tucked within Gavin's waistband.

"At the end of the aisle…" she stammered, bravely angling her eyes in that direction. Only to find him gone.

"No one's there—" Gavin said, gazing in that direction. He faced her. "What makes you think it was Evigan that you saw?"

"It was just his general appearance and the way he seemed to be studying me, as if sizing me up for the kill…" Nikki swallowed the lump in her throat. "Maybe I was mistaken," she suggested, suddenly questioning her own interpretation.

"Maybe, or maybe not…" Gavin pursed his lips thoughtfully. "Wait right here where I can see you…"

"Okay," she obeyed.

Nikki watched as he hurriedly headed down the aisle and past an elderly female shopper. Gavin kept his hand close to his weapon, without removing it. At the end of the aisle, she saw him look in both directions, before quickly making his way back to her. "Stay put," he directed, and went down the other way to the end, where Gavin peered one way, then the other, before rushing back to her and stating evenly, "I didn't see any sign of anyone who resembled Evigan. But that doesn't mean he wasn't there."

Again, having second thoughts, she wondered out loud, "How would he have found us? Even as he was at the same time trying to avoid recapture?"

"Those are good questions, and there are no easy answers." Gavin rubbed his chin while contemplating this. "My guess is that you saw someone else and thought it could have been Evigan. If he had followed us out of Owl's Bay, I'm pretty sure that either I or Marshal Ulbricht would have noticed a car that was trailing our vehicles."

Nikki wrinkled her nose. "You're probably right," she

conceded, feeling foolish in causing him to panic unnecessarily. "Guess I just got spooked for no reason…"

"You had a very good reason for being spooked," Gavin said, wrapping his hands around the cart's handle. "I'll never fault you for that. Let's pay for these items and go get that pizza."

Nikki nodded and they headed down the aisle, still feeling a bit strange about the entire episode, as if there was an itch that wouldn't go away where it concerned the escaped serial killer.

THOUGH GAVIN WAS fairly certain that Perry Evigan had not found their location and was stalking Nikki as a prelude to kidnapping her again, it still made him nervous about the fugitive, while Evigan remained on the loose. The fact that Nikki had been freaked out at the grocery store in what appeared to be an unprovoked and unreal sighting of the escapee, told Gavin, if nothing else, that Evigan still loomed large in her psyche. That was not likely to change for the time being, in spite of them being thirty miles away from Owl's Bay. And presumably far enough from Evigan's crosshairs to be in a safe space.

Still, Gavin found it incumbent upon himself to reassure Nikki that she needn't worry about the serial killer while they were at the cabin. He wanted the worry to fall on his shoulders instead. "Don't let him get to you. Why don't we just try and relax and enjoy this, to the extent possible," Gavin told her in a gentle tone as they sat in ladder-back side chairs across a pine solid wood trestle dining table from one another in the cabin, eating pizza with soft drinks.

"I will if you will," Nikki countered, lifting a slice of

the pizza topped with cheddar cheese, ground beef, onions and green peppers.

"Deal." He gave her a convincing grin, wanting to shift the mood to one that was more agreeable—as if they were on vacation together, which he hoped to turn this outing into.

"Good." She bit into the pizza. "Mmm, this is delicious."

Gavin took a bite from his own slice and had to concur. "It is." *But not even close to being as delicious as you are to kiss and make love to*, he told himself, knowing it was coming as much from the heart as his libido. He only needed to show her that more and more, so she knew he meant business in wanting what they had to continue to progress into something truly special when this was over.

While Nikki was clearing the table, Gavin checked the windows and front door to make sure they were locked, then went upstairs, where he called Jean O'Reilly for an update on the situation. "Hey."

"Heard you had gotten out of Dodge," she quipped.

"Seemed like the smart thing to do, with Evigan proving to be so difficult to pin down and take into custody," Gavin said honestly.

"You're probably right about that."

"What's the latest on the search for the fugitive?"

"We haven't captured him yet, if that's what you're asking," Jean told him.

"Didn't think you had." Otherwise, Gavin would know that Nikki was finally out of harm's way for the long-term. "Anything at all I can work with…?" Before she answered, he added ruefully, "Nikki thought she might have seen Evigan at a store in town. Though I never laid eyes on him to confirm this and am thinking it was a case of mistaken identity, I'd like to know that all signs point toward him still being holed up in Owl's Bay…"

"The signs do suggest that to be the case. But we both know they can be misleading at times."

"How so?" he pressed.

Jean paused. "Surveillance video footage from yesterday picked up a man we believe to be Perry Evigan getting into a blue Toyota Corolla Cross outside of a strip mall in town. We got the license plate number and saw that the car had been reported as stolen. Evigan never bothered to switch plates. There's no reason to believe he's not still driving the vehicle—when out on the road at all—and we've issued a BOLO on it and him."

"All right." Gavin hoped they were that much closer to nailing the bastard and putting an end to the nightmare he'd put Nikki through. "If you get anything at all on his where-abouts or his capture—"

"I'll definitely keep you abreast on all fronts," Jean promised him, before Gavin disconnected.

Nikki had come upstairs and regarded him suspiciously. "Everything okay?"

"Yeah," he said in a calm voice. "We're good."

Chapter Fifteen

"I was thinking that we should make the most of this situation," Gavin uttered erotically to Nikki, while resting his hands on her hips as they stood in the main bedroom.

"Oh, really?" Her lashes fluttered coyly. "And just what did you have in mind?"

He grinned, turned on by her in every way. "Well, this…" Gavin kissed her right cheek. "And this…" Next came the left cheek. "And, of course, there's that—" He went for her abundant mouth, and she reciprocated in kind, letting him know she was more than amenable to what he was suggesting.

"I'm all yours, Agent Lynley." Nikki tsked, wrapping her arms around his neck and bringing their mouths together again for a passionate kiss.

"Since you put it that way, let's see what we can do about that," Gavin teased her.

They wasted no time undressing and he took her to bed, getting cozy atop the matelassé bedspread, where Gavin went to work making sure that he tapped into every sensitive spot on Nikki's perfect body and shapely breasts to give her the hands-on treatment she deserved. Only after the undulating tide of satisfaction came for her amid deep sighs and quivering, did he let go and complete the overwhelming joy of their lovemaking. It sent them both to new heights of ecstasy that was only solidified by their circumstances.

Catching his breath as he lay beside her still and slick body, matching his own, Gavin kissed Nikki's soft shoulder and said truthfully, "I wish we'd had the chance to experience this long ago."

"So do I," she cooed, draping a silky-smooth leg across his thigh. "But it wasn't our time then. I guess it is now."

"Yes, I'd say so." Gavin was in complete agreement. He couldn't very well argue with fate as it were. Maybe they weren't meant to be together ten years ago. Or maybe they were, but were prevented from doing so by forces beyond their control. He wouldn't overthink it. Instead, he was grateful that the universe gave them a second opportunity to find each other and they had. If he had his way, they would never let this slip away.

As soon as the danger that Perry Evigan posed had subsided, Gavin wanted nothing more than to work on a future with Nikki. After all, wasn't that to be expected when two people had fallen in love? Not that he could speak for her, but he could for himself. And when she was ready to tell him how she felt, he would be there to listen.

For the moment, all Gavin wanted to do was hold Nikki, listen to their heartbeats synced and see what tomorrow brought in the hunt for a serial killer escapee.

NIKKI IMAGINED THAT she had known from the moment she first saw Gavin Lynley that she had fallen in love with him. She hadn't exactly been in denial about being in touch with her feelings. It was more that she couldn't act on them with Gavin seeming to be totally hooked on Brigette. Now it was clear that this hadn't been the case. At least not to the extent that he wouldn't have been open to giving someone else a chance.

The problem had been more of going after someone that her best friend was involved with. Nikki would never have tried to come between Brigette and Gavin—no matter the serious cracks in their relationship—as long as they were together. But now, somehow, some way, Gavin had come into Nikki's life a decade later and things had heated up between them, in and out of the bedroom, telling her that what they had was real. And, from her point of view, it had the potential to be lasting, if she was reading Gavin correctly in his body language and mentality. Now, if only they could put the saga of a dangerous serial killer on the prowl in the rearview mirror.

Slipping from beneath Gavin's protective arms as the morning sun filtered in the window above the cellular shades, Nikki allowed him to get a bit more shut-eye, as she got up and left the room quietly. She hoped to take advantage of this time of the day to sketch the magnificent landscape and breathe in the fresh air.

After washing her face and pulling her hair together into a messy pineapple ponytail, she threw on a white scoop neck tunic tank top, some dark blue shorts and her running shoes. Downstairs, she had a glass of water and then grabbed her sketch pad and drawing pencil from her straw tote bag. Peeking out the window, Nikki saw nothing that alarmed her. She had decided earlier that Perry Evigan had not followed them to the cabin after all. It was just her panicking, unreasonably so. As such, it was likely safe for her to step onto the wraparound deck, where she would do the sketching, before having breakfast with Gavin.

No sooner had she gone out on the deck and began to sketch, observing some ducks and rabbits out and about by the lake, than Nikki heard a sound that she couldn't quite decipher. Realizing it was the cedar deck boards creaking, she turned in that direction only to come face-to-face with her worst nightmare.

Perry Evigan stood there with an eerie grin playing on his lips and sporting a patchy beard, as he said coldly, "Nice to see you again, Nikki. We have some unfinished business to take care of…"

"No, we don't!" she shot back with defiance, glaring at the man who was unmistakable, in spite of being ten years older.

Just as she attempted to use a self-defense technique, then make a run for it and scream at the same time, Nikki was grabbed roughly and felt a needle pierce her neck. Before everything went black, she heard the Gulfport Nightmare Killer remark smugly, "Don't fight it, Nikki. The ketamine I injected you with will make you mine as we get out of here and go to a safe place where we can get down to business uninterrupted."

GAVIN AWOKE WITH a start when he thought he heard the sound of screeching tires. Expecting to find Nikki beside him—in a dreamy sleep after making love much of the night—he instead realized her spot on the bed was empty. For whatever reason, his gut instincts kicked in that something wasn't right. He shot out of bed, slid into some slacks and went in his bare feet looking for her. But he couldn't find her in the cabin.

Where was she? Why didn't she wake him up? How could he have not heard the creaking of the stairs?

Gavin resisted the urge to panic, hoping that Nikki had simply gone outside while not going too far. Hadn't she talked about wanting to sketch the scenery? Maybe she had fallen and hit her head? He opened the door and walked out onto the wraparound porch. At first, he saw nothing that got his attention to suggest Nikki was in trouble. But then, near the side of the deck, he spotted what looked to be... her sketch pad and drawing pencil lying there.

Would she have left them there voluntarily?

Gavin called out to her, "Nikki!" He went around the entire deck on the chance that she was there somewhere and hadn't heard him. But she was nowhere to be found. He called her name again. No answer. Would she really leave him hanging if she were able to speak?

Now it was time for panic to set in.

He stepped off the deck and checked the perimeter of the cabin, but saw no sign of Nikki. Realizing that without his firearm and shoes on, he was at a disadvantage, should she be in danger.

Sprinting back into the cabin, his heart racing, Gavin hurriedly scaled the stairs, finished dressing and grabbed his loaded FN 509 MRD-LE 9mm semiautomatic duty pistol. He went back outside and started to look for Nikki, calling her name, while holding out hope that she wasn't in jeopardy.

But when he reached the dirt road and saw fresh tire tracks, Gavin recalled thinking he'd heard tires screeching when he awoke. It hadn't been his imagination after all. Someone had taken Nikki.

No, not someone.

Perry Evigan had her.

The mere thought that the bastard had kidnapped Nikki

made the hairs curl on the back of Gavin's neck. He needed to regroup and find the woman he'd fallen in love with. Before Evigan was able to murder someone else Gavin cared for.

AT FIRST, Nikki thought she was in some weird dream where everything was fuzzy and nothing was as it seemed. She was trapped under water and sinking fast. As she tried to scream, her mouth filled with muddy water and death seemed imminent. Then she opened her eyes and saw nothing but darkness and felt herself lying in a fetal position in a tight space. She realized she wasn't dreaming at all. She was caught in a living nightmare.

Though groggy, she came to the conclusion that she was trapped inside something... A trunk. And the car was moving.

Everything began to come back to her. She was on the wraparound deck of the log cabin of Gavin's friend—about to sketch the surroundings—when she was accosted by Perry Evigan, who injected her with a date-rape drug.

It was the last thing she remembered. Till now.

He'd kidnapped her and was taking her somewhere. Nikki quickly realized that the trunk emergency release lever had been ripped out. She tried to push and kick open the trunk lid, to no avail. And though she wanted to scream, nothing seemed to come out of her sour throat and dry mouth but a whimper.

Where were they going? Was Gavin aware that she was missing? Or was he still asleep, oblivious to what had happened to her?

Am I going to be able to get out of this alive? Nikki asked herself fearfully. Or would Evigan make good on his pledge of revenge, doing to her whatever ghastly things he had in mind? Finishing with strangling her to death and maybe burying her where she could never be found. And leaving Gavin and her parents to mourn her death, just as they had Brigette's. While their killer remained free to go after other young women, with no end in sight.

This frightening scenario chilled Nikki to the core and was one that she needed to do everything in her power to avoid. Now if only she could overcome the dizziness and trouble breathing in the enclosed space to formulate a plan of action.

PERRY EVIGAN COULD barely believe his good fortune. First, he executed a timely escape from the Mississippi State Penitentiary—dodging every close call in the effort to recapture him. Then, he managed to avoid the fate of fellow escapees, Craig Schneider and Aaron Machado, who literally went up in flames rather than go back inside.

And now, Perry had gotten hold of his prized possession, Nikki Sullivan. He'd found his way to her in Owl's Bay, where she had thought she was safe from him. She had become his for the taking—and he fully intended to do just that—before ending her life once and for all, as he had intended to do a decade ago. He could hear her squirming inside the trunk, hoping to find some miraculous way of breaking free. He was confident that wasn't going to happen.

Perry glanced at the rearview mirror to make sure he wasn't being followed. There was no one behind them. Good. He had dumped the Toyota Corolla Cross he had stolen for a green Dodge Charger GT. By the time they figured out it had been carjacked by him, he would have done what he set out to do with Nikki Sullivan and moved on.

So much for her protector Special Agent Gavin Lynley keeping her safe from harm. Perry laughed at the thought. He remembered learning that Lynley had been dating Brigette Fontana ten years ago—only to come up short in preventing her death. Now he was about to go 0 for 2 in the saving a damsel in distress department.

You lose again, Perry mused wryly, as they neared the destination for his latest kill. He salivated at the thought, knowing it would be even more of a thrill when the deed was done.

"NIKKI'S MISSING," Gavin spoke glumly over the speakerphone to Marvin Whitfield while driving.

"What do you mean she's missing?" the director asked, ill at ease.

"He took her," Gavin hated to say, feeling nauseated picturing Nikki in the clutches of the serial killer. "Somehow, Perry Evigan managed to lure Nikki out of the cabin. Or she went out unsuspectingly and he was waiting for her… and kidnapped her."

Whitfield spat out an expletive. "I thought we had him boxed in," he groaned, "if not in custody."

"Instead, Evigan's outfoxed us in being able to slip out of Owl's Bay and track down Nikki." Gavin frowned and sucked in a deep breath, blaming himself for placing her in harm's way and allowing the escaped con to nab Nikki under his watch. "I don't know where he's taken her, but they couldn't have gotten very far," Gavin said, driving in the direction the tire tracks suggested Evigan went. "Only a few minutes passed before I realized that Nikki was gone."

"Tell me exactly where you are and we'll have the Fugitive Apprehension Strike Team and other law enforcement converge on the area and try to cut Evigan off."

Gavin gave his GPS coordinates and said, "If Evigan is still driving the Toyota Corolla Cross, we should be able to narrow down—"

Whitfield cut him off by saying forlornly, "We found the Toyota a few hours ago. It had been abandoned by Evigan. He's obviously using another vehicle right now."

"Figures," Gavin muttered sarcastically, then remembered Nikki believing she had seen him yesterday at the grocery store, as he approached it. "Let me get back to you. I may be able to pin down what Evigan is driving…and has Nikki inside against her will."

The director sought no explanation as he deferred to Gavin's potential new lead, while both moved into high gear, trying to find Nikki alive, before it was too late.

PACING IN HIS OFFICE, Marvin Whitfield was on pins and needles as he contemplated the dire situation with Perry Evigan. In no way should it have gotten to this point, where this serial killer seemed to be calling the shots. And not him as the Director of Investigations at MDOC. He couldn't let this stand, as the buck stopped with him. Last thing he needed was to have Evigan do to Nikki Sullivan what he did to her friend, Brigette Fontana. Not to mention give Gavin Lynley another reason to shoulder the blame, should this go south on him.

Whitfield wondered if it was wise to send Gavin to do bodyguard duty of the artist. Maybe this was a little too close to home for him, causing the special agent to lower his guard just enough to allow Nikki to slip through his fingers for Evigan to nab. And now had them all at a disadvantage in a race against time to stop him from killing her.

But as the director reconsidered this, he knew deep down that Gavin Lynley was where he needed to be. He had every right to confront the enemy—no matter the cost. And to play a role in rescuing Nikki Sullivan from the grasp of Evigan and his evil intentions.

Whitfield was determined to do everything in his power to stop the escaped convict from continuing to circumvent the law by remaining free to wreak havoc in their state and flaunting this in their faces. He got on his cell phone to speak with the Fugitive Apprehension Strike Team Commander, Eddie Prescott, to talk strategy in converging on Osweka County and holding Perry Evigan accountable for his crimes and bringing him to justice.

Chapter Sixteen

Nikki felt the car driving onto gravel, before coming to a stop. She heard Evigan get out and approach the trunk. Holding her breath, she waited for it to open and have to face her tormentor again.

When the trunk lid was lifted, Perry Evigan stood there smugly, wearing a dark blue fleece pullover hoodie and jeans. His short brown-gray hair was uncombed and his face had become weathered after a decade.

"I see you're awake," he said with a laugh, while holding a gun. She wondered if it was the one he'd used to shoot to death Kenan Fernández. "Good to see I didn't overdo it with the ketamine." She sneered but said nothing as he grabbed her with one hand and pulled her out of the trunk. "Welcome home, Nikki."

It took her a moment to recognize the setting. It was the same two-story Greek Revival house on Robinson Road that he had first brought her and Brigette to ten years ago, after also being drugged. Only now it was overgrown with weeds and looked more dilapidated. Was anyone actually living there these days?

"I see it's all coming back to you now," Perry expressed, grinning wickedly as he clicked together his scuffed brown

Chelsea boots. He kept the gun on her and pushed her toward the house. "Get inside and I'll try to make this as painless as possible."

Yeah, right, Nikki told herself doubtingly. She expected it to be just the opposite, knowing that, based on his history—including the rape and murder of Miriam Broderick—the serial killer got his kicks out of inflicting pain and humiliation on his victims, before he strangled them to death with ligatures. Or even his bare hands.

I have to play along for now, Nikki thought, biding her time till she struck back. Or died trying. Assuming Gavin was unable to come to her rescue in the nick of time.

"You won't get away with this, Perry," she spat, if only to try to reach his sense of self-preservation.

He chuckled, shoving her again. "Watch me."

As they neared the porch, Nikki took a quick glance at the shed and then nearby woods, and tried to map out an escape route, should the opportunity present itself.

That thought had to be put on hold as Perry Evigan forced the front door open and made her go inside.

GAVIN FLASHED HIS identification as he said to the grocery store manager in an official tone of voice, "Special Agent Lynley."

Sarah Yarborough, fortysomething and petite, with red hair in an angled short cut and blue eyes behind oval glasses, asked, "How can I help you, Agent Lynley?"

"I need to take a look at your security footage from yesterday, inside and out." He gave her a time frame to work with. "We have reason to believe that an escaped prisoner may have been seen in the area…"

"Sounds scary."

"And for good reason—if it's him," Gavin told her point-blank, while trying to hold it together, knowing that every second counted where it concerned Nikki's survival.

Sarah furrowed her brow uneasily and said, "Follow me."

She led him through the store to a back room with surveillance equipment. Standing before a laptop, the store manager pulled up security video footage at the store's entrance.

Gavin waited till he saw what—or whom—he was looking for and asked her to stop. "Can you zoom in on that man?"

"Sure." Sarah did just that, giving Gavin a closer look. "Do you recognize him?" she asked.

"Yeah, I'm afraid I do," Gavin muttered, his nose wrinkling in disgust. The man was clearly on edge, his big hazel eyes shifting this way and that, for fear of being recognized, even with the hood of his dark-colored sweatshirt over his head. It was him, undeniably. "His name's Perry Evigan."

Though years removed from when Gavin confronted the serial killer in court, he would recognize Brigette's killer anywhere. Nikki had been right in believing she spotted Evigan at the store yesterday.

I should have trusted her judgment and been better prepared to deal with it when he came for her, Gavin told himself, knowing that if Evigan laid one hand on Nikki, he would never forgive himself.

"I heard about him," Sarah confessed. "Can't believe he was actually here."

"Believe it." Gavin jutted his chin. "Let's switch to the outside surveillance camera…"

"All right."

She pulled up the footage from just after the time Evigan was inside the store and Gavin spotted him walking to a green Dodge Charger GT. He got inside and started to drive away.

"Stop it there!" Gavin ordered her, and asked her to zoom in on the license plate. He took a photo of it on his cell phone and said, "I've seen enough." He knew that with Evigan having a head start on him with his deadly plans for Nikki, there was no time to waste in going after the serial killer before the damage done was irreversible.

MINUTES LATER, Gavin was in his car as he passed along to Jean the license plate number of the green Dodge Charger GT that Perry Evigan had sped off in from the supermarket parking lot the day before.

"Got it," she said and was able to quickly run the plates and determine that the vehicle had been carjacked. "The thirtysomething owner of the Dodge Charger, Karl Shimomura, who was also robbed but not physically harmed, had reported the car stolen at gunpoint by a man wearing a hoodie."

"Perry Evigan," Gavin thought out loud, recalling the hoodie Evigan was wearing at the store, coupled with him being the one who fled in the stolen vehicle.

"We'll issue a BOLO immediately on the Dodge Charger GT," Jean stated, "which shouldn't be too difficult to track down—if Evigan is still in the area—with the tremendous amount of manpower that's out in full pursuit of the escapee."

Gavin twisted his lips. "I've heard it all before," he voiced cynically. "Evigan knows we're onto him—making him all the more dangerous and desperate, as his kidnapping of Nikki was conniving and deliberate."

"If he had wanted to kill her right away, Evigan would have done so," the special agent surmised cautiously. "That tells me Nikki Sullivan is probably still alive."

But not for much longer, unless I can find her in time, Gavin told himself, trying hard not to panic at the thought of being too late. He only needed something to go on for a sense of direction in discovering where Evigan was headed with his captive.

"If the BOLO alert comes up with anything," Gavin told Jean as he drove, "hopefully, I'll be close enough to get to Nikki." Before Evigan could put into action the horrible ordeal he'd put Brigette through, culminating in her death.

THE PLACE HAD a musty smell that suggested it hadn't been lived in for a while, along with the dusty contemporary furnishings and even a few cobwebs that Nikki spotted in corners and hanging from the ceiling. As she was pushed forward across the dark hardwood flooring on the main level, she knew she had to buy time before the escaped serial killer went on the attack.

Rounding on her kidnapper, who was still brandishing the firearm and sizing her up like a piece of meat, Nikki asked point-blank, "It was you who killed Kenan Fernández, wasn't it?"

Evigan cracked a grin. "Yeah, I confess—little good it's going to do you."

"But why?" Not that she needed to know what went on inside the head of an obvious psychopath. However, she was still curious as to what had prompted him to go after Kenan.

"Why? Because I could tell that he wanted you too," Evigan argued. "I saw him through the window at the art gallery. The way he was all up in your face and the way you reacted, told me that the man was a problem. You were mine and I had to eliminate the competition."

Nikki sneered. "Kenan wasn't competition. I rejected his advances and wanted nothing to do with him."

Evigan laughed. "I don't think he saw things that way. Kenan Fernández got what he deserved." Evigan's brow wrinkled. "So too would've Brigette's former boyfriend, Special Agent Lynley, who really rubbed me the wrong way at my trial—just as you did—except for the fact that I wasn't able to get the jump on him without putting my own life at risk. Lucky dude."

Nikki was given a start at the thought that Evigan had wanted Gavin dead apparently as much as he wanted to kill her, in spite of the fact that Gavin had every right to be angered at the sexual assault and murder of his then-girlfriend by Evigan. Nikki could only feel relief that the escaped inmate hadn't succeeded in killing Gavin and destroying his life in the process. Even if she was unable to avoid this fate, with Evigan clearly planning to finish what he started ten years ago.

"Why did you go after Miriam Broderick?" Nikki shot him a hard look. "Was it because of me?" She needed to know if his obsession with her caused Miriam to lose her life, no matter how the forces of fate might work in death.

Evigan threw his head back and roared with laughter. "Sorry to have to tell you this, but the world doesn't just revolve around you, Nikki. The truth is I had sized her up for the kill when I spotted her walking on campus. Miriam fit the bill as someone who met my criteria as a fresh victim—young, attractive, naive and unsuspecting, till it was too late to change what I had in store for her. Much like the predicament you're in now, Nikki—again." He chortled, giving her a lascivious look, ogling her from head to toe, then turning demonic in his facial expression.

I'll see you again someday, Nikki, and finish what I started. Trust me.

She recoiled at the threatening words he'd said to her during his trial and his intentions of making good on his vow, even as she took solace in learning that Miriam's death hadn't been preventable, per se, as Nikki related this to herself and the prison escapee.

I can't give up fighting for my life, Nikki thought resolutely, while eyeing the demented killer and trying to find the slightest chink in his armor.

As though he was reading her mind, Evigan knitted his thick brows and said meanly, "In there."

Nikki looked toward a downstairs bedroom and back at him, her heart pounding. "I know you want to make up for lost time with me, but can't we just talk about this, Perry…?"

"I'm afraid the time for talking is over, Nikki." He made a menacing sound. "Time to get this over with. Now move."

She weighed whether or not to comply. He was still holding the gun on her and seemingly daring her to try to take it from him. Having the serial killer shoot her on the spot and still likely carry out his other sick plans, Nikki thought better of it.

She would obey him while knowing the will to survive was just as strong as ever. Meaning that she would need the courage to do whatever it took for that to happen. Assuming that Gavin would not be able to swoop in and save her—even if Nikki sensed that he was moving heaven and earth to try to do just that.

WITHOUT PREAMBLE, the director said with an edge to his voice, "Fifteen minutes ago, a traffic camera picked up the Dodge Charger GT stolen by Evigan, headed toward Gulfport."

"Gulfport?" Gavin repeated into the cell phone, pensive. It was where Perry Evigan had abducted and taken Nikki and Brigette a decade ago. Why go back to the scene of the crime?

"Yeah," Whitfield confirmed. "With the walls closing in on him, I'm guessing that Evigan may be headed to familiar territory to hide out."

"Not just familiar to him," Gavin remarked, as a light bulb suddenly went off in his head. "Evigan's taking Nikki back to the house where he did his dirty work—and where she was rescued by FBI and other law enforcement."

"Hmm… I'd heard that the house had gone into foreclosure a few years back," the director pointed out. "Don't know what's happened to it since."

"Whoever owns the property or doesn't—my gut instincts tell me that's where we'll find Nikki—and the serial killer," Gavin said worriedly.

Whitfield responded sharply, "I'll notify the Fugitive Apprehension Strike Team, Gulfport Police Department and the rest, along with the Mississippi Department of Public Safety crisis negotiator, to head there."

Knowing he couldn't afford to put Nikki's life solely in their hands, Gavin told him with a sense of sheer determination, "I'm only a few minutes away from Gulfport. I'll meet them there."

"All right. Just be careful, Lynley," he warned. "I don't think I need to remind you that Evigan can be considered armed and dangerous—meaning it puts Nikki Sullivan at that much greater risk as both a victim and human shield."

"I know," Gavin allowed, as he pressed down on the accelerator. "Which is precisely why I need to do this. I won't let Evigan have his way with another woman I want in my life when this is over."

He disconnected and put on even more speed in what had literally become the race of Gavin's career and life, knowing that the life of the woman he loved now hung unsteadily in the balance.

Chapter Seventeen

Nikki was shoved into the room. It was barren, aside from a platform bed with only a soiled mattress, as if left for this moment in time. Dusty faux wood blinds were drawn on the windows. She obviously didn't like where this was going, but had no way out, as he had her at a decided disadvantage.

I need to get him talking more, Nikki told herself, believing that this might be her last chance to not only buy time—that she hoped to sell to Gavin and the others in law enforcement, who were undoubtedly doing everything in their power to locate her and Evigan—but get him to lower his guard somewhat, taking away his inflated sense of invincibility and superiority.

"Take your clothes off, Nikki," Evigan ordered her snappily.

"Okay, okay," she said, turning toward him and seeing that he was still pointing the gun at her. While delaying this demand as long as possible, Nikki stared at her kidnapper and asked curiously, "Just let me ask you a question, Perry... How is it that you didn't end up with the other escaped prisoners at the farmhouse that caught on fire?"

Evigan regarded her thoughtfully and laughed. "I'm a hell of a lot smarter than they were," he said unashamedly.

"They didn't want to separate—strength in numbers and all that silliness. Whereas, that's all I wanted, to go it alone and stick to the game plan I had all along, which was to come after you and take what I was deprived of ten years ago when the cops showed up at my door."

I'll see you again someday, Nikki, and finish what I started. Trust me.

His chilling words once again resonated in her head. Nikki's knees nearly buckled under the weight of his lascivious gawk. Instead, she stood her ground and, peering at Brigette's killer, asked flippantly, "So, now that your wish is about to come true, what happens after that, Perry? Do you intend to go on, sexually assaulting and strangling other women? Or will you simply sail off into the sunset and rest on your laurels? Better yet, maybe you'll turn yourself in, knowing that the authorities will never stop looking for you—wherever you go or try to hide."

Evigan chuckled. "Hadn't really thought that far ahead, to be honest. But if you must know, as a natural-born serial killer, chances are that I'll keep at it for as long as I can—handpicking new victims to go after, feeding my thirst for what I can get from them." His eyes narrowed. "Enough of the questions and answers. Now, take your clothes off! Or I'll rip them off myself."

Nikki pretended that she would voluntarily remove her tank top before stopping. "Maybe you should do it," she dared him. "Or are you afraid to drop the gun and handle me with your bare hands?" She knew this was taking a big risk by incurring his wrath even further and challenging him to get rough with her. But it was better than trying to fight someone who could shoot her at any time.

Evigan took the bait and tucked the gun inside his waistband. "Okay, if that's what you want, you've got it." He pushed her down hard on the filthy mattress. "This is going to be fun—at least for one of us. I'll even strangle you afterward with my bare hands. Just like I did your friend, Brigette."

He tossed out a sickening laugh as if to really rub it in just how cold-blooded he was as a serial killing monster. The thought of what he did to Brigette and intended to do to her the second time around, only fueled Nikki's anger. Along with her strong will to not give in to victimization again from the same perpetrator. When he relaxed his body while overconfident, and started to bend his knees to lower himself onto the bed, Nikki used the self-defense class mechanism she had been taught. In one quick motion, she lifted her right foot in a running shoe and slammed it as hard as she could against the side of his left knee—immediately dislocating it.

As the leg buckled badly, Evigan screamed an expletive at her and tried to grab his leg to keep from falling. The momentary distraction was enough for Nikki to use her other foot to thrust it with all her might smack-dab against his aquiline nose. The wicked crunching sound told her she had broken it.

While Evigan wailed like a wounded animal as he raised his hands to his bloody face, he lost his balance and fell onto the floor. Not taking any chances of a quick recovery, Nikki wasted no time in jumping off the mattress, knowing she needed to get out of there. She started to race toward the bedroom door, when she felt her leg being grabbed from behind. It was twisted just enough so she lost her balance and tumbled to the floor.

Before she could recover, Nikki was dragged toward Evigan, who said acrimoniously, "You're going to pay for this, bitch, and I'll enjoy every second of it."

Nikki's pulse raced wildly as she tried to fight off the serial killer, who was now more intent than ever to make her suffer, before strangling her to death.

GAVIN DROVE UP to the Greek Revival-style home on Robinson Road. He spotted the carjacked green Dodge Charger GT parked in the driveway haphazardly. It appeared to be empty. Meaning that most likely Evigan had already forced Nikki inside the house.

I pray I'm not too late, Gavin mused worryingly, as he climbed out of his Chevy Tahoe. Taking the FN 509 MRD-LE 9mm semiautomatic pistol from his tactical thigh leg holster, he checked the Dodge Charger and then approached the foreclosed property cautiously. He refused to believe that Nikki was already dead. There was too much left unsaid for their journey to end prematurely. Evigan could not take away everything that had become most important to Gavin—the chance at love and a lifetime of happiness.

Resting on that optimism and having faith in Nikki's ability to hang in there as long as she possibly could, Gavin stepped onto the porch, which squeaked. In spite of being fearful that he had tipped his hand in warning Evigan that they had company, this didn't prevent him from going full steam ahead as Gavin went inside the broken door that was left partially ajar.

With his pistol out in front of him, he saw signs—such as footprints in the floor dust—that indicated someone was in there. Just as he was about to head up the stairs, Gavin heard Nikki's voice as she called out for help. It was coming from a downstairs bedroom.

He raced toward it and stepped inside, where Gavin saw Perry Evigan halfway atop Nikki on the floor. The serial killer's nose was a bloody mess and one of his legs was awkwardly bent. When Evigan grabbed a handgun from his waist and pointed it at Nikki, Gavin never gave him a chance to use it.

He aimed his pistol and fired twice, hitting Evigan both times in the head, causing brain matter to spray out. The dead man slumped over, falling off Nikki, who was still clothed and appeared unhurt, but clearly shaken as she sat up.

Looking at Gavin, she said softly, "You found me."

"Yeah." He stepped over to her and grinned, helping her to get to her feet, and then hugged her, happy to be able to touch her again. "Are you all right?"

"I think so." Nikki hugged him back for a long moment, then glanced over at Evigan. "Is he…?"

"Yes, Evigan's been neutralized," Gavin spoke confidently. "He won't hurt you or anyone else, ever again."

"That's good to know."

Gavin regarded the serial killer. "Looks like you did quite a number on him before I showed up."

"He really didn't leave me any choice," she said matter-of-factly. "Either fight back or give up. That wasn't an option."

Gavin gave a satisfied smile. "Glad to hear it."

Nikki paused. "He wanted to come after you too."

He arched a brow. "Excuse me?"

"Ever since the trial, Evigan has apparently been caught up in some vindictive vengeance mindset against both of us," she informed him. "But as an armed special agent, you were harder to corner. Though he would likely have never given up trying."

"Wow." Gavin let that roll around in his head for a moment. The idea that Evigan wanted to put him and Nikki in the grave, alongside Brigette, only made it more comforting that he had been stopped cold, before carrying out the rest of his agenda. "The man was obviously the worst kind of human being. Neither of us have to watch our backs anymore, where Evigan's concerned."

Nikki's voice broke as she uttered, "It's a relief, for sure." Her eyes watered. "I thought I might never see you again."

"That wasn't going to happen," Gavin assured her with a straight face. Never mind that, at times, that frightening thought had crossed his mind too. "Not if I had anything to say about it."

"He was waiting for me outside the cabin when I went onto the wraparound deck to sketch the landscape," Nikki explained.

Gavin nodded. "I gathered as much." He only wished he had gone out there with her. And had been able to take out Evigan sooner.

"Before I could react, Evigan had injected me with ketamine and thrown me into the trunk of his car—and brought me here." She looked at Gavin curiously. "How did you figure it out anyway?"

He turned to Evigan and what was left of his head, before Gavin decided that Nikki didn't need to see any more of the man who kidnapped and tried to kill her. "I'll explain in a moment," he told her, taking Nikki's hand to lead her out of the room. Then he said, "You were right about seeing Evigan at the grocery store. After he abducted you, I had a hunch and went back to the store to take a look at their surveillance video. I saw not only Evigan inside, but outside—where he got into a green Dodge Charger GT. Found out that it was carjacked. The vehicle was picked up heading toward Gulfport. I was able to put two and two together that he was taking you here—the scene of the original crimes against you…and Brigette."

"Your instincts were spot-on," Nikki declared. "In his warped mind, Evigan wanted to try and re-create what happened ten years ago—only this time succeeding in his plans to finish me off. Just like he killed Brigette."

"But Evigan failed again," Gavin told her, with a catch to his voice. "He overplayed his hand and lost. Brigette can now have the peace she has long sought. And so can we, Nikki."

She nodded with teary eyes, and said quietly, "It's what I'd always hoped for."

"Same here." Gavin gazed into her eyes soulfully as they heard the sounds of sirens approaching. "But there was always something else I'd always wished for—"

"Oh…" Nikki met his eyes. "What's that?"

"To truly fall in love with someone and be able to tell her that."

"Oh," she repeated. "Is that what you're saying to me?"

"Yes, it is." Gavin's voice fell an octave. "I have fallen in love with you, Nikki Sullivan. Not just young love like I may have felt for Brigette," he made clear, "but adult love for a beautiful and talented artist, who gets me and made me get her. I never thought it would happen this fast, but it has and you need to know that."

"There's something you need to know too," Nikki said, and took his hands, her own trembling. "I think I've been in love with you for the past ten years—or since we were first introduced. But I tried to ignore it for obvious reasons. I felt all along that there was a real connection there, even if your attention was on someone else. After Brigette's death and being blamed for it by you, I thought our moment had passed. That seemed even more the case after the trial, when it seemed like I would never see you again. Then, just days ago—which somehow seems like a year—you showed up at my house..."

"And the rest, as they say, is history," Gavin finished, while looking squarely toward the future, elated to hear that she loved him too and had for some time.

"Yeah." She flashed her teeth. "Something like that."

"And like this," he said, as Gavin cupped her cheeks and they kissed, before putting everything on hold when the Fugitive Apprehension Strike Team and support team showed up and took over the crime scene.

THREE MONTHS LATER, Gavin was driving his Chevrolet Tahoe, with Jean O'Reilly in the passenger seat. They were en route to the Mississippi Department of Corrections Central Office headquarters to discuss with the director of investigations an ongoing probe into gang violence and narcotic violations in the state's prison system.

"Director Whitfield will be happy to know we're making serious progress in getting to the root of the problem and offering constructive solutions," Jean said.

"You think?" Gavin suspected that making progress and really rooting out the dual problems of gangs and drug-related offenses among inmates were two entirely different things that Whitfield, a stickler for actual results, likely wouldn't have much trouble differentiating.

"Hey, have you forgotten how we nailed Titus Malfoy to the wall and made Whitfield look good in the process?"

"I remember." Gavin considered that the probation officer

they had investigated for embezzlement and other crimes had pleaded guilty and implicated another probation officer and a parole agent for the bargain. Whitfield had used this to tighten procedures and accountability for those working in these fields in the MDOC.

"Then there's Perry Evigan and the other escapees that came to a satisfactory conclusion under the director's watch," she mentioned.

Gavin thought about Evigan and just how close he came to murdering Nikki—to add to the eleven other women he strangled to death and the four men he killed as well for good measure. The fact that Evigan was now dead and buried gave Gavin only a limited amount of placation. His death could never bring back Brigette or the other victims. But it could bring closure to survivors, such as Nikki, who had gotten an added measure of payback in shattering Evigan's nose and messing up his leg, before the serial killer's time on Earth ran out.

A firearms examiner was able to positively link the SIG Sauer P365 9mm pistol Perry Evigan tried to shoot Nikki with to the murder of Kenan Fernández, to tie up one loose end. Another was to hold those responsible for the prison escape of Evigan, Craig Schneider and Aaron Machado accountable—with Whitfield reassigning Mississippi State Penitentiary superintendent, Crystal Rawlings, and warden, Zachary Livingston, in an effort to reduce the chances of this from happening again in the future. Whitfield went public with this to show both his commitment to prison reform and to take credit for the fugitives being taken off the streets.

"I take your point," Gavin told Jean, with a slight grin. "Maybe we can score some points with the director—and vice versa."

"Yes, I'm game for a basket or two, if you are." She laughed. A minute later Jean asked him, "So, when do you plan to pop the question?"

Gavin glanced her way. "Pop the question?" he asked, as though befuddled.

"Uh, ask Nikki to marry you?"

He didn't need to give this any thought. "As a matter of fact, I plan to do it today."

Jean's eyes widened. "Seriously?"

"Yeah. It's time." Gavin knew, and already felt giddy about tying the knot with the woman he was in love with. "I just hope she says yes."

"There is that." Jean gave a chuckle. "From what I've seen of you two, the *yes* part is a mere formality, Lynley."

He grinned crookedly, while eager to put that to the test.

AT THE OWL'S BAY FITNESS CENTER on Tenth Street, Nikki was on a treadmill, enjoying a good workout. She welcomed being able to do one of the things she loved most in staying fit, without the ominous shadows of Kenan Fernández and, even more, Perry Evigan, hanging over her. She was still coming to terms with the fact that the serial killer who murdered her best friend and was on the verge of sending her to an early grave as well—had Gavin not intervened— was now dead himself. Meaning that he wouldn't get the chance to escape from prison again to wreak havoc on her life or the lives of other innocent people.

Justice was definitely served here, Nikki told herself, as she turned toward her friend, Blair Roxburgh, who had been there for her throughout the ordeal that included them losing another friend to Evigan, Miriam Broderick.

"Having trouble keeping up, are we?" Blair joked, as Nikki had inadvertently slowed down her pace during the reverie.

"Sorry about that." She laughed, while picking it up again. "I'll try not to drift off any more."

"You're entitled," Blair said. "Especially if you're fantasizing about that hot boyfriend of yours, Special Agent Lynley."

Nikki colored. "Maybe I was," she confessed, at least to some degree. "Can you blame me?" She knew that Blair, who had recently gotten engaged to her boyfriend, Oliver Pascal, was hoping Nikki and Gavin would follow suit. Though they were rotating spending long weekends at her place and his, the subject of marriage hadn't come up. For her part, Nikki was more than ready and willing to walk down the aisle with the man she loved. But pressuring Gavin to want the same wasn't in her nature. Should it be?

"Not one bit." Blair grabbed her water bottle and took a sip. "You know, you could just go out on a limb and ask Gavin for his hand in marriage. I'm guessing that he would never want you to get away."

"Hmm…" Nikki drank water thoughtfully. Was Gavin ready for that? Or was he content to keep things as they were for now, while still expressing his love for her? "We'll have to see about that," she told her friend noncommittally. "All I know for certain at the moment is that I never want to let Gavin slip away from me."

"That's never going to happen," Blair reassured her. "Whatever else I may think of your special agent, he definitely knows a great thing when he sees and touches it."

"Ditto." Nikki cherished the thought of a future together with Gavin, in whatever form both could live with.

WHEN GAVIN SHOWED up at Nikki's cottage that evening with a dozen long-stemmed red roses, it was fully intended to woo her. "For you," he said coolly.

She blushed. "Thank you." Her nose took in the fragrance. "They're lovely."

"So are you." Gavin grinned, resisting the urge to kiss her for the time being.

Nikki smiled. "I'll go put these in some water."

"Before you do—" he lifted one rose from the bouquet that held something hidden in a leaf and removed it "—you might want to see if this ring fits…" Falling to one knee, Gavin held up the 2.5 carat princess-cut engagement ring with a diamond band in platinum and said affectionately, "Nikki Sullivan, I don't think it's any secret that I've fallen madly in love with you. That's only grown these past few months. I'd like nothing more than to make it official by becoming your husband and father to any children that come our way. Will you marry me and make my happiness level off the charts?"

Without ado, Nikki cried, "Yes, yes, I'll marry you, Gavin Lynley. I love you too, just as madly!" She put a hand to her mouth at the joy of the moment, then stretched it out for him to slide the ring onto.

"I'm delighted to hear that," he professed, and put the ring on her finger. "How does it feel?"

"Like it belongs," she uttered, gazing at the engagement ring admiringly. "Like we belong."

"We do." Gavin got to his feet, finding it difficult to take the smile off his face. "For the rest of our lives," he swore.

"Yes, the rest of our lives," Nikki repeated blissfully. She tilted her face upward. "Kiss me and we'll make this official."

"With pleasure." He puckered his lips and brought them upon hers that opened slightly in anticipation for that sweet kiss, which was stirring and gave Gavin something to definitely look forward to time and time again. He broke their lip-lock just long enough to say sweetly, "I think that definitely makes our engagement to marry and live happily thereafter official."

Epilogue

Gavin watched as his sister, Lauren, and her husband, Rory Nolden, along with their two little girls, Ellen and Miley, appeared on the laptop screen for a Zoom video chat.

"Hey, everyone," Gavin said evenly.

Ellen and Miley, seven and eight, respectively, both with long curly dark hair and brown eyes, and resembling both parents, said in unison, "Hi, Uncle Gavin."

"What's up, man," Rory said merrily, wearing round reading glasses over brown eyes. His brown hair was styled in a spiky quiff cut.

Lauren, who had already picked up on his closeness to Nikki during other conversations, still looked on with anticipation, behind her own geometric-shaped glasses, when she said wryly, "It's so nice to visit with my big brother. Anything special happening in your life these days?"

Gavin laughed. "As a matter of fact, there is…" He took a breath while standing over the marble countertop in Nikki's kitchen. "I wanted you all to be the first to know that I've asked Nikki to marry me…"

"Did she say yes?" Miley asked animatedly.

"Yeah, did she?" Ellen pressed impatiently.

"Come on, out with it," Lauren demanded.

Gavin chuckled. "I thought I should let Nikki tell you herself."

Nikki, who had been standing just out of view of the laptop's camera, moved beside him. "Hey, guys!" She flashed a brilliant smile and stated enthusiastically, "I said yes!" She lifted her hand to show off the engagement ring for everyone to see.

"Congratulations," Lauren said lovingly. "I'm so happy for you both and applaud you, Nikki, for finally being able to make an honest man out of my brother."

Nikki chuckled. "Believe me when I tell you, the pleasure is all mine. Well, maybe a little bit is left over for Gavin."

He laughed, kissing her on the cheek and giving them an opportunity to get to know one another better now that they were about to become family.

ON HER WEDDING DAY, Nikki had butterflies in her stomach with the wonderful anticipation she felt in knowing that she would be spending the rest of her life married to Gavin Lynley. She only wished in an odd way that her first best friend, Brigette, were alive to be there. Though Brigette and Gavin were once an item, Nikki was certain that Brigette would have wanted them both to be happy in her absence.

The wedding was held outdoors on a gorgeous and sunny day in Jackson, Mississippi, where Nikki and Gavin would live. They had already begun home shopping, in search of a property that both could put their stamp on as a place to raise a family. Nikki was thrilled that Jackson was also a wonderful place for artists. She'd already begun to establish herself there with a few pieces on display at various art galleries.

Nikki felt honored that her stepfather had agreed to give

her away and was already bonding with Gavin—as both were into jazz music and such great artists as Billie Holiday, Duke Ellington and Sarah Vaughan. Blair was Nikki's maid of honor and the bridesmaids were Gavin's sister, Lauren, and his equally beautiful cousins, Madison and Annette. With Lauren's daughters, Miley and Ellen, serving as the flower girls. All had been very welcoming in having Nikki join their family.

Gavin had asked his college friend and log cabin owner, Jake Kendrick, to be his best man, while choosing his handsome cousins in law enforcement, like Gavin—Scott, Russell and Caleb Lynley—to be his groomsmen. Nikki was elated to be on the threshold of becoming a Lynley herself and hoped to have at least one son to carry on the family name for the next generation, joining their cousins.

As her stepfather walked her down the aisle, Nikki felt beautiful in a white floral lace, V-neck sleeveless mermaid gown with a side cut and white peep-toe high heel sandals. When she stood before her fiancé, Nikki was enamored with him, as he was resplendent in a black tuxedo and matching patent leather Oxfords.

"You look incredible," Gavin told her, a generous grin on his handsome face.

Her teeth shone. "So do you."

"You ready for this?"

"I've never been more ready," Nikki told him, meaning it with all her heart.

"Same here," Gavin promised her.

They brought their own vows to read and did so without missing a beat, while gazing into each other's eyes. When they were finished and exchanged diamond wedding bands, the female pastor pronounced them husband and wife and gave them permission to kiss one another. It was short, sweet and satisfying to Nikki as her husband took her by the hand and they headed down the aisle joyously. Nikki stopped briefly to give her mother a hug.

"I'm so proud of you, Nikki," she told her tearfully. "And Gavin too."

"Thanks, Mom." Nikki received a kiss on the cheek from her parents and then proceeded on with the man she intended to have a great life with as Mrs. Gavin Lynley.

Their wedding night was everything Nikki could have asked for and so much more. It felt like both the first time and a comfortable sense of familiarity that she looked forward to relishing for years to come.

FOR THEIR TWO-WEEK HONEYMOON, Gavin surprised Nikki by fulfilling her dream of going on a cruise. He wanted to make the start of their marriage a memorable occasion and a shared adventure that could propel them to further outings in keeping the romance alive through the years.

As the riverboat cruised the Upper and Lower Mississippi River, its ports of call included fascinating small towns in multiple states including Missouri, Tennessee, Minnesota, Louisiana and, of course, Mississippi. In each place, they enjoyed the cuisine, culture and music of the locals, all while discovering more about each other.

Halfway through the voyage, Gavin and Nikki stood on the private veranda in their stateroom, while appreciating picturesque landscapes and astounding views of the Mississippi. They were sipping Manhattan cocktails, when Gavin had to ask, "So, is this everything you thought a riverboat cruise would be?"

"How could it not be?" Nikki beamed. "Getting married

and then taking this journey with the man of my dreams is more than I could ever have asked for."

"Really?" Gavin was delighted to hear her say that, eager to please in every way he could.

"Well, actually, there is one other thing I could think of that just might truly make it complete."

He tasted the cocktail and gazed curiously into her lovely eyes. "And what might that be?" he asked nervously.

"Only this—" Nikki stood on her tiptoes and laid a mouthwatering kiss on his lips that left Gavin breathless and wanting for more.

"Oh, was that all?" he quipped once their mouths had separated.

"Hmm…" She licked her lips. "Well, maybe there is one last bit of business to absolutely make the cruise unforgettable…"

Gavin regarded her keenly. "Name it."

"In that case," Nikki said flirtatiously, "here's precisely what I had in mind…"

She whispered sweet and sensual words in his ear and the rest spoke for itself.

* * * * *

LAST MISSION

LISA CHILDS

For my hotshot hero and amazing husband who
inspires all my heroes: Andrew Ahearne

Prologue

Sixteen months ago...

The flames consuming Charlie Tillerman's corner tavern lit up the whole town of Northern Lakes, Michigan. The fire cast a sunrise-like glow over Main Street. The arsonist had struck again, setting the bar on fire where it was well-known that the Huron Hotshots, a team of elite firefighters, hung out. That son of a bitch had been coming after them for the past six months.

But some damn firebug wasn't going to beat them. They got out while making sure the other customers got safely out as well. Except for one...

Nobody could find the superintendent of the hotshot team. Not that *everyone* was trying to find him. Someone would be damn happy if Braden Zimmer was never found.

The hotshots were out on the street now, hooking up the hoses, working together to put out the flames before they spread to the other buildings on the block. The noise of the engines was loud, so loud that this particular person didn't immediately hear the shouts. Then they turned and saw hotshot Ethan Sommerly barreling out of the smoke, carrying a small blonde woman over his shoulder. Owen James, the paramedic on the team, rushed forward to help, pressing an oxygen mask over the woman's face.

"Braden's in the alley!" Ethan yelled.

The woman, the arson investigator, pulled down her mask and shouted, "Get in there! Please, save him!"

She wasn't the only one yelling, though. Another hotshot, Michaela Momber, emerged from the front of the building. She was dragging the bar owner, Charlie Tillerman, out with her. "Clear!" she yelled. "The building is about to collapse!"

Just as she said it, the structure shuddered and imploded on itself, sending out flames and a thick cloud of acrid smoke.

This was it.

An eerie silence fell like the building just did. Everybody had to know. There was no way that even the great Braden Zimmer could have survived a building collapsing on him.

But then someone gasped and pointed to the alley between the burning remains of the Filling Station Bar and Grill and the building next to it that had flames licking at its roof and walls. From that narrow space and all that thick smoke, a man emerged. Like Michaela had carried Charlie, Braden was carrying someone, too. The body of Matthew Harrison, that damn kid who'd wanted so badly to be a hotshot, too. He was the arsonist. He had to be the person who'd targeted their team and Braden specifically for not hiring him for the last open position on the Huron Hotshots.

Owen and Ethan and the others rushed forward to help Braden and the kid. While the paramedics treated them, the other hotshots stepped back and cheered and applauded. Tears rolled down soot-streaked faces, tears of relief that their fearless leader was okay.

Everybody was so happy—everyone but one person.

While the others were happy about Braden, they were probably also relieved that the arsonist targeting the Huron Hotshots team of elite firefighters was going to jail. The team should have been safe and might have been if the arsonist was the only one after the team, the only one trying to hurt them.

But there was someone else. And while the arsonist was going to spend a lot of his life behind bars, this person had no intention of ever winding up there and had no intention of ever stopping either.

They weren't going to rest until the Huron Hotshots team was destroyed, even if they destroyed themselves in the process...

Chapter One

Sixteen months later...

What the hell am I doing?

Mack McRooney tried to focus on the meeting his brother-in-law, Braden Zimmer, had called in the conference room on the third floor of the Northern Lakes fire station. But while he stood behind the dark-haired man, that question—*what the hell am I doing here*—kept running around Mack's mind like his younger brother Trick used to run around the house when he had too much sugar.

Even though Mack was only thirty-seven, he was supposed to be retiring from all of this. From danger. From any more missions. He'd turned in his *official* paperwork. He'd gone home six months ago, not to Northern Lakes since he had never lived here. He'd gone home to the house where he'd grown up on the Pacific coast, in Washington.

But what was that damn saying?

You can't come home again...

He'd spent a few months in the Pacific Northwest, in the national forest in Washington where his dad had raised Mack and his siblings pretty much on his own while training smoke jumpers and hotshots to fight wildfires. While it had taken a couple of months for his dad to train Mack how to be a hotshot and a smoke jumper, it hadn't taken Mack long to realize that place wasn't home anymore and hadn't been since he'd left.

Hell, it hadn't been *home* since his mom had left, abandoning her husband and kids in order to find herself. But Mack was really the last person who could judge her for that since instead of staying to help his dad out with his younger siblings, he'd taken off, too. He'd left right after high school graduation because he'd already enlisted in the army. Instead of finding himself, though, he got lost somewhere... maybe even before he left home.

He sure as hell wasn't here, in Northern Lakes, Michigan, looking for himself, though. He was looking for a saboteur. For the person who'd been messing with his brother-in-law's hotshot team. The equipment, rigged to malfunction, might have been a prank, but with a job as dangerous as a hotshot, pranks like that could kill. Then there had been some blatant attacks on the team members. The threats and the violence had escalated to the point where someone was definitely going to die.

That was why Mack was here. So that the person who died wasn't someone he cared about, like his younger brother Trick, who already had some close calls thanks to the saboteur and also an obsessed stalker. But the stalker, Colleen Conrad, their sister Sam's former college roommate, was behind bars now.

Trick wasn't the only one Mack was worried about. He liked his brother-in-law, too, and he knew how devastated his sister would be if she lost him. Sam had finally found happiness, and she was due any day now to give birth to her and Braden Zimmer's son. Sam didn't need the stress of worrying about her family.

And neither did Mack.

"So let's all welcome the newest member of our team, Mack McRooney," Braden said, and he stepped back to pat Mack's shoulder. Then the hotshot superintendent clapped his hands together to lead the applause.

There was a slight hesitation before the other firefighters on the twenty-member hotshot team joined in. Instead of being offended, Mack grinned. They had to suspect why he was really here. It wasn't to just fill the spot Michaela Momber had opened up on the team when her pregnancy compelled her to go on medical leave.

His hire wasn't even nepotism, which was probably what the other hotshots thought when Braden hired Trick—Patrick McRooney—onto the team months ago. Trick was younger than Mack and looked like a younger version of their dad before the old man had shaved off what was left of his red hair. Trick's hair was thick and long and more auburn than red. Mack didn't look anything like his dad or his brother except for size. He was probably even a little taller and broader than them. He didn't resemble their sister either, who had their mother's petite build and blonde hair. Mack's hair was black, buzzed short like he was still in the military, and his eyes were dark.

Sometimes, he wondered about his actual paternity. But that was something he'd rather not know because it didn't matter. The man who'd raised him was his dad and after their mom took off, Mack Senior had been their mother as well.

And what actually mattered was catching this saboteur. When Trick came onboard eight months ago, the other

hotshots hadn't realized then that there was a potential saboteur among them. Braden had begun to suspect, though,
and a mysterious note he'd received had made him even
more suspicious. So he'd brought in Trick to be objective
and investigate the other members of the team to find out
who wasn't, as the note claimed, whom Braden thought
they were. Well, one of them might have known why Trick
had been hired if the saboteur was actually a member of
the team.

Mack wasn't sure about that, though. He wasn't sure
about anything yet except for the same thing everyone was
well aware of by now: they were in danger.

Some of them had nearly died because of the sabotage
and those outright attacks. Fortunately, the ones who'd been
attacked, like Ethan Sommerly with an exploding stove,
and Rory VanDam, with an axe handle to the back of the
head, had survived. Unfortunately, they hadn't seen who
had attacked them.

They were applauding along with Braden nearly as hard
as he was. Probably because they had no secrets to hide
anymore since their true identities had come out. And they
wanted another identity revealed—that of the saboteur.

Rory, or Corwin Douglas, as Mack had known Rory Van-
Dam, was well aware of the work Mack had done in the special forces and other branches of the military and homeland
security. While Mack's family didn't know as much about
what he'd been doing all these years, they were aware that
he'd participated in top secret missions.

This mission was no secret though. Someone had to catch
this saboteur. Nobody was any closer, after all these months,
to figuring out who that was. So if the team suspected Mack
was here to investigate, they all should have been happy, not

just Braden, Ethan and Rory. If Rory had shared what he knew about Mack, how he'd successfully completed every mission, then they had to know that he was damn well going to figure out who'd been terrorizing the team. And in order to do that, he was going to have to uncover every secret any of them had left.

After the meeting concluded, only a few of the other team members, besides Rory and Ethan, approached him. Trent Miles, Carl Kozak and Ed Ward joined him, Rory and Ethan near the table of coffee, bagels and fruit.

Trent was a big guy, like Ethan, and was that kind of movie-firefighter-good-looking that a lot of people expected real-life firefighters to look like. But there was no expression on his handsome face. "So you're the one who saved Rory's life?"

Mack shrugged, surprised that word had spread like it had. He'd tried to stay under the radar five months ago when he'd dipped into town to check on Rory. He hadn't known for certain then how he was going to help Braden, from a distance or like he was now, up close and maybe a little too personally. Although he'd been able to save Rory while watching from afar, it hadn't brought him any closer to learning the identity of the saboteur.

"I don't know whether I should thank you or not," Trent continued.

Instead of being offended, Rory laughed. "He's just pissed that his little sister has fallen for me."

Trent held out his hand to Mack who shook it. "I do appreciate that you saved *her* life that day, too. And because, for some reason she has fallen for this loser, I am glad that you saved Rory's ass."

Rory laughed again.

"So, you're what?" Ed Ward asked. The guy was in his mid-thirties, the kind of guy that was average in every way. Height. Build. Coloring. He probably blended into every crowd, but in this one, he stood out more for being nondescript in comparison to all the other larger-than-life people. "Retired military or something?"

"Something," Mack said. "I've always gone where I was needed."

"We need you here," Rory said, and he slapped his back. Rory was thinner than the other guys, with pale blond hair and a cleanly shaved face, but while he didn't look quite as strong as the more muscular guys, Mack knew very well how tough the guy was. "We need you to figure out who the hell is messing with us."

"Yeah, before my sister tries to investigate any more and gets herself killed," Trent added.

Rory flinched as if just the thought brought him pain.

Mack was surprised that a guy like Rory, who'd lived like Mack had, under different identities for different agencies, had let himself get attached to anyone, let alone fallen for her. Mack couldn't imagine ever doing the same. But his aversion to relationships had less to do with his career choice and more to do with his childhood, with how his mom had so easily abandoned their dad and them. He knew how shallow and selfish people could be, so it would be hard to trust anyone with his heart.

And maybe it would be even harder to let anyone trust him with theirs. He had already hurt his family when he'd taken off like he had. He didn't want to hurt anyone else, especially when he had no idea what he was doing after this mission. His last one. And it wasn't just to find that saboteur, it was to make up to his family for taking off, by making sure they stayed safe.

"Is that why you're here? To investigate?" Carl Kozak asked. Most of the team called the older guy Mr. Clean because of his shaved head and muscular body. "I heard you were retiring from all that."

Mack wondered how he heard. Had Rory told him? Or maybe Trick or Braden? They were all too trusting of their team members, but that was why they needed him. He could be objective.

"I am retiring," Mack confirmed. "I turned in my papers months ago." Against the wishes of his superiors, who'd begged him just to take some time off instead since he rarely had. But he'd been able to stack up that vacation and personal time in order to retire early. That hadn't been his reason for not using it, though. He'd worried that if he went home more often, it would have been too hard for him to leave again. Or maybe too easy...

And then he would have that confirmation that he was just like his mother.

"Shh," Carl said. "Don't let my wife hear you say that word. She's been harping on me to retire. Now that the kids are all grown up and out of the house, she wants to travel, go on cruises." He shuddered. "But I figure you have to be old to retire."

"You are old, Mr. Clean," one of the younger guys joked as he walked up to join them. Bruce Abbott or Howie Lane. They were the youngest guys on the team, hired just before Cody Mallehan had filled the last open spot. Until the death of hotshot Dirk Brown had opened up another seven or eight months ago. Trick had filled his spot.

Most of the other hotshots gradually stepped forward and

welcomed him except for Trick. Mack's younger brother held back, talking quietly to Braden near the podium of the conference room. Maybe they were just talking about the next assignment, like these guys were talking about the job they were heading to after this meeting.

Another fire had recently threatened the town, so the team had to make a few more breaks in order to protect it. Because of that fire, Braden had taken them out of the wildfire rotation for a while. They were going to stay local instead of heading off to wherever they were needed or back to the day jobs most of them had in addition to being hotshots.

Mack was the one who had actually asked Braden to make sure they all stayed in Northern Lakes. That way he could fully investigate every member of the team at the same time that he investigated every person in town who could possibly be the saboteur.

If anybody on this team—hell, if anyone in this town—had any secrets, Mack was going to find them out. And he was going to find the saboteur. But this, one way or another, was going to be his last damn mission.

WYNONA WELLS HAD a secret. A big one.

One that could potentially affect her career if anyone found out. But the state trooper didn't know what to do. People already suspected her of being complicit in the sabotage happening to the hotshot team that operated out of their headquarters in Northern Lakes. And if they knew what else she'd done...

They wouldn't believe she wasn't involved, that she wasn't as corrupt as her training officer who was now in jail. The only way to prove her innocence in all of this was to find the real saboteur.

She parked her police SUV at the curb near the fire station and stared up at the three-story concrete block building. Was he or she in there right now, thinking that they were going to get away with it?

With everything they'd done?

She had to make certain that didn't happen, and that she was the one who finally brought the perpetrator to justice. Her career depended on it.

And maybe even her life…

Because lately she had a strange feeling, like she was being watched. As she stepped out of her vehicle and walked around the front of it toward the fire station, she felt it again, and the skin between her shoulder blades tingled as if a chill was racing down her spine despite the warmth of the June day.

Someone was watching her.

From where?

She peered around, but the people walking on the sidewalk across the street from the firehouse seemed uninterested in her. They were engaged in conversation either with each other or with someone or something on their cell phones.

So where was the watcher?

In one of the buildings across the street? In an alley? She looked around, and then with that sensation intensifying to the point that her chill became a bead of sweat rolling down between her shoulder blades beneath her dark blue uniform, she looked up.

On the third story of the firehouse, in the conference room where the team meetings were held, stood a dark shadow behind the glass. Big, broad, imposing. Quite a few members of the hotshot team were big and broad. But nobody else was quite that imposing…at least not to Wynona.

He was back.

She'd only seen him once, five months ago, coming out of her boss's office after the shooting at this very firehouse. He'd barely glanced at her then, as if she was insignificant to him, and maybe she was. So why would he be staring at her now? Or watching her over the past few days when she had that strange feeling?

A couple of days ago, she'd been standing outside the house she owned on the biggest lake in the Northern Lakes area, and she had noticed a glint in the distance, like sunlight reflecting off glass. At first, she'd suspected someone was watching her with binoculars, but there was just one glint, like a scope. Like the one on the long-range rifle that had been used to kill an FBI agent five months ago, that *he* had used. And ever since that day, he'd been on her mind entirely too much. Something about him had frightened her then. And so, once she'd thought a scope might have been trained on her, fear had raced through her, and she'd ducked down, expecting a bullet to come toward her.

But if someone had fired at her, it had been silent and had missed. After, she hadn't been able to find any bullet near her or any casings where she'd seen that glint, and she concluded that it must have been something else. Maybe even a camera lens. Because she knew if this man had fired at her, he wouldn't have missed. If he hadn't hit that FBI agent all those months ago, a few other people would have died that day: Rory VanDam, Brittney Townsend and the kid who helped out around the firehouse, Stanley.

Probably even his dog would have died. That massive bull mastiff-sheepdog mix now bounded out of the open overhead door of one of the firehouse garage bays. Annie rushed toward her as if they were old friends and jumped on her, knocking off the trooper's hat as she tried to lick Wynona's face. Instead of being annoyed like some of the other troopers were with Annie whenever they had a call at the firehouse—which had been all too often over the past almost year and a half—Wynona was charmed.

Once Annie had warmed up to her, and it had taken a little while for her to get used to both the gun and the uniform, they had become fast friends, probably because Wynona always brought her a little treat. She pulled the doggy dental chew from her pocket.

"Here, girl," she said as she pushed it between Annie's drooling jowls. "We can all use a little fresher breath." The only kisses Wynona had gotten recently had been from this dog. She had officially sworn off dating and had no intention of changing her mind.

Annie dropped back down to all fours as she gobbled up the treat. Then she sniffed Wynona's pocket for another. Wynona chuckled. "You are so spoiled."

And the dog knew her well enough to assume that she wouldn't have brought just one treat.

"Hey, Trooper Wells," Stanley said as he bounded out of the open garage door with nearly as much energy as the dog. The teenager was tall with a mop of blond curls and a big smile. That smile quickly slipped away as he peered fearfully around them. "Did something else happen? Is that why you're here?"

She assured him, "Nothing's happened." At least not to a hotshot. But she was pretty convinced that someone had been following her lately. Not here though. But now she knew why. The person following her was probably already here, on the third floor of the firehouse.

She continued, "I'm here to make sure that nothing else bad does happen." Not to anyone else and not to her either.

That was her plan anyway, to find out just who was responsible for the bad things that had happened to hotshots— that had nothing to do with the people already in jail or dead. And she knew there were other incidents but the hotshots had been reluctant to share any of those details with her. They were either determined to handle everything on their own, or they didn't trust her to handle anything at all. Sometimes she suspected her own co-workers felt that way about her, like she couldn't handle the job.

The teenager nodded, tousling his curls. "That would be good. That's why Braden hired Trick's brother Mack. He's going to make all the bad things stop."

"Mack..." So *he* was definitely back. Her stomach lurched with the confirmation.

Stanley gave another vigorous nod, knocking some of those curls into his blue eyes. "Yeah, you know. He's the guy who saved me and Rory and Brittney."

"Yeah, I know." Or she would have known if he'd agreed to talk to her, but he'd disappeared from the scene before she could take his report. Then he'd shown up at the state police post where he'd talked to her superior instead. Was that because he didn't trust her, like the hotshots, or because he didn't respect a woman in law enforcement?

Stanley bent down, picked up her hat from the ground and handed it to her. "Sorry Annie knocked it off," he said. "She sure loves you now."

Wynona pulled back the long red hair that had escaped the pins she used to keep it in place and shoved it all under the hat she settled back on her head. Then she reached into her pocket and gave Annie another dental chew. "I've been bribing her."

"So you do know something about bribes." That deep voice didn't belong to Stanley. And while she hadn't heard it before because he'd refused to answer any of *her* questions, Wynona instantly knew to whom it belonged: *him*.

Mack McRooney. Her boss had told her his name after he'd passed her in the hall that day. He was some kind of military hero with special security clearances that apparently made him exempt from answering her questions or explaining any of his actions.

While she appreciated his service, she didn't appreciate him using it to ignore her. But she shouldn't have been surprised that he would since most of the hotshots did. They didn't trust her. Did they actually think she was taking bribes?

At least *he* seemed to be implying that she'd sold out. If he only knew…

But she wasn't sure if the truth would make people feel less suspicious of her or more. Especially if they knew the other secret she wanted to keep.

But she wasn't sure that she would be able to keep that truth hidden much longer, not with him here watching her. He definitely wasn't ignoring her now.

She looked up from the dog and stared into eyes that were nearly as big and deep as Annie's. There wasn't any affection in this gaze for her like there was in the dog's. There was just suspicion.

What did he know?

Had he already discovered her secret?

A MEMBER OF your team isn't who you think they are...

Several months ago, Braden Zimmer had found that note folded up on his desk where he sat now in his windowless office in the firehouse. He still had no idea who the writer had been talking about, but there were many possibilities. So many of his team weren't the people he'd once thought they were.

Ethan Sommerly was really Jonathan Michael Canterbury IV, heir to a vast fortune and a family curse. Rory VanDam was really a former undercover DEA agent. And those were just the two whose names were different from what Braden had first known them as.

But there were other ways that people could be someone he didn't think they were. Like if one of the team was actually the saboteur who had hurt and betrayed the others.

Just a few days before calling the meeting this morning with the rest of the hotshots, Braden had turned over that note to Mack along with all the video footage from the cameras he had installed after Rory was attacked just outside the bunkroom. Braden had also given his brother-in-law a detailed report of all the things the saboteur was probably responsible for and the list of people that he and Trick had already ruled out as possible suspects.

While Mack had thanked him for turning everything over, he'd also been succinct. "Nobody is ruled out as a suspect until I rule them out."

Mack was the fresh eyes and objectivity this investigation needed. Braden knew that, but he couldn't help being a little uneasy about his team. Not everybody had secrets that anyone else needed to know about, like Michaela with her unexpected pregnancy, and Luke Garrison and his wife's former marital issues.

But the person Braden was most worried about was Mack, especially as the new hotshot was heading out with the others today to cut back some trees for fire breaks. The first time Trick had gone out with the team to do that, something had happened to the lift truck's bucket while Trick was in it. If not for the safety cable he'd been wearing and Henrietta's quick thinking, Trick might have fallen to his death with a chain saw landing on top of him. That malfunction of the bucket coming loose from the truck was like so many other things that had happened over the past several months: sabotage.

Messing with the bucket had been the saboteur's initiation for Trick joining the team. What was Mack's going to be? Because Braden had no doubt that the saboteur knew why Mack was here, and that he or she had something planned for him. While Mack had survived some dangerous missions in the military, Braden was worried that this might be Mack's most dangerous mission yet.

Chapter Two

While Mack had avoided the state trooper the last time he'd
been in Northern Lakes, this time he wanted to talk to her.
Hell, he wanted just to look at her. She was beautiful with
her deep green eyes and pale skin and all that red hair that
kept slipping out from beneath her hat.

She was staring back at him, too. No. She was glaring
at him, obviously offended about his bribe comment. She
wasn't hotly denying it or defending herself either, but that
made her look more innocent to Mack than if she'd dramati-
cally reacted to his comment.

"Mack!" Trick shouted at him from the pickup truck he
pulled up in front of her police SUV. The passenger window was down, and he was leaning across the console, so
he didn't need to yell. He probably just wanted to. "We have
to get going," Trick said, his voice sharp with irritation.

"You're leaving again already?" she asked.

Mack grinned. "Why, Trooper Wells, you sound disappointed."

"I didn't get a chance to talk to you yet," she said. "I have
questions I'd like answered."

He did, too. He reached out and touched the tendril of

hair that had slipped out to slide down her cheek. It was just as silky as it looked. He pushed it back behind her ear.

"Don't worry," he told her. "I'm not going anywhere this time. I'm sticking around Northern Lakes." And, since she was one of the people from town who had come up as a suspect, he intended to stick close to her until he ruled her out as the saboteur.

"Mack!" Trick yelled again. "C'mon!"

He hesitated one moment, as much to annoy his younger brother as that he didn't want to leave her. Not yet. There was something intriguing about Trooper Wynona Wells, and it wasn't just how suspicious everyone else was of the woman. She was as mysterious as she was beautiful, like she was trying hard to act tough. Like she'd been hurt and was determined not to let that happen again.

He understood that all too well.

"We will talk later," he promised her. Then he crossed the sidewalk and pulled open the passenger's door of his brother's truck and hopped inside with him. "What's the rush?" he asked Trick.

"Everybody else is going to be at the site we're supposed to clear for that fire break," Trick said as he sped off. "And if someone on the team actually is the saboteur, we're giving them time to mess with the damn equipment again."

Mack swiveled around in his seat for one last look at the beautiful trooper. His gaze met hers, and his pulse quickened. With excitement, with anticipation even though he had no idea exactly what he was anticipating with her.

"I thought Trooper Wells was your chief suspect," Mack said.

"Michaela's," Trick said. "And Henrietta's too. While I agree there's something not quite right about the trooper, I don't see how she could have done everything that's happened to the hotshots."

"Sounds a little sexist of you," Mack chastised him.

Trick chuckled. "My fiancée and our sister would kill me if I was at all chauvinistic. I meant that I don't know how Wells could have gotten to the equipment so easily and had such free access to the firehouse, too."

"I've heard that Stanley doesn't keep the doors locked." But was that just an accident? The kid had been hanging around the trooper looking as besotted as that dog of his was with the woman. Not that he'd left the doors open for her—unless he was helping her with the sabotage.

But why? What reason could either of them have for going after the team?

Trick sighed. "Love that kid but he can be a little scattered. He's really sweet, though."

Or was that just an act?

Mack knew that at one point Sam had thought the kid could be the arsonist that had terrorized the hotshots and Northern Lakes over a year ago. While he hadn't been, he had been friends with Matt Hamilton who actually was the arsonist. Of course, that friendship had nearly gotten him killed, but still Mack wasn't entirely convinced of Stanley's innocence. He wasn't entirely convinced of anyone's innocence yet.

Trick glanced over the console at him. "Stanley is not the saboteur."

"How do you know?"

"I just… I know…he's not capable of purposely hurting anyone."

"You'd be surprised what people are capable of doing," Mack muttered. Worried that some old images would flash through his mind, he resisted closing his eyes. But when he had to blink, the image he saw was *her face*.

"I heard what you told Braden," Trick said. "That you're going over everything we did, everyone we eliminated, like we don't know what we're doing."

Mack could have chosen to be diplomatic, but with the attitude his younger brother had been giving him since his arrival in Northern Lakes, he decided to goad him instead. So he asked, "Did you catch the saboteur yet?"

Trick cursed and braked abruptly.

Mack didn't know if his brother had done that because they arrived so suddenly at the site, where other trucks and equipment were already parked alongside the road, or if Trick was just pissed at him. He suspected he was just pissed.

Trick drew in a deep breath and turned to him. "You know I'm not that little kid anymore that you left behind when you took off all those years ago."

"I didn't take off…" Not like their mother had, but Mack wasn't sure his brother saw the difference. "I graduated and started my career."

Trick shrugged. "Whatever. You left. And while you were gone, I grew up. Like I said, I'm not a naïve little kid anymore, Mack. Sure, I didn't catch the saboteur, but it wasn't for lack of trying."

"I know." Mack reached across the console to pat his brother's shoulder, but Trick threw open the driver's door and stepped out before Mack's hand touched him, as if he was avoiding it.

Then he turned back. "And while I know I'm not much of an investigator, I am a damn good hotshot. I know what

I'm doing. So out here, you need to listen to me and do what I tell you to do."

"Why? You don't think I know what I'm doing?" Mack was getting annoyed now.

"You haven't been doing this work all these years," Trick said. "You're new to it, and you're going to get hurt if you're not careful."

"You don't know what I've been doing all these years," Mack pointed out. "But if I hadn't been careful, I wouldn't be here now." He wouldn't even be alive. He was not about to get killed doing the hotshot job that was in his DNA. And he was going to catch the saboteur before he or she could hurt anyone else.

WYNONA HATED THAT her skin tingled where Mack McRooney had touched her. She hated that she'd let him touch her when she should have, instead, dropped him with a knee to the groin. But she hadn't wanted him to think that he affected her at all.

She didn't want him to affect her at all. She wasn't even sure why he had.

Sure. He was the epitome of tall, dark and handsome with a whole lot of mysterious, too. And it was that mysteriousness of his that she wanted nothing to do with. No. It was any attraction at all, any *distraction* at all, that she wanted nothing to do with. She didn't have time for things like that, for a personal life. Especially after that disastrous experience the last time she'd tried to date…

She kept a note on her fridge from that *mistake* to remind herself that her judgment was off. And because of that, she couldn't risk having a personal life. She needed to focus on her career and close some cases.

She had a couple of outstanding ones, like who had attacked Rory VanDam and put him in a coma. And who had rigged the stove to explode on Ethan Sommerly? And who had thrown the Molotov cocktail in the parking lot that had sent Michaela Momber and Charlie Tillerman to the hospital?

She was sure there were plenty of other instances that she knew nothing about because the hotshots hadn't reported them. For some reason they figured they could handle this on their own, or they just didn't trust the police anymore.

She stood over Braden Zimmer's desk now, trying to stare him down like she had tried with Mack. But damn...

She let Mack McRooney get to her. And she wasn't happy about that. She hadn't been happy in a long time, though. She'd counted on her new career and moving to Northern Lakes to change that, but it had just made things worse for her. She felt even more alone now than she had when she lost her parents a few years ago.

She drew in a deep breath and willed away the tears that threatened whenever she thought of them. Instead, she focused on her job and on the hotshot superintendent.

"I don't know why you're thwarting my investigation," Wynona said. "It seems like you, more than anyone, would want to know who's been hurting members of your hotshot team."

"I do want to know, *more than anyone*, who has been doing that," Zimmer agreed.

"Stanley said that's why you brought in your other brother-in-law. The older one." *The sexy as hell one.* Wynona bit her lip at the thought, as if she was worried that she might actually let it spill out.

Braden sighed. "Stanley talks too much."

"Stanley knows that I'm trying to help," Wynona said. "Why won't the rest of you believe that?" They'd frozen her out of every investigation just as Mack McRooney had frozen her out that day he'd killed the FBI agent. But, with just that touch on her cheek as he pushed back her hair, he'd thawed her. Maybe a little too much…

"You know what your sergeant, Marty Gingrich, did to us," Zimmer said.

"He was my training officer," she said. "Not my friend. And I had no idea what he'd done until…"

"Until he nearly killed Luke and Willow Garrison," Braden finished for her. "You worked that closely with him and had no idea what he was capable of?"

Unfortunately, Martin Gingrich wasn't the only person whose evilness Wynona had been unaware of since she'd moved to Northern Lakes. And there was someone else out there yet. The saboteur.

"Did you have any idea?" she challenged the superintendent. "You were the one who knew Martin Gingrich the longest, since you were kids in school together."

"And he'd always been a jerk," Braden said. "He was a bully back then. And as he got older, he got more bitter and resentful."

"But still," she said. "You wouldn't have suspected that he would actually try to kill someone." Martin Gingrich wasn't the only one who'd done that recently, though. There were a lot of would-be killers in Northern Lakes. And now that Mack McRooney was in town…

She didn't believe that the corrupt FBI agent was the only person McRooney had killed. Was that what he'd done in the military or special forces or the CIA or whatever he'd been?

Braden sighed again then shook his head. "I didn't know how deranged Marty is."

"And what about this person hurting members of your team?" she asked. "Don't you think that has to be someone close to you?"

He stared at her the way that his brother-in-law just had, with such suspicion.

"Why would any of you think it was me?" she asked. "What the hell would my motive be for messing with the hotshots? For messing with anyone? I barely know anyone in this town." And after her poor judgment regarding the couple of people she had gotten to know, she wasn't willing to risk getting any closer to anyone.

Braden just shrugged.

"I want to catch and stop this person," Wynona said. "Before anyone else gets hurt. So I need everything you have. Every incident report you filed with the US Forest Department. Every bit of surveillance video you've taken. Everything."

Braden shook his head. "*I* don't have any of that stuff."

"You should have reported all those incidents to your superiors at least, and I've seen the cameras you installed after Rory was hurt." Then she realized what he meant. "You already turned it all over to Mack McRooney, didn't you?"

He didn't answer her, but he didn't have to. She knew. "He is not an officer," Wynona said. "He has no jurisdiction here in Northern Lakes."

"He's now an official member of the Huron Hotshots," Zimmer said. "He took Michaela Momber's spot on the team."

"Of course he did." No wonder he'd said he was sticking

around. Michaela had months and months of medical and maternity leave coming.

"And as a member," Braden continued, "he can look at the incident reports, video footage, and he can check up on other members of the team."

Wynona had a feeling it wasn't just the other hotshots that Mack was checking up on, but on anyone he considered a suspect. He had to be the one who'd been following her, so he was already investigating her.

What had he found out?

THE BUZZ OF chain saws echoed throughout the woods like a swarm of killer bees. The air vibrated with the noise, and the ground shook as trees fell for the new fire break that would protect the town.

They'd already made some breaks earlier in the spring, but after the last fire, Braden had decided to add more. His efforts to protect anyone were useless, though.

Because there were people in town who would not be protected. Like Wynona Wells. The saboteur had started to worry about Trooper Wells. She'd been getting more persistent, more determined to catch him.

Not that she could.

Not that she was a real threat. But her hanging around the firehouse would become a complication eventually. And complications needed to be eliminated.

But whatever concerns he had about Wells were nothing now. Mack McRooney was a much bigger complication. A much bigger threat…

And the saboteur could not wait to eliminate him. This McRooney had to go as soon as possible. Through the same scope that had been used to watch the trooper, McRooney was being watched now. If only the saboteur had attached the scope to a gun…

But he couldn't risk any bullet or casing getting traced back to one of his registered weapons.

So he was just using the night vision scope to watch his next victims…like he was watching McRooney now.

And when the new hotshot, brandishing a chain saw, finally stepped into the perfect position, the saboteur put down the scope and picked up a chain saw, too. The enormous oak tree had been cut earlier, even before the meeting this morning. Its wide trunk was nearly severed in two. Just enough of the trunk was left to hold it into place so no one would notice.

This tree hadn't been marked like the other ones, with blue paint. It wasn't supposed to be cut, so no one had come near it but the saboteur.

No one knew what he'd planned.

When this enormous tree fell, it was going to land on something—on *someone*—before it hit the ground. It was going to land on Mack McRooney.

And from the height and breadth of the mighty oak, there was no place that the brand-new hotshot would be able to go to escape from being struck with the limbs or that massive trunk. There was no way for Mack McRooney to survive.

Chapter Three

Mack had spent most of his adult life in the wrong place at the wrong time. Mostly because that had been the assignment. Sometimes he'd survived because of his skill and sometimes because of pure dumb luck.

Like now. Because he didn't hear anything, not with the earmuffs on, but he caught sight of the tree and of its branches moving toward him. He was looking around because he had a feeling someone was watching him...

And when those tree branches began to rustle, he shut off his chain saw and jumped toward the shallow ravine he'd noticed earlier, like his career had taught him to scope out every place for somewhere to hide if necessary. Or to escape...

He dove for that shallow ravine, jumping into it and lying low. And that tree fell, striking the ground so hard that it shuddered like an earthquake. Branches covered him, scratching his skin, sticking through his clothes, and the leaves were so thick he could barely breathe. Or maybe that was because of how close a call he'd just had.

A couple of hours later, he still couldn't believe how close it had been. And how it was sheer dumb luck that he was alive now. Because if he hadn't jumped into that shallow ravine when he had...

He would have been crushed for certain. The tree that had come toward him had been massive. Once it had fallen, the other hotshots had rushed around him, all well aware of how close it had come to killing him. But nobody had admitted to cutting it down or even seeing who had cut it down. Not that it could have been done while they'd been out in the woods. It had been too big. Someone would have had to precut it enough that it wouldn't take much more to send it toppling down toward him.

A few other ones had been cut like that, too, around the perimeter of where they'd been supposed to make that break. They hadn't been cut enough to fall but just enough that it wouldn't take much to topple one over, probably when Mack had been in front of it.

And while he hadn't seen who did it, Mack knew who had: the saboteur.

He couldn't see anything for a moment as he stepped inside the corner bar. Coming from the bright sunlight of the early June afternoon into the dim lighting made everything so dark that he had to wait until his eyes adjusted. And until his legs steadied a bit after he just relived those moments in the woods.

He'd had closer calls before, but this one unsettled him more because he hadn't expected it to happen here. Sure, he knew what had been going on, but Northern Lakes just seemed like such a safe place. But he, better than anyone, knew no place was safe.

And Trick had warned him.

A warning he should have heeded. Just because the saboteur hadn't killed before didn't mean that he or she wouldn't.

Obviously, they'd tried to kill before or Rory, as tough as he was, wouldn't have spent so many days in a coma. He was lucky to be alive at all.

And so was Mack after what had happened.

His eyes adjusted enough that he could scope out everybody who was in the bar. That corner booth in the back of the dining room area was filled with hotshots.

Once the tree fell where it shouldn't have, the operation had been shut down. While one of the assistant superintendents had remained at the scene, the other one, Dawson Hess, had already flown out that morning to be with his wife in New York City. Braden and Trick had already cleared him, but Mack had made certain Dawson's alibi was valid for when the other things had happened to hotshots. And he'd been far from the scene then, usually on camera at some red-carpet event with his wife.

The other assistant superintendent, Wyatt Andrews, was back in the woods with Cody Mallehan, probably trying to figure out who the hell had cut down that tree that wasn't marked to be cut.

Mack knew they weren't going to find anything out there that he hadn't already found, like those other trees that had been precut. And he was pretty certain that the saboteur was here, probably in that corner booth. He could have walked over to join them, but he knew that groups like this were a lot like high school. You had to be invited to "sit at the table" with the cool kids.

So he headed toward the bar instead and settled onto a stool. An older guy sat at one end of the bar, a fishing hat on his head, and a defeated sag to his shoulders. He'd obviously not been any more successful than the saboteur had been that morning.

The bartender, who was also the mayor, chuckled as he put a cup of coffee in front of the older guy. "Retirement not all you thought it would be, Les?" Charlie Tillerman said. "Thinking about taking back your mayor job?"

"Nope, it's all yours."

But instead of serving as mayor, Charlie was serving drinks. Mack had considered him a suspect, like the other hotshots had, but the bar owner, along with Michaela Momber, had been victims of the saboteur.

A big hand smacked Mack's shoulder. "After that near miss you had, McRooney, you're probably thinking the same thing about retirement, eh?" Carl Kozak asked. "Not all you thought it was cracked up to be?"

The man standing next to Carl, Donovan Cunningham, shot a cold glare at Mack. But when he saw the bartender staring at him, his face flushed and he hurried off. Carl didn't wait for Mack's reply before ambling off behind Cunningham toward that corner booth that neither of them had invited Mack to join.

Tillerman stared after Cunningham for a long moment. Then he turned his attention back to Mack. "Retirement? Didn't you just start a job? You're the one taking Michaela's spot on the team, right?"

Mack nodded.

"Good thing he did," a husky female voice remarked, and he found Henrietta "Hank" Rowlins standing on one side of him while his brother stood on the other. They were recently engaged, but Mack hadn't had much of an opportunity to get to know the woman who would be his sister-in-law. She was tall and attractive with her long dark hair bound in a thick braid.

Like Henrietta, Wynona Wells was pretty tall, too, with

that gorgeous red hair of hers. Mack used to tease Trick about his red hair, but the female trooper was beautiful with it and her pale skin and delicate features. Damn, he had to stop thinking about her.

"What do you mean?" Charlie asked Hank.

"He had a close call just a little while ago with a very big tree," Hank said. "If that had been Michaela…" She shuddered. She must have been close to the only other female hotshot.

Charlie Tillerman, who was definitely close to the former hotshot, shuddered, too. "What can I get you?" he asked Mack. "It's on the house."

While he probably could have used a drink after the morning he had, he ordered an iced tea instead. He was going to need the caffeine to keep him focused. And after that attempt, he definitely needed to stay focused.

The younger guys, Bruce and Howie, called out to Hank from the booth. She clearly had the respect of the rest of the team. She glanced uneasily between her fiancé and Mack. Trick nodded at her to join the others. She offered Mack a small smile of encouragement before she walked off in the direction of the corner booth.

From the look on Trick's face, he clearly wasn't inviting Mack to join them. "What the hell are you doing here?" Trick asked.

"I'm getting a drink," Mack said. And he really wished he had gone for that alcoholic beverage now.

"Why didn't you stay at the scene?" Trick asked. "You took off right after some of the others did."

"The saboteur isn't back in the woods," Mack said.

"How the hell do you know?" Trick asked.

Mack shrugged. "I just do." He was pretty certain that

the saboteur was here. At that corner booth or at least back in town somewhere if it hadn't been a hotshot who'd cut down that tree.

While he'd ruled out Charlie Tillerman as a suspect, he wasn't convinced that Stanley was as innocent as everyone thought he was. And then there was *her*.

The outside door opened, letting in a spotlight beam of sunshine. Out of that beam stepped Wynona Wells. And Mack wasn't the only one staring at her. But before he could acknowledge her, his brother drew his attention back to him.

"You think you know everything," Trick said. "But you're underestimating the danger that the saboteur poses. You could have gotten killed out there." His gruff voice cracked, and he shook his head as if disgusted with Mack—or maybe he was disgusted with himself for caring.

"Why are you so damn mad at me?" Mack asked. Was his younger brother angry with him for leaving all those years ago? Or was he angry with him for coming back now?

Trick just shook his head again and walked away, over to join his fiancée in that booth full of suspects. Mack had already ruled out some of them, the same ones that Braden and Trick had ruled out: Trick's fiancée, Henrietta Rowlins. She'd been with Trick when that bucket had come loose and she'd saved his life. The multi-hyphenate hotshot Owen James, who was also a paramedic as well as a veteran, had had his own brushes with the saboteur. Luke Garrison and Trent Miles, like Ethan and Rory, were also crossed off Mack's list of suspects because of the saboteur piling on them with the hell they'd gone through with their own enemies.

But too many of the others were still on his list and in that booth. The younger guys, Howie Lane and Bruce Abbott. And the older ones, Donovan Cunningham, Ed Ward and Carl Kozak. Ben Higgins and a couple of others didn't have alibis during all the acts of sabotage or at least alibis that Mack had been able to verify yet.

Mack had narrowed his list of potential suspects down to include eight of the hotshots in that booth with Trick. So it was damn ironic that he'd warned Mack not to underestimate the saboteur when he could possibly be sitting right next to him. And Trick was much more vulnerable than Mack was because he trusted them. Mack trusted no one.

He felt a twinge of concern for his brother's life. And he felt another twinge of concern for their relationship. He'd already realized he couldn't go home again.

Home wasn't just a place, though, it was people. Family.

And apparently, he'd neglected them for far too long. He'd come back to try to make that up to them, though. He'd had so many close calls over the years that had warned him that time was running out for him to do that, and so he'd retired except for this last mission which was twofold: to find the saboteur and to make amends with his family.

THE TWO MEN were both McRooneys, both Braden Zimmer's brothers-in-law, so that meant they were brothers. While they were both big and muscular, they didn't look much alike beyond their intimidating size. And the tension between them had been palpable the moment Wynona had walked into the bar. That tension was there between her and Mack McRooney, too. It had been there earlier this morning, and it was there when he'd looked up as she'd walked into the bar. But that was a different kind of tension entirely.

Mack was staring so intently after his brother that she

wasn't sure if he was even aware that she'd settled onto the stool next to him at the bar.

"Are you okay?" she was compelled to ask.

He jerked his head around to her then, his dark eyes wide. "How did you hear?"

"Hear what?" she asked, and now dread tightened her stomach. "What happened?" Because something obviously had.

He shrugged. "Nothing. Just…nothing…"

She wasn't as good an investigator as she wanted to be, obviously, or she would have known that her training officer was more than an obnoxious jerk. She would have known he was a criminal. Unfortunately, he wasn't the only one she'd misjudged, though. So she probably shouldn't rush to judgment on Mack McRooney. But she couldn't help but let one word slip out. "Liar."

His lips twitched as if he was trying not to grin. "What did you call me?"

"Something happened," she said. It had to have happened after he'd left with his brother earlier. "And you're trying to keep it from me just like your whole damn team tries to keep everything from me."

"My team? Yeah, right…" he muttered, his voice thick with sarcasm, and he glanced toward that corner booth again where his brother was sitting with the other hotshots.

"You're not joining them?" she asked.

"I haven't been invited," he remarked.

"Your brother-in-law said you took Michaela Momber's spot," she said. "He actually admitted to me that you're not just working as a hotshot. Apparently, you're moonlighting as an investigator."

He grinned. "Ah, that's what you're talking about." Then

he glanced toward that booth again, and his grin slid away from his handsome face.

"Oh," she said. "You're talking about *their...*" She held up two fingers on each hand to make air quotes, "...booth. Your own brother didn't invite you to join them?"

He chuckled. "It really is like high school, isn't it?"

She sighed. "I wish it was. I was popular in high school."

"You're definitely not popular in Northern Lakes," he said. "Apparently you've been hanging with the wrong crowd..." He arched a dark brow as he teased her, but it was more than that.

And she knew it, dread settling heavily in the pit of her stomach. He *knew*.

"But then I guess Gingrich was your boss," he said, "so you didn't have much choice about hanging with him."

Not about Gingrich.

"I had no idea what he was doing," she insisted.

"That's not exactly a ringing endorsement of your investigation skills," he remarked.

Heat rushed to her face with a wave of embarrassment. "I just didn't think the man training me to be a police officer would be breaking the law." She drew in a deep breath. "But just because I missed what he was doing doesn't mean that I don't know what I'm doing now. I am a better investigator than any of the hotshots."

"Apparently not better than Luke Garrison," Mack said. "He and his wife figured out how dangerous your former boss was pretty quickly."

He hadn't been living in or even visiting Northern Lakes then, but he obviously knew everything that had happened in town over the past several months.

That heat was burning up her skin now, but she drew in

another deep breath to force down the embarrassment. She didn't have to answer to this man. He had to answer to her.

"Can I get you anything, Trooper?" Charlie Tillerman asked her, albeit reluctantly.

She shook her head. "No, thank you. I was just looking for Mr. McRooney here."

Tillerman walked away then.

"You got about the same reception from him as Donovan Cunningham did," Mack remarked.

He was observant. She bristled though at the comparison between her and the hotshot. "I'm surprised he would serve the guy at all after his kids broke in here a couple of weeks ago."

Mack didn't look particularly surprised to hear that. "What's going to happen to those kids?"

"That's for the judge to decide," she said.

"This break-in all they did?" he asked.

She shrugged. "I don't know. If you're thinking they're responsible for some of the other stuff, I don't think they could have pulled it off. They could have slashed the tires in the parking lot and lobbed that Molotov cocktail at Michaela and Tillerman. They probably could have even struck Rory over the head. But I don't think they could have rigged the stove to explode like it did on Ethan Sommerly."

"Or for the bucket to come loose on my brother," he murmured. "But their dad probably could have…"

She sucked in a breath with the confirmation that things had happened that they hadn't reported to her, like that incident with his brother. "What? When did the bucket come loose?"

He shrugged. "I don't know…"

"Bullshit," she muttered as irritation chafed what was

left of her nerves. "Braden gave you all those incident reports and evidence. No matter what he thinks, you're not an investigator. You need to turn all that stuff over to me."

"What evidence?" he asked.

"Are you calling your brother-in-law a liar?"

He shook his head. "No. I don't call people liars until I have evidence. And right now, I don't have any *evidence*—" he made air quotes with his fingers now "—of anything. If I did…"

"If you did, what?" she asked. "You better not be considering acting like a vigilante." But that was basically what he was if he really had retired from his previous career and was investigating on his own.

"If I had any evidence, I would turn it over to you so that you could make your arrest, Trooper Wells," he said, but he sounded more like he was humoring her than being honest with her.

She narrowed her eyes and studied his face. "Somehow I don't believe you."

He grinned. "So you're calling me a liar again?"

"I've learned that some people find it easier to lie than to tell the truth," she said.

"Some people? Not just Sergeant Gingrich?"

Damn. He probably was as good an investigator as his brother-in-law must think he was since Braden had turned everything over to him. Mack McRooney was already getting more information out of her than she'd intended to give up while she'd gotten nothing out of him. Yet.

"I'm in law enforcement," she said. "A lot of people lie to me."

"Why?" he asked.

She sighed. "Because they don't want to get in trouble or don't want to get someone else in trouble."

He leaned closer to her and lowered his voice. "Are you going to get me in trouble, Trooper Wells?" he asked, his breath warm against the skin of her cheek. Then he leaned in even closer, until his lips almost touched her face. "Or are you trouble?" he asked in a deep whisper.

She resisted the urge to jerk away from him, to show him how much he was affecting her, how aware she was of him and of that attraction she felt for him. Instead, she just smiled. "Not me. I'm not trouble." But he was. Ever since he'd shown up in town, he'd been trouble at least for her, with how he'd unsettled and upset her.

And if he was actually going to stick around Northern Lakes for a while, he was going to prove to be even more trouble for her to deal with and to resist.

DESPITE THE BEER he'd just guzzled, Trick couldn't stop shaking. That had been such a damn close call for Mack. If he hadn't moved when he had…

He would have died for certain. There was no way even the indomitable Mack McRooney could have survived that tree falling on him.

But Trick really had no idea what his brother had already survived. He had no idea about his older brother at all. And that infuriated and frustrated him.

"Are you okay?" Henrietta asked, leaning close to whisper it in his ear.

He shook his head. "No. That was so damn close…"

Under the table she covered his hand with hers. "He's fine," she said. "He didn't get hurt."

"This time."

But he knew that there would be a next time. With the saboteur, there was always a next time. Mack wouldn't necessarily be the target again. But someone else Trick cared about would probably be.

And Mack…

Trick was going to lose his older brother one way or another. If the saboteur didn't take him out, Mack was going to leave again just like he'd left before, like their mother had left.

Like Trick used to leave, going from team to team as a temp, before he'd fallen in love…with Northern Lakes, the Huron Hotshot team and most deeply in love with Henrietta Rowlins.

Now he didn't want to go anywhere.

And he didn't want his brother going anywhere either after all these years of being away from the family. But Trick couldn't get over the feeling that he was going to lose Mack again.

And maybe this time, it would be forever…

Chapter Four

Someone was following him. Mack knew it even before he glanced into his rearview mirror to see the dust rising up from the vehicle that had turned onto the same dirt road as him. That vehicle had been behind him since he'd left the Filling Station a short time ago. Staying a safe distance back but close and steady enough that he knew it was the same one, the same driver trying not to lose sight of his truck.

He could have lost them. If he'd wanted to.

But he wanted to see who it was. If they got a little closer, he would be able to identify the vehicle and the driver. Even though its automatic headlights had come on, it wasn't dark out. Just overcast, as if a storm was brewing this afternoon.

Mack felt it. He'd felt it in the woods with the ground shuddering beneath him as trees fell. He'd felt the darkness coming, threatening to suck him in like it had before. And maybe that was what had made him move at just the right time.

He hadn't just stepped aside, he'd jumped over the edge of that shallow ravine which had served as his protection, like a foxhole during an air raid. And maybe because he'd jumped into so many foxholes in the past that was why he'd already scoped out the ravine, why he'd already known where to take cover if he needed to.

While he'd done that this morning in the woods, he didn't want to do that now. He wanted to see the danger coming, and he wanted to face it head-on. His hands gripped the steering wheel of the truck, as the temptation to spin it nagged at him. He could have turned around, could have pursued his pursuer.

But then the person would run like they had earlier. While Mack had jumped into the ravine, the person who'd sawed down that tree had slipped away. They had either blended in with the rest of the hotshots who'd gathered around him with concern. Or they'd taken off toward town.

Was this person following Mack to finish what they'd started earlier in the woods? Were they going to try to finish *him* off now?

He chuckled. Whoever the hell this saboteur was had never dealt with someone like him before. He continued on, turning off the dirt road onto a dirt driveway that led to the cabin in the woods that he'd rented. Sam and Braden had offered to let him stay with them. But he'd known this might happen, that he might become the saboteur's next target, and he hadn't wanted to put them or anyone else in danger.

So it was better that he was out here, away from town, away from everyone. Except whoever was following him...

That vehicle behind him slowed down when he turned. It wasn't going to pass. It was waiting. And he had no doubt that it would turn onto the driveway behind him, just as it had turned onto the dirt road from the main one. Or maybe it would park on the road and the driver would head through the woods to his cabin.

And when they did, Mack would be ready. He reached

under the seat and pulled out his weapon. And he really hoped that was the saboteur following him.

He really hoped he could end this now.

WHERE THE HELL had he gone?

One minute he was there, turning his truck onto the driveway off the dirt road, and the next...

It was like his truck had vanished. Was there a garage behind the cabin? Was this even his place? But if it wasn't, where had the truck gone? Because the road seemed to stop at the cabin, and the trees were pretty thick on either side of that driveway. How could he have driven off between them?

No. He had to be here. Somewhere.

Wynona had no idea where, but she intended to find out. She intended to find Mack McRooney and find whatever Braden Zimmer had handed off to his brother-in-law instead of turning it over to the police like he should have done.

Like he would have if he'd trusted them or her...

After how Gingrich had targeted him and his hotshot team, he had every reason to be a little distrustful. She would like to think she hadn't done anything to earn that distrust. But she hadn't figured out what the sergeant had been doing, and they'd been working together. How had she missed it? And not just what he'd been doing, but what someone else had been up to as well...

Maybe she should be happy that the other hotshots considered her complicit and crooked like Gingrich instead of what she'd really been: inept.

She had to prove herself now. Not to the hotshots. But to *herself.* That was why she didn't call in to dispatch and share her location, why she didn't report what she was about to do...

Break and enter.

But as she approached the door to that cabin, she found it ajar. It wasn't locked. It wasn't even closed tightly.

"Ma—" Even though she thought of him that way, she couldn't call him that, by his first name or nickname or whatever *Mack* was. "Mr. McRooney?"

Nobody answered her. There wasn't even a bird chirping outside. The forest around the cabin had gone as silent as it sounded inside the small building with its board-and-batten siding and metal roof.

She reached out and pushed the door inward a bit and peered through the wider crack. "Hello?"

Nobody answered her. But she noticed something just a short distance inside the door. A big whiteboard on wheels like the detectives used, more so on TV than on any actual case she'd helped with. Not that she'd helped much...

She had to do more than just help now, though. She had to solve this, or she wasn't only in danger of losing her job. She was going to lose all of her self-respect, too.

She stepped through the door then and glanced around to see if anyone else was inside before she moved closer to inspect that board. The cabin was small. A kitchenette against one wall. A bathroom was probably behind the two walls partitioning off a corner of the open area. And a king-sized bed was behind that board, sticking out on both sides.

She moved closer to the whiteboard to inspect the pictures and names written on it in bold handwriting, like someone had pushed the marker hard against the surface. All the hotshots' names were written on it, some with lines already through them. And Stanley was there, too. And Charlie Tillerman. And...

She heard a gun cock and turned back toward the door

and to the man who'd stepped out from behind it, a gun in his hand. Pointed at her.

She could have pulled her weapon from the holster strapped to her belt and would have if she'd considered Mack McRooney a physical threat to her. But she was pretty sure that he wasn't going to shoot her.

"Where did you park your truck?" she asked Mack.

He didn't lower his weapon. "There's a gap in the trees midway between here and the road. I'm surprised you missed it with as close as you were following me."

"I wasn't following you that closely," she said. "Or I would have seen it. And you have some nerve complaining about that when you've been following me."

He snorted and finally holstered his weapon.

"I should ask to see your permit for that," she muttered more to herself than to him. He'd been wearing it that day he came into the police post, and he wouldn't have been allowed inside with it on him if he hadn't shown his permit at the front desk. She hadn't noticed him wearing it earlier today, though.

"I'd be happy to show it to you," he said. And he actually pulled out his wallet and flipped it open to a laminated card on one side.

On the other side was another type of card. Something with an official looking shield and his picture, but before she could read the details, he flipped his wallet shut again.

"Who are you?" she asked.

"You just saw my ID," he said.

"I saw your name," she said. It was Mackenzie McRooney. "But what are you? That wasn't a driver's license." It had probably been something indicating his level of security clearance. Was he a CIA agent? Special forces? Homeland security?

"I'm a hotshot," he said.

"What were you before you were a hotshot?"

"Retired," he said, and his mouth curved into a slight but still infuriating grin.

"Retired from what?"

"I'm not applying for a job," he said. "So why are you checking my résumé?"

She wished he would give her his résumé. She turned back and pointed at that board. "Apparently you have applied for a job. And it's not as a hotshot."

"Are you afraid I'm going to take your job, Trooper Wells?" he asked, and that infuriating grin widened.

But she couldn't deny that was a fear of hers. *She* needed to be the one to solve the open cases in Northern Lakes. But she needed that more for herself than for anyone else. She needed to prove to herself that she wasn't the fool she felt like she'd been. And she needed to prove that she could take care of herself as well.

"Is that why you've been following me?" she asked. "You are after my job?" A lot of the officers at her local post were retired from some branch or another of the military. Maybe that was what she should have done before going into law enforcement. Maybe then she would have been better at her job.

But it was really the first one she'd had despite being thirty-one years old. When her parents were alive, she didn't have to work. After they died a few years ago, she had even less reason to work. It wasn't as if she needed money. But she needed a purpose.

So she'd gone back to school, once again, and instead

of another degree in philosophy or art or French cuisine, she'd gone into criminal justice. Nursing or medical school would have taken longer, and she'd wanted to help others as soon as possible. While she did that with writing checks, she'd wanted a more active role—she wanted to personally protect and serve others. Once she'd completed the police academy, she'd applied for jobs in remote areas where no one would know her so that she could start over fresh. And she'd wound up in Northern Lakes.

"Why do you keep thinking *I've* been following you?" he asked.

For one, his crack about the bribes...

She'd been very careful to make sure that nobody knew exactly where she lived because they would probably think she was supplementing her public servant salary somehow in order to be able to afford the lake house she owned. She hadn't become a police officer to get rich, she'd done it to help people that needed help, to make a difference.

But she hadn't made much of one. Yet. People were still getting hurt in Northern Lakes, they were still in danger.

"Wynona," he said. And he reached out like he had earlier that day and pushed back a lock of her unruly hair. "Why do you think I've been following you?"

She stepped back and pointed toward his board. "Because I'm on your suspect list."

"A lot of people are on my suspect list," he said. "I'm not following any of them."

The photo he had of her was a copy of her driver's license picture. He hadn't gotten that from Braden Zimmer. So he probably had access, with that security clearance, to personal records.

"What makes you think you're being followed, Wynona?" he asked, and he stepped closer to her again as if he was concerned.

But he didn't even know her. Nobody really did. The couple of people she'd spent the most time with after she'd moved here, Sergeant Gingrich and another man, had wound up being such horrible men that she hadn't risked getting close to anyone else.

"I just…have this feeling that I'm being followed, watched…"

He moved closer and touched her shoulders, turning her to stare up at him instead of at that board where he'd crossed off names and circled some other ones. "Has anyone tried to hurt you? Or made any threats?"

She shook her head then shrugged, and his hands fell away, but it was as if she could still feel them on her, lightly holding her. "I really don't know. If they did, obviously they failed."

"Not the last time they failed…"

"What?" she asked. "What happened earlier today that you thought I heard about?"

"Another miss," he said with a sigh.

Alarm jolted her. "Did someone shoot at you?" And nobody had reported it. What the hell was wrong with his team?

He shook his head. "Nobody shot at me unless you consider a tree a bullet."

"What are you talking about?" she asked. "Tell me what happened."

He sighed again. "When we were cutting that firebreak, a tree nearly hit me. It might not have been intentional, though. I might have just been in the wrong place at the wrong time."

"Bullshit," she said because she could tell that he was downplaying the incident. "You know it was no accident. This saboteur, or whatever you guys are calling him, is more dangerous than you thought he was."

"Him or her," Mack said. "Don't be sexist."

She laughed. It just kind of slipped out of her at the irony of him saying that. A big man like him usually considered women like her too weak and emotional to handle the job. At least that was the way Gingrich and some of her co-workers and superiors treated her. Michaela Momber had recently been treated the same way by one of her co-workers, so it was no wonder she'd gone on medical leave. She couldn't trust her fellow hotshots to have her back any more than Wynona could probably trust hers.

"What's so funny about me saying that?" he asked as if he was offended now.

"The saboteur could be a woman," she acknowledged. "But it's not Michaela Momber." The saboteur had gone after Michaela and Charlie Tillerman. But she noticed he'd already crossed out the former hotshot's name and Henrietta Rowlins's name as well. That left Wynona as his only female suspect. She grimaced. "You really can't believe that I would go after the hotshots."

"I don't know," he said, and that grin was back. "You followed *me* home."

"Not to hurt you," she said.

"So I don't have to watch out for falling trees?" he asked, and that grin was back.

She didn't know how he could laugh about what had happened, what could have happened. While she'd purposely chosen a career that was dangerous, she certainly would never be able to joke about the danger. "You're lucky you didn't get hurt. Someone was obviously trying to hurt you."

"Or they just cut down the wrong tree in the wrong area," he said.

"So it wasn't marked to be removed like they do, and it nearly fell on you?" she asked for clarification. When he nodded, she continued, "That wasn't an accident, Mack." She pointed back to the board, to the names he'd circled. "Two of these guys, Bruce Abbott and Howie Lane, work as arborists."

His brow furrowed. "Arborists?"

"They take care of trees, cutting them down mostly. That's their day job."

"So they would have known how to precut that tree at some earlier time so that it wouldn't have taken much to make it topple over on me," he mused.

She nodded. "Yes, but with all the tree removals the hotshots do to make breaks, probably everyone on the team knows how to do that."

"So you haven't narrowed it down any more than I have," he said, and he was grinning again, like he wasn't affected or concerned at all over what could have happened to him earlier today.

"Someone tried to kill you," she said, spelling it out since he seemed to not be understanding what had happened and what could have happened to him.

He shrugged. "Not the first time someone's tried," he said. "I'm harder to kill than you think."

"And cocky and arrogant and condescending, too," she added. And infuriating and attractive and so intriguing, but she kept those adjectives to herself.

He chuckled. "So you and my brother have something in common. Your opinion of me."

She'd felt the tension between them. And no wonder Trick had been upset with him for not taking that attempt on his life seriously. But if Mack was special forces or any of those other departments that would have high security clearances, he probably wasn't exaggerating the number of times someone had tried to kill him.

"Don't you care about your life?" she asked. "Do you have some kind of death wish? Is that why you went into whatever career you retired from?"

"You went into law enforcement," he pointed out. "Don't you care about your life?"

"I care," she said. "I know that life is precious." And she knew how good she'd had it growing up with loving and supportive parents who she missed every day. But because of them, she felt like she had to give back somehow and not just by writing a check. She wanted to be more involved in helping others while being more independent and self-reliant, too. She had to put herself out there even if it put her in danger.

"I retired from that…career," he said.

"And then you became a hotshot," she said. "That's not a whole lot safer. Even if whatever happened with that tree today had been an accident, and I think we both know that's not damn likely, you still would have died if it had hit you." At least that was the impression he'd given her, and from his brother's frustration with him, she was probably right.

He shrugged. "The world is a dangerous place, Wynona. Bad things happen everywhere and for no reason at all."

Tears rushed to her eyes then as she thought of her parents. She had to close them so he wouldn't see.

But then his hands were on her face again, tipping it up toward his. "What's wrong? What did I say?"

She willed the tears away and opened her eyes. "Nothing... I just...lost someone like that..."

"Who, Wynona?"

She shook her head. If she talked about her parents, she would start sobbing for sure. She'd only told one person in Northern Lakes about them, and that had been a mistake. "I'm not here to talk about that," she said. "I followed you here to get back the stuff Braden gave you, the stuff that should have gone into evidence."

"And like I told you, there is no evidence," Mack replied. "Not yet. I just have all these names written down, and I've eliminated some because there was no way they could be both the victim of the saboteur and the saboteur. But if you want to work together..."

She narrowed her eyes, surprised at the offer. "What are you suggesting?"

"That you tell me whatever you're holding back," he said, "because I can't work with people I don't trust."

"Me neither," she said. "Not anymore..." Then she stepped around him and headed toward the door since it was obvious he wasn't really willing to work with her. And even if he agreed, he wasn't a police officer. He was a hotshot, and as one, his job was to put out fires, not to investigate crimes.

THE SABOTEUR WASN'T sure why the trooper had followed Mack McRooney home. They'd been talking at the bar earlier. Had he invited her home with him?

If that was the case, though, she probably would have followed more closely. It was almost as if she hadn't wanted him to see her, which was how the saboteur had followed the trooper, far enough back that she hadn't seen his vehicle. Trooper Wells had been followed twice. Because the saboteur already knew where she lived and had a picture to prove it.

A picture and a plan were in place for her, in case she started to pose a problem. And since she was pushing her investigation, she was a problem.

Just like Mack McRooney was going to be a problem. How the hell had the tree missed him?

How had he guessed that it was about to fall?

It was as if he possessed that sixth sense his brother-in-law was legendary for having. Braden Zimmer was supposedly able to predict when a fire was about to happen. That was why Wells's former training officer had been so convinced that Braden had been the arsonist. Even Braden's wife, when she'd first come to town to investigate those fires, had suspected him.

Then she'd fallen for him.

Because that was how things worked out for Braden. He always got everything he wanted. Or maybe he was just lucky like his older brother-in-law, but that luck was about to run out for both of them.

And for Trooper Wells, too.

She and McRooney had no idea that the person they were looking for was standing right outside that cabin that was conveniently remote. And in these woods, there was nobody else around that might see him. That might be able to identify him later.

And now the saboteur had a gun, one taken from a pickup

parked in the firehouse parking lot. A weapon that couldn't be traced back to him if any bullets or casings were recovered. So, this time, the saboteur was ready to take them out.

Chapter Five

Wynona Wells had secrets she obviously wasn't willing to share with him. And that made Mack all the more determined to find out what those secrets were.

But she was already heading toward the door he'd left partially ajar in order to lure her inside when she'd driven up earlier. Now he wanted to entice her to stay. But just to learn her secrets.

He couldn't deny that he was attracted to her. She was beautiful, but what drew him even more than her beauty was her determination and her guts. She truly seemed intent on catching and stopping the saboteur. So he doubted that she was the saboteur. But he wasn't ready quite yet to cross out her name on the suspect list.

"I thought you wanted this stuff," he said, gesturing back at the board she'd found.

"You won't give it to me."

"If you leave now," he said, "you'll only be able to come back if you have a warrant, Trooper Wells." He'd already called her Wynona, but at the moment, she seemed determined to keep up her walls, to act all official, in order to keep her distance from him. And maybe she was the smarter one of them to do that because he shouldn't be drawn to her as anything more than a suspect.

But the way she'd looked just moments ago, the tears that had sparkled in her eyes...

She'd lost someone she loved. Mack had lost some people who mattered to him, too, and that had hurt a hell of a lot. But he suspected whoever she lost had mattered even more to her.

"Don't think I won't get one," she said.

"How? I'm the one person in Northern Lakes who absolutely can't be the saboteur," he pointed out. "I wasn't even in the country when most of this stuff happened."

"Yet you have a knack for turning up when you're needed, like when you shot that FBI agent."

"He was corrupt," Mack said. "And my dad reached out to me when that reporter started asking questions about Rory and I got worried." He'd been right to worry about his old military friend. The minute the FBI agent had learned the former DEA agent was still alive, Rory had been marked for death.

"And you showed up just in the nick of time," she said. But she didn't make it sound like a compliment.

"Like you said, I turn up when I'm needed," he said. But that was just because he was trying to make up for taking off when he'd been needed, just like his mom had taken off on their family. While his dad and Sam might forgive him, he doubted that Trick was ready to any time soon, if ever at all. But catching the saboteur and making sure that Trick and his fiancée and Sam and Braden were safe mattered even more than their forgiveness. He had to eliminate the threat to their safety. And once he did...he had no idea what he would do in his *retirement*. "And, Trooper Wells, you just might find that you need me, too."

She snorted now. "I don't need anyone."

He'd thought that once, too, himself, when he'd been so bitter and angry about his mom deserting them. Then he'd taken off so that he wouldn't get attached to anyone else. But he knew now that everybody needed *someone*. That being alone was too damn lonely.

He needed his family. Friends.

He'd lost so many friends already.

Wynona didn't seem to have many in this town, either. If he thought he could trust her, he might have asked if she wanted to be friends and work together. But he couldn't trust her. And he couldn't trust himself to keep their relationship just as friendship. Not when he was so attracted to her. And trying to have a romantic relationship seemed much more dangerous than trying to find the saboteur.

Before he had the chance to say anything else to her, she stepped through the door. And the minute she did, shots rang out.

Panic struck him, thinking that she was hit and that he hadn't lost a friend, but someone who might have come to mean even more to him…

ONE MINUTE WYNONA was standing, the next she was face-down on the ground. It wasn't a bullet that had knocked her flat, though, but a big, muscular body.

"Are you okay?" A deep voice rumbled in her ear as those shots echoed all around them.

With the wind knocked out of her, she couldn't draw a

breath. She couldn't answer him. Then he arched up to roll her over beneath him.

"Where are you hurt?" he asked, his voice gruff with concern.

She shook her head. "I'm not—"

But another shot rang out, this one striking the doorjamb near his head. She pulled him down on top of her. "Are you okay?" she asked now, fear making her heart beat so fast and hard.

"No," he said.

She reached up to check his head, to make sure he wasn't bleeding. His short hair was soft against her palm, but she felt no blood, no wound.

"I'm not hurt," he said. "I'm pissed." He scooted back through that open door, sliding her over the threshold with him. Once they were inside the house, he slammed the door shut. And just as he did, another bullet struck it, splintering the wood on its way through to that board with all the names and photographs taped to it.

Wynona started to lift her head up as she reached for her holster. But Mack was still hovering over her, as if trying to cover her body with his like he had outside the door. His body was so big and muscular and close. But it wouldn't stop a bullet.

"You have to stay down," he whispered as another shot rang out. And finally he moved, rolling off her.

Wynona pulled her weapon from the holster on her belt. "I've got this," she said. Then she drew in a deep breath to brace herself to go back out there.

Mack had drawn his weapon, too. Instead of heading toward the front, though, he was walking, crouched low, toward the back.

"Stop, you can't go back out there," she said, her pulse quickening even more with the fear and adrenaline rushing through her. He seemed so unfazed compared to her. But he'd probably been shot at more times than she had.

"I've got this," he said, throwing her words back at her along with a crooked grin.

He was so damn cocky. Too cocky.

And too sexy.

"You're not a cop," she said. "You need to stay inside and let me handle this."

"You take the front," he said as if he was in charge. "But give me ten seconds."

"Mack—"

The sound of the back door opening and closing cut off her protest. And then the gunfire rang out again.

Fear gripped Wynona. Was he the one shooting or the one getting shot?

She had to get out there, had to try to protect him before he got killed. She cracked open the front door, and gun drawn, started out. She just hoped that she wouldn't be too late to save Mack.

Or even the shooter because she had a feeling that Mack would shoot to kill just like he had with that FBI agent. Her whole reason for going into law enforcement was to save as many lives as she could while not losing her own. Because she hadn't been able to save the people she'd loved the most.

BRADEN USUALLY COULDN'T wait to get home when his wife was here in Northern Lakes instead of off investigating an arson somewhere like she usually was. She'd gone on maternity leave a few weeks ago in anticipation of her due date that had passed the week before.

With her so very pregnant, he would have been even more eager to get home if today hadn't gone like it had. If it hadn't happened again…

He'd just closed the door behind himself when she called out the question he'd been dreading, "So how was my big brother's first official day on the job?"

Braden's stomach muscles tightened, but he forced a smile for his wife as he walked into the kitchen where she was standing at the island cutting up something. "Sam, you're supposed to be taking it easy and staying off your feet as much as possible. I was going to make dinner."

She smiled at him. "I know you prefer your cooking to mine, but it was getting late."

"You didn't have to wait for me to eat," he said. He crossed the kitchen to where she stood and wrapped his arms around her. He just wanted to hang onto her. Forever.

She chuckled. "I didn't. I've been eating all day. I shouldn't even be hungry right now."

He moved his hands down, sliding them over her protruding belly. "You're eating for two," he said.

"It better be just me and him," she said. "But I'm beginning to have some doubts about that from the size of me. I think he could have a friend in there…"

Braden chuckled now. "I love you so much."

She turned then and wrapped her arms around him. "If you do, stop trying to distract me and answer my question, my darling husband."

"Question?" he asked, but he was smiling as he feigned ignorance.

She lightly jabbed his chest. "Hey, buddy, answer me. How'd Mack do?"

"Mack did great." Or he wouldn't be alive if the situation had been as serious as Trick and the others had made it sound. Mack hadn't talked to him about it at all, as if it was no big deal that someone had probably tried to kill him.

Sam narrowed her pretty blue eyes and studied his face. "Out with it."

"With what?"

"I can tell you're holding back," she said, and she poked his chest again. This time a little harder than she had before.

He flinched. While she was petite, she was strong. "Hey, there…"

"I'm already frustrated with this kid," she said, and she poked her belly now but gently. "If he doesn't get out of there soon, I'm going to drag him out just like I'm going to drag whatever you're keeping from me out of you."

He chuckled. She was so tough. But with her dad and her brothers, she had to be. And knowing that, he knew she could handle what he told her. "There was an incident with Mack. A tree got cut down and would have hit him if he hadn't moved when he did…"

She sucked in a breath and then nodded. "Of course the saboteur would try for him just like they did for Trick when he first came on the team. They know why he's here."

"To catch them," Braden said. "It's so damn overdue…"

"Just like me," Sam said with a heavy sigh.

Braden steered her away from the counter and toward the couch. "Sit down. I'll finish dinner."

"I'd rather finish this pregnancy," she said. "I've heard that sex sometimes induces labor."

He chuckled. "I'm more than willing to test that theory," he said.

"Good," she said. "But I'm going to call Mack first… while you finish dinner." She grabbed her cell phone from a table beside the couch. She punched in a number. Then she grimaced.

"What? Are you okay?" he asked with alarm. "Did you have a contraction?"

"No. Damn it," she muttered. "His phone went directly to voice mail."

Braden shrugged. "You know Mack has always been hard to reach."

"Yeah, because he was off on some top-secret mission or another," Sam said.

"He's retired from all that," Braden reminded her.

"Yeah, sort of, but he's still on a mission."

"For me," Braden said with regret. This was his team. He should have been able to stop the threat against them without involving anyone else.

"For us," Sam said. And she patted her belly. "For all of us."

Braden couldn't wait to become a father. He wanted to be able to focus on that, on his wife and child, and not on the threat against his team. He didn't want to lose anyone else like he'd already lost one of the members.

The saboteur hadn't killed Dirk Brown, the man's wife had. But the saboteur had nearly killed Rory VanDam and could have killed so many of the others with the dangerous stunts they'd pulled.

Like that one today that had put Mack in danger.

Sam must have hit redial because she cursed. "Went to voice mail again."

Why wasn't Mack answering his phone?

Braden felt that uneasiness again, that concern that of all the dangerous missions Mack had probably been on, this might prove the most dangerous of all of them.

Chapter Six

Mack squeezed his trigger, firing off a couple of shots, trying to draw the attention to the back of the house because he had no doubt that Wynona was going out the front. Just as she had moments ago.

Maybe this time she wouldn't be as lucky as she'd been the first time. Maybe this time she would get shot. Mack shouldn't have left her. He should have stuck with her until backup arrived.

But she hadn't called for it. Sure, there hadn't been much time. But still…

Mack wondered. He rounded the corner of the house, firing a few more shots in the direction where the shooter had to be. Somewhere in the trees between the cabin and the road. But there was no return fire.

"Put your gun down."

He recognized that voice, her sexy, uptight tone. "I'm not a threat, Trooper Wells."

She snorted. "Yeah, right." She gestured at the cell in her hand. "I'm calling it in. Backup will be here soon."

"A little late," Mack said, wondering again why she'd waited to make that call. "The shooter is gone." Tires squealed in the distance, probably as the shooter's vehicle left the gravel side road and hit the asphalt of the main road that led back to the heart of Northern Lakes.

"Then we'll bring in techs to go over everything, get bullets and slugs and see if there's any evidence that will lead us to the shooter," she said.

He didn't know if she was talking to him or to whoever she had on her cell phone.

He shrugged. "Why bother? It was probably just a hunter," he said, trying to downplay it. The hotshots hadn't trusted her to investigate the saboteur probably because some of them suspected she was the saboteur. He knew that wasn't the case now, but even though he'd teased her about working together, he wasn't sure that he really wanted her or anyone else interfering in his investigation, especially if she didn't even trust her co-workers enough to call for backup before now.

For Mack, the best part of retiring was that the only orders he had to carry out now were his own. Except for Braden's—he respected his brother-in-law as the hotshot superintendent.

She snorted again. "The only thing that person was hunting was us."

"Us?" He'd thought he was the target, but he realized now that she was the one who'd been shot at first. And there was no way anyone could mistake her for him.

She glanced back at the splintered doorjamb and shuddered. It had been close, she could have been hit.

So could he, but that had been only when he'd knocked her down, when he'd tried to protect her. Now he was wondering how badly she needed protection. So he didn't protest anymore. He was glad now that she called for backup to go over the scene and to make sure she was safe, too.

He was also glad that they wouldn't be alone much longer because he had a feeling if he spent much more one-on-one time with her, he might be the one needing protection. Not just because she was getting angry with him, but also because of how he reacted to her.

Sirens wailed in the distance. Maybe her backup had been closer than he realized. But when they arrived, he wasn't that impressed with how they talked to her. Or rather talked down to her like she was inferior to them.

He tensed with irritation. Some of the best operatives he'd worked with over the years had been female. And like his sister, they'd been smart and strong. He suspected Wynona was just as smart and strong. But he seemed more aware of that than her fellow officers.

"What are you doing here, Wells?" a man asked.

Mack recognized the sergeant he'd talked to after the shooting at the firehouse. "Hughes," he said. "Trooper Wells was here at my request."

Hughes was probably in his fifties with graying hair and lines around his eyes and mouth—frown lines. He'd been in the service, too. So he had respect for Mack. When he heard him, he stood up a little straighter. But he was smart enough to look a little skeptical too. "You called dispatch?"

"No. I saw her earlier today at the firehouse," Mack said. "And I wanted to talk with her about the things I heard had been happening to the hotshots."

"Your brother-in-law didn't fill you in on all of that?" Hughes asked.

"I've heard they've been having a hell of a run of bad luck," Mack said. "So, of course, I wanted to know if there was an official investigation going on."

The sergeant glanced at Wells, and that frown was back

on his face, as if he wasn't happy with his subordinate. "Trooper Wells has been insisting that we investigate further, but she forgets that every time something has happened, arrests have been made."

"Even one of your own, I've heard," Mack said.

And the sergeant's face flushed. "Gingrich was a little too obsessed with the hotshots." Now the man looked from Wells to Mack. "Sometimes I wonder if Trooper Wells is getting a little too obsessed as well…"

"I'm not, sir," she said. "I'm just not certain that everything that has happened to the hotshots can be blamed on whoever is in custody."

"Or dead," the sergeant said. "Like Jason Cruise. He was responsible for a lot of things, and then he took his own life before we could determine everything that he'd done."

Wells sucked in a sharp breath, and her face flushed. And Mack wondered…

Who the hell was Jason Cruise? The guy who'd gone after Charlie Tillerman and Michaela? He'd also gone after the mayor, too, if Mack had the story straight. He clearly hadn't been the saboteur, though, so Mack hadn't paid as much attention to the story about him as he probably should have.

Wells lifted her chin and stood up straighter, her pride obviously smarting right now with the way her sergeant was talking to her and about her to Mack. "And if the person responsible for everything that happened was already in jail or dead, who took those shots at us?" she asked.

The sergeant glanced back at Mack, and he just shrugged and replied, "I have no idea what happened." That much was true. "I don't know if that person was firing at me or Trooper Wells or maybe some prey they were hunting…"

Because he had no idea which of them had been the prey

this time, and he needed to make sure that what happened had only to do with the saboteur and that nobody from his past had found him. Though he highly doubted that since nobody involved in his previous missions had had a clue who he really was.

"You told me that someone tried to drop a tree on you earlier today," Wells reminded him. "That had to be the saboteur."

He shrugged again, and he could see the fury rising in her along with the flush in her pale skin. "Nah, that was probably just a mistake." The mistake had been his assuming it was the saboteur. If it wasn't, and someone from his past had tracked him down like that corrupt FBI agent had tracked down Rory, Mack didn't want her involved. He didn't want her getting hurt like she nearly had been earlier.

Wynona sucked in another breath. She obviously knew he was lying, and she wasn't happy about it. He couldn't help but think again that she was holding something back, too, keeping some damn secret that he was even more determined to discover now. Now that they both could have died. But first he had to make sure that wasn't because of him. That he wasn't the one who'd put her in danger.

WYNONA WAS FURIOUS. As usual, her concerns had been dismissed by her boss. She should have been used to that. Sergeant Hughes had been resisting her efforts to fully investigate everything that had happened to the hotshots. He would rather blame the people who had already been arrested or had died for everything and just close those cases. That would help improve the closing rate for this post as well as make Northern Lakes seem safer.

But it wasn't safe. She could have died today. That bullet

had come so damn close. Even Hughes must have realized that because he'd told her to go home early and he'd called techs to go over the scene and collect the bullets and casings.

When she stepped out of her car onto her driveway, her knees shook so much that she nearly dropped to the ground like she had dropped at Mack's house. No. Mack had dropped her. And because he'd knocked her down, out of the line of fire, he had probably saved her life.

But shortly after that, he had lied to her boss. And he'd disappeared before they'd even wrapped up at his house. Or at least before the sergeant had dismissed her, too, but at least Hughes had promised to make sure the techs processed the scene. Even though he acted like she'd overreacted, he saw the holes in the door, he knew how close she'd come to getting shot. Not that he seemed to care all that much.

And that was why she hadn't immediately called for backup. She wasn't sure who she could trust.

Even though Mack McRooney couldn't possibly have fired those shots at them, she didn't trust him, especially after how he'd downplayed everything despite knowing damn well that someone had tried to kill them.

And yet he acted like it was nothing and then he'd taken off. What? To return to the bar? Throw back some drinks and pretend nothing happened?

Like he'd acted earlier. Maybe it wasn't a big deal to him. Maybe he was used to people trying to kill him. Maybe that was who'd fired those shots, someone after him...

But why was she the one the bullets had come the closest to hitting? And would she ever get used to someone shooting at her, to the danger? She hoped not.

But she did intend to open a bottle of wine for herself and to cuddle with her kitty. Though if Harry smelled Annie on her, Wynona wasn't sure that the snooty Siamese would let her get close. But when Wynona neared the side door of her house, she found it like she'd found his earlier…unlocked and slightly open.

She reached for the holster on her belt, drawing her weapon. She could have called for backup, but she didn't for the same reason she hadn't called earlier today. She didn't trust her backup any more than the hotshots trusted her. She needed to prove herself. First, to herself.

As she drew closer to the opening to peer inside her house, a deep voice called out, "The door's open. Come on in."

She'd been irritated earlier, now she was furious. So she didn't holster her gun before she stepped inside her own damn house at his invitation. She didn't point the gun at him, though, and she was glad she hadn't when she saw that her cat was curled up on his lap where he sat on her couch. Harry, Harriet her Siamese cat, did not like strangers and usually hid from them, like she would hide from Wynona if she smelled Annie on her uniform. But the little traitor seemed quite taken with this stranger.

And Wynona was irritated that she understood all too well the fascination with this intriguing but infuriating man. She focused on him instead of her traitorous feline now. "What the hell are you doing here?" she demanded to know.

He gestured, with a wineglass in one hand, toward the bottle of red on the table in front of her white leather sectional. "I opened a bottle of wine. Figured you could use a glass."

It was like he'd read her mind. And she was so tempted to join him. To join them…

Harry peered at her through slitted eyes as she purred

from his lap. The cat rarely sat on Wynona's lap let alone a stranger's. She usually avoided strangers. And pretty much everyone was a stranger now that Wynona's parents were gone.

"What the hell are you doing in my house?" she asked. How had he even known where she lived?

Unless…

"You said you weren't following me," she said. And she'd stupidly believed him, just as she had stupidly believed Martin Gingrich and…someone else she shouldn't have.

"I wasn't. I already knew where you lived," he said. "It's easy to search property records."

She narrowed her eyes with suspicion. "This property is not deeded in my name." It was in a trust.

"You're listed as a trustee of that trust," he said.

He was right. But he would have had to do some work to discover that—or maybe, with his security clearances, he just had access to more databases than the average person. Either way, he unsettled her. He unsettled her in a lot of ways.

"That doesn't answer how the hell you got inside," she pointed out. She had a good security system. An alarm should have gone off and alerted her to anyone breaking inside, and if she didn't respond with a code, then a call would go out to the local emergency number.

"The door was open," he said.

She gazed around the room. Nothing looked out of place in the big living room. The wide-screen TV was still mounted over the fireplace. All of the artwork was still hanging on the walls. And through the French doors to her office, she could see the big monitors for her computer. Nothing had been touched. But that bottle of wine…

And the cat was lying on his lap instead of out prowling as she was prone to do whenever she managed to slip outside, which she would have been able to do if a door had been left open. Despite her pampered upbringing, Harry still thought she was a badass. The cat was a lot like Wynona. But until now, Wynona was the only one who'd been aware of that, of how pampered she'd been growing up.

Did Mack McRooney know now? Had he figured out everything she'd wanted nobody else to know? She had enough problems trying to get people to take her seriously, so she wasn't about to divulge how wealthy her family had been.

Because of how she'd been raised, they'd always had good security systems and safety practices. She always locked her doors and windows and activated the alarm.

"The door wasn't open," she insisted.

He sighed as if he was getting tired of this conversation. "So you're calling me a liar again?"

"Yes," she said. "You're lying now just like you did when you told my boss that you thought the gunfire could have been coming from a hunter."

He arched a brow over one of his dark eyes. "You don't think that's who it was?"

"I think it was someone trying to kill us," she said. "And you damn well think the same thing I do, especially after someone just tried to drop a tree on you. You have to know someone is after us."

The brow arched higher. "I do?"

The urge to scream nearly overwhelmed her. But instead of giving in to it, she holstered her gun and reached for the bottle of wine instead.

"There's a glass there," he said, gesturing toward it.

"I'd pour for you, but I don't want to disturb the cat. She's so comfy."

Wynona glared at him, ignored the glass, and lifted the bottle to her lips, chugging some back.

"Classy," he said.

He had no idea. Or maybe he did. If so, he was the only one who knew about her past. The only one who was still alive...

The wine slid smoothly down her throat. He'd picked a really good bottle of Cabernet Sauvignon from her collection. Somehow he knew about wines just like he presumably knew about her.

"Why are you here?" she asked. She dropped down onto the couch next to him and Harry who barely spared her a glance as she continued purring on his lap.

"You stopped by my place earlier," he said as he continued to stroke Harry's fur. "So I figured it was only fair that I stopped by your place. You know, return your hospitality."

"You were not very damn hospitable at your house," she said. "Instead, I got shot at and then you lied about it so that nobody would take me seriously."

"I didn't lie," he said. "I really have no idea who it was. Could have been a hunter."

"You know it wasn't a hunter," she said. "And now you know that I have nothing to do with everything that's been happening with the hotshots."

"That doesn't necessarily mean that," he said. "You could have someone else after you like Rory did and Ethan."

She shook her head. "I have no corrupt FBI agent out to kill me or a greedy brother-in-law." She had no family left now. "It's more likely that you had someone from your former career coming after you…" But he wasn't the one those bullets had nearly struck.

"Even though I'm pretty sure there is no way that is possible, I checked all my sources," he admitted. "There's been no rumblings, no chatter. Nobody from my former career knows where I am. And not even that many people in Northern Lakes know but my fellow hotshots and *you*…"

"Well, you know I didn't fire those shots at myself," she pointed out. "So you should be crossing my name off that suspect list."

He just smiled. "We'll see."

"Is that why you broke into my place?" she asked. "You're looking for something incriminating?"

"I wanted to make sure your place was safe," he said.

Something shifted in her chest. No one had cared about her for a very long time. Not that she believed he really cared. She wouldn't make that mistake again.

"And clearly it is. *Someone* would have to be very smart and have a lot of experience bypassing high-tech security systems in order to bypass yours." His lips curved into a slight grin or a smirk.

"Someone? Yeah, right." Had he done it just to test her system and her safety? Or… "What are you really up to?" she asked.

"You were the one who wanted us to work together," he said.

"No," she said. "I want to work the case on my own. But I want everything that Braden gave you." While the whiteboard had still been inside his place when the techs started going over it, she hadn't found any of the incident reports.

"Your boss doesn't think there is a case," Mack said. "He

thinks everybody who was responsible for the things happening to the hotshots is behind bars or dead."

"And you know that's not true," she said. "You damn well know that someone purposely tried to hurt you with that tree and then purposely shot at us. So why did you lie?"

She waited, but she wasn't about to hold her breath for him to finally answer her.

THEY COULD HAVE DIED. Both of them. Trooper Wells and Mack McRooney. It wasn't so much that the saboteur had missed but that it probably wasn't time yet.

Maybe it would be more fun to play with them. Because now they knew that he knew where they lived, where they worked, and the saboteur could find them, could get to them, whenever he wanted.

And soon he would want them dead.

Chapter Seven

Wynona waited, but Mack wasn't any more forthcoming than he'd ever been since she'd met him months ago. Or actually hadn't met him. He just kept sitting there on her couch with her cat, refusing to answer her question.

"Why did you lie?" she asked again. "About the shooter and about what happened with you and the hotshots?"

He shrugged. "I don't know what you're talking about…"

She cursed him then and said, "I should arrest you for breaking and entering." But instead she took another swig of the wine. It had been a hell of a day.

After the sergeant had told her to clock out early, she just wanted to come home and curl up on the couch with her cat. She never would have imagined Mack McRooney here with them, opening her wine, petting her cat…

Was she dreaming this?

Because it didn't seem real.

But Mack hadn't seemed real since the first time she'd heard about him, swooping in to save his friend and Brittney Townsend and Stanley and Annie. He'd saved her earlier tonight, too. That was why she wouldn't arrest him. That reason and that her boss probably wouldn't believe her that the hotshot had broken into her home. He would accept Mack's lie that she'd left the door unlocked.

"You have a very good security system," he said.

She snorted. "Not good enough."

"Not good enough to keep me out," he said with a grin. "But it'll keep most people out."

"Most people don't know where I live," she said.

"Somebody followed you to my place," he said. "I'm sure somebody could have followed you here. Or looked up your address the same way I did."

She'd felt that here, that strange sensation of being watched. So he probably wasn't wrong.

"But why?" she asked. "I'm not a hotshot. And I really don't have any enemies. So why would anyone want to follow me or come after me?"

He stared at her for a long moment as if considering her question. Then he shrugged those broad shoulders of his. "I don't know. Why would they?"

"Maybe they think I have some idea who they are." If only that were true...

"Or maybe they're worried that you'll figure it out," he said.

She nearly laughed. It had taken her too long to figure out so many things. She was lucky that people hadn't died. At least because of the saboteur. People had died because of other people, like Mack killing that FBI agent. And Jason killing himself.

She was lucky *she* hadn't died earlier today at Mack's cabin.

"Thank you," she said.

"For what?" he asked. "Opening the wine?"

She took another swig from the bottle. It had been a

hell of a day. It had been a hell of a year since she'd moved to Northern Lakes, since she'd started working as a state trooper. It had been hell longer than that, though, ever since she'd lost her parents who'd been the only family she'd had and had also been her closest friends. That was why she'd wanted to start over somewhere new. She'd been hopeful when she'd started her new career and found her new home that she could find happiness again.

She'd been so wrong.

"What are you thanking me for?" Mack prodded her as if he really wanted to know, as if he was interested in her as more than a suspect.

And surely, he could no longer suspect her of being the saboteur, not after she'd nearly been shot dead in front of him.

"Thank you for saving my life earlier tonight," she said. If he hadn't knocked her down when he had...

He shuddered, and Harry let out a soft hiss of protest at his movement. "I was scared. The shots rang out just as you stepped outside."

She shuddered, too, and she wasn't sure if it was because of how close a call she had or because she had that strange sensation again. Like someone was watching her...

Mack was. His dark gaze was intent on her face, as if he was trying to see inside her head, to see what she was thinking. Maybe that was why someone else was watching her, to figure out if she considered them a suspect.

She glanced at the big windows of the living room that looked out over the lake. She loved to watch the sunset over the water, but she'd missed it tonight. Mack probably hadn't showed up in time to see it either.

While it wasn't that late, probably just nine thirty or ten, it was too dark for Wynona to see if anyone was standing out there looking in, watching not just her now but the two of them: her and Mack.

Mack looked from her to those windows, too. "You feel like someone's watching you…"

She shrugged. "Maybe I'm just paranoid."

"After what happened earlier, after those shots fired at you, you're not paranoid," he said. "But you need to be careful."

"So you admit those shots weren't fired by some random hunter?" she asked.

"I don't know who was shooting at you, but I do intend to find out." And he glanced out that window again like he felt it, too. Felt that they were being watched…

"Why not have the police help?" she asked.

"Your techs are processing the scene," he said. "They're going to find whatever evidence the shooter might have left behind."

"And obviously you don't think they're going to find anything?"

He shrugged. "Maybe they'll find some slugs and casings. But somehow, I doubt that will lead us back to the shooter."

"Not us," she said. "Just me."

"Happened at my house," he said. "I'm entitled to know who was shooting on my property."

"Then why weren't you straight with the sergeant?" she asked. "Why not tell the truth about everything and share with us the information that Braden Zimmer gave you?"

"Martin Gingrich couldn't be trusted," he reminded her.

"That doesn't mean that I can't be," she said. She was sick of being judged by her professional association with another man. And since she'd been judged for that professional one, she was certain to be judged for the personal one she'd had with someone else, even as short-lived as it had been.

"What about the rest of your co-workers?" he asked. "How do you know they can be trusted?" He studied her face intently now, his dark eyes narrowed. "You don't. That's why you didn't call for backup when you came to my place or even when those shots were first fired. You don't trust them either."

"I don't trust anyone anymore," she said. Not after everything that had happened. The only people she'd truly been able to trust were gone: her mom and dad.

He grinned. "Not even me?"

"You least of all," she said, but she couldn't help but smile back at him. And she couldn't help that her pulse quickened. He was as good-looking as he was infuriating. Maybe being so attracted to him was why he infuriated Wynona so much.

"Then I better leave," he said, and he moved Harry from his lap. The Siamese let out a soft hiss in protest at being moved. Harry always had to be the rejector, not the rejected.

Mack stood up and grinned. "I need to leave before I'm tempted to do something that proves you can't trust me."

She stood up then, too, just to walk him to the door. That was all. To make sure that he really left...

And that the door was locked and the security system was engaged. But she found herself asking, "What are you tempted to do?"

He stepped a little closer to her and stared down at her face, his focus seemingly on her lips. Then, his voice gruff, he replied, "Kiss you."

Her heart started beating as fast and furiously as it had when those shots had been fired at her. "Kiss me?"

Then, as if she'd made a request instead of just parroting

his words back to him, he lowered his head and covered her mouth with his. And Wynona suddenly felt as if she had a lot more than a few sips of wine as her world tilted, and she had to clutch his shoulders to hang on while she and her emotions spun out of her control.

MACK SHOULD HAVE come here first before going to her place. But he'd wanted to make sure that Trooper Wells would be safe, that she had a security system, because someone had taken those shots at her. And he believed her, too, that someone was watching her. He'd felt that way as well back at her house.

And when he walked into the bar, he felt it again as everyone looked up at his entrance. Northern Lakes was that kind of town where everyone knew everyone else, and the tourists and strangers stuck out like he stuck out. But he wasn't going anywhere, not until he caught the saboteur, so they were going to have to get used to him.

There were only a few of the hotshots left in that corner booth. Maybe they'd gone home for the night or back to the firehouse. Or maybe they were sitting outside Wynona's house like they'd been sitting outside his earlier.

With the security system she had, she was safe. Even her windows were special tempered glass. The builder had probably used them because they could withstand birds flying into them. Hopefully they would withstand bullets, too.

While she was safe in her house, it hadn't been safe for Mack to be there. Kissing her had been a mistake. She'd probably just been repeating his words, but he'd taken them as an order. One he hadn't wanted to refuse. But when his lips touched hers, a current had passed through him, making him so damn aware of every feeling, of the silkiness of her lips, the heat and sweetness of her breath...the scent of her like a fresh rainfall.

God, he was an idiot.

"Hey," he called to the bartender. "Have I missed last call?" Didn't bars close early during the work week in towns like this? Or maybe, since the tourism season finally started given that it was June, they would stay open later.

"We have a couple of hours yet before last call," Charlie Tillerman replied. "Do you want another iced tea? Or can I get you a drink or something to eat now? It's still on the house for taking Michaela's place on the team."

"That's not necessary," Mack said.

"It is," Charlie said. "I hate thinking about what happened to you today and how that could have been her instead. I appreciate what you're doing here. I know you're not just taking her place."

"No, that's not the only reason I'm here," Mack admitted.

Charlie grimaced. "There's that person after them, pulling the dangerous stunts. You need to be careful. Extra careful. They all need to be."

Charlie had cause to worry. Mack was concerned too, but not just about the hotshots. He was worried about Wynona Wells for more than one reason, though. He was concerned about her safety, and he was especially worried about how dangerous she was to him. Because he knew more about her than just how sweet her mouth was, how silky her lips...

He knew something that made him trust her even less than he had before.

"I heard about what happened to you and Michaela in the firehouse parking lot with the Molotov cocktail getting tossed at the two of you," he told Charlie.

Fortunately, they had not been hurt too badly. But Mack

knew all too well how badly that could have gone, how badly they could have been burned.

Charlie shivered. "Yeah, that was awful."

"The local police sergeant, Hughes, thinks Jason Cruise was responsible for that, too."

Charlie snorted. "I doubt that. That seems petty even for him."

"Do you think it was the kids who broke in here?" Mack asked. "Donovan Cunningham's kids?"

"Or Donovan Cunningham," Charlie said.

"You're not a fan either?" he asked. He'd picked up on Wynona's low opinion of the guy.

Charlie shook his head and glanced over to that corner booth again. But Cunningham wasn't there now.

Was he outside Wynona's house, watching her?

Charlie shrugged. "I don't know now. Cunningham was there for us during that big fire, and he's been really apologetic to Michaela since he said some horrible things to her. I should forgive him."

"But you can't forget," Mack said. Maybe that was the problem between him and Trick. His younger brother couldn't forget that Mack had left just like their mother had.

"I'd rather believe that Jason Cruise was behind everything," Charlie admitted. "He did keep trying to kill me and Michaela using methods that the saboteur or other people after the hotshots had used in the past. Maybe whatever happened to you today with that tree was just an accident, and Cruise really was the saboteur."

Mack knew that wasn't the case. What had happened with that tree had not been an accident. It had either been meant as a warning or to kill him, and those gunshots could have killed Wynona. A dead man hadn't done those things.

But Mack pulled out a magnet he'd found on Wynona's refrigerator when he'd been looking for that bottle of wine. It had been holding something else to the side of her stainless-steel fridge, something he left in his pocket. He put that magnet with Jason Cruise's smiling face on the counter. "Tell me about him."

"He was smart and determined and greedy," Charlie said. "He was trying to get rich off Northern Lakes. His plan was to increase the property values of places he already owned by rezoning it to commercial and then he was going to bring in developers."

"What developers?" Could one of them be going after Wynona now? But Wynona hadn't been the one who'd killed Jason Cruise. When the Realtor realized his plan had failed, he'd killed himself.

Charlie shrugged. "I don't know. They all backed off after he died."

"How do you think he knew about all those things the saboteur did?" Mack asked.

"You don't think he was the saboteur then?" Charlie asked, and he groaned as if in pain. "I was hoping it was him…"

"So that it would all be over," Mack finished for him. But it wasn't over. For Mack, it was just beginning. Like whatever he'd started with Wynona. But the minute he'd made that mistake, that he'd kissed her, he'd pulled away and rushed off. He wasn't one to mess around with relationships. He knew relationships were riskier than any mission he'd ever undertaken.

"He knew so many of the things that had happened," Charlie continued as if trying to convince Mack.

And Mack had a feeling he knew how Jason had known

about those things. Because of the card that the magnet had been holding up...

The card had probably come with a bouquet of flowers, since it had been from a florist, and the words on it had read: *Welcome to Northern Lakes, beautiful. I think our personal relationship has even more promise than our professional one.*

Wynona had been professionally and personally involved with the would-be killer. Mack wasn't just suspicious of her now, he was also jealous...of a dead man.

CHARLIE LEFT THE Filling Station in the capable hands of the bar manager and bartender and headed upstairs to his apartment and to the woman he loved, the woman pregnant with their baby girl. He'd never been as happy as he was now or as hopeful for the future.

But the conversation he just had with Mack McRooney had unsettled him.

"What's wrong?" Michaela asked the minute he stepped inside the door. She was in the kitchen scooping cookies and cream ice cream into a bowl. Fortunately, her months of nausea were gone and she was eating more now for her sake and their baby's.

He grinned at her. "Nothing unless you add some pickles to that, then I'm going to be nauseous."

She grimaced. "No weird cravings here. And you're not distracting me from what's bothering you. What's wrong?"

He stepped closer and kissed her. "Distracted yet?" he teased when he lifted his head from hers.

She smiled. "Nope. You're going to have to do better than that."

But when he reached for her, she stepped back and

held up her bowl of ice cream between them. "Spill it, Mayor Tillerman."

He sighed. "It's nothing. Just Mack McRooney asking some questions."

She groaned. "He doesn't think you're the saboteur now, does he?"

He shook his head. "I don't think so. He didn't ask any questions about me beyond what happened to us, about the break-in and Donovan and his sons."

"The hoodlums," Michaela remarked. And she was probably referring to Donovan as well. Like Mack had said, it was harder to forget even if you were able to forgive.

"He was most interested in what Jason Cruise did to us," Charlie said. "I think he suspects that he could have been the saboteur."

She sighed. "No. He doesn't. Hank told me that the saboteur went after Mack today. If he hadn't gotten out of the way, a tree would have crushed him."

"That could have just been an accident," Charlie said. He hoped. He really wanted this to be over, for his town to be safe and especially for his soon-to-be wife and baby to be safe.

Michaela shook her head, and her blonde hair brushed across her cheek. "Nope. The tree wasn't marked to get cut down and nobody would admit to even being in that area when it happened."

"So you think someone tried to kill Mack?"

Michaela nodded.

"He didn't seem really shook up about it," Charlie said. "He seemed more focused on asking about Cruise, about how he tried to kill us using the same methods that had already been used against other hotshots."

Michaela's brow furrowed. "I suspected that Jason wasn't working alone," she said. "Maybe Mack suspects the same thing."

"He asked about the developers."

Michaela snorted. "It wasn't the developers. They wouldn't have known about those things. But I know one person who would have…"

"The saboteur," Charlie said.

"And Trooper Wynona Wells," Michaela said. "Or maybe they're one and the same."

Charlie shrugged. "I don't think *we* have to worry about any of that anymore," he said. "Mack McRooney is determined to get to the bottom of it all."

"Probably even more determined after someone tried to drop that tree on him," Michaela agreed. "I just hope that he manages to escape next time."

"Next time?"

"You know there will be a next time until the saboteur is finally stopped."

Hopefully Mack McRooney would catch them soon before anyone else got hurt. Charlie had taken on the role of mayor to make sure the town was safe, but now, with his daughter coming into the world in a few months, he was even more determined to make sure there were no dangers around her.

The saboteur had to be stopped. Soon.

Chapter Eight

Wynona hadn't slept well the night before and not because of someone taking shots at her, but because of that damn kiss. She probably should have slapped Mack McRooney for doing that, but she could see where he might have misconstrued her "kiss me" as an order rather than the question she'd intended it to be. Actually, if she was honest with herself, and she always was, she hadn't intended it as a question at all because she really had wanted him to kiss her.

And once he'd kissed her, she hadn't wanted him to stop. His lips had been so firm, and he tasted like dark chocolate and red wine. There had been this sizzle between them that had had her senses reeling, her skin tingling. She'd wanted that kiss to go on and on, but he'd pulled away. And then he'd walked away, leaving her wanting more.

And more…

But not kisses.

She wanted justice. That was why she'd forced herself to get out of bed after just tossing and turning in it the night before. And she'd gotten ready and rushed to work with one purpose.

She wanted to find out who the hell had taken those shots at her, who'd been going after the hotshots and who'd been watching her. And she wanted to put them behind bars with her old training sergeant.

But first she had to convince her *current* sergeant to let her investigate. Since he'd sent her home from the scene of the shooting the night before, she didn't have much hope that he would agree. But before she could even knock on the door to his office, it opened, and a man stepped out and nearly ran into her. His muscular chest just about touched her face.

She stumbled back a step, and his hands reached out and grasped her shoulders. Last night those big hands had cupped her face when he'd leaned down and kissed her. Her skin tingled and heat streaked through her at just the thought of his mouth moving over hers. She took another step back, so that his hands fell away.

"Why are you here?" she asked.

"Just following up with the sergeant," Mack said. "Letting him know that I might have misread that situation yesterday. I could have been mistaken about the hunter and the hunted, especially given the things that keep happening around Northern Lakes."

A sudden chill washed away the heat she'd felt moments ago. And the little hope she had that Hughes might agree to let her lead the investigation dissipated.

Had he told her boss she was being hunted?

Was she?

And who was doing the hunting? The saboteur or Mack McRooney?

She'd initially suspected he was the one following her, but getting shot at while she was with him had proven her wrong about him. There was no way that he was the one who'd tried to hurt her physically.

But she still didn't feel safe with him, especially after

that kiss. And she felt just as hunted by him as by whoever was watching her.

She also couldn't be certain about what she was going to lose. Her job or her life?

Or maybe even her heart...?

BEFORE MACK COULD say anything else to Wynona, her sergeant called her into his office. As she passed Mack in the doorway, she shot him a look full of indignation and maybe a little hurt. She must have thought he'd betrayed her.

But he hadn't told Sergeant Hughes everything he knew about her. He really hadn't told him anything at all about her except that she was right. Somebody dangerous was out there yet, and the more people looking for them the better.

Once the door closed behind them, Mack headed off to the next sergeant he intended to speak to, but this one was behind bars at the local jail, which was in the same building as the state police post. This was where the sergeant was being held while awaiting trial. At the moment, he was behind Plexiglass, his pudgy body stretching the snaps on his orange jumpsuit.

Mack picked up the phone, and the guy waited a moment before he picked up the receiver on the other side.

"I don't know you," Sergeant Martin Gingrich said. "I thought you were Trick McRooney."

"Trick is my younger brother," Mack acknowledged even though Trick didn't seem too proud that they were related right now.

The guy grimaced, then his sigh rattled the receiver. "You're another one of Zimmer's brothers-in-law."

Mack nodded. "Yeah, I am."

"Why did he send you here?" Marty asked. "Is he afraid to face me himself?"

"Braden is a little busy right now," Mack said.

The balding guy smirked. "Yeah, with that traitor on his team."

"You think the saboteur is on the team then? That he's one of the hotshots?" Mack asked.

The guy shrugged, but then nodded a little eagerly. "Probably. Nobody was that happy when that suck-up Braden got the job."

"What do you mean?" Mack asked. All of the team seemed to respect Braden. And they were all loyal to him. That was why they'd tried to keep the problems quiet, so that Braden wouldn't lose his job.

He shrugged again. "Let's say a lot of us had to work a lot harder than Braden Zimmer has ever had to work in his life." He made woo-woo noises. "His legendary sixth sense about fires is why he got promoted. Not because he put in the time or the work. He had the same luck with school and sports. He always got what he wanted."

And apparently what Gingrich had wanted too, which was undoubtedly why the guy was so bitter and jealous of his old high school rival.

"What about Wynona?" Mack asked. That was whom he really wanted to talk about, probably because he couldn't stop thinking about her and hadn't been able to even before that kiss. After that…he'd thought about her even in his sleep, dreaming about her.

The guy's face was blank like the expression in his beady dark eyes. "Who?"

"Trooper Wells."

"Oh, Wells..." He snorted. "Yeah, stuff probably comes easy for her, too. Money. Looks."

The deed to her house being in a trust had tipped Mack off, even before he saw the house, that she had some money. Once he saw the ultra-modern house on an extra-large lot on the biggest of the lakes in Northern Lakes, he'd realized that she had some *serious* money.

Mack tried to sound casual as he asked, "Anything else I should know about her?"

"What? Are you looking for me to give a recommendation for her?" Gingrich snorted again. "I don't really know her. I don't think I was in her league. She dated that Realtor for a while, the one who bought up half the town."

"Not anymore," Mack murmured.

"Did he sell out?"

"Something like that," Mack said. "He's dead. You didn't hear about that? Don't get a lot of visitors?"

The guy's face flushed a deep red.

Nope. He didn't. So it was unlikely anyone from the local police post was carrying out the vendetta he obviously still had against Braden Zimmer. But was Gingrich the only one with a grudge against the hotshot superintendent? Or did other people resent Braden Zimmer's rapid rise to his leadership position with the Huron Hotshots?

"Is Wells still a trooper?" Gingrich asked the question now.

Nobody was keeping the former sergeant apprised of anything anymore. So it wasn't likely that he was a factor in any of the incidents that had happened since his arrest. And Wynona obviously wasn't in cahoots with her former training officer either since he didn't even know if she was still working in law enforcement. But still…this wasn't an entire waste of Mack's time.

He nodded.

And those beady eyes widened in reaction.

"That surprises you that she's still on the job?" Mack asked. Had Gingrich thought his successor would fire her? Or that she would quit?

Gingrich nodded. "She doesn't have the instincts for police work."

Mack wanted to argue with him, but since she hadn't picked up on how evil this man was, he couldn't. And Jason Cruise…

How long had she been involved with him? And how deeply? Deep enough to help him hurt Charlie Tillerman and Michaela Momber?

"What about sabotage?" Mack asked.

Gingrich snorted again. "What?"

"Could she be the one sabotaging the hotshot team?"

Gingrich laughed. "You think she would get her hands dirty? She's too soft. Too pampered."

"To be the saboteur?"

The former sergeant nodded. "And to be a cop. She's going to get hurt or worse."

God, Mack hoped Gingrich was both right and wrong about Wynona. He didn't want to suspect that she was the saboteur, and after last night, after she'd been shot at, he really didn't think she was. So the former sergeant was right about that, but Mack didn't want him to be right about anything else. He really didn't want her getting hurt or worse.

USUALLY, BRADEN SENSED when a fire was about to happen, but he had no forewarning about the fire he'd just taken a call about. Maybe that was because it wasn't that big. Because he usually only got the forewarning about the big ones, like the one Jason Cruise had set recently.

And all the fires that arsonist, Matt Hamilton, had set. His premonitions seemed to come about the dangerous fires...

But as long as that saboteur was on the loose, every fire was dangerous. Hell, everything was dangerous. Mack could have been killed yesterday when they'd been cutting that break to protect the town from another fire like the one Jason Cruise had set and they'd barely been able to get under control.

Braden couldn't help but worry that this fire was going to give the saboteur the chance to make another attempt on Mack's life. Maybe it had even been set for that purpose and that was why Braden had had no premonition about it, because it had been set on the spur of the moment.

But Mack hadn't showed up at the firehouse yet. And Braden was kind of hoping that he wouldn't show up. But that thought had no more entered his head than he heard the squeal of tires as Mack's truck turned abruptly into the parking lot next to the firehouse.

When Mack had agreed to help Braden find the saboteur, he'd insisted on being one of the team in every way. He wanted to work the fires, and he'd even gone through hotshot training with his dad before he'd joined the team.

Braden had trained under the older Mack McRooney himself, and so had several other members of the team. Mack Senior was the best, so Braden had no doubt that Mack junior was prepared to do the job.

Despite how badly Braden wanted the saboteur caught, he wouldn't have hired either of his brothers-in-law if they weren't damn good at what they did.

The best of the best.

But no matter how good they were, the job was still dangerous for a lot of reasons. The saboteur was only one of them.

There was always danger with a fire because they were so unpredictable. They could turn without warning. And they could fight back at the firefighters trying to extinguish them. Braden had no doubt that Mack was a fighter, or he probably wouldn't be alive.

But eventually the man was going to come up against something or someone even stronger than he was. A fire or the saboteur...

Chapter Nine

A billboard-sized real estate sign was nailed to the side of the burning building. And on that sign was Jason Cruise's smiling face just like it had been on the magnet Mack had taken off Wynona's fridge with the card from a flower store. Wynona had kept that card.

That was probably what bothered Mack most, that this man, this would-be killer, had meant something to Wynona. Was he the reason she'd gotten teary-eyed when they'd talked about losing someone?

Was Jason Cruise the one she missed so much that it still affected her? And why did that bother Mack so damn much? The man was dead. He was no longer a threat to anyone.

The fire was a threat, though, because of the possible exposure and risk. While the burning building was an abandoned warehouse, it was close enough to other structures that it could spread to inhabited businesses and buildings. There was also the threat of backdrafts in a building like this, and it was possibly a Class D fire if there were any chemicals or metals left in that warehouse.

Knowing all those things, because of his training and because Braden had warned them before sending them out,

Mack knew he had to stay focused. He couldn't keep thinking about her now. Or even about the saboteur.

He had to focus on the fire only.

Because of the risks with this fire, Braden had chosen only hotshots to respond to it and not any of the volunteers. And despite the risks, it was a fire that the hotshots should have easily been able to handle if there wasn't also the concern that it was a trap.

Mack had that concern, too, but he still wanted to go inside that building. In all the cities where he'd lived and even in some of the remote rural areas, no vacant building was ever truly vacant. Somebody had usually taken up residence inside it, or teenagers might use it for a hang-out. And that could have been how the fire started. Maybe it hadn't been deliberately set.

"It has to be checked," he insisted to Braden. "You know it."

"I'll go in with the rescue company to check it," Braden said.

Mack shook his head. "You're the boss. You don't run the rescue company."

Dawson Hess ran that because he was also a paramedic like Owen James. Dawson was gone, though, on a trip to New York where his reporter wife lived. Since Dawson had long ago been eliminated as a suspect because the saboteur had also gone after him, his leaving Northern Lakes wasn't an issue.

Owen was in charge. And Mack, with his medical training and evacuation training, had been assigned to the rescue company as well. Owen, standing near the back doors of the building, gestured for Mack to come and join him,

Luke Garrison and Ben Higgins, who were also assigned to the company.

Braden hesitated for a moment as if reluctant to send Mack, then he nodded. And Mack rushed off toward that burning building. Knowing that it was probably a trap, he would be careful of his safety and the safety of the rest of the rescue company.

While he'd gone through his intense hotshot training with his dad, the older Mack had told a lot of stories of the rescue companies who'd needed rescuing. Mack didn't want that to be the case here. But he couldn't help but think this was a trap. Just before he followed Owen inside the building, he glanced back toward the staging area in the parking lot.

And he saw *her*.

Wynona was here. And if this was a trap, she might be in as much danger as he was. He had to make it out to make sure that nothing happened to her.

Then he adjusted his mask to make sure he had oxygen and he headed inside, letting the door slam closed behind him.

WYNONA STOOD IN the glow and the heat of the burning building, but a chill rushed over her. When that door closed behind Mack, her heart sank with dread. Would she see him again? Would he make it back out of the fire?

She rushed up to Braden and tapped his shoulder. "What are you doing?"

He glanced at her, his brow furrowing. "What? We got called out here."

"Why would you let Mack go in there?" she asked, her pulse racing with the urgency gripping her.

"Because it's his job."

"No, no, it's not," she said. "You brought him onto the team to investigate those acts of sabotage, to find out who's after you. He's not a firefighter."

Braden smiled slightly, as if it was all he could manage. "Don't let him hear you say that. Every McRooney has the firefighter gene, and thanks to their dad, they have the best training, too."

That pressure on her chest eased a bit, letting her draw a deeper breath. But then she coughed and sputtered as smoke burned her lungs. The air was thick with it, making the sky look dark already like night had come before noon.

"You need to get back," Braden said. "And please establish a perimeter with police barricades to keep people away."

"I already have some other troopers blocking off the streets around here," she said. But this fire was even more dangerous than she'd been worrying that it was. "Do you suspect there are chemicals in that building?"

"I don't know," Braden said. "The rescue company goes in first. They'll establish if there are any dangerous chemicals inside when they make sure that there are no people in the building."

There were people in that building. Mack and three other firefighters had gone through that door. They were going into the main level, but the whole structure was burning, flames consuming it and that billboard that hung on the side of it. Jason's face melted, fading into black with flames shooting through where the eyes might have been and his mouth like he was some demon coming back from the dead to destroy them.

But Jason was gone. Even the magnet and that note she had on the side of her fridge, to remind herself not to be sweet-talked and fooled again, was gone. Harry had probably knocked it down between the fridge and the cabinet next to it. But while Jason was gone, the threat was still out there. Or maybe the saboteur was in that building with Mack, waiting for an opportunity to try to kill him again.

"Trooper!" Braden shouted at her. "I need your help."

She nodded, and despite all the smoke, she tried to clear her head, tried to think. She had to secure the scene, had to protect as many people as she could. That was why she'd gone into this career.

After being helpless to save her parents when that virus had ravaged their bodies, she'd vowed then to help as many other people as she could. But she had this horrible feeling that she wouldn't be able to help the person who probably needed it the most.

Mack.

He was already in the fire. And she couldn't get him out of there. He and his team would have to find their own way through the flames.

But then the ground and the building shuddered and fire blasted out the side of the structure, spraying bricks and debris into the parking lot, some of it landing dangerously close to where she and Braden stood. She felt the heat, but more than that, she felt the fear that overwhelmed her.

Not for herself but for Mack.

Because she had an answer to the questions she'd asked Braden. There must have been chemicals inside that had caused that explosion. There had also been firefighters inside that building.

Had they survived?

Had Mack?

TRICK WAS LATE to the scene. Since Michaela had taken medical leave, he'd taken her "day job" at the St. Paul fire department. By doing that, he was able to work with Henrietta and live with her in the apartment over the firehouse. But that meant that if the hotshots were called up to report to a fire, he and Henrietta would have to drive nearly an hour south to Northern Lakes. That meant that he was an hour late for the fire and the explosion that they'd heard when they'd still been miles from town.

Maybe he was too late to save his brother. Because he doubted that building had exploded on its own. The saboteur was at it again and was getting more and more dangerous the longer he or she eluded justice.

Debris from the building had expanded the cordoned-off area, so Trick had to park more than two blocks away from the scene. He threw open the driver's door and ran toward the old warehouse. Henrietta, as always, was right beside him with her hand in his.

"He's going to be okay," she said.

And he was surprised that she would make that claim, that she would lie to him when she had no way of knowing. He wanted it to be the truth. He wanted Mack to be okay, or Trick would never forgive himself for how he'd treated his older brother. How he hadn't been able to bring himself to forgive him for leaving.

And now Mack might be gone forever...

Chapter Ten

The blast rocked Mack, knocking him down, knocking off his helmet. He scrambled around in the smoke, fumbling around the ground for the helmet and the mask. That smoke filled his lungs, and a cough racked him as he gasped for breath. Through his thick gloves, he found the helmet and mask and shoved them on his head again.

"Hello?" he called into the mike built into his helmet. "Hello?" Not even static emanated from the speaker. Were the others unable to speak? Even those outside the building? It looked like more debris and bricks had blown out that side instead of flying around inside...

But where were the others?

"Hello? Hello?" he called into the mike, but there was no reply.

From the rest of the rescue company and from Braden. Were they all hurt? Braden and Wynona were in the parking lot. Had the debris extended that far? Had she or his brother-in-law been struck by anything or by the heat and the flames?

The fire burned brighter now. Hotter. Even with all his gear, Mack could feel the heat. He had to get the hell out of here, but not without the rest of the rescue company. Luke and his wife had just had a baby. He had to be okay.

"Hello? Hello?" he called out again, but the only thing he heard was the roar of the flames and the rush of water from hoses. The others were still out there, pumping water from the outside. And then there was the loud buzz as a plane overhead dipped low and dropped a deluge of fire retardant onto the site, beating down the flames, killing the fire.

Like someone had probably intended to kill him. But had someone else died instead?

As the smoke dissipated, the others emerged. Ben Higgins. Owen. Luke. They made hand gestures, so their radios weren't working either. But they worked, as a team, to avoid the fallen beams and bricks. And finally they made it to an exit. Before the explosion, they'd determined that they were the only humans inside. The rest of what they'd found had been boxes and containers of leftover material of whatever had once been stored or manufactured in the warehouse. Apparently something highly combustible.

While they all had suspected it might have been a trap, they had had to make sure that there hadn't been any other innocent people in that building. Braden hadn't known about the chemicals, though, but Mack had a feeling that someone else had been well aware of how combustible the warehouse was: the saboteur.

That was why they'd chosen it for their next stunt, their next attempt on either his life or the lives of any hotshot. But Mack and his company escaped unscathed, their masks and gear protecting them.

That didn't mean that there hadn't been other casualties, though. Outside...

Once Mack was out of the building, he peered through

all the smoke billowing around outside and he tried to find her. Where the hell was Wynona?

Two guys, in gear, ran up and grabbed him. Despite the masks they were wearing to protect them from the possible fumes, he recognized his brother and brother-in-law.

Trick and Braden led him and the others farther away from the building, farther away from the heat and the smoke. And Rory made another pass over the building, dousing it with something other than water, with the special retardant that would extinguish chemical fires. Smoke and heat rolled out of the structure which was collapsing in on itself and dis-integrating into a pile of broken bricks and scorched metal.

Braden and Trick led them farther into the parking lot. Mack peered around them now, trying to catch a glimpse of her. She'd been here earlier. He knew that had been her, in her uniform, standing near Braden just as Mack had walked into the warehouse.

But unlike Braden, Wynona hadn't been wearing any protective gear. Just her uniform, her badge and her gun. He removed his mask to ask about her but a cough racked him for a second as the oxygen he'd been inhaling was re-placed with the smoke.

"Are you all right?" Braden asked. He wasn't looking at just Mack but at the entire company.

The others nodded, but Mack coughed again when he tried to speak. Despite the intensive training he had re-cently done with his dad, he wasn't quite as ready to jump into fires as he thought he was. And in that blast, he'd lost his damn helmet and mask for a minute.

Trick had been right—being a hotshot was much more dangerous than he'd realized and not just because of the saboteur. He needed to tell his brother that. He needed to make whatever this tension was between them go away... because they were both in danger now.

But when he opened his mouth, he sucked in more smoke and coughed again.

"You need an EMT," Trick said, his voice gruff either from the smoke or the concern Mack could see in his eyes.

What Mack needed was Wynona, to make sure that she was all right. But he still couldn't see her. When he tried looking around the parking lot, his eyes teared and his vision blurred for a moment.

"We'll get you to the ER," Trick said.

Mack shook his head and reached out and clasped Owen's shoulder. Owen was a former Marine and tough as hell as well as a damn good paramedic. He'd probably saved Rory's life more than Mack had since Rory had still gotten shot that day in the firehouse garage, the day that Mack had shot the crooked FBI agent.

"My EMT's right here," Mack told his brother. "And he'll tell you we're all fine." Or at least Mack would be once he found her. But with Braden and Trick and the rest of the rescue company standing around him, he couldn't see much beyond them. He couldn't see through the smoke to the rest of the parking lot.

And then she was there, shoving her way between his hotshot team members. Then she shoved him back with her hands on his chest. "What the hell were you thinking to go in there? You know you're in danger!"

Then, right after she finished shouting at him, she coughed and wheezed slightly. While she didn't seem to be hurt, she might have inhaled too much of the fumes already. And with the chemicals that were in them, those fumes could be especially toxic.

Lethal even.

Mack stepped forward and reached for her, intending to pick her up and carry her toward one of the rigs. She was the one who needed to get to the hospital as soon as possible. Because she might have once again become the one that the saboteur nearly killed.

Or depending on the toxicity of those fumes, the saboteur could still succeed this time.

WYNONA HAD BEEN so scared that she hadn't been able to control her reaction to seeing Mack. Or to stay away from the building despite Braden's warning for her to get back as well. When the explosion had blasted that huge hole through the side of the building, she had been so worried about him, so terrified that he had died. And when she saw him acting as if nothing was wrong, emotions overwhelmed her. Her relief got swept up in anger that he was being so blasé again, and she lost her temper.

Shoving him wasn't smart, though. But now he was reaching for her, trying to pick her up right in front of the other hotshots. She shoved him back again. "What are you doing? Have you lost your mind?"

Just moments ago she'd been so damn worried that he'd lost his life. Didn't danger affect him at all? How could he seem more concerned about her than about himself?

"You need to get to the ER," he said.

"I wasn't in that burning building," she said, but she coughed again as the smoke overwhelmed her. Other troopers were holding back onlookers, keeping a wide perimeter around the fire. She hoped it was wide enough.

"The smoke could be toxic," Mack said, and now he

coughed, too. "And you don't have a mask." He'd taken his down to talk to her.

"You need to get back, Trooper Wells," Owen James told her. "He's right. We need to check air quality levels before anyone should be inhaling this without masks." After he said it, he pulled his up again.

Mack reached for her again, but instead of trying to lift her up, he just guided her farther from the fire. From the fumes. "You need to be careful, too," he told her. "I'm not the only one the saboteur has targeted."

She wanted to deny that it was true, but she couldn't, not after those shots had been fired at her the night before. That hadn't been a hunter.

And now…

She could feel that gaze on her, the one that made a chill race down her spine despite the heat. The saboteur was out there somewhere, watching them…

From the shadows outside the perimeter of the fire?

Or from closer? Was the saboteur one of the hotshots fighting the fire, the fire that he or she had undoubtedly set to try again to kill Mack McRooney?

The saboteur might have known that she would show up, too, since Northern Lakes was her primary coverage area and a fire this big would need a police presence to secure the scene. And while she was securing the scene, she was putting herself in danger, too.

"Maybe you're right," she agreed with Mack. "Maybe we both need to get out of here."

Because what if the saboteur started shooting again? They might not because there would be witnesses now, but if they didn't care about that, then those witnesses could become casualties of whatever war the saboteur had decided to wage against her and Mack.

THE EXPLOSION SHOULD have finished off Mack McRooney. The saboteur had known that the new hotshot was part of the rescue company. McRooney would have to go in first. But he wouldn't be going in alone. Others could have died with him.

But now…

With as long as this had gone on, with as deep as the saboteur was in, he just didn't see a way out that didn't include casualties.

But the first ones who had to die were Mack McRooney and that damn state trooper. While the fire and the explosion hadn't taken out either of them, the saboteur, as always, had a backup plan.

Chapter Eleven

Standing under a spray of water in the firehouse locker bathroom, Mack wanted to shower off the stench of the fire and the chemicals that had burned up in it. Hell, he wanted to shower off the whole damn day that had finally ended after spending hours at the scene. And after showering off the stench, he wanted to start over again.

Hell, he wanted to do last night over, at least that kiss. And this time he didn't want to stop kissing Wynona. This time he didn't want to leave her.

If he'd had any idea that this could have possibly been his last day alive, he would have wanted to spend that last night with her.

But that hadn't been his last night, and Mack knew all too well that he couldn't undo the past. That he couldn't stay after he'd already left...which Trick's resentment had proven to him all too well.

So instead of getting rid of his whole day, he would have to make do with just getting rid of the soot and the grime. For now. But once he figured out who the hell the saboteur was, he would get rid of him or her, too. And the son of a bitch would be lucky if they just wound up behind bars with Martin Gingrich or...

They wound up in hell.

Mack reached out and turned the tap to cool off the water rushing over him. He had the showers to himself. Everyone else had come back to the firehouse before him, cleaned up and left. He'd stuck around the scene to make sure that the fire was out and to make sure that Wynona didn't get hurt stubbornly trying to investigate it. That was a job for an arson investigator like Mack's sister Sam. But with Sam being as pregnant as she was, she had no business investigating this fire.

Not that it would take much to determine it had been deliberately set. There had been no sign of anyone living in or even hanging out in that abandoned warehouse. So it wasn't as if someone had accidentally started the fire with a discarded cigarette or something.

And there'd been flash marks from where an accelerant had caught fire. Someone had wanted the fire to keep burning until those containers exploded.

And probably until some people exploded along with them and the building.

Mack wanted to explode with anger like Wynona had vented at the scene. But she'd been angry with him, not the saboteur. She'd been upset that he'd taken chances even knowing that he was in danger.

But that was the story of his life. That was what he'd done for years, and even though he'd retired from that life, apparently he hadn't retired from danger.

Wynona was also a threat to him and not just because of how angry she'd been with him. He kind of liked that she'd been upset with him because that seemed to indicate that she cared. But he liked that, and her, a little too much for his peace of mind.

He needed to focus on catching this saboteur. Not on her and what she made him feel. She was focused on catching the saboteur too. After she'd insisted she was fine and kept working the scene with the other troopers, he hadn't had a chance to talk to her again. And by the time he and Braden had left, she was already gone.

Where had she gone?

Back to the police post? Or home?

Once he was done with the shower, he would swing by her place just to make sure that she was all right. That was the only reason why. And maybe to ask her questions about Jason Cruise, like why she'd kept that card on her fridge, and this time, he would make sure that he got answers.

Those were his intentions.

Not to kiss her again.

He chuckled. She was right. He was a liar, and now he was even lying to himself.

The lights went off, plunging the showers into darkness, but the water kept running.

And then he heard it…

The snap and the crackle of electricity.

Specifically of a bare wire snapping with it. Sparks appeared in the darkness, and he knew that current was racing toward where he stood in the water on the wet floor, and if he didn't think of something fast, he was about to get electrocuted.

WYNONA WAS OFF duty now. Her shift was over, but she couldn't stop working because she could not stop worrying.

After going back to the police post, she'd gone home and showered off the soot and smoke from the fire. She'd also filled up Harry's automatic feeder and water fountain because she knew she had to go out again and she wasn't sure how long she would be gone.

After what had been happening recently, she wasn't even sure she would be able to make it back home. But she was absolutely sure that she wouldn't be able to rest until she checked on Mack again. She was clearly not the only one in danger now—he was too.

She'd driven past the warehouse, or what was left of it, but the fire was out, and crime scene tape and cones blocked off the area. Nobody was there anymore.

Maybe, since the techs had finished processing his house and the area around it last night, he'd gone home. But she thought of swinging by the firehouse first before making the drive out to his place. She was just pulling up to the firehouse when the lights went out, momentarily plunging the entire area into darkness.

Then the lights flickered and came back on, but she was still uneasy. There was no storm. No reason for the lights to have gone off and come back on unless someone was messing with them like the night the saboteur had slashed the tires of the trucks in the lot and thrown that Molotov cocktail. He or she had messed with the lights then. But the only truck Wynona saw in the lot was the one she'd followed home the night before.

Mack's. He was here. But was he alone?

She parked at the curb and rushed out of her car, leaving it running while she ran up to the side door of the firehouse. She pounded on the steel surface. "Hello? It's Trooper Wells. Let me in."

There was no sound inside, but she picked up on a strange sensation from that metal, like a vibration or a current. She pounded again then tried the knob. As the others had said, it was often left unlocked.

Thanks to Stanley. Or at least everybody blamed it on the kid. But if the saboteur was a hotshot, then he or she had keys to the firehouse anyway. Maybe they were the person leaving the doors unlocked and blaming Stanley in order to cover up that the saboteur was a hotshot.

The knob turned easily, and the door creaked open. "Thanks, Stanley..." she murmured, although she was beginning to doubt that the teenager was the one leaving the door unlocked, especially tonight. Someone else might have deliberately left that door unlocked. Maybe to lure her inside, too.

She almost reached for her collar and for the radio that was usually clipped to it. Unlike last night, she would have used it this time, because she wasn't the only one in danger now, Mack was too. But after showering, she'd changed out of her uniform into jeans and a sweater, so she didn't even have a collar. But she had her weapon, and she drew that out of the holster on her belt loop.

Holding it in both hands, she pushed the door open farther. As she stepped inside, she called out, "Hello?"

But nobody answered her. The fire trucks filled the bays. They were all back. But where were the firefighters? Where was Mack?

That had to have been his truck. It had a Washington state plate instead of a Michigan one. It was the one he'd driven here from where his dad lived on the West Coast. Mack had a place here now, so he wouldn't have to sleep in the bunkroom like some of the other hotshots, the ones who had day jobs in other areas of the state or the country even. Those hotshots had other places to stay now, or they'd found other places. After that attack on Rory in the firehouse, hotshots rarely spent the night in the bunkroom anymore.

But maybe, after his long day, Mack had been too tired to drive home. Maybe he was asleep in that bunkroom on the second floor. But he had to know about what had happened to Rory there, so he shouldn't have taken the risk of staying here, especially since the saboteur was clearly targeting him now.

She crossed the garage to the stairwell of concrete steps that led up to the second and third stories of the three-story cement block building. The lights were dim in the stairwell, as if they were emergency lights only or maybe working off a generator instead of an electrical source.

But she had this strange feeling, almost as if there was electricity in the air. There was a crackle to it and her hair was starting to stand up, but maybe that was with fear.

When she reached the second-story landing, she heard the crackle and the sounds of running water and she saw the sparks coming out of a door that had been jammed open with a trash can. "Hello? Mack?" she called out again.

"Wynona?" a gruff voice called back.

And she started toward that open door.

But now he shouted at her, "Get out! Get out of the building!"

Was it rigged to blow like the warehouse might have been?

Her heart pumped fast and hard with fear. "What is it? What's going on?"

"There's a live wire in the shower room," he said. "You gotta get out of here."

She wasn't going anywhere, but she was reaching for her

cell. She had to phone for help because she had no freaking idea how to deal with this.

And how the hell had he not been electrocuted if there was a live wire in the shower with him? Mindful of the water starting to trickle out the open door, Wynona kept the rubber soles of her boots out of the water, and she peered inside the room.

She couldn't see much in that dim emergency lighting. Just the water coming out of the showerheads, and then she saw the man clinging to the top of a ceramic privacy wall that didn't reach all the way to the ceiling, but it was high and his body was clearly wet, water dripping off his broad shoulders and his bulging arms.

How long was he going to be able to hang on without slipping off the ceramic onto the floor where sparks danced from the end of the stripped-out wire that was lying there?

"You have to get out of here," Mack said again.

"Don't worry about your modesty," she said, trying to keep the panic from her voice. She didn't want him to panic and slip. And she didn't want to panic and slip either. "I'm going to figure this out…"

"You're going to get electrocuted too or maybe even shot," Mack said. "Whoever rigged this could still be around here somewhere."

She sucked in a breath at the thought and peered around the shower area again. But she didn't see anyone but him. While the person could still be hiding somewhere in the building, she wasn't as concerned about the saboteur or her own safety as she was about Mack.

"Get out of here!" Mack shouted again. He clearly didn't want her help.

Or he didn't think she could give it without getting hurt

herself. She didn't care about her safety right now. But she backed out of the shower area. Once she was in the hall, she reached for her cell.

But instead of calling emergency dispatch, she called someone else. Someone who knew this building better than she did. Someone who might have a clue how to save his brother-in-law because she wasn't certain how to do it without getting them both killed. All she knew was that she needed to find the breaker box where the electrical current came into the building. But there was a good chance that whoever had set all this up was there, making sure that the breaker didn't go off and break that flow of electricity.

So while she talked to Braden, she tightly grasped the weapon she held in her right hand, and she headed back down the stairs to the main level where Braden was telling her that the box was.

"I'm on my way," he said.

But if the saboteur was waiting for her in the utility room, the hotshot superintendent wasn't going to get here in time to help either her or Mack. Because if the saboteur was waiting for her, Wynona might not be able to shut off that breaker. She might not be able to save Mack.

TRICK HEARD THE call come out over the hotshot radio frequency. SOS at the firehouse. At the cottage Henrietta had inherited from her grandfather, she was in the shower, washing off the soot and smoke from the fire.

"What the hell happened now?" he wondered aloud. But he didn't need to ask to whom it had happened.

It had to be Mack.

Why hadn't he hugged his big brother when Mack and the rest of the rescue company had come out of that warehouse earlier today? He hadn't, though. He'd just stood there with Braden, letting his brother-in-law do all the talking.

Why hadn't he told Mack how sorry he was for being such a dick to him since he'd come back?

Trick had to let the anger and resentment go, he knew that now. But he didn't want to let his brother go.

He was afraid that he might not have a choice.

Chapter Twelve

Mack might have been embarrassed that he was hanging, bare-assed naked, from a shower wall, when Wynona had stepped into the shower room. But he was too worried about her to care about modesty or anything else. Even himself right now.

What if this was a trap? And that son of a bitch was somewhere inside the building yet, waiting to get Wynona alone. Minutes ago he'd yelled at her to leave, but now he wanted to call her back.

But those damn sparks kept bouncing up from the end of that wire. If he stepped down onto the tile floor, into the water, he was going to get electrocuted for certain.

While Wynona had a chance to save herself…

And maybe even him…

But then the lights flickered and shut off again, leaving him in darkness. Complete darkness.

Maybe that live wire had finally blown a breaker. Or Wynona had found and shut off the main switch. He didn't hear anything now but the water running, spraying out of the faucet and onto his back and onto the floor.

His arms started to shake from the exertion of holding up his body weight for so long. And he found himself starting to slide down from that half wall. As his foot touched the wet tile, he cringed in anticipation of the shock of electricity.

But nothing happened...until the lights flashed on again. And he let out a curse as he waited for that wire to spring back to life again.

But it lay limply in the puddle on the floor, like a dead snake. The lights that had flickered on were just the security lights, which would have been on a different circuit than the one that someone had rigged that wire to, so he breathed a sigh of relief.

Until he heard the squishing sound of shoe soles against the wet tile. He glanced up from that wire to confront whoever had walked in, but it was her.

"You're okay?" he asked Wynona.

She held her gun yet, as if she was worried that they weren't alone. He could hear other voices now. Other people were in the building, and in the distance, he could hear sirens.

She nodded, but she wouldn't meet his gaze. Her attention seemed to be elsewhere...

On his body. His naked body. He hadn't grabbed a towel yet. And right now, he wanted to grab her instead, especially with the way she was staring at him, making him even more aware of her than he'd already been, more aware of the attraction that sizzled between them. But he felt more than attraction for her now, he felt gratitude.

"You saved me..." he murmured. He wasn't used to that, to being the one who needed saving.

"Don't sound so surprised," she said, her lips curving into a slight grin. "I *am* capable..." But she sounded a little surprised herself.

"Mack!" Braden called out from below.

"Are you capable of handing me a towel?" Mack asked. The one he'd brought into the shower with him had dropped off the half wall he'd been hanging onto just a short while ago. And it was as wet as he was. But he wasn't cold, not with the way she was staring at him.

And if he hadn't heard other people inside the building, he definitely wouldn't have minded being naked with her.

Her smile widened even as her face flushed. She picked a towel off one of the hooks near the door that had been propped open to the hall. But she held it just a bit out of his reach.

Like she was just a bit out of his reach...

He couldn't quite figure her out. And he didn't have the chance because before he could take that towel from her, Braden was in the showers, too. And he wasn't alone. Owen was with him. And the young guys, Abbott and Lane. Cunningham and Kozak were there, too.

"If this is your SOS, you need more help than us," Kozak said.

"Stand back!" she said, holding up her hand, with that towel, to direct them all back into the hall. "This is a crime scene."

"What's the crime?" Abbott asked. "Indecent exposure?"

"You going to cuff him, Trooper Wells?" Lane asked.

"I'm kind of wondering why she's here at all..." Cunningham murmured.

So was Mack, but he was damn glad she'd showed up when she had.

"Someone tried to electrocute McRooney," she said.

And they probably would have succeeded if not for her showing up when she had.

Trick, who'd just showed up, gasped. "Mack?" he called out to him over Braden's shoulder. "Are you all right?"

"I'm fine," Mack said with a nod. "Or I will be once you all get out of here and let me get dressed." He wasn't sure about that, though. He wasn't sure that he was fine, and it wasn't just because someone had tried to kill him yet again. It was because of her and how much she unsettled him.

Wynona turned back toward him then, and her gaze dipped down once, over his body, before she handed him the towel. And just under her breath, so that he barely heard her, she muttered something that sounded a lot like, "You are fine…"

And now his face flushed. His hands shook a bit as he wrapped that towel around his waist. But that was just from the exertion, not because she affected him so much. And now he was lying even to himself.

The police joined the others out in the hall. "What's going on? What happened?" Sergeant Hughes asked.

He wanted the son of a bitch caught who'd done this, so Mack quickly shared what little he knew. He'd thought he was alone in the firehouse, in the showers, when the power had gone out only to come back on moments later with that damn live wire sparking across the water toward him.

"I want everybody out of here," Hughes said with a hard glance at Wynona.

"Sir, I was—"

"Wynona saved my life," Mack said, though he wasn't sure exactly how she'd managed that.

"Braden directed me on where to find the breaker box," Wynona said. "It had been jammed to keep that breaker on…" She gestured toward the one into which that wire had been plugged. "I had to pry it out with a crowbar. I'm afraid I might have damaged evidence."

"You shouldn't have done anything until on-duty officers arrived," Hughes admonished her.

"If she'd done that, I would probably be dead," Mack pointed out. "Unless that's what you wanted, Sergeant."

Hughes's face flushed. "I don't want anyone to die," he said.

"Then let Trooper Wells do her job," Mack suggested.

She drew in a deep breath that seemed to make her grow a couple of inches taller, and she nodded. "Yes," she said, but she was looking at the hotshots who'd been backed into the hall. "Let me do my job."

While they were all talking, Mack slipped through a side door into the locker room. But he wasn't alone in there—the other hotshots gathered around him. The younger guys catcalled a bit, razzing him. And Trick...

His brother looked like he wanted to say something, but before he could, the sergeant stepped inside the room. "I want all of you out of this building," he said. "Not just the shower rooms. Out. Now."

With varying sighs and muttered comments, the other hotshots filed out. And Mack couldn't help but wonder if the sergeant hadn't just let the saboteur go. But then the crime scene techs arrived, and the sergeant turned his attention to directing them.

Where had Wynona gone? Wasn't she supposed to be doing her job? Or had she, like the saboteur, slipped away?

Mack dressed quickly and headed downstairs to Braden's office. That was where the security footage would be, but when he approached the open door, he overheard the conversation between Braden and Wynona and her sergeant.

"The cameras were taken offline somehow," Braden said, his voice gruff with frustration. "There's nothing on here…"

"Not even Wells saving McRooney," Hughes remarked, as if he doubted that she had.

"The power had already gone out before I walked in," Wynona said.

"Through an unlocked door?"

"Yes," she replied.

And Braden groaned.

"You don't know that Stanley left it unlocked," she said, defending the kid.

And making Mack smile that she did. But he wasn't sure Stanley deserved it. He needed to check out the kid a bit more, make sure that he was as sweet as he seemed.

"If he left it unlocked, I'm damn glad that he did," Mack said.

Braden and Hughes turned toward where he was standing in that open doorway. But Wynona didn't look away from the blank screen on Braden's computer, as if she didn't want to face him. And her face was flushed.

Even though she was ignoring him, he continued, "I probably wouldn't have been able to hang on much longer." He had in fact slipped off the wall, but thankfully only after Wynona had gotten the breaker to the wire shut off. With as strong as that current was, it easily would have killed him if it had still been on.

"We'll have our techs go over the footage," Wynona said to Braden, not to him. "See if there's anything they can recover."

"It'll be hard to recover what isn't there," Hughes chimed in. "If the cameras weren't running, they weren't recording."

Mack hated to admit it, but the guy was right. The saboteur was smart and knew the firehouse and even the security system pretty well, which made him think of the hotshots who'd just showed up. Braden had probably called Owen since he was a paramedic. But why had Carl Kozak and Donovan Cunningham and those younger guys showed up? And Trick?

Had they just been responding to the call? Or had one of them been around the firehouse, waiting to see if this act of sabotage had caused a casualty? Instead of banishing them from the scene, Hughes should have been questioning all of them about their whereabouts earlier so he could check their alibis.

The sergeant should have taken Mack's advice to let Wynona do her job, but it was clear now that he intended to run the investigation. He glanced at Mack with more annoyance than anything else, though.

"You've given your statement," he said. "You need to leave now. Let us finish processing the scene."

The radio on his collar sputtered something at him, not about the case but apparently about his wife. The man's face flushed, and he pushed past Mack to step out of the office. He continued down the hall, though, before taking out his cell phone, probably to call his wife.

He definitely should have left the investigation to Wynona. But maybe it was a good thing that he hadn't because she was in danger, too.

While Mack was glad that the techs were here, he didn't think they would find anything that would lead to the saboteur. This person was too damn smart. Smarter than Hughes.

But maybe not Wynona. She'd known Mack was still in

danger and had showed up in time to rescue him. But she wouldn't even look at him.

Braden was studying his face though, and there was concern in his dark eyes. "You should go home, Mack. It's been a hell of a long day for you. I'm going to stick around here until the techs are done—"

"Me, too," Wynona said with a glance past Mack, as if she expected her boss to overhear and insist on taking her off the case.

She had saved Mack, and if she hadn't been careful, she could have died doing that. She was the one he could trust the most right now.

"What about me?" he asked.

"You should leave, like the sergeant said. There is no reason for you to stick around," she replied as if letting him off the hook. Obviously she didn't have to stick around either since she was not in her uniform now. She must have clocked out some time ago. And her boss was here to supervise those techs.

"You're just going to let me drive off on my own?" he asked. "You're not providing police protection?"

"I'm actually off duty," she said, gesturing toward her black sweater and jeans.

But that hadn't stopped her from saving him. And why had she stopped by anyway since she was off duty?

Her lips curved into a slight smile. "And you actually want police protection?" She made a soft sound, like a snort. "I already intended to have a trooper follow you home, one who is currently on duty."

"I want a trooper I can trust," he said. "I want you." He had a feeling from the way her face was so flushed and that she kept looking away, that she wanted him, too.

BLOOD WAS RUSHING through Wynona's entire body now,
not just in her face like when she hadn't been able to stop
blushing over the image of Mack she would never get out
of her mind. Naked. He was so damn big and muscular and
also so strong and fearless.

So why had he wanted a police escort home?

He hadn't seemed fazed at all over nearly getting electrocuted. He hadn't even seemed as angry as she was that
someone kept putting his life and other lives in danger. She
was furious that this saboteur cared so little for human life.
Cared so little about everyone but...

What was the saboteur's motive?

She could almost understand him or her going after Mack
since it was pretty obvious that Braden had hired him for
the sole purpose of finding and stopping the saboteur. Not
that he couldn't fight a fire because he had handled himself
well at the warehouse, too.

He'd survived that explosion. But the saboteur had obviously not been happy about that and had tried again almost
immediately after the warehouse fire failed to kill Mack.
Obviously he or she wasn't going to stop trying until Mack
McRooney was dead.

So it was smart that she followed him home. She pulled
her SUV up behind his truck and hopped out quickly, her
gun drawn to protect him should the shooting start again.
This was why she'd become a cop, to protect people. She'd
figured out that there was no protecting someone from an
illness, like the one that had claimed her parents' lives, but
she could protect people from other threats.

He held up his hands. "Don't shoot," he said, but there
was the rumble of laughter in his deep voice. He obviously
didn't consider her a threat. "I'm not armed."

She rushed him toward the door. "Hurry," she urged him, "get inside." She covered him while he unlocked the door. But then when he pushed it open, she stepped in front of him. It took her only moments to clear the small cabin. "It's safe," she said. The crime scene techs had collected and cleared the house just hours after the shooting. She holstered her weapon. "And why the hell would I have gone to the trouble of saving your life if I intended to shoot you?"

"I was just joking," he said. "Guess not everyone gets my gallows humor."

She enjoyed gallows humor. Usually. But she was so damn on edge. He could have died too many times over the past couple of days, and that bothered her probably way more than it bothered him. Probably way more than it should bother her. He would only be as blasé as he was about danger if he'd been in it many times before.

And while he claimed he was retiring, she wondered if he would be able to stay away from it. Or if that life, and living on the edge like that, had become an addiction to him. Knowing that he wasn't going to stick around was a good reason for her to not get attached or addicted to him. But there was something about him that had fascinated her even before she'd seen him naked. Now that she had…he was all she could see when she closed her eyes.

"You did save my life," he said. "Thank you."

She shrugged. "Just doing my job."

"Is that why you came back to the firehouse?" he asked. And that look was back on his face, the same expression she'd seen on so many other people's faces in Northern Lakes since her training sergeant's arrest.

She groaned now. "Oh, my God, I can't believe you're

still suspicious of me like the rest of your hotshot team. You were here when someone shot at me."

She pointed at the door he'd closed and locked behind them. There was duct tape over the hole the bullet had come through on its way to the board of suspects. She walked over to it now, and her unflattering driver's license picture was still hanging there. The techs had probably gotten a good laugh at seeing her as a suspect.

"And if you're still so suspicious of me, why did you ask for me to specifically be your police protection?" Especially when it was clear he could take care of himself. At least as long as there was no live wire in the shower with him.

"I don't think you tried to hurt me," he said. "But I do have some suspicions about you that I wouldn't if you were more forthcoming."

She felt a little frisson of unease that he already knew her secret. But she forced herself to laugh. "That's interesting coming from you. You won't even tell me who you used to work for."

"The government."

"Which department?"

"Military affairs," he said, but he was grinning slightly now. He knew he was being vague.

"And you're sure nobody from your past could be here in Northern Lakes, coming after you?" she asked. From the scars she'd seen on his muscular body when he'd stood naked in front of her, she knew that he'd had some close scrapes before. That someone else had hurt him. And she suspected that might not have been just physically with the way he seemed to hold himself aloof from the team and even from his brother Trick.

She understood that. Her co-workers probably thought

she was aloof, too. But after what could have been the fatal mistakes in her judgment regarding Gingrich and Jason Cruise, she hadn't known whom to trust, and had decided that it was easier to trust no one.

"I checked," he said, then sighed. "And double-checked. Nobody's looking for me." But his jaw clenched as if he was gritting his teeth when he said it.

"Really?"

"Nobody who wants to kill me," he said.

"An old lover?"

He snorted. "No. I didn't even think my bosses liked me much. But…"

"They want you back on the job," she presumed.

And his jaw seemed to clench tighter, so tightly that a muscle twitched in his cheek.

"Will you go back?" she asked.

He hesitated a moment. A long moment. Then he shook his head.

And her stomach muscles tightened. She suspected that he would go back. If he was able…

First, he had to survive his job here in Northern Lakes, which was as much about catching the saboteur as it was about fighting fires.

"I answered your questions," he said. "Now you answer mine."

She swallowed a groan. She wasn't sure if answering his questions would get her name crossed off his suspect board or if it would get it circled. Right now, the only names he'd circled belonged to hotshots, an interesting collection of the older and the younger ones. She turned her attention to the board to see if he'd crossed off or circled any more names, but Mack's big hands cupped her shoulders.

He turned her toward him and asked, "Will you answer my questions?"

Maybe it was time for it all to come out…

She drew in a breath to brace herself and nodded.

"Did you want me to kiss you last night?"

That was not the question she'd expected, so her mouth dropped open.

"I'm really sorry—"

"Don't apologize," she said. She didn't want him to regret it when she didn't. She didn't want to admit to wanting it, to wanting him, either, but she didn't want him thinking he'd crossed a line. "You would have known if I hadn't wanted you to kiss me. I would have dropped you."

His lips curved into a sexy grin. "And instead, you kissed me back…"

She groaned as heat rushed to her face. "I know. That was unprofessional and stupid." And yet she still didn't regret it. The only thing she really regretted was that it had ended with just the kiss. After what they'd been through, how close they'd both come lately to dying, she hated that she might have denied herself pleasure she'd gone a long time without feeling.

He groaned, too, then sighed. "I don't understand this… attraction…myself."

She flinched. "Ouch."

He chuckled. "You know you're gorgeous," he said so matter-of-factly.

She felt like she used to be pretty, but with her unflattering uniform and all the stress of her job, she hadn't felt as if she'd looked well, let alone pretty, for a while. So his comment affected her, had something that felt suspiciously like butterflies somersaulting in her stomach.

He continued, "But usually I don't notice stuff like that..." He brushed one of his hands over his short dark hair, and it almost looked like there was a slight tremor in his fingers. But after how close he'd come to getting electrocuted, it was understandable.

She was shaky, too, but it had nothing to do with that and everything to do with him.

"You're just...you're impossible to ignore," he said. "There's just something about you...something that draws me closer to you..."

She knew that feeling. She felt the same way about him, like something was pulling her closer to him. And closer... every time they were in the same vicinity.

"Something that fascinates and mystifies me," he said. Then he shook his head. "God, I sound like an idiot. It's just...been a while since I've been involved with anyone."

If she was as jaded as she should have been, she might have thought that he was just putting on an act to get to her, to get her into bed. But she actually believed that he was sincere, and she was touched.

And she was so damn attracted to him, too.

"It's been a while for me, too," she said. "Not that we're involved, we're just trying to find this person..." She gestured behind her at the board. "And not get killed." But they could have been, both of them, too many times. "It looks like you've come closer in your past than you have here..."

His brow furrowed. "What do you mean?"

She pointed at his chest. And his shoulder. And even though he was wearing a shirt now, she could see the ridges of the scars marring the sleek skin that had stretched taut over all those sculpted muscles. "You have so many scars..."

He shrugged. "I've had some close calls in the past," he said. "A helicopter crash. An explosion…"

She shuddered at the thought of how close he'd come to dying. She might never have met him. Even if she hadn't, she had a feeling she would have felt a loss, like the one she felt at the thought of him dying now or leaving again.

He would probably leave again, if those old bosses of his convinced him to come back.

And then she would be alone again. But she wasn't alone now. And she didn't want to be alone tonight.

He stepped a little closer to her, as if he was as drawn as he'd told her he was. "So, when you didn't hand that towel over when I asked, you were just checking out my scars?" he asked, and his lips were curving into that sexy grin again.

She felt a twitch in her lips with the urge to grin back at him. But that wasn't all she wanted to do with him. "Yes, I found your scars very interesting," she said. And she'd wanted to trace each of them with her fingertips and her lips…

And the desire to do that, the desire for him, intensified now to the point she was almost in pain. A pain she knew that he could relieve…

So she reached out, wrapping her hands around his neck to pull his head down to hers. And she kissed him.

The kiss went from a light brush of lips across lips to something much deeper, much more intimate, and passion overwhelmed her. She couldn't remember ever wanting anyone this much.

Maybe it was because of the danger they'd been in and the adrenaline that her feelings were so much more intense than anything she'd ever felt before.

When his tongue slipped inside her mouth, she moaned.

He tasted so good, so dark and rich and dangerous. She found herself tugging at his shirt, pulling it up, so that she could see what she had in the showers. His sleek skin marred with an old scar here and there that had healed over long ago, his muscles so hard and well-defined, like he worked out all the time. Or used them all the time.

"You really have been through hell, haven't you?" she murmured, wondering how he had survived everything that had obviously happened to him, all those explosions and crashes.

"That wasn't even the worst of it," he muttered.

"What was?" she asked, wanting to know him more, to know him deeply.

He shrugged and shook his head. "Something that happened a long time ago…"

"What?" Because she knew that was what had hurt him the most.

"You probably heard the story…how my mom took off, left my dad to raise me and my siblings on his own…"

She instinctively knew that was the biggest scar he carried with him. The emotional one. She carried one of those herself.

As if he was embarrassed by the admission he'd just made, he picked her up, using all those muscles of his, and carried her over to that big bed in one corner of the open cabin. As he laid her down onto it, he followed her, his mouth still fused to hers.

Finally, he pulled back, panting for breath, and asked, "What are we doing?"

"I don't know," she admitted. After the fiasco with Jason, she'd vowed to focus only on her professional life and give up trying to have a personal life. But she'd nearly lost her life the day before in the gunfire.

And today he had nearly lost his.

Twice.

"No, *tell* me," he said, his voice gruff with desire, "tell me to stop if you want to stop."

She shook her head. "I don't want to stop. I want you." And she did, more than she could ever remember wanting anyone. The desire was overwhelming, probably because the man was so overwhelming.

He stepped back then and pulled off the shirt she'd only managed to pull up a bit. Then he unbuckled his belt.

She was so eager to be skin to skin with him that she shucked off her jeans, being careful of the holster strapped to the belt. And then she pulled off her sweater, too, leaving her wearing only her underwear, which she had chosen for comfort. She hadn't considered that anyone else might see her in it. It had been so long since she'd even had a date for coffee or dinner let alone a night in. So she wore a sports bra and granny panties rather than some of the sexy stuff she owned, but with the way he looked at her, she felt sexy. His gaze skimmed over her body like a caress. Then his fingers were there, trailing across her skin.

"You are so silky," he said. "So beautiful…" And his voice was even gruffer with the passion burning in his dark eyes.

He was the beautiful one. The one with the perfect body, the chiseled facial features. Even his head, with his dark hair clipped so short, was perfectly shaped. She trailed her fingers along his jaw, down his neck to his chest. When she pressed her palm to his chest, she could feel how hard his heart was beating, how hard he was breathing. He wanted her as badly as she wanted him.

She wound her arms around him and pulled him down onto the bed with her. But he braced himself, putting his weight on one arm rather than on her. And in that arm, the impressive bicep bulged.

"I'm going to crush you," he said.

"I'm stronger than I look," she said. She hoped that was true, and that she could resist letting this attraction between them become anything more. Because she doubted he was going to stick around after he caught the saboteur. So she would be a fool, again, to get attached to him. To fall for him…

But at the moment she wasn't strong enough to resist the desire she felt for him, the need for him that burned inside her. She arched up and kissed him, his lips, his jaw, and then she slid her mouth down his neck.

He shivered despite the heat of his skin, of his body, and then he kissed her back. First he kissed her lips then he moved his mouth down her throat, and as he did, he pushed up her sports bra and freed her breasts.

She arched up to pull it over her head and toss it down beside the bed. Then she wriggled out of her panties. And there was nothing between them but his boxers. He got rid of them, too.

She sucked in a breath of appreciation and anticipation. The man was big everywhere. She reached for him, but he drew back.

"I'll go right away," he warned her, and he was already gritting his teeth and clenching his jaw as if he was struggling for control.

"I'm ready," she said. "I want you."

But it was as if he didn't believe her because he pushed her back onto the bed. Then he moved his mouth down her body, over her breasts, licking and tugging at her nipples before he moved lower.

He barely touched her, and she felt a rush and quivering of her inner muscles as pleasure streaked through her. The orgasm was intense but still it wasn't enough. She needed him inside her.

She reached for him again, sliding her hand around his pulsating erection.

"Wynona…" He fumbled in the table beside the bed and pulled a condom out of the drawer. The packet tore and then he moved her hand aside to sheathe himself.

She pushed him onto his back, and he chuckled, his chest rumbling so much that the bed vibrated. Then she swung her leg over him, and guided him inside her, taking him deep. A moan slipped through her lips at the intensity, the pleasure…

He felt so damn good. He was exactly what she hadn't known she needed. This was exactly what she hadn't known she needed.

He clutched her hips, helping her find a rhythm as she rocked back and forth and slid up and down. And he thrusted against her. Sweat beaded on his upper lip, as he continued his battle to hold on to control.

But that was a battle she wanted him to lose. She leaned down and kissed his lips, his chin.

His hands moved up to cup her breasts. He flicked his thumbs, rough from hard work, across her nipples. Tension wound from them to her core until it finally snapped, until she finally snapped. She rode him in a fury, screaming his name as this orgasm overwhelmed her.

He clutched her hips again, thrusting deep, and groaned as he pulsed inside her, joining her in that mind-blowing release he'd given her.

She collapsed onto his chest, embarrassed to look at him after how totally she'd lost it. But still she had no second thoughts. No regrets. Because she'd never felt passion like that before…

IT HAD BEEN late when Mack and Wells left the firehouse. It was even later when Braden got home after waiting for the techs to finish up and then for an emergency electrician to fix the damaged breaker box. The Northern Lakes firehouse was the only one within an hour, so it couldn't be shut down for any reason. They had to be able to keep working out of it. But they had to survive the saboteur to be able to keep working.

Braden was surprised he'd survived the night himself, just from exhaustion. But even with as late as it was, when he opened his door, he found Sam on the couch, waiting for him. "You were supposed to go back to bed," he told her.

"I hear Trooper Wells telling you that someone is trying to electrocute my brother and you expect me to go back to sleep?" she asked, her voice a little sharp.

Braden had expected his wife to try to go with him. But Sam was as protective of their baby as she was her family. And she had also heard that Wells was handling the situation, that she'd gotten the breaker out of the box to stop the current of electricity.

"Before I even left, you knew that Wells had everything under control," Braden said. "She made sure he wasn't in any danger."

Wells had saved Mack's life, so it probably shouldn't

have surprised him that Mack had wanted her to follow him home. But still…

"What is it?" she asked. "You said he was okay!"

Braden had called his wife and verified that her brother was fine the minute he'd gotten to the firehouse. "Yes, he is," he said. "He even has police protection for tonight."

Sam narrowed her eyes. "Don't tell me Trooper Wells…"

He nodded.

"Why did he let that happen?" Sam asked. "I know she saved him tonight, but that doesn't mean that she couldn't have been the one who set it up, too. She could still be the saboteur and was just trying to prove her innocence. I don't trust her, and I didn't think Mack did either."

"He was the one who asked her to go home with him."

Sam sucked in a breath. "What?"

Braden shrugged. "She did save his life."

Braden was beginning to wonder if his older brother-in-law was a cat because he certainly seemed to have more than one life. He'd used at least two of them in one night. Braden hoped he wouldn't have to use any more of them. But that hope was dim, because the saboteur seemed fixated on Mack now, on making sure the former special forces operative couldn't catch them.

And they probably knew what Braden had come to realize about his brother-in-law. The only way to stop Mack McRooney was to kill him.

Chapter Thirteen

Sunshine warmed Mack's bare skin and burned like an orange flame behind his closed lids. He opened his eyes to the brightness of the new day, surprised that he'd actually survived the night and not just because of those attacks.

But because of Wynona...

He hadn't been able to get enough of her, and she had seemed just as insatiable as he'd suddenly become. Maybe it was that he'd denied himself a personal life for so long that he hadn't been able to stop reaching for her, kissing her, filling her, and she had done the same, waking him up a couple of times with her lips on his skin.

Just thinking about it had his body tensing up all over again. Hell, he was surprised he'd slept at all and not just because of having sex, but because he usually couldn't sleep around other people. He couldn't let himself be that vulnerable, not in the situations he'd been in during his past missions. But he'd found himself in that situation again here in Northern Lakes.

Danger.

But that threat wasn't just from the saboteur anymore. It was because of *her*. She was standing by the board, studying the pictures he'd tacked to it. She was wearing one of his button-down shirts over her bra and panties. Her red hair was tousled around her shoulders, and she had a cup of coffee in her hand. The scent of fresh ground beans was strong, and he turned his head to find a cup sitting on the table beside the bed.

"You're still here," he mused as he reached for the cup.

"You wanted police protection," she reminded him with a small smile.

"We both know that's not what I wanted." He'd wanted her, and he'd thought that once he had her, maybe he would be able to control his attraction to her. But now it was even more intense, his body even more aware of hers. She was so damn sexy.

And he hoped she was as strong as she'd claimed as well because he had a feeling that they were both going to get hurt one way or another. He didn't want to hurt her like his mom had hurt his dad, like she'd hurt all of them. He didn't want to be like her, but Trick wasn't the only one afraid that Mack was. Mack was afraid, too.

"Thanks for the coffee," he said, and he took a long sip. "Hmm…really thanks."

She chuckled. "You're really welcome."

"And really thanks for coming back here last night," he said.

She grinned, and her green eyes twinkled. "Were you afraid to be alone?"

He sighed. "I think I'm more afraid to not be alone." Which was why he couldn't believe he'd fallen asleep with her in his house, in his bed. On some level he had to trust her, and he wasn't sure why.

Her smile slid away then. "So you're not going to stick around once the saboteur is caught." It wasn't a question—

it was as if she knew something he wasn't certain of himself. Because he really had no idea what he was going to do after the saboteur was caught. He had no plan for retirement beyond making sure that his family was safe by making it up to them for leaving like their mom had.

He shrugged. "I don't know what I'm going to do," he admitted. "I've never let myself really think about the future before…" He'd always just focused on the current mission.

"The saboteur seems to want to make sure that you don't have one," she said. She pointed at all the circled names. "You have some really good suspects here. The arborists especially, given that first attempt on your life. And I think one of them has a dad who's an electrician…"

He did need to catch this bastard. So he had to focus on the mission instead of how damn sexy she was. "I know. I need to figure out who this son of a bitch is." She'd brought up an interesting point about the arborists. Either Bruce or Howie could have cut that tree to fall on him. And they'd been at the warehouse fire and at the firehouse right after the attempt to electrocute him.

"Are you going to cross my name off the suspect list now?" she asked. "Like you have so many of the others?"

"I want to," he said with a yearning that surprised him. But he didn't want to make the same mistake that his dad had, trusting a woman he shouldn't any more than he wanted to be like the woman his dad shouldn't have trusted.

"What's it going to take?" Wynona asked. She could have flirted when she asked it. After last night, after what they'd done to each other, she could have used that to her advantage, to distract him, to persuade him.

He was that susceptible to her. And that scared him nearly as much as that live wire in the shower had…because he wasn't just susceptible—he was vulnerable in a way he'd never been before.

So he drew in a deep breath, bracing himself, then replied, "Honesty."

All the color drained from her face. And his stomach sank with dread and the realization that he'd been right to have doubts about her. She definitely had something to hide.

MACK HAD THROWN that word at her like a challenge. And Wynona didn't shy away from a challenge. Or she wouldn't have gone back to college, got her criminal justice degree and entered the police academy. But she had.

And she knew she had to answer this challenge, too. She just took a moment to compose herself and to get dressed. And when she came out of the bathroom, she told him what she suspected he already knew. "I was seeing Jason Cruise."

"When he was trying to kill Charlie Tillerman?" Mack asked.

Clearly he knew everything since he didn't seem a bit surprised—just cautious and maybe disappointed with a slight bowing to his broad shoulders. He'd pulled on his jeans while she'd showered, but he wasn't wearing a shirt, which just wasn't fair. He made it harder for her to focus.

She shook her head. "No. I only went out with him a few times after he helped me find my house. He was probably only interested in me because of that..." Because of her money. Too many men and so-called friends had been only interested in that when she was growing up, so she'd trusted few people as friends and especially as potential partners. "And I realized quickly that he was a narcissist. But before I did, when he was trying so hard to woo me, I know I told him too much about my job, about things that had been happening on my job."

"The things that had happened to the hotshots?"

She nodded. "I know it was unprofessional and stupid. And I know Michaela Momber already thinks I was taking bribes or something from him. If they saw my house and knew that I'd been going out with him..."

"Most people don't know you were personally involved with him," Mack said. But clearly he had. "Most people question how close you were to Martin Gingrich."

She grimaced. "That makes me sick to think anyone believes I could have been personally involved with him. He was assigned as my training officer. I had no control over that. Just as I have no control over people thinking whatever they will about me." She drew in a deep breath and let it out in a sigh. "And I guess I shouldn't care what these people think of me. I should just want to do my job."

But she cared. Ever since her parents had died she felt so alone, and she'd wanted to make connections here in the town she'd chosen for herself. She'd wanted to make a life here, not just professionally but personally as well.

"I talked to Martin Gingrich," he said. "I visited him in jail."

Gingrich was still awaiting trial, still trying to push it off as long as he could. Wynona almost felt sorry for him. "Did he know about Jason?" Was that who had told Mack?

"Not that he was dead, but he knew you were going out with him," he said. "But I already knew before I talked to ole Marty." He pulled out a magnet and a card.

"He sent me a lot of flowers," she said. "I think love bombing is what that's called." But after last night, after that warehouse exploded, bombing had a whole different connotation for her. Both types were dangerous, though. Thankfully she hadn't been so lonely that she'd fallen for Jason Cruise's phony charm or for him.

Now Mack McRooney…

He wasn't trying to love bomb her unless he considered an interrogation a version of that.

"I kept one of those notes to remind myself of how I shouldn't trust anyone," she explained. "Something I should have learned when I was a kid and people just wanted to get close to me because of my money. That's probably all that Cruise was after, too. My money and the information I stupidly shared with him."

His gaze was intent on her face, as if he was trying to figure out if she was telling the truth now. Or maybe if she actually cared about Jason…

"I didn't have any idea how dangerous he was," she said. "Just like with my former training officer. Is that why you talked to Gingrich about me? You asked him about Jason Cruise? I wasn't even sure he knew that I was seeing the guy. It was just a few dates." She sighed again. "A few too many…"

"I talked to him about you because you're on the suspect board," he said.

"And you didn't find any reason to cross my name off yet?" she asked, and she turned back to the board. Instead of focusing on the crossed-off names, she focused on the others. "Why are Ed Ward, Bruce Abbott, Howie Lane and Carl Kozak on the board with Donovan Cunningham?"

He cocked his head. "That was an unusual way to say that."

"What?"

"Like you're not surprised Donovan isn't crossed off, just the others."

"Donovan Cunningham is a jerk," she said. "And he's raising his hellions to be as misogynistic and entitled as he is. Michaela Momber may not respect me, but I respect her. Her former co-worker did not."

"And you know how that feels," he said. "Thanks to Marty."

She flinched again at the mention of Gingrich. "He's an entitled, misogynistic jerk, too."

"I agree with the entitled," Mack said. "I just don't know about the rest…"

"You don't think he's a jerk?"

"Oh, he is, but he's so bitter and hateful and jealous of Braden, like the guy's still stuck back in high school and can't get over Braden being more popular than he is."

"Well, Gingrich is in jail," she reminded him. She pointed at the board. "And I assume it's because of that that he didn't even make your list?" But he'd talked to the man anyway to check her out. "But yet, here I am…did you think I was working with him? For him?"

"No. If that was the case, he would still be on there," Mack said.

"So he was on it, but you took him off?"

"I checked his visitor logs. Nobody is going to see him, not even his wife," Mack said.

"He cheated on her during their entire marriage, so that's understandable," she said. "And I sure as hell haven't gone to see him either."

"Neither has anyone else from the post," Mack said. "But if they did, maybe they don't sign into the visitor logs if they're on duty. Although the guards claimed that they would have made them." He didn't seem to trust them any more about that than he trusted her, though. "But Gingrich didn't seem to know a lot about what has been happening since he's been incarcerated, so maybe no one has been visiting him. But I don't know for sure, especially when it comes to your new sergeant."

She nodded. "I don't know for sure about him either," she admitted, especially with how reluctant he was to pursue an investigation into the saboteur. "Just like you don't know for sure if you can trust me…" Yet he had no problem sleeping with her, not that they'd done much sleeping. She felt like a fool though for getting so involved with him when they still knew so little about each other.

"Where did your money come from?" he asked.

The coffee she'd drunk churned in her otherwise empty stomach. "I told you just a minute ago that I grew up with that money." Because it had affected every relationship she ever had, tainting it. "But you probably think I took bribes."

"No, I wasn't sure what to think about you," he said. "And I'm very curious. You fascinate me."

Maybe she should have been pleased. Even though they'd slept together, he wasn't bored. That must not have been all he wanted from her: a one-night stand. But then he hadn't known about the money. From seeing the house, he knew she had some. But some people were house poor with huge mortgages. She didn't have a mortgage, and the house had not hurt the balance in her bank accounts. Usually, people tried to latch onto her because of her money, like Jason Cruise had tried.

"That money is the reason that *I* can't trust a lot of people," she admitted.

He grinned then. "You think I'm a gold digger?"

She looked down at his hands. "Where's your shovel?"

"I don't have any interest in your money, Wynona."

"Then why ask about it?"

He sighed. "I don't want it, but I do want to know how you got it."

"Not through bribes," she said. "And I would give up the money in a minute if I could have back what I had to lose to get it." Tears rushed to her eyes, but she furiously blinked them back.

"What—who did you lose?" he asked.

"My parents," she replied. "They were world travelers and picked up some illness that they couldn't beat. They were older when they had me and had underlying health issues. So it hit them hard. They were out of the country when it happened, and I couldn't get to the hospital in time. But the nurses told me they died holding hands." She'd always longed for a love like theirs. But she'd never been able to trust anyone to love her for her and not for that damn money.

And now she had even more.

"Wynona," he said, his dark eyes warming with sympathy. As he started toward her, her cell rang.

She was grateful that it had because if he had hugged her, she probably would have lost it. As it was, she was barely holding back her tears. She drew in a shaky breath and answered, "Trooper Wells..."

"I know you're not on duty yet," Sergeant Hughes said. "But somebody said that they might have seen a vehicle down in a ravine near where you live. I wondered if you could check it out on your way into the post."

"I'll check it out," she said.

She'd already worked last night after clocking out, but she didn't need the money or the overtime. She just needed to make a difference. And right now, she just needed to get the hell away from Mack McRooney before she started falling for him.

TRYING TO KILL them together had not worked. One rescued the other instead of dying with him or her. So the saboteur had had to come up with another plan.

A way to separate them.

And since Trooper Wells seemed like the weaker of the two, she would have to die first. Hopefully there were no recordings of the non-emergency police post number. But if there was, he had disguised his voice, hopefully enough that it couldn't be matched. That nobody would figure out *he* was the one who had spotted what might have been a car deep down in that steep, rocky ravine.

He peered down over the edge now, and as he did, a pebble slipped over the top, struck off the shale side that was as hard as granite, tumbled down and broke apart on the big, jagged rocks at the bottom of the ravine.

If a car had gone down there, the occupants wouldn't have survived. The car would have crumpled and broken apart just like he intended for the trooper's body to crumple and break apart when he tossed her over the edge. It would be easier than shooting her, especially since he'd already returned that gun he'd *borrowed*. He wanted his patsy to have it on him in case it was traced back to him. He hadn't wanted him to be able to claim it was stolen, even though it had been.

The patsy hadn't even noticed it was gone. And as far as he knew, it hadn't been traced back yet. Maybe the crime lab was slower than what they showed on TV.

But the saboteur couldn't be slow. He had to get rid of

Wells and McRooney before they could figure it out, before they could figure out who he was: the saboteur.

When Wells showed up at this possible accident site, she was definitely going to have an accident of her own.

A fatal one.

And this time, nobody would be able to save her.

She was going to die. Then once she was dead, he would go after Mack McRooney next. And once the hotshot ex-military man was out of his way, he would take down everyone else he'd been wanting to take down, everyone else who deserved to die.

Chapter Fourteen

Mack hated how quickly and easily Wynona had left him. Obviously, she hadn't wanted to answer any more of his questions. And he couldn't blame her.

He'd pried and pushed even though he knew in his gut she had nothing to do with the sabotage. He didn't have his brother-in-law's rumored sixth sense about things, but Mack had learned over the years and through the dangerous missions that he'd had to trust his gut.

But in this case, Mack had more than that to go on. Wynona had proved last night and the night before that she couldn't be the saboteur. Otherwise, she wouldn't have rescued him, and she wouldn't have been in danger herself. Those instances proved she was innocent, but still he wanted some reason not to trust her.

Some reason to keep his distance from her. But when he'd learned more about her, he wanted to get closer. He wanted to console her, to comfort her…but that brought him little comfort. He didn't want to get attached to her because he always tried to stay unattached.

So that he didn't let people down who loved him like their mother had let them down. And like he'd already let down his family.

It was almost easier to deal with Trick's resentment than it was to deal with Sam. She looked so much like their mother that he felt better keeping his distance from her. But her last text had left him no choice, so he crossed the small front porch and knocked on the door to her and Braden's house.

"If that's you, you better damn well not be knocking," she called out, her voice sharp and grumpy sounding.

He breathed deep through his nostrils, in and out, calming himself so that he wouldn't react as he always did to seeing Sam. Then he turned the knob and pushed open the door. "I'm assuming I'm *you*, or did you summon someone else here?" he asked.

She didn't get up from where she was lying on the couch, a bunch of pillows stacked all around her. She should have been able to see out the front windows and watched him walking up, unless she'd been napping.

Alarm shot through him. "Are you okay?"

"No," she fairly growled. "I'm pissed at you, and I'm pissed at this nephew of yours."

"What did he do?" he asked. "He's not even out yet."

"That's why he's pissing me off," she said. "He was supposed to be out over a week ago."

"What does your doctor say?"

"That maybe the dates were off, that maybe we should just wait another week…" She tried to shift on the couch, but her belly looked like it was holding her down.

"I should have called your bluff," he said. "You wouldn't have been able to come to me if I hadn't come to you."

She smiled then. "Sucker. If I could move around, I would be out at the warehouse, checking for signs of arson."

"It was arson," he said. He doubted there was any other explanation.

"Then it was definitely a trap," she said. "And the live wire in the shower was, too."

He nearly shuddered but resisted the urge. He didn't want to upset her, especially now. That was why he'd shown up even though seeing her took him back into the past when he was a kid. When their mom had been pregnant with either Sam or Trick, she'd looked exactly like Sam did now. He'd loved her so much, but she'd had no problem just walking away from all of them.

He'd done the same thing, though, and he still loved his siblings and his dad. He wasn't always sure the feelings were reciprocated anymore. At least not with Trick.

Sam still loved him. And he loved her. While she looked so much like their mother, she was nothing like her. She was probably the most like their father of any of them. Smart. Strong. Good.

If only he could be confident that he was the same...

But sometimes he wasn't even confident he was Mack McRooney's real kid. And having all that doubt just fed into his doubts about himself.

It was safer for him to focus on his career, no matter how dangerous it was, than to focus on his personal life. Maybe he shouldn't have retired. And he might not have...

If he hadn't known that his sister and his brother had been in danger.

"You should not be worrying about any of this," he admonished her. He'd retired so that she wouldn't have to worry or put herself in danger. He would do it instead. "You're supposed to be resting, getting ready for that baby."

"He's determined to never come out," Sam said with a ragged sigh.

"He has no idea how good he's going to have it out here," Mack said. "How much he's going to be spoiled."

"I won't spoil him."

"I was talking about Braden," he said.

She smiled with such love for her husband that Mack felt a twinge in his chest. Not of envy like other people seemed to feel for Braden, if Gingrich was telling the truth that he wasn't the only one. No, Mack was worried about his sister, worried that she would be heartbroken if something happened to her husband.

And Mack's gut was beginning to tell him that this saboteur was after more than him and Wynona. This saboteur was maybe after Braden or his job or his downfall or something.

But if someone really wanted to hurt Braden, they would go after the people he loved more than anyone else in the world. His wife and unborn baby.

"Uh oh, you have that look," Sam said then sighed.

"What look?"

"The look you get just before you head off to something dangerous."

"You think I looked scared?" he asked. Because he had a feeling that was why he'd taken off all those years ago, because he'd been scared of disappointing the people he loved, like their mother had. But he'd probably disappointed them more by leaving than he would have done had he tried to stay.

Could he stay anywhere? Wynona had asked him what he was going to do once the saboteur was caught, and he really had no idea. But the thought of staying anywhere unsettled him.

Sam stared up at him, her head cocked and hair brushing

across her cheek. She reminded him of Wynona studying the board so intently, trying to figure out who the saboteur was. Sam's blue eyes widened. "Now you look scared."

Wynona scared the crap out of him. No. The way he felt about Wynona scared the crap out of him. But he wasn't about to talk to his sister about *her*.

"I'm worried about you," he admitted. "Are you being careful?"

She sighed a long-suffering sigh. "Yes, I'm staying off my swollen feet as much as possible. I'm sleeping just about all the time...unless fear for my idiot brothers keeps me up."

"I'm sorry about that," he said sincerely. "I did not mean to worry you."

"I should be used to it." She sighed again but softer now. "I've been worrying about you since you left home all those years ago, Mack. I was scared I would never see you again. And then you came here to help me and I'm even more worried that I'm going to lose you. And I'm sorry about that, about talking you into this. You're supposed to be retired."

He snorted. "I retired from that career." From danger he'd thought, but he realized that wasn't truly possible. There was danger everywhere, no matter what career one had. There was danger just sitting home alone like Sam. "I wasn't going to spend the rest of my days fishing and drinking beer."

"Were you going to spend it fighting fires?" she asked.

He hadn't chosen to go into the family business like everyone else had. In fact, Mack had left to escape from that because as a kid, he'd blamed it for driving their mother away. But he knew now it hadn't had anything to do with the hotshots.

He shrugged. "I don't mind putting out fires," he said.

Or starting one like he had with Wynona Wells. That fire was probably going to burn him more than any physical one could. He'd never experienced that intense passion or pleasure before.

"I want to get over to the warehouse and check it out," she said.

"You need to take it easy," he reiterated. "And you need to be *careful*, Sam."

She smiled. "Now you sound like Braden and Trick. They're worried about me over more than the pregnancy. And like I told both of them, it doesn't matter how pregnant I am, I can still take care of myself." She lifted one of the pillows propped around her and showed him the holstered gun she'd stashed beneath it.

He chuckled as pride for her suffused him. "You are a badass, little sister."

"I hope you didn't think you were the only one in the family," she said.

"Nope. Dad's the OG," he said. He'd had to be to do what he'd done, raising his kids alone while training so many hot-shots. Most of the ones that Mack was working with now had been trained by Mack Senior. That was why Braden's team was so good. So hopefully one of them wasn't the sab-oteur, but that didn't leave many other options on his ever-narrowing list of suspects.

Stanley and Wynona.

And he felt like Wynona was in more danger than she posed to anyone. Like even now, he had a strange feeling about the call she'd taken that morning to check on some-thing on her way to work.

Had that been as innocent as it sounded?

Or was it a trap?

THE BLOW KNOCKED Braden back as he was struck walking inside his own house.

"Sorry," Mack said after colliding with him in the doorway. "I was just on my way out." And true to his word, he rushed across the porch, down the steps and out to the truck parked at the curb.

Braden stared after him for a second before walking in to greet his wife. "Was it something you said?" he teased her.

She shrugged. "I don't know why he suddenly had to leave in such a hurry." She narrowed her eyes as she stared up at him. "Or why you've come back in such a hurry..."

"I can't stay away from you," he said. Because he was so damn scared of losing her, of something happening to her like what kept happening to the hotshots.

"Like I just had to tell my big brother, I can take care of myself." She tapped the pillow under which she kept her gun.

So Braden wasn't the only one worried about Sam being in danger. Mack was too. Mack's investigation was probably leading him to the same conclusion that Braden was drawing, that no matter who the saboteur went after, the person was ultimately trying to destroy Braden.

WYNONA KNEW THE area where the caller had reported seeing a vehicle. Not only did she pass it every day on her way from her house to the state police post, but it was also where Stanley had been found after the arsonist tried to kill him over a year ago. She'd been new to the job then, acting more as a ride-along than even as a trainee.

That was the only time she'd actually stopped and studied the area, while they'd been looking for evidence to lead them to the arsonist. But she remembered how dangerous the ravine was, how steep the sides.

After leaving Mack, she'd headed straight there, parked along the road, and was once again studying that ravine. It was even more dangerous than she remembered. After another winter and more rains, there was no slope down, just a sheer drop off, and the side of the ravine by the road was shale and rock, not just dirt. And there were big boulders poking out of the grass and underbrush at the bottom of the pit.

She wasn't sure what had formed the ravine. Had there once been a river flowing through it, or given how much rock was in it, had the area been mined for something? For iron or copper or granite? The side of the ravine and the rocks at the bottom looked that hard, like granite.

Like Mack McRooney's body. Heat rushed through her as memories from last night played through her mind, like they had played with each other in that big bed of his.

She had never before experienced anything like that. She'd never felt as much pleasure as he'd given her. But she knew that it hadn't been smart. They were in danger and couldn't afford any distractions.

And knowing that he was unlikely to stick around Northern Lakes once the saboteur was caught, falling for him would cause her as much pain as if she fell into this ravine.

But she wouldn't let herself worry about that.

Right now, she had to find this vehicle. But from the road, she couldn't see anything down below except those rocks and trees and brush at the bottom. There was no glint of the sun off glass or metal.

No tire marks going off the road and over the edge.

If someone had been driving past here, as she did nearly

every day, how had they even seen into the ravine? She hadn't been able to see anything from her vehicle. She hadn't been able to see anything until she'd parked and walked to the edge.

And even standing at the very end of the solid ground before it dropped away, she couldn't see anything like the caller had described to dispatch. There was absolutely no sign of a car accident in this area.

Maybe dispatch had gotten the area wrong?

Or her sergeant had when he called her?

She reached for her collar and realized that her radio wasn't there. She was still in the sweater and jeans she'd worn to Mack's last night but that she hadn't worn for long once she'd gotten there.

She still didn't know if being with him had been a mistake, or if it would have been more of a mistake if she hadn't given in to her desire for him. He could have died twice last night. First at the warehouse and then in the firehouse showers. She could have died, too, had he not called out and warned her about the live wire. And maybe all those brushes with death had just been too much.

She'd either lost her mind, or she'd been caught up in the rush of adrenaline and attraction. He was too much. And he made her feel too much. She wasn't ready to fall for anyone.

To risk her heart.

She knew all too well how it felt to love someone and lose them. She'd lost her parents much too soon.

And with the life he led, and the scars he carried from that life, Mack was too big a risk. Whoever fell for him would probably lose him one day, either because he took off like his mother had or because he came out of retirement to return to his dangerous life. A life that he wouldn't be able to survive forever.

And she still had so much to figure out in her life, with her career, with trying to find this saboteur before *anyone* died.

Now was not the time for her to be seeing *anyone*. But especially not *him*.

Because once again, he'd distracted her even though he wasn't here. She couldn't stop thinking about him, but she had to focus.

She drew in a shaky breath and reached into her pocket for her cell. She needed to call dispatch and verify the location where the caller claimed they'd seen the wreckage.

But when she pulled the phone from her pocket, hands pressed against her back, shoving her. First the cell flew out of her grasp, flying over the edge and down onto those rocks below where it broke apart into pieces.

Then her feet skidded and slipped across that loose gravel at the top of the ravine and suddenly Wynona was the one going over the edge.

And like her cell phone, would she be broken on the rocks below?

Chapter Fifteen

Mack's call to Wynona's sergeant hadn't relieved that horrible feeling he had. In fact, it had only confirmed to him that he'd been right to worry about her.

She hadn't shown up at the police post or even checked in yet from the site of the supposed accident that had been reported. If she'd found something, she would have called in for help.

If she'd been able to make that call...

Maybe Mack should have requested that the sergeant send a police unit to the scene where he'd sent Wynona. But he couldn't help but think that the sergeant was the only reason Wynona had gone out there at all. And it was only his word that an actual report had come in...

Mack wasn't entirely sure if he should trust Hughes or anyone else who worked for him with Wynona. She was in a worse situation with her job than he was with his. At least he had a few people he could trust on his team—Rory and Ethan and maybe Trick depending on how pissed his little brother was at him. And he could definitely trust his boss, Braden.

Because Mack couldn't trust Wynona's boss, he wasn't sure if the sergeant had even told him the right road and location for him to find her. He figured he'd driven past where he was supposed to be when he caught a glimpse of a vehicle out of his side mirror.

It wasn't in the ravine, though. It was parked alongside the other side of the road where there was more than just the gravel shoulder. There was some grass on which she'd parked her vehicle. Hers was the only one there, so the pressure on his chest eased some.

But then he noticed something glinting farther out in the trees beyond that grass. Like metal or…

Was someone out there with a gun? Or was that where the vehicle was that the caller had seen?

But the ravine was on the other side of the road…

Still feeling uneasy, Mack reached down and pulled out his weapon from beneath the driver's seat. He had to be careful. Had to make sure that, if this was a trap, he didn't fall into it, too.

But if it was a trap, it might already be too late for Wynona.

AFTER THOSE HANDS on her back had propelled Wynona over the edge, she'd reached out and grasped at whatever she could on the side of that rocky wall of the ravine. Her fingers were scraped and bleeding, but she'd found the roots of something that had been strong enough to break through the shale. Hopefully the roots would be strong enough to hold her weight. While she dangled, she shifted her feet around, trying to find a toehold as well to ease the stress on her aching shoulders and her scratched up hands.

Blood oozed from the scratches and soaked into those roots she grasped. Hopefully the blood didn't loosen them, didn't make them weaker or her weaker.

But she wasn't bleeding much.

Yet.

If she fell...

She glanced down below her, and now she saw a glint, the sun reflecting off the broken pieces of her cell phone. She didn't want to wind up like that. But she couldn't call anyone for help now.

Not that she knew who she would call...

She couldn't trust anyone at her work or any hotshot either. And Mack...

She could trust Mack. Probably. With her life, just not with her heart.

But without her phone, she couldn't call him. She couldn't reach out for help. She was even afraid to yell because whoever had pushed her might be up there yet. And if whoever shoved her was the same person who'd shot at her, she knew that they had a gun.

And shooting her now would be like shooting fish in a barrel. There was no way that they could miss.

Even when she heard an engine on the road above her, she didn't call out. She hadn't seen a vehicle earlier when she'd been looking for the one in the ravine. So whoever had pushed her had parked somewhere out of sight.

And maybe now, after retrieving their vehicle, they were coming back to make sure she'd fallen all the way down. And when they saw that she hadn't...

She had no doubt that they would make sure she fell. Either by shooting her or reaching out to push her off the tree roots. She could probably be reached from the top yet if someone had long arms.

She could be rescued if whoever was up there with the idling vehicle was not the person who'd deliberately lured her here with that false report to the police. She had no doubt now that this had been a trap.

Like the burning warehouse and the shower had been traps for Mack.

At least he hadn't come with her. Because she had no doubt that if they were both here, the saboteur would start shooting for sure.

And now, along with the hum of that idling engine, she heard something else. Like the soft cock of a gun...

Then the crunch of gravel as someone started across the shoulder of the road toward the ravine.

She held her breath, holding back a scream of frustration. She was so helpless, and she hated it. If she reached for her weapon now, she'd have to let go of the root with one hand...

And she was afraid that one hand wouldn't be enough to hold up her weight. But as those footsteps got louder and closer, she knew she had to be able to defend herself. So she tightened her grasp with her left hand, shoved the toes of her boots hard against the shale wall of the ravine, and took one hand loose to reach for her holster.

But the movement had her left hand slipping down the root.

A scream tore free of her throat with the horrifying certainty that she was about to fall. That the person coming toward her wasn't even going to have to shoot her to kill her.

THE SABOTEUR QUIETLY CURSED. He should have made damn certain that she'd fallen all the way into the ravine. But he hadn't wanted Wells to see his face just in case she survived the fall.

Hell, he should have shot her and dumped her body down

there, but after stashing the patsy's weapon back in their truck, he hadn't dared to use one of his own. But if he couldn't kill the trooper and McRooney any other way, he might not have a choice.

But she had to have died. There was no way that she could survive a fall into that ravine. He hadn't actually killed anyone yet despite having made some attempts lately on her life and on Mack McRooney's life.

He knew that he would have to kill, but maybe just hurting her would have been good enough to get her out of his way. And then he could kill the person that he knew he needed to kill. The one who was going to mess up his whole plan if McRooney wasn't stopped.

Mack McRooney might have been a military hero if the gossip about him was true. And according to Rory Van-Dam, it was. But he was no hotshot.

At least his brother Trick had been trained and was working as one before his nepotism hire onto the team to replace Dirk Brown.

Using Dirk's death to his advantage was just one more thing Braden had done that proved he had never deserved to be superintendent. He didn't care about the team at all, or he would have stepped down months ago.

He would have been able to figure out that was all it would have taken for this to end. His resignation.

But now it was going to take a life.

His brother-in-law's.

Through the trees where he'd parked well off the road, he could see Mack's truck where it sat with its engine idling while the new hotshot started across the road toward the ravine.

Of course McRooney was here to rush to Trooper Wells's rescue just as he had the other night. But instead of rescuing her, he was going to die with her.

Chapter Sixteen

Mack approached the ravine with caution, his gun drawn, as his stomach clenched with dread. Where the hell was she?

She wasn't on the road anywhere that he could see her. She wasn't walking along the edge, looking into the ravine for the wreckage her sergeant claimed someone had seen down there. Had a vehicle struck her and hit her so hard that she'd fallen over the edge?

He glanced back over his shoulder. Or was she in the woods where he'd seen that reflection bounce off something metallic?

Maybe she'd had seen that, too, and had gone to investigate. He probably should check that out as well. But something compelled him closer to the edge of the ravine. He wanted to at least look inside the deep gorge and investigate if that wrecked car someone had reported was actually there. When he looked down, he caught another reflection like he had in the woods. But it was small, just something glinting among the boulders and the brush.

Then he heard the scream, and he looked at the side and saw her dangling there from one hand. "Oh, my God, Wynona!" Her hand was slipping down whatever she was clutching on the side of the rock.

Her other hand must have already slipped off it because she was wriggling now, trying to reach the branch or roots that she was clutching, that was about the only thing keeping her from plummeting to the bottom.

He holstered his weapon and dropped down to his stomach along the top. His legs were probably out in the road, but he didn't care. He didn't care about anything except for saving her.

But her fingers kept slipping, and he was about to lose her, maybe forever if she hit those rocks below. He leaned far over the edge, stretching as much as he could without sliding off. He reached down and clasped her wrist just as her fingers lost their grip.

His shoulder jerked with her weight as her body swung against the side of the ravine. She grimaced as she hit the rocky edge. But then she was reaching again, trying to catch those roots.

He tightened his hold on her wrist, locking his fingers around it. "Oh, my God," he muttered again. "What the hell happened?"

And how was he going to get her up?

He was strong, and she wasn't that heavy, but the way she was dangling like dead weight pulled at his muscles, pulled at his body. He started sliding across the gravel at the top, leaning out dangerously far.

So far that he might slip and fall headfirst down into that gorge. And if he did, he would take her with him, sending them both down onto those rocks.

"I got pushed," she said between pants. "Did you see anyone?"

He thought of that glint between the trees but shook his

head. "I've got to get you back up here. Can you get a foot-hold? Anything?"

"I… I had some roots…"

From the sweat beading on her forehead and dampening her hair, he could tell she'd been hanging on for a while. And when she reached her free hand up, trying to clasp those roots again, her arm was shaking.

Her muscles were obviously cramping. And he was afraid that his would soon, too, if he didn't hoist her up and over the edge. His legs slipped a bit more, the gravel grinding and biting through his jeans.

He flinched now. "Let me try to get your other hand," he said. Because he was so damn afraid that he was about to lose his grasp on her wrist.

Like her face, his hand was starting to sweat or maybe her wrist was sweating, her skin getting so slippery that he wasn't sure he could hold onto her much longer. He had to do something. He couldn't lose her.

WYNONA HADN'T FELT this helpless since she had lost her parents. She hadn't been able to do anything to save them or to even ease their suffering. Because of how far away they'd traveled and how remote the hospital was, she hadn't even been notified of their illnesses until they were too sick. She'd made it to the hospital before they died, but because of the contagiousness of their disease, she hadn't been allowed to see them. She hadn't been able to say goodbye to them or tell them that she loved them. At least they'd had each other, and according to the nurses, they'd been holding hands when they passed away within min-utes of each other.

She wanted a love like that one day, a love like her parents had had. But Mack wasn't holding onto her out of love. He was holding onto her because he was a hero, and that was what heroes did: rescued people.

That was why she'd wanted to become a cop—to be the hero for others that she hadn't been able to be for the ones she'd loved the most.

But she was afraid that she was about to be the reason Mack got hurt, too. He was leaning so far over the edge that eventually he was going to fall off. And then neither of them would be able to rescue anyone else ever again.

She'd already slipped too far down to reach the roots anymore. And the side of the ravine she kept slamming against was rock hard and slippery now. It must have been granite or something mined here that made it difficult for her to get a toehold on anything.

She didn't want to give up, but she didn't know how to get out of the ravine. Maybe going down was the only way to make her way out somewhere where it wasn't as steep as it was here. She would just have to figure out a way to slow her descent.

Her hands were already bleeding, and her jeans were torn. Hopefully the rock wall wouldn't tear her up anymore and hopefully she wouldn't hit one of those boulders like her phone had.

But she'd rather take her chances sliding down into the ravine than risk pulling Mack into it with her. He would go down headfirst and get hurt far worse than she would.

"You have to let me go," she said, "or you're going to fall."

"I'm not letting you go," Mack said, his jaw clenched so hard that there was a muscle twitching in his cheek. And a vein was popping out on his forehead, too, and another one zigzagged along his temple. "Come on, give me your other hand…" He held out his other hand toward her. "If I have both of them, I can try to hoist you up."

He was too far over the side already. If she grabbed his other hand, she was afraid that she would just be pulling him down with her. But if she tried to wriggle her wrist free of his grasp, she was afraid that would send him toppling over with her, too.

"If you let me go, I'll just slide down," she said. "I'll be fine." She hoped. "But if you fall headfirst down…" He would free fall right into one of those boulders, and his head would break like her cell.

"You're already bleeding," he said. "You're already hurt. Now give me your damn hand!"

He must have slipped out even farther because it was as if a shadow fell across her. She looked up with alarm, and she saw that the shadow had fallen across him, too.

Whoever had pushed her over the edge had returned, probably to make sure she was dead. And now they would have an opportunity to get rid of him, too.

"Mack!" she yelled. "You're in danger! Someone's behind you."

"I'm not letting go," he growled.

Then she would have to protect him if it was the last thing she did. With her free hand she reached again for her holster, and this time she drew her weapon and pointed it right over the edge at whoever the hell was sneaking up on Mack.

While he was trying to save her, she intended to save him. And if she could hit the saboteur, she would be protecting Mack and the rest of Northern Lakes from any more of the saboteur's dangerous games.

TRICK'S CELL RANG, and he grimaced as he saw who was calling. Maybe it was good news, though. Maybe Sam had gone into labor and his new nephew was here. "Hey, Braden," he answered.

"Hey," Braden said, and his voice was low as if he was whispering.

Maybe Sam was sleeping. Or Braden didn't want her to hear him.

And the dread that he'd felt when his phone had initially lit up with his brother-in-law's contact came back. "What is it?" he asked. "A fire?"

The warehouse fire had been a monster. And that explosion...

And then the stunt with the stripped wire in the shower that...

Mack had survived the explosion though. And then, of all people, Trooper Wells had rescued him at the firehouse, saving him from electrocution.

He shuddered and Henrietta, sitting next to him in that corner booth at the Filling Station, grabbed his free hand, already offering him comfort. Like him, she must have figured he would need it.

"No, no, no fire, at least I don't think so," Braden said. "It might be nothing..."

Might be.

Probably wasn't.

Trick didn't think Braden's sixth sense was just for fires anymore. Sometimes the superintendent just seemed to know when one of the team was in danger whether it had to do with a fire or not.

"What is it?" Trick asked, bracing himself.

"Have you seen your brother?"

Trick's heart pounded faster with fear. He'd known that call was about Mack. He cleared his throat to reply, "No, I haven't."

But he should have. After Mack had two near misses the day before, Trick should have talked to him. But those near misses were like getting all his childhood fears confirmed, that everyone he cared about was going to leave him.

As if she read his mind, Henrietta's grasp on his hand tightened. She wasn't leaving him.

"Yeah, of course, you wouldn't have seen him," Braden muttered. "You're in St. Paul with Hank—"

"No, Henrietta and I didn't go back to St. Paul last night after the warehouse fire and not after the call went out about the showers." He'd wanted to be close in case his brother needed him. In case something happened again. And it sounded like maybe it had. "We stayed at her cottage last night. We're at the Filling Station now."

"So Mack's not there?"

"Nobody is," Trick said. But it was late for breakfast and early for lunch. That was probably why the bar was so dead even though they served three meals in addition to drinks. "Why are you looking for Mack?" he asked over the pounding of his heart. "What happened?"

"Probably nothing," Braden said. "I just...he was leaving here when I brought Sam breakfast this morning. And he was in a really big hurry when he left, and now he won't pick up his phone."

Trick cursed. Not that it was out of character for Mack to ghost them. He'd ghosted them most of his adult life, just like their mother had. That was why he was so angry with Mack, not because he'd left but because he hadn't come back.

Until now…

Until he was in as much danger here as he'd been wherever he'd been all those years he'd been gone. So Trick understood Braden's concern because this time, Mack failing to pick up his cell felt different to him, too.

This felt like the saboteur again.

Had Mack found him or her?

Or had the saboteur found him? And had they managed this time to get rid of him for good?

Chapter Seventeen

"What the hell!" Mack exclaimed.

When she pulled that gun, he nearly lost his grasp on her wrist and just managed to catch it with his other hand before he lost her completely. But as he grabbed for her, he slipped farther over the side, sending gravel toppling down with him, onto her.

She flinched and cursed. "Let go of me!" she shouted. "You have to!"

But he kept sliding over that edge until someone grabbed him. That was why Wynona had drawn her weapon. Someone had come up behind him, and he'd been so focused on her that he hadn't heard them until she'd called out. But if he wanted to defend himself, he had to let her go. And he couldn't bring himself to do that.

Then a deep, familiar voice rumbled, "What the hell are you doing? I nearly ran you over!"

"Ethan!" Mack exclaimed.

"Rory's here, too. He saw your legs or you'd be under my truck tires right now," Ethan said.

"Hang onto him," Rory said as he plopped down on his stomach beside Mack. "What the hell is going on with you two? Is she trying to jump?"

"Someone pushed me!" Wynona said.

"Maybe because you were trying to shoot them," Rory remarked.

"I… I just pulled this…" And now it was as if she didn't know what to do with it.

"You don't need it," Mack said.

"I'm not dropping it," she said. "I slid the safety off…"

Rory groaned. "Great. Two people hanging off the edge and a loaded gun about to go off, too." He jumped up, and Mack thought for a moment that his old military buddy was deserting him.

Ethan must have thought the same thing because he said, "Uh, I could use a little help here. He weighs more than I do. Where the hell are you—"

But then Rory was back with some ropes and a harness. And between the four of them, they managed to get Wynona up from the edge without them or the gun going off.

But once they were lying in the road, Mack could see the scrapes and bruises on her, some from his hand where he'd gripped her wrist so tightly. She rubbed at it, almost absentmindedly, smearing blood across her skin.

"Let me call Owen," Rory said, "and get him in the rig over here to check you guys out."

"We should just take them to the hospital," Ethan said as he studied them both, his face tight with concern.

"I'm fine," Mack said, and he barely had a scratch on him. "But Wynona should get checked out."

"Wynona?" Rory muttered the question as if he hadn't known her first name, or maybe he was just surprised that Mack had used it.

She shook her head. "No…" She released a shaky breath and shook her head again.

Mack was worried that she might have gone into shock. "We definitely need to get you to the hospital," he said.

"No, I have to call this in, report what happened here—"

"You can call it in on the way to the hospital," Mack suggested.

"I just have some scrapes and bruises," she said, dismissing her injuries. "Nothing serious."

"Your wrist could be sprained," Ethan said. "I don't think Mack here knows his own strength." Sommerly was a big guy, too, like Mack. He would know how easy it was for them to hurt someone without meaning to.

"I don't care if he broke it," Wynona said. "He saved my life." She smiled at the other hotshots, her green eyes sparkling a bit with tears of emotion. "And so did you two. Thank you."

Warmth spread through Mack's chest. Maybe it was just relief that she was all right. Or maybe it was appreciation for her gratitude. Or maybe it was because she was so beautiful. And while he hadn't gone over that edge, he still felt a bit like he was falling. But he couldn't let himself do that for so many reasons.

He turned toward the other two hotshots. "What were you doing out here? Does Braden have you following me?"

Rory shook his head. "Yeah, like that would work, like anyone could follow you without you noticing. No. We were out on this road because we were heading to Donovan Cunningham's place to talk to him."

Wynona perked up then. "About what?"

"Just going to ask him some questions," the former DEA agent remarked.

Mack shouldn't have been surprised that Rory was looking for the saboteur, and Wynona didn't seem to be either.

But after the person had nearly killed him, Rory had to want justice and answers.

She asked, "So he's your suspect for the saboteur?"

"That's who she suspects, too," Mack said, and she shot him a look.

He shrugged. "Like they don't know what I'm doing here? Or that they don't know what you want to do?"

"I want to catch the saboteur," she said.

"Is that who pushed you?" Rory asked. "Did you see him?"

Her face flushed a bright pink and she shook her head again. "No. I was told there was a car down in the ravine and I was looking for it when someone pushed me from behind."

Ethan sucked in a breath.

Rory nodded. "Well, at least we can eliminate you as a suspect now, Trooper Wells."

She laughed instead of being offended like she'd seemed when she'd seen her picture among his other suspects. Then she turned toward Mack. "Going to take my mugshot off your board now?"

"Board?" Ethan asked.

"Mugshot?" Rory repeated.

"Her DMV photo," Mack said. "The trooper has no record and no reason to go after the hotshots." He'd believed that even before someone had tried to push her into the ravine. He'd believed it before he slept with her. He must have somehow instinctively known that she was a good person, or he wouldn't have been able to fall asleep with her in his house, in his bed. "So yeah, I will be taking your photo down from the board and crossing out your name."

"What is this board?" Ethan asked. He was obviously

stuck on it. "Is this like a murder board the detectives use on TV?"

She nodded. "Yes, Mack thinks he's a detective instead of a hotshot."

"With the saboteur after us, every hotshot has become a detective," Ethan said.

"Or you could let the police handle it," Wynona suggested, but with a teasing smile. "Not that I'm not damn happy that you guys were doing some investigating on your own today."

Mack chuckled. He liked seeing her like this, especially with guys he considered friends. She was relaxed and friendly instead of the uptight trooper they'd previously thought she was. He'd somehow always known that was who she really was. Just like he wasn't as unemotional and unattached as he pretended to be.

"So who's your prime suspect?" Rory asked him.

"Well, there's me," Wynona answered before he could. "But you two can rest assured your names were crossed out right away. You didn't get circled."

Rory chuckled. "I would hope not after all we've been through." He extended his hand down to help Mack up from the ground.

Ethan reached out to help Wynona up. She flinched when he touched her, and given how good-looking the guy was, it wasn't because she was repulsed. She was hurt.

"If you won't go to the hospital, at least let us find Owen," Mack said. He was counting on the paramedic telling her she needed an X-ray to make sure that he hadn't broken anything when he'd held her so tightly. Not that he wanted to know—he would feel horrible if he had hurt her however inadvertently.

"Owen's out here somewhere checking out Bruce and Howie," Rory said. "He should be close. They were supposed to be doing an arborist job around here cutting down trees around someone's cabin."

"So they were in the area," Wynona mused, totally focused on the investigation instead of herself. "And I assume Owen is checking them out because he figures that stunt with Mack and the tree could have been one of them?"

Rory nodded as he pulled out his cell to call the paramedic. "Yeah, Bruce's dad is an electrician, so he could have been responsible for the thing in the showers, too."

"He was certainly amused by it," Mack said. "But let's put the investigation on hold now and get Owen to check out Wynona's arm."

"I need to call this latest incident in to the police post, too," Wynona said. "But I need to use someone's phone. Mine fell…"

When she'd fallen…

While Rory made the call to Owen, Mack checked his cell and found a bunch of missed calls from Braden and Trick. Instead of calling them back, he shot them a text. I'm good. Talk later.

But he wasn't good, not after yet another close call, one where he could have lost Wynona. Where she could have slipped right through his fingers…

He handed his cell over to her to call the police, and then he stepped closer to the edge and looked over to where the pieces of metal and glass reflected back light from down below. That was probably what was left of her cell. She could have fallen there on those rocks.

She'd wanted him to let her go, and he knew why. She'd been trying to protect him. To save him…

She really was an incredible person, determined and generous and self-sacrificing. And so damn beautiful that his chest ached just looking at her when moments ago she'd been talking and joking with his friends.

And even though they were on solid ground now, he still felt like he was falling. Maybe not into a ravine, but maybe he was falling for her.

WYNONA WAS GRATEFUL that Mack and his fellow hotshots had saved her. But she was also irritated that Mack and Owen had talked her into the trip to the ER because now her left wrist was in a brace, and she had to go on desk duty for the next three to six weeks while the sprain healed.

It could have been worse, though. Much worse. It could have been broken or she could have been dead. Even if she hadn't been injured, though, Sergeant Hughes would have sidelined her. He'd told her that it was too dangerous for her to be investigating anymore, after this latest attempt on her life. He promised he would lead the investigation, check and see if the call had been recorded that had lured her out to that ravine. But she still wasn't sure he could be trusted any more than his predecessor should have been.

"Thank you," she said again as she and Mack walked into her house. He'd driven her vehicle home for her, even though she could have driven, and Rory and Ethan had brought his truck. So both vehicles were parked in her driveway.

And the hotshots would all know about her house now. Not that Ethan Sommerly could judge her for having money. His real name was Jonathan Michael Canterbury the IV and he was heir to a fortune a lot bigger than what her parents had left her.

They'd also already told her that she was off his and Rory's suspect list now, after being pushed into that ravine. If she hadn't caught herself…

But she shouldn't have been put in that situation. She shouldn't have let herself be lured there like that. But she had to check out the report because it could have been legit. There could have been a car down there with crash victims inside needing help.

Like she'd needed help…

That was another reason she'd become a cop, so that she would be stronger. More independent so that she wouldn't need anyone to help her like her parents always had. She hadn't realized how reliant she'd been on them until they were gone, leaving a gaping hole in her heart and her life.

"You didn't have to give me a hotshot escort home, though," she said to Mack, who was walking through her house with the cat winding around his ankles like she was starving for affection and food.

When Wynona had come home to shower after the fire the night before, she'd given Harry lots of love and had filled the feline's automatic feeder and water fountain. But Harry had clearly forgotten who took care of her. Or maybe she just felt that same draw to Mack that Wynona felt, that even now, scraped and bruised, she felt to him. She wanted to be close to him, too. As close as she could get…

"I wanted to make sure that you were safe," Mack said, his voice a bit gruff.

"You told me that my security system is good," she reminded him. "That it would keep out everyone but you." She expected him to smile, but he turned toward her with his face nearly as tense as it had been when he was holding her wrist on the side of the ravine.

"I shouldn't have let you go off to that call alone," he said.

"I'm a cop," she said. And in a rural area, she always rode alone. She didn't have a partner like they showed on TV. The only time she'd ridden with anyone else had been Sergeant Gingrich during her training. She'd been uncomfortable with him, but she'd thought it was just because he was misogynistic, not that the man was actually dangerous. But now she knew anything and anyone could be dangerous.

Even Mack McRooney...

Maybe most of all Mack because of how he made her feel, how much he made her want him, and she was afraid that she would come to rely on him too much. And he hadn't promised to stick around. He hadn't promised anything except to find the saboteur and stop him.

"You can't go to work with me," she said. Then she lifted her arm with the brace. "And even if you could, I don't think you would want to ride a desk with me for the next six weeks."

He grimaced at the mention of desk duty.

"So much for you retiring," she murmured with a smile. But it was forced because she suspected there was no way he would be able to stay away from the danger of his old career, no way that he would be able to stay retired. With the very real probability of him leaving again, she had to protect her heart from him. She had to make sure that she didn't get hurt as emotionally as she'd nearly been physically. "You're not going to be able to give up your old life."

"I already have. And there are days that I wouldn't mind a desk job," he said.

She would. She wouldn't be able to help as many people as she wanted to from a desk. So maybe she shouldn't begrudge him his old career. She was certain he'd helped a lot of people like he'd helped her.

"Then what's wrong?" she asked because she could see that he was troubled, his strong jaw tense as if he was gritting his teeth.

"I'm just…" He drew in a deep breath. "I'm really sorry about your wrist."

"You saved my life," she said.

"You told me to let you go and that you would be fine," he reminded her.

She shrugged. "Might have been…" But she doubted it. Her phone certainly hadn't survived. With giving her statement to Sergeant Hughes and being seen in the hospital, she hadn't had time to even think about replacing it yet.

"I… I…" he trailed off, his voice even gruffer. Then he wrapped his arms around her and pulled her against his chest. His heart was beating fast and hard like they were still dangling over that ravine.

Hers started beating just as fast and hard because of him. All that adrenaline came rushing back, not over what had happened on the side of that wall of rock, but over the night before. And she wanted him again.

She *needed* him. Despite how badly she hadn't wanted to need anyone anymore, she couldn't deny herself this. Couldn't deny herself *him*. "Mack…"

She barely whispered his name before he kissed her, and she kissed him back. And then she fumbled with her brace as she tried to take off his clothes.

He chuckled and pulled back. Then he picked her up. "Let me take care of you…"

With as determined as she was to be self-sufficient now, she shouldn't want that. But somehow, because he was the one making this offer, she did. So she pointed him toward the bedroom.

He nearly tripped over the cat, and they both laughed while Harry hissed and ran off. The feline knew that Wynona had stolen his attention, at least for the moment.

But after all the horrible things that had happened to them, Wynona wasn't going to allow herself to think beyond the moment. Now was all that mattered.

He was all that mattered.

Instead of laying her on her bed, he carried her through the open door into the en suite bathroom. He lowered her to a bench that sat next to the enormous bathtub which was probably the whole reason she'd bought the house. And then he drew her a bath.

"What are you doing?" she asked with a smile. She wanted him, not a bath.

"You're all scraped up and..."

She glanced down at the torn and dirty clothes she was wearing. "I'm a mess," she agreed. But that wasn't just on the outside. On the inside, she was shaky and unsettled and not just because of having yet another brush with death.

It was him. And how important he was already becoming to her. After losing the last people who'd been important to her, she didn't know if she could risk her heart again, especially on someone who was probably leaving as soon as the saboteur was caught.

But the past few days had been nice, having someone take care of her, drink wine with her, play with her cat. All of that had made her all too aware that she didn't want to be alone anymore. Yet she couldn't count on him to stay.

But with the way he was looking at her, his face so tense but his eyes so warm, she couldn't resist him or the feelings flooding her heart.

He gently removed the brace from her wrist. And when he

saw the bruises, he flinched as if the sight of them physically hurt him. He ran his lips gently over the swollen skin, and her fingers tingled and not because of the sprain. Then he removed the rest of her clothes and lowered her into the tub.

"This is big enough for the both of us," she said.

"Just relax for a moment," he told her. And then he stepped out of the bathroom.

She closed her eyes and sank down to her chin in the warm water he'd scented with her bath salts. Moments later, he was back with a tray of cheese and grapes and an open bottle of wine. And he was naked.

Gloriously naked.

She moaned at just the sight of him.

"Hungry?" he asked as he held a big purple grape to her lips.

"You know what I'm hungry for," she said. Him. But he fed her the grape and then a nibble of gouda cheese before he poured her a glass of another Cabernet Sauvignon. They definitely had the same taste in wine. Or maybe he had just figured out what hers was since she had more bottles of that than any other.

"You're going to get cold," she said. "You need to get in the tub with me."

And finally he did, lowering himself into the water with her, his legs on the outside of hers, rubbing against them. He was so big that water sloshed over the rim onto the marble floor.

But she didn't care. She launched herself at him then, winding her arms around his neck. And she kissed him, rubbing her breasts against the hair on his slick chest.

He groaned, and his cock pulsated against her. "Wynona, I didn't bring a condom."

"I have an IUD," she said.

He tensed for a moment then chuckled.

"You thought I said IED." It shouldn't have been funny, not after the explosion in the warehouse. But she giggled too. "No. That wouldn't make me safe at all to have sex with you. But I am safe. I've been checked recently, and I'm fine."

"Me, too," he said.

She reached down and guided him inside her as she straddled his lap. As she rode him, he played with her hair and her breasts and kissed her over and over again.

She came once, softly keening his name.

Then he reached between them, caressing her core. And the pressure wound up again. He moved, thrusting while she arched. More water sloshed over the rim, pooling on the floor around the tub. And she came again, the orgasm so intense that it shook her.

He tensed then uttered something like a growl, and his big body shuddered as he came, too. "Wynona..." he groaned her name like he was in pain.

Maybe pleasure this intense was painful, especially when she was so worried that it wouldn't last. That eventually the saboteur who kept coming after them was going to succeed.

Or Mack was going to leave. Either way she was going to lose him.

BRADEN SHOULD HAVE been relieved he heard from Mack, even though the text had been short and hadn't provided much information. Unfortunately, Ethan and Rory had just filled in the rest, and Braden was reeling now. And it wasn't just because he had that damn feeling, that sizzling of his nerve endings, that tightening in his gut, like a fire was starting.

His senses had to be all out of whack, though. He hadn't predicted that fire last night at the warehouse or the incident in the showers. Or even what had happened now with the latest attempt on the lives of Wells and McRooney.

"Hey, boss, this is good news," Ethan said. "They're all right."

"And we can write Trooper Wells off the suspect list now," Rory said, "since someone clearly lured her out there to try to kill her."

Ethan shrugged his broad shoulders. "I could point out that we all had enemies of our own in addition to the saboteur. Someone could be going after the trooper for another reason. Like how she could afford the place we followed her to?"

"Says Mr. Moneybags," Rory teased.

"Yeah, family money." His dark eyes widened. "Oh…"

"Brittney did some digging," Rory said, referring to his reporter girlfriend who was also his fellow hotshot Trent Miles's sister. "Wells is an older rookie because she spent a lot of time going from fancy college to fancy college. She doesn't have as much money as the Canterburys, but she inherited a lot when her parents died a few years ago."

Braden felt a pang of sympathy for her. His parents were alive and well and hopefully safe in Florida because he was worried that nobody close to him was safe. Hell, nobody in Northern Lakes was safe. He really needed to send Sam back to Washington to stay with her dad until the saboteur was caught. But he'd learned long ago that Sam wouldn't go anywhere she didn't want to go or stay anywhere she didn't want to stay. All the McRooneys were like that.

Trick hadn't intended to stay either. But he wasn't going anywhere now. Mack…

He was the one who was least expected to stick around anywhere. Hell, none of his family even knew where he'd been for the last twenty years, and, from what Braden had heard, Mack's visits home had been few and far between over the years.

"Did Brittney find any enemies in her past?" Braden asked, but he knew he was clutching at straws. He would still rather hope it was Wells or anyone else not on his team that was attacking the others.

Rory shook his head. "No. I think it was the saboteur that went after her. She hasn't been a cop long enough to make enemies here. Though her boss wasn't too warm to her when he took all our statements for the report."

Braden groaned. "If this person is brazen enough to go after a cop…"

"Nobody's safe," Rory finished for him, confirming his worst fear.

And that feeling intensified. A fire was starting…

Chapter Eighteen

Mack awoke with a start and cough, smoke burning his nostrils and drying out the back of his throat. "What the hell…"

For a moment he was so disoriented that he didn't know where he was. Which mission was this? What country was he in? What war?

Then everything came rushing back to him. He reached out and touched the bed next to him, looking for her. But there was nobody lying beside him—not like she'd been when he'd fallen asleep with her curled up against him.

"Wynona!" He coughed and sputtered again. Something was burning. Her house?

Fully awake, he grabbed his clothes and pulled them on, his heart hammering in his chest with the panic gripping him. How the hell had he fallen asleep?

He knew they were in danger. He'd stayed to protect her, and now he didn't even know where she was. Had the saboteur gotten past her security system? Had he abducted her? Or worse…

Was she already dead?

Panic gripped him so tightly that he could barely breathe. He gasped for air and coughed some more as smoke filled his lungs.

Mack flipped on lights in the bedroom, which made the smoke hovering in the air appear dusky.

"Wynona!"

He coughed again and it seemed to echo, coming from somewhere else in the house. He pushed open the door of the en suite bathroom, but it was empty, the floor still slick with water. He picked up the towel that was lying in the water and pressed it over his mouth to block some of the smoke. Then he turned toward the hall, moving through the smoke toward the main living area.

"Wynona!" he shouted.

He heard a cough. Was it hers? Or was someone else inside the smoky house with them?

Someone who'd already hurt her?

He needed his gun. But he'd left it in his truck earlier, beneath the seat. He'd been so worried about her injuries from the ravine that he hadn't thought to grab it. And while he'd checked her house for her, he hadn't believed that anyone else was able to get inside.

But now...

Unless the fire had started outside, someone must have gotten in somehow. Then he heard a gun cock, and he knew that someone else had found their way inside despite that damn security system.

They must have already gotten rid of Wynona, and now he was going to be next. But he wasn't going out without one hell of a fight. And hopefully he could find Wynona, get her out of the fire, and get her medical help.

WYNONA UNCOCKED HER gun just as Mack lunged toward her. "Stop!" she said. "It's me." With all the smoke and her eyes watering because of it, she hadn't been certain the big shadow moving toward her was him until he got closer.

"What the hell is going on?" Mack asked.

"I heard something and got up to check it out. There wasn't any smoke then. I don't know where this is coming from." She coughed.

"We have to get out of here," Mack said. "Now."

She pointed at the cat carrier on the ground. Harry was already listless which had made the cat easier to catch and put in the carrier. And she'd draped a wet towel over that, but the smoke just kept getting worse and worse. "But the fire…"

"What fire? I don't see any flames. I don't feel any heat," he pointed out. Then he tensed. "Oh, my God…"

"What is it?" she asked.

"Smoke bomb. Somebody set off a smoke bomb in here," he said.

There could only be one reason for that, which Wynona voiced aloud. "To get us out…"

"It's going to work," Mack said. "We can't stay in here." He coughed again.

But the minute they stepped outside a door, Wynona knew what would happen. And Mack had to know, too. The saboteur was going to shoot at them like he had outside Mack's cabin that first time Wynona had followed him home.

But Harry emitted a pitiful, weak cry, and Wynona knew she was going to lose her cat and maybe her own life if they didn't at least try to escape the smoke.

"This way," Mack said, his voice gruff.

He took the cat carrier from her and headed through the

kitchen to the French doors that opened onto the brick patio that stretched nearly to the sandy beach.

"The lakeside will give the saboteur fewer places to hide," he said. "And we can take cover behind the outside fire-place and kitchen."

It was like he'd already assessed the situation, like it was one of his military missions. And it did feel to Wynona like they were at war. She didn't want her pet and her house to be casualties of it, though.

She knew they had to get out of the smoke-filled house. Her lungs and throat were burning, and her eyes kept watering. She had her weapon in one hand, but she wasn't sure she would be able to see well enough to shoot anything, especially since it was so damn dark outside. After the long, dangerous day they'd had, they'd fallen asleep after making love, and must have been out for hours, long enough for day to slip into night.

The saboteur could be out there now, waiting to shoot them even through the glass. Mack must have thought the same thing because he pulled her down so that they were crouching lower to the hardwood floor as they crossed the kitchen to the breakfast area. He passed a wet towel to her. "Put this over your mouth."

Then he opened one of the French doors. As the fresh air came in through it, the smoke billowed and seemed to thicken around them.

First, he slid the carrier outside through the patio door, using the long handle of a broom that she hadn't even seen him grab. He pushed Harry across the patio behind the outside fireplace.

Hopefully the wind blowing in off the lake would clean

out the cat's lungs. Wynona lowered that damp towel from her face, but no fresh air reached her yet. A cough racked her.

And somewhere, too close to them, a gun cocked.

Wynona tried to raise hers, but with her coughing, she couldn't even hold the Glock steady with just one hand able to grip it.

"Let me have the gun," Mack said. He took it from her hand.

But the saboteur had already started firing, and bullets struck the house and the patio doors, shattering glass all around them. She felt something nip at her skin and flinched at the sting.

Mack fired her gun with one hand while he used his other to pull her through those shattered doors and into the shadows of the fireplace and the outside kitchen. Bullets pinged off the built-in grill and stainless-steel counter.

No matter how good a shot Mack was, Wynona wasn't sure he would be able to save them. That he would be able to stop the shooter before one of his bullets struck them instead of the house.

So much gunfire went back and forth, and then all of a sudden Mack crumpled forward and collapsed onto the patio bricks.

A scream clawed up the back of Wynona's throat. He must have been hit!

GETTING THE GUN from the patsy's truck again had been the smart thing. He should have had it earlier, at the ravine. But it worked now.

The saboteur was pretty certain he'd hit one of them, maybe even both of them. But the problem was that he had been hit, too.

He didn't think the wound was bad. He hadn't even felt it until he saw the blood. Would anyone else notice it?

Could he cover it up? Keep anyone from seeing that he'd been hit?

Chapter Nineteen

Mack awoke again with a start and no idea where he was. Bright lights blinded him, and he tried to talk, but something was covering his mouth. What the hell had happened? He reached up to push at it, but someone caught his hand.

"No. You need that oxygen."

The sight of the blonde peering down at him rattled him more than not knowing where he was. He pulled off the mask. "Mom?"

"Not yet," Sam said with a heavy sigh. "But hopefully soon…" Then her face flushed. "Oh, you meant…you thought I was…"

"No, no," he said when he could tell that he'd hurt her feelings for thinking that she was anything like their mother. He was the one who was most like her, just as Trick had accused him of being.

Then Trick leaned over Sam and asked, "Are you all right, big brother?" Instead of the usual resentment, there was affection and relief in Trick's green eyes.

Just like he'd thought Sam looked like their mom, Mack murmured to Trick, "You look so much like Dad…"

Tears glistened in Trick's eyes for a moment before he blinked. "You're the one who's the most like him," Trick said. "You're so damn tough. And I'm so damn glad that you are. I don't want to lose you."

Was this his brother? The one who'd been acting so resentful since his arrival in Northern Lakes?

Mack touched his head again. He hadn't hit it. Why the hell was he so confused? "What happened?" he asked his siblings.

"You passed out from that smoke bomb," Trick said, his voice gruff.

Then he wasn't that damn tough. He'd needed to stay conscious. For her. To protect her.

He jerked upright on the hospital gurney and looked around. "Where's Wynona?" Because if he'd passed out, she must have too.

"I think she loves another more than you," Trick said, but he was grinning and teasing him.

Did his younger brother know how Mack felt about the state trooper? Did Mack know? With the way his heart was pounding with fear for her, he suspected he knew, but he didn't want to face it yet. Not until the saboteur was caught and they were out of danger.

But maybe even not then because despite what Trick had said, Mack knew he was more like their mother than their father. He wasn't the McRooney that could be counted on, he was the one who would probably run.

"Where is Wynona?" he asked, his voice gruff as his concern for her choked him. "Is she okay?"

"She will be if her cat is okay," Trick said. "She insisted on taking it to the animal hospital before she would come here to get stitched up."

"Stitched up? She got hit?" And she'd gone to the veterinarian first? But that was just like her to think of others before herself, like when she'd urged him to let her go in that ravine.

"Just with some broken glass Owen told us," Sam shared. "She isn't hurt badly at all. You're the one who passed out."

He remembered firing her gun into the shadows. And then…nothing. "Did I hit him?" he asked. Or had the shooter kept firing after he'd passed out?

"Who?" Sam asked.

"The saboteur," he said.

"Who was it?" Trick asked. "Did you see who it was?"

He shook his head. "I don't know. I didn't see him. Just his damn shadow…" But he was pretty sure he'd hit him, or the person wouldn't have stopped shooting and he and Wynona would probably be dead.

"Did you hit him?" Trick asked.

Mack shrugged.

"There are troopers out at her house going over the scene right now," Sam assured him. "If someone else is out there, they'll find him."

"He'll only be there if I did hit him," Mack said, and then he started coughing again. But it felt more as if his lungs were clearing the last of the smoke out.

"You have to put the oxygen back on," Sam said, mothering him now as she reached for the mask and tried to pull it over his mouth and nose again.

But he resisted her efforts even as he coughed again. "The smoke was so bad…"

"Those bombs are brutal," Trick said. "Somehow the saboteur got his hands on some of the training ones. Braden went to check at the firehouse, and he confirmed that a couple of them are missing."

Somehow…

The saboteur had to be one of them or at least someone who had free rein to the firehouse, like Stanley or one of the volunteers. "What about the cameras? Did he see who was hanging around? Who could have taken them?"

"He checked the footage," Trick said. "But there were a lot of people coming and going. He couldn't see anyone actually holding one of the smoke bombs, but that didn't mean one of them didn't take it."

"Who?" Mack asked then coughed. "Who was there? Stanley?"

"Stanley's always there," Trick said.

Mack nodded.

"No," Sam said. "I suspected him once of being the arsonist, but that kid loves everyone too much to hurt anyone. And just suspecting him nearly destroyed him. So don't go there, Mack."

"You're getting soft," Mack mused. Must have been love that had made her less cynical than she used to be.

She flushed and touched her belly. "Yeah, I am. I'm also worried. My husband shouldn't be off on his own," she said, her brow furrowing with concern. "Not with how all these attacks have been stepped up."

The saboteur was getting more and more dangerous and more and more determined. What was his end goal? To kill Mack and Wynona or all the hotshots?

"Your husband is already on his way back," Trick assured her, sliding his arm around her shoulders.

Mack envied them that closeness. They clearly had a tighter bond than he had with any of his family. With anyone except maybe for...

"Wynona," he said, rasping out her name. "Somebody needs to check on her. See if she made it to the hospital yet."

The smoke could have snuck up on her the way it had him. It could have damaged her lungs.

What if she collapsed somewhere on her own? And there was no one there to help her like when she'd been hanging off the side of that ravine.

"She shouldn't be off on her own either," Mack said. After nearly getting killed so many times, she should have realized that. He wanted to be angry with her over taking chances, but he was too scared that she was hurt.

"She's not alone," Trick assured him. "She's with Owen. He wanted to keep an eye on her, so he used the rig to drive her cat to the animal clinic. They're probably on their way back here now."

He hoped so because he didn't like being separated from her. Every time they had been, something happened to her. Something bad.

WYNONA PUSHED DOWN the oxygen mask Owen had put on her and asked, "Can you drive faster?"

He glanced across the console at her. "You told me you were feeling fine."

"I am." The oxygen had cleared the smoke from her lungs. And the emergency vet at the animal clinic had assured her that Harry's lungs looked good as well. She was worried about Mack, though. He was the one who'd passed out. But his siblings were with him and would make sure he was being taken care of. Even Trick had been so scared when he'd shown up with Owen. Mack had family to care for him. Harry only had her.

And she only had Harry like the stereotypical crazy cat lady she had vowed to become after she'd realized what a narcissist Jason Cruise had been. Wynona wasn't crazy, she was just cautious now after that near miss with a would-be killer. And if she gave her heart to anyone, it wouldn't be someone like Mack. Clearly, he wasn't going to stick around once the saboteur was caught. He was only here on a mission for his brother-in-law, and then he'd be off somewhere else. Probably back to the excitement of his old life and new missions.

But first he had to survive this one.

"I just want to get to the hospital," she said.

"Eager to get those stitches?" Owen asked.

She reached up and touched the bandage he'd affixed over some liquid bandage. "I don't need any. You took care of that cut."

"You're not worried about having a scar?" he asked.

"I'm not worried about that." She wasn't worried about herself at all.

Owen smiled as he must have figured out whom she was worried about. "I checked on Mack while you were back with the vet. He's fine," he assured her. "His oxygen levels are back up. He'll be released soon."

But that worried her even more. "I don't want that shooter trying for him again."

"Was he after Mack or you?" Owen asked. "You had that close call by the ravine."

Too close.

"You know he's gone after Mack, too," she said. "That warehouse fire had to be a setup and then the live wire in the showers..."

Owen groaned and pressed his foot down a little harder on the accelerator, but as he rounded a corner, bright lights flashed in their faces. Owen cursed then twisted the wheel as that vehicle headed straight at them, right in their lane.

The paramedic rig bounced off the shoulder of the road and into the ditch. Airbags deployed, but Wynona hadn't buckled up after she'd crawled into the passenger's seat from the back. She went flying.

Then everything went black.

BRADEN WAS IN a hurry to get back to the hospital. While he knew that Mack was tough and would undoubtedly be all right once his oxygen levels were brought back up, he was more worried about Sam.

She should have stayed home with her feet up, resting. But she'd sworn she wouldn't be able to relax until she saw for herself that her brother was all right. And so she'd insisted on going to the hospital.

But Braden wanted to get her home to rest. She was going to go into labor soon—he didn't need a sixth sense to know that since she was already overdue. And the added stress of the saboteur going after her brother wasn't helping the situation at all.

With as worried as he was about his wife, he pressed his foot down harder on the accelerator and sped toward the hospital. He was drawing close to it when he saw the lights.

Off the road.

In the ditch.

One of the paramedic rigs.

Owen. And he wasn't alone.

He had Wynona in the rig with him on the way back to the hospital. But they hadn't made it. And Braden was concerned that now it might be too late to get them there.

Chapter Twenty

"Where is she?" Mack asked Trick. "You said she needs stitches." How badly had she been hurt? Or was it that her cat wasn't okay?

God, he hoped she hadn't lost her cat, too. Not when she was still hurting from the loss of her parents. He knew Wynona cared about that cat. Hell, he cared about the fluffy little ball of affection. If something happened to her, Wynona would be upset.

And she would be even more alone than she already was. Maybe that was why he'd been so drawn to her from the first moment they'd met. Not because she was aloof like he was, but because she was lonely like he was.

He hadn't even realized how lonely he was until he'd started spending time with her and with his family. He'd been alone too long. And while it might have been safer for him and for the people he cared about, it had been…lonely.

"Where the hell is she?" Mack repeated the question, his voice getting gruffer with the frustration and the fear that were overwhelming him.

Trick wasn't answering him. He was staring down at his phone instead and the color drained from his face as he read whatever text he received.

Dread settled heavily in Mack's stomach. Sam must have noticed his reaction too because she pressed up against their younger brother's side and tried to read his phone. "What is it?" she asked. "What's going on? Is it Braden?"

Mack shook his head. He knew from the way that Trick glanced at him and then quickly looked away.

"The text is from Braden," Trick said. "Nothing happened to him. *He's* okay, Sam."

"But Wynona isn't," Mack said, that dread so heavy that he struggled to sit up. But he managed and then swung his legs over the side of the gurney.

Sam rushed forward and tried to shove him back. "You shouldn't be up."

"I'm fine," he said. But he coughed again. That might have been more with panic than anything. "What the hell is it, Trick? What happened?"

Instead of answering him, Trick glanced at Sam. She sighed and nodded. "Tell him."

"Braden just found the rig in the ditch."

Mack gasped now, and it wasn't for air. It was with concern for Wynona. He knew it. He knew something had happened to her, that she shouldn't have been off on her own. Well, she hadn't been quite alone—she'd been with Owen. But she hadn't been with *Mack*. "Tell me everything you know!"

Trick shrugged. "I don't know much more than you do. Owen said some vehicle came straight at him. He went in the ditch to avoid a head-on collision."

"So he avoided the head-on crash," Mack said. "That's good."

But Trick looked away from him again. "Wynona wasn't belted in."

"No!" Mack yelled. Because now he didn't want to know. If she was gone, if he'd lost her, he didn't want to know.

"They're on their way in now," Sam said, her voice soft with sympathy for him.

Like he was the one hurting. But he was hurting over just the thought of her being hurt. She had to be okay, she had to be…

And then he heard them, the commotion outside the curtained-off area where his gurney was. He heard the nurses and doctors rushing around, and he knew it was bad.

HANDS CAME OUT of the darkness, grabbing at her, trying to get to her, trying to pull her even deeper into the abyss. But in that all-encompassing blackness there were rocks and boulders with jagged, sharp edges and Wynona could feel herself plunging toward them and then breaking into little pieces.

She awoke with a scream. The darkness was gone, replaced with lights so bright she flinched, and her head pounded.

"Are you okay?" a deep voice rumbled.

She turned her head to find Mack seated beside her, his hand on hers. But it wasn't his hand she'd felt in her dream. He'd held her up, he'd saved her.

"What happened?" she asked, her voice a rasp.

"Owen said—"

"Owen!" Everything rushed back. "Is he all right?"

Mack nodded. "Yeah, he was wearing his seat belt." He reached out and touched her forehead. "You weren't. You're lucky you didn't go through the windshield. The airbags saved you from any more cuts and bruises than you already had. But you have a slight concussion. That's why you've been unconscious."

"Are you okay now?" she asked. He had dark circles beneath his eyes, and his face was tense. "When you passed out, I thought you were shot…" Her voice cracked as it trailed off with the fear she'd felt then. How scared she'd been that he was gone.

He smiled at her. "Nope. I'm just a wuss who passed out," he said with self-deprecating humor.

But she felt compelled to defend him to himself. "Because your lungs were full of smoke."

"Well, my lungs are fine now," he said. "Yours are too. They checked them. They did all kinds of X-rays and MRIs on you."

She glanced down at her body then and saw that she was wearing a hospital gown beneath the sheet covering her. She patted her sides. "Where is my gun?" She remembered those hands tugging at her.

"Your gun?" Mack asked, his voice cracking a bit with alarm.

She nodded, and pain radiated throughout her skull for a moment. Spots danced in front of her eyes, and she had to hold her breath for a moment until it passed. Until her vision cleared again.

"I'll find it," Mack said. He reached under the gurney, probably where his stuff had been stored, and pulled out the bag that held her clothes and her belt and holster. But the holster was empty. "Maybe the staff took it and locked it up somewhere safe. Or Owen or Braden took it from you in the ambulance."

She closed her eyes, trying to remember, but those hands

came back to her again, reaching out of the dark. When she opened her eyes, Mack was gone.

She felt a flash of panic because she knew. Someone had taken her gun, but not Owen or Braden or a hospital staff person. The saboteur had taken it.

She looked at that empty holster, and she saw the blood on the snap that had held it shut. Maybe it was hers. The glass from the broken patio door had cut her. But that had been on her head, not her hands. And she hadn't even been aware of the cut until Owen pointed it out.

So she couldn't imagine that, when she'd taken her weapon from Mack after he'd passed out, she would have gotten blood on her holster. She wouldn't have had any blood on her hands then. So where had the blood come from?

Unless Owen had been hurt worse than Mack had admitted...

She remembered the lights coming right at them, in their lane, forcing the ambulance into the ditch. But Owen had been wearing his seat belt whereas she'd just switched from the back to the front.

But that didn't mean Owen wasn't hurt. Or maybe something else had happened to her gun. Maybe someone else had taken it. That thought scared her so much she forced herself out of bed. The room tilted despite the fact that her feet were flat on the floor. The blackness threatened again. She gripped the side of the gurney, riding out the wave of dizziness. Then she grabbed her clothes Mack had dumped out of the bag, and she dressed quickly. Before she could pull back the curtain around her area in the emergency room, Mack was back, and he wasn't alone.

"I'm sorry, Trooper Wells," Owen said. "I didn't know how to avoid that vehicle heading right at us."

"Did you see it?" she asked him. "Do you know what kind it was?"

He shook his head. "The lights were so bright, they were blinding."

She nodded, and her head pounded harder. "I know. I couldn't see anything either. Just that it was big." And coming right at them.

"But then whoever was driving it came up to the rig," Owen said. "They got the back doors open somehow, and then I think they were trying to get you out of it."

Mack cursed.

"Did you see them then?" she asked.

He shook his head. "With the airbag and all the stuff from the back flying around, I couldn't see anything but a shadow. Then there were lights coming up behind us, and whoever it was ran off."

"With your gun, Wynona," Mack said, stating what she'd already deduced for herself. "Neither Owen nor Braden saw it on you, just the empty holster."

"I didn't see him take it, but I figured he might have been grabbing other stuff out of the back, maybe trying to steal drugs. But then it didn't make sense that he was grabbing at you in the passenger seat," Owen said with a slight shudder. "I thought he was trying to pull you out of the back with him, so I held onto you."

Mack squeezed the paramedic's shoulder. "Thanks, man. You did good. You kept him from abducting her."

"Why didn't he just kill me?" she asked. "That's what he's been trying to do."

"Has he been trying to kill you or scare you off?" Mack asked. "Gingrich said something that day I visited him—"

"You visited Marty Gingrich in jail?" Owen asked,

sounding horrified. But then Gingrich's mistress had tried to kill Owen, and Marty had probably helped her with some of those attempts.

Wynona chuckled. "He was trying to find out if I was working with the creep."

While Owen stared at her with wide eyes, Mack just shrugged. "Anyhow, he said something…"

When he trailed off, she finished for him. "Something I'm probably not going to like."

"He didn't think you'd last as a police officer, that you'd be too soft for the job."

"Because I'm rich and spoiled," Wynona said. Then she sighed. "He's not wrong. I am rich and spoiled."

Mack snorted. "You work damn hard and you're pretty fearless."

Owen nodded. "And relentless. You don't give up no matter how much crap we've all given you."

"But is that what someone is trying to do?" Mack asked. "Get you to give up? Could they just be trying to scare you off the case?"

"Why take my gun though?" she asked. "What reason could he have for doing that? Unless…"

"What?" Mack and Owen asked at the same time.

"What if he was shot?" she asked. "What if you hit him, Mack? That could have been why he was going through the back of the rig, too. Getting stuff for his wound."

Mack tilted his head as if considering it. "I hope like hell that I did hit him, but why take your gun, especially since he has his own?"

"It was the gun you were using…" Maybe he'd seen that, had seen Mack take it from her and when she took it back.

"But still…why?" Mack asked, his brow furrowed as he tried to figure out the reason.

"I don't know," she said. "But we better call and report all of this to Sergeant Hughes."

"Braden already called him," Owen said. "I gave him my statement a while ago."

How long had she been unconscious?

Mack nodded. "I did, too. He's probably around here somewhere waiting to take yours."

"We need to find him," she said. "To warn him about that gun…"

Because she had a feeling that something very bad was about to happen. And after everything that had already happened, that was saying a lot. But why else would the saboteur have taken her gun unless he intended to use it?

But on whom?

HE SAT IN that corner booth laughing and joking with so many members of his team. And maybe he should have felt guilty for what he was about to do or for the things he'd already done, but all he felt was…

Rage.

The rage that had been driving him for over a year. And after getting shot earlier that night, the rage was even more intense. He didn't just hate Braden Zimmer anymore. He hated all of them.

And they all deserved what was about to happen…

But he smiled and joked around, like he always did. They didn't suspect anything.

None of them had.

And none of them would until it was too late.

He wasn't sure if they knew that he'd left or if they

thought he was in the bathroom. None of them knew he was waiting for them outside the door of the Filling Station until he started shooting them as they walked out.

And one by one, they dropped to the pavement.

Chapter Twenty-One

Wynona would have preferred to take a report rather than giving it, but since she was a victim now, and stuck yet in the ER bay until the doctor released her, she had to answer her boss's questions.

Heat flushed her face because it was clear from his smirk that he knew why Mack had been at her house earlier that night. And he probably also thought the only reason she'd lost her weapon was because she was a girl, not because she'd been unconscious at the time.

Fury bubbled up inside her over that smirk and over his entire treatment of her since he'd taken over for Gingrich. She was flushed with anger, not embarrassment.

"Sergeant Hughes, I have some questions for you," she said. "Like, why was I the one you sent out to that ravine? Why not another trooper? I wasn't even on duty yet. And since you and Gingrich were so tight for many years, how the hell didn't you know what he was up to?"

The smirk slid away into a tight-lipped grimace. "I would be very careful, Trooper Wells."

"I have been," she said. "And I've had to be because I can't trust anyone I work with. I just started at this job. But you were doing it for a while. How the hell did you not know what your friend was up to? I want an answer."

"You're being insubordinate, Wells. I'll allow it this once because I can tell you're overwrought—"

"I'm furious," Wells said. "And if I were a man, there is no way in hell you'd be calling me overwrought."

Which reminded her so much of what Michaela Momber's co-worker Donovan Cunningham had said to her when the female hotshot had encouraged her boyfriend Charlie Tillerman to press charges against Cunningham's teenage boys for breaking into his bar. She and Michaela had both wondered if those teenage boys and Cunningham himself might have been responsible for all the horrible things that had happened to the hotshots.

"And you haven't answered her questions," Mack pointed out as he pushed back the curtain around her gurney and joined them.

She was glad she'd gotten dressed even though the doctor hadn't actually released her yet. Dr. Smits wanted to make sure that the follow-up CT scan she'd ordered after the initial one showed no swelling or bleeding on the brain. But it seemed as if the doctor had forgotten about her since Wynona had been back from radiology for a while now.

"I'm taking a report, not giving it," the sergeant remarked.

"I'm sure we can find out from the jail just how often you actually have been by to talk to your friend."

The sergeant shrugged. "Go ahead. I haven't been there. And I can admit when I've misjudged someone, like I misjudged Marty." He turned back to Wynona then. "And maybe you, too. Maybe you are tougher than I thought."

She was battered and bruised nearly from head to toe. So she wasn't feeling that tough at the moment.

"She is damn tough, or she wouldn't have survived the crap she's been put through," Mack said.

"But she lost her weapon—"

"While she was unconscious!" Mack shouted. "Are you a moron? How can you hold her accountable for that? Or are you just looking for a reason to harass her? Because I've found one to har—"

Wynona jumped up from the gurney and stepped between them. She didn't want Mack to get arrested, and she had no doubt that her sergeant would book the hotshot for assault if Mack so much as laid a finger on him. But before either of the men could say anything else, a commotion outside the curtains drew all their attention.

And the sergeant's radio started squawking at him.

"Déjà vu," Mack muttered. "This is what it was like when Braden brought you and Owen in. I wonder what the hell happened now."

"I guess we know where your gun turned up, Wells," the sergeant said. "Someone used it to shoot a bunch of hot-shots as they were coming out of that bar they all hang out at. They're being brought in now."

"Oh, my God…" Wynona murmured. "Are there any casualties?"

"All I know is that the gun was recovered at the scene and the serial number matches yours."

Son of a bitch.

While Mack said the sergeant couldn't hold her account-able for it being taken, Wynona would hold herself respon-sible if anyone was killed with her gun.

From the way all the color left Mack's face, it was clear he was worried about a particular hotshot or two. His brother and brother-in-law. And probably all the others. Even though he hadn't worked with them long, he had already formed a close connection to a few of them, like Rory VanDam.

Like he'd formed a close connection to her. So close that Wynona could feel his distress.

MACK FELT LIKE he was trapped in a nightmare that would never end. Even during wars, he would have more of a break between battles than he'd had here in Northern Lakes. And the fear was overwhelming.

Not for himself but for those he cared about. Trick and Braden had left a while ago with Sam, making sure that she got safely home. But what if, instead of heading straight back to their house, they'd all stopped at the Filling Station first?

Sam was hungry all the time. She could have wanted something to eat. Then she would have been there with the hotshots.

And if something had happened to her and her baby...

No. He couldn't even let himself think that. His whole reason for coming here had been to protect his siblings, but his arrival in town had done the opposite. The saboteur had gotten even more dangerous.

Wynona pulled back the curtain of her area of the ER to watch as the others were brought in.

"I'm sorry," a nurse said as she noticed Wynona and Mack. "You two are free to leave. You're fine."

And they probably needed the bed.

But Mack wasn't fine.

Wynona squeezed his hand and used it to guide him away from her area toward the door that marked the exit to the waiting room. But Mack stopped. He wasn't going anywhere until he saw who'd been hurt.

Or worse…

"Were there any casualties?" he asked Sergeant Hughes who was leaning against the wall near where they were. He was listening to his radio.

The sergeant shook his head. "No. Doesn't sound like anyone was seriously wounded either. A couple shoulder wounds and a couple of leg wounds. Sounds like whoever was firing wasn't trying to kill."

"Thank God…" Mack murmured.

And then he saw Trick…

He wasn't on one of the gurneys, thank God. He was pushing one with Owen on the other side of it.

"Who is it?" Mack asked, trying to see around them to who lay on that stretcher.

Braden?

Sam?

"Carl," the man on the stretcher answered for himself. "Like I told you, McRooney, I should have retired, too. Don't tell my wife she was right, though."

"You'll be back fighting fires in no time," Owen said. "You've gotten hurt worse shaving your head bald."

Carl chuckled then grimaced.

Another stretcher came in behind him with one of the young guys, tears trailing down his face. "It hurts so bad!" he said, his voice cracking.

Was it Howie or Bruce?

Mack wasn't sure yet who was whom, but they were usually together. And sure enough the other one followed, grasping his bloodied shoulder as he cursed. "Son of a bitch."

"Did any of you see the shooter?" Wynona asked the question that her sergeant should have been asking, but he seemed a bit overwhelmed at the moment. Fortunately, there was a crew of officers and crime scene techs back at the Filling Station where the shooting had happened. She'd managed to get that confirmation out of her boss before he'd clammed up.

Maybe she and Mack had put him on notice regarding his harassment of her and his lack of judgment regarding his friend Marty, and he was being more careful now. At least he couldn't be the shooter unless he'd left the scene at the Filling Station in a hell of a hurry to get to the hospital.

It was probably possible. And maybe that was why he held back. Either way, Mack didn't trust him. And he would definitely be making some calls to Hughes's superiors.

"There was no time to see anything," the other young one said, his words a bit slurred.

Mack wondered if he was sober enough to be able to identify anyone.

Two more stretchers came in, and more color drained from Wynona's already pale face. She closed her eyes for a moment, and Mack was worried that she was blaming herself for this. But he noticed something when he identified the new arrivals: Donovan Cunningham and Ed Ward.

Like Bruce and Howie, one had a shoulder wound and the other a leg wound.

But all five of the injured hotshots were the ones whose names were already circled on his suspect board. His gaze met Wynona's, and he knew she'd noticed that, too. Had the saboteur seen his board?

It was possible. After following them there, he knew where Mack lived. And maybe he'd made certain to hurt them all so that they would have no more suspects.

Sergeant Hughes finally spoke again. "You're not just on

desk duty anymore, Wells. You're going to be suspended until this can all be figured out."

"You're really not going to try to blame her for this," Mack said. It wasn't a question, it was a warning. He wouldn't let that little weasel get away with pinning this on Wynona.

"I don't want her getting killed," the sergeant said. "Maybe you should take a vacation for a while, Wells. Leave town." He met Mack's gaze. "You, too."

Was that what this all was? An attempt to get him and Wynona to drop their investigation?

From the look on her face, she had no intention of doing that any more than he did. But she smiled at her boss and replied, "Thanks for the time off." And she started walking away.

Mack followed her. He would talk to the other hotshots later, when the sergeant wasn't around. But for now, he didn't intend to be separated from Wynona again. He wasn't letting her out of his sight until the saboteur was caught or killed or…killed Mack.

BRADEN KNEW HOW Sam must have felt with her morning sickness. Because when he learned what had happened at the Filling Station, he got physically sick.

"They're going to be fine," Sam said. "All of them. Owen said the injuries weren't life threatening."

"This town wanted the hotshot headquarters out of here," Braden said. "And now I understand why. I guess I always understood why. We just seem to attract danger and are putting others in it, too."

"Only hotshots were harmed," Sam said. "No innocent bystanders."

That was the problem. It didn't feel like the hotshots were

innocent anymore. It definitely felt like it was all about them. At least all about one of them.

"I should have stepped down months ago," Braden said. "This is probably about me. Somebody wants me gone."

"Nobody's even tried to come after you," Sam said. "Or after me. You're taking responsibility for something that isn't your fault."

"Your brothers have both been in danger because of this saboteur—"

"That's just because they're trying to figure out who he is," Sam said. "People will take drastic measures to protect themselves."

"I can't imagine anything much more drastic than tonight," he said.

But he was worried that it was going to get even worse before it got better. If it ever got better...

Chapter Twenty-Two

Mack's intent for bringing Wynona home with him was to make sure she stayed safe. And that, with the concussion she had, she needed to rest. But the minute they walked into his house, she headed for the suspect board.

"You narrowed it down to these guys," she said. "And all of them were shot tonight. That can't be a coincidence."

"It wasn't me," he said, trying to lighten the heaviness gripping him. And that must have been gripping her, too, because her shoulders were bowed as if she carried a heavy burden. Guilt. "And it wasn't you," he added.

"But it was my gun," she said. "You heard Sergeant Hughes. They confirmed it with the serial number."

"Why take it when they had a gun of their own? They used it to shoot at us," Mack pointed out. "And then why shoot so many people with your gun?"

"It has to be one of them," Wynona said.

He tensed. "What?"

"You shot whoever it was who threw that smoke bomb into my house," she said. "So to cover up the fact that you'd shot them, with my gun, they had to shoot more people with my gun." She pointed to his board. "Maybe they saw this or heard about it somehow. Maybe they knew who all your suspects are. Why are the names of these guys circled on the board?"

Some of the others, like her and Stanley, were off to the side. Sergeant Hughes's name was on the board, too, but like hers, it wasn't circled like those five.

"They've consistently been in the area or at every scene of sabotage. The night Rory was hit. The night that Molotov cocktail was thrown at Michaela and Tillerman and things dating back even further than those incidents. While some of the other hotshots or you or Hughes might have been in the vicinity of one incident or another, these five were the only ones that were at all of them."

"And tonight, all of them were shot," she said.

"He must have gotten a look at the board, or maybe he heard Ethan and Rory talking about it after we filled them in," he said. "But either all of them are working together or you're right and one of them is trying to cover up getting shot tonight."

"And they could still all be working together," Wynona said.

He shrugged. "I don't know. Then I think they wouldn't have all been a possibility for every incident. They would have split up the sabotage. One does one thing, one another…" He shook his head. "No, it's one of them. Just one of them working alone."

"They're all in the hospital for tonight," she said, and she yawned. "We can interview them tomorrow."

"You're suspended," he reminded her.

"You're a hotshot," she said. "You can talk to your own team members."

"And what about you?"

"I can go with you when you talk to your team members," she said.

"As my what?" he asked. After what had happened, after he nearly lost her, he wanted to know what they were. What he would have lost...

He had a feeling that he knew, though. His heart.

She shrugged. "I don't know, Mack. I don't even know if you're sticking around Northern Lakes after you catch the saboteur."

Neither did he really. He wanted to make her promises, but his mom had made those promises to his dad. And she'd broken them and his heart and his and Sam and Trick's when she left.

"Hell, I don't even know if I'll be sticking around," Wynona said. "Maybe the sergeant will make my suspension a termination."

"He'd be an idiot if he did."

"Why?" she asked. "Gingrich told you that I'm not cut out for this job. And I bet you didn't argue with him."

"I didn't know you then," he said. "Now that I do, I know how tough and determined you are."

"But I still haven't caught the saboteur."

"Nobody has," he said. "He's been messing with the whole team for over a year and nobody has caught him."

"They're firefighters, not police officers," she said. "Except for you. Or maybe you are. It's not as if I really know you."

"Yes, you do," he said.

He was a little afraid that she knew him better than most people did. She knew how much it meant to him to be able to help people, to save them, just as much as it obviously meant to her.

"And you also know my sister Sam," he said. "She's an arson investigator, a damn good one, and she's been helping Braden look for the saboteur and hasn't succeeded."

She shrugged as if it didn't matter who else had failed, just that she had. She was tough on herself. That was another thing they had in common. But she was too tough.

"We have to figure out which one of them it is," she said. "Because I have a feeling someone is going to die if we don't stop him."

He gestured at those five again. "They're all in the hospital tonight. So they're safe. There will be extra security there. And since they're all in the hospital tonight, we're safe, too."

"I can go home then," she said. And she glanced toward his front door.

"Your house is full of smoke," he reminded her.

"It should be cleared out by now," she said.

He slid his arms around her and said, "I don't want you to leave, Wynona." And he was starting to fear that he would never want her to leave.

But as she'd pointed out, he wasn't even sure he was going to stay in Northern Lakes. He wasn't sure what he was going to do after this mission, after finding the saboteur.

But for tonight...

There was no place else he wanted to be but with her, reminding himself that she was alive. That he hadn't lost her. And she must have felt the same because she closed her arms around him and kissed him. Then she started tugging at his clothes but flinched.

He remembered that she didn't have her brace. She must have left it at her house, after he'd taken it off her, so she could relax in her bath. But they hadn't relaxed. They'd made love.

"You have to be careful," he said.

Her lips curved into a slight smile. "If I was being careful, I wouldn't be here."

But she was. They'd had to borrow Trick's truck to get back here, but she hadn't protested. And with the way she tugged at his clothes, she wanted him as badly as he wanted her. But maybe that was the reason she didn't think she should be here with him.

Maybe she knew him too well, and she knew that it wasn't in him to stick around. That he was too much like his mother, that he would let down the people who loved him like she had let down the people who'd loved and depended on her.

He had already let down people he loved, his dad and his sister and his brother.

"I don't want to hurt you," he said as he drew back slightly.

She smiled. "You're the one who told me I'm tough," she reminded him. "A few bruises and sprains aren't going to stop me."

"You have a concussion, too," he said. "You should be resting."

"I'm fine," she said. "The nurse just about threw us out of the ER."

Because they'd needed her bed. And Mack needed her, too much to deny himself any longer. But he took it slowly, trying to be as gentle as he could be with her. He undressed her, kissing every silky inch of skin he exposed.

And the marks on her skin, the scratches and bruises, had his heart clenching with regret over the pain she'd endured.

He didn't want her to feel anything else but pleasure. So he laid her down onto the bed and he made love to her with his mouth and his hands.

Even after screaming his name as she writhed around on the bed, she reached for him, pulling him against her, into her. He tried to go slowly yet with sweat beading on his forehead and sliding down his spine, as he struggled for control.

But she kept touching him and kissing him. And his control snapped. The passion and the pleasure were just too intense. And all the feelings that pummeled him as he filled her and reached his own climax, one that shook him to his core, were too intense, too.

That climax, and those feelings, shook him more violently than any of the explosions he had been in. It was all too much, and even after his release, he couldn't relax while she fell asleep in his arms.

What was he going to do? After catching the saboteur...

That had to be what he did next. He had to make sure that all the people he cared about were safe from that bastard. But after the suspect was caught...

What would he do? Could he break the cycle his mother had started? That he'd continued? Instead of running, could he stay somewhere for once? For someone?

Right now, he intended to stay awake. He really did. But with all the suspects in the hospital, he could rest, too. And he would probably need it for the following day, for trying to figure out which one of his fellow hotshots was the saboteur. Because he had no doubt that when the guy was cornered, he wasn't going to go down without a fight.

But maybe Mack was wrong about the suspects, or at least about them staying in the hospital, because he woke up to the sound of someone messing with his door, trying to jimmy the lock.

He reached for Wynona, but the bed next to him was empty. She was gone.

GUILT WEIGHED HEAVILY on Wynona over losing her gun and over leaving Mack so early this morning. But with all the saboteur suspects in the hospital, he had to be safe. She had left him without a vehicle though, since she'd taken his brother's truck.

But she'd awoken with such a feeling of panic to find herself naked in his arms. He was like an addiction to her, something she just couldn't resist no matter how much she knew it was going to wind up hurting her. Like alcohol or sweets. Wynona wasn't addicted to either of those things though. But Mack…

He might prove worse than any sweet, than any spirit or drug. Maybe if she wasn't so distracted by the desire she felt for him, she might have figured out who the saboteur was, especially since he kept trying to hurt her.

Like last night.

She'd turned over her holster to her sergeant to have forensics check that blood on it. And even though the techs had been all over her house and the grounds, too, she wanted to look for herself to see if any of the techs had marked the area and found any blood around the vicinity where the saboteur would have had to be standing last night when he'd fired all those shots at her and Mack.

It was probably a miracle that they hadn't been hit except for the shard of glass that had nicked her face. And Mack passing out from the smoke inhalation.

He'd been fine last night, though. Once he'd gotten the

oxygen. He'd been better than fine later when they'd made love. At least that was what it was beginning to feel like for her. She wasn't sure how he felt about her, if he even really liked her all that much, at least enough to stay.

Of course, she didn't know if she would stay either. The new life and career she'd wanted for herself in Northern Lakes hadn't turned out like she'd hoped. But she couldn't think of anywhere else she'd rather be now that her parents were gone. This was one of the few places she hadn't traveled with them, so it had felt like she could make a fresh start here, a new life for herself.

Instead, she'd nearly lost her life too many times. After taking his truck, she'd stopped in town to replace her phone, but she hadn't called him yet to let him know where she'd gone. Or that she'd left.

She hadn't called anyone else either.

When she pulled up to her house, there were more vehicles than hers and Mack's parked in the driveway. There was another US Forest Service vehicle. She automatically reached for her weapon, but it wasn't on her belt. She didn't even have the empty holster anymore.

Nothing to defend herself.

Mack had a gun in his truck, though, stowed under the front seat. If she could get into the locked vehicle…

She jumped out of Trick's truck and headed toward Mack's. But just as she reached the door, she heard a gun cock. She was too late.

"I'm sorry," a female voice said. "I wasn't sure who had driven up…" Sam McRooney-Zimmer stood between Wynona and the house. The arson investigator re-engaged the safety on her gun and dropped it into her cross-body purse which rested on the big swell of her belly.

The woman had treated Wynona as coldly as most of the hotshots had in the past, so Wynona wasn't particularly happy to see her here. At her home.

"What are you doing here?" Wynona asked the arson investigator. "There wasn't a fire last night." *Thank goodness.* "Just all that smoke…"

"From the smoke bomb," Sam said. "I know it wasn't arson, but I thought maybe I would find something else here, some clue…"

"That would lead to the saboteur," Wynona finished for her. "I was thinking that, too. I think Mack hit him last night. I think that's why…"

"Some of them were shot last night," Sam finished for her and shuddered. "Braden was so upset about so many of his team getting hurt. He's blaming himself."

And that was obviously the reason his wife was here, trying to help her husband.

"It's not *his* fault," Wynona said. "None of this…but especially not that…"

"It's not your fault either," Sam said. "I've tried to catch this person for a long time, and while I've never not caught an arsonist, I haven't been able to figure out who the saboteur is." A grimace, probably of frustration, crossed her pretty face.

"I hope to find something here that might lead to him, too," Wynona said. "If Mack hit him, there might be blood where he was standing when he was shooting at us."

"Where?" Sam asked. "And wouldn't your techs have found it?"

"I don't know what all they found and didn't find at the scene," Wynona said. "Mack and I were at the hospital. And then, after I lost my weapon, Sergeant Hughes suspended me, so I can't get an update on the investigation directly from the techs."

"Hughes is an idiot then," Sam said, and she grimaced again. "What happened last night wasn't your fault. Any of it."

Wynona wanted to believe that, but she couldn't help but think that she could have done more. "I need to make it right," she said. "No matter what."

"We'll find this saboteur," Sam said. "We will." She glanced at the truck Wynona had driven here and asked, "Where is my brother? He's usually not far away from you lately."

Heat rushed to Wynona's face with embarrassment over how far she'd crossed the line with Mack. Not that he was a suspect but he had suspected her at one time. "I left him sleeping at his cabin."

"Don't be embarrassed. You have no reason to be," Sam assured her. "I totally understand that sometimes we get caught up in the adrenaline and the danger and the love."

Wynona shook her head as panic gripped her. "I barely know your brother. I don't think anyone does. Maybe not even him."

Sam sighed and nodded. "You're right. I just hope…"

"What?" Wynona asked.

Sam shook her head. "No, I'm sorry. It's not any of my business."

"I've learned in Northern Lakes that everyone's business is everyone else's business," Wynona said. There had certainly been a lot of gossip and speculation about her. Unfortunately, most of that had more to do with Gingrich and how much she'd known and how involved she'd been with the evil, little man.

Sam sighed. "True. Small towns. And family..."

"And family," Wynona repeated wistfully. She had no family anymore.

"With me and Trick, sure," Sam said. "We've always been in each other's business. But Mack has always been a loner. And now..."

"Now what?" Wynona pressed. "You obviously want to warn me or something."

"I don't know if he'll stick around," Sam said, and she flinched again as if the thought caused her pain. "And I know that there are people who want him to un-retire. They've been trying to find him."

"Do you think someone else could be trying to find him?" Wynona asked. He'd assured her that nobody was looking for him for revenge or whatever, but how could he know for certain? "From that old life of his, from whatever he did that had all those high security clearances?"

Sam smiled then, but even that looked a little pained. "You don't know any more about that life than the rest of us, huh?"

Wynona shook her head. "No. He just assured me that whoever was after him here wasn't from his previous life. That everybody he'd encountered back then had no idea who he was." Which was kind of how she felt now. Like she had no idea who he was.

"But his superiors know," Sam said. "And they want him back. They tracked him down through my dad."

A heaviness settled on Wynona's heart with the certainty that he would probably un-retire just like Sam seemed to suspect. "I had no expectations that he was going to stick around. I knew he was just here to help your husband. The only thing we really have in common is the same goal." And their inability to resist their desire for each other. "We both want to find and stop this saboteur."

"Is it a competition?" Sam asked. "Since you're here without him?"

"I just… I needed some space…"

"I get that," Sam said. "I had to get away from Braden for a while when I first fell for him, clear my head before I figured out what I really wanted."

"It's not like that," Wynona insisted. She was not falling for Mack McRooney. He was just a distraction. Like Sam and this conversation was, too. "And I need to check for that blood—"

Sam reached out and grasped her arm, squeezing, and a low growl slipped out of her mouth.

"What?" Wynona asked with alarm.

"I'm… I'm in labor," Sam said. "I think I have been for a while now but I was thinking they were just Braxton Hicks contractions again. And now my water just broke…"

The grimaces. Sam hadn't been making those faces over their conversation, the arson investigator was having contractions. Ones that were close together from how often she'd flinched.

Wynona pulled out her cell phone to call for help, but she had a feeling it wouldn't get to them in time. That, with as close as those contractions were, the baby was going to beat the paramedics. And Wynona had to figure out how she could help Sam so that neither the mother nor the baby was lost.

THE PLAN HAD gone to hell, just like where he was probably going to go as well. But at least he wouldn't go alone.

The saboteur had a backup plan to his original one, which

had been to get Braden fired in disgrace. So that everyone would know that he hadn't been the best man for the superintendent job. When that hadn't happened, the plan had escalated.

And so had his rage. He was so damn angry that he didn't feel any remorse anymore. He didn't feel anything but that rage. And it was in that rage that he'd made his backup plan.

When it looked like the authorities, or Braden, were finally closing in on him, he wasn't going down without one last fight.

Without one last act of sabotage…

Chapter Twenty-Three

Mack glanced across the console at the person who'd tried breaking into his cabin. "I can't believe you're here."

"You thought I would miss the birth of my first grandchild?" Mack Senior asked from the driver's seat of his pickup truck.

"No." His dad was always there for his family no matter how busy he'd been with his career. He'd always made his kids a priority. Unlike their mother...

Unlike Mack himself. That was why he'd come here, to help his siblings, to try to make up for all the years he hadn't been there for them. Trick had seemed to thaw the night before. Hopefully he was ready to forgive him. But if he did and Mack left again...

There would be no hope for their relationship. But that wasn't the only relationship Mack was concerned about ruining. Not that what he and Wynona had was a relationship. He wasn't sure what they were to each other, especially since she'd slipped out while he was asleep.

"I would have been here sooner," his dad said. "But I was busy fielding all those calls and visits from people looking for you." He arched his reddish brows over eyes that were the same green as Trick's. "A lot of very official looking people."

Mack shrugged. "They're wasting their time. I'm not going back." Especially now, not when Wynona was in danger. And even when she wasn't, Mack wasn't sure he would be able to leave her. "It's up here…" He directed his dad to drive toward her house, which was easy to find because of all the flashing lights and emergency vehicles. He cursed.

The police should have finished up at the scene last night, especially after the shooting at the firehouse. There should have been no need for an ambulance now. Unless…

Had Wynona been attacked again?

"This is the state trooper's house?" his father asked.

Mack didn't know if it was because of the house or because of the emergency vehicles that Mack Senior was questioning him.

"Yeah," Mack said. He knew for certain that he had to stay in Northern Lakes and as close to Wynona as he could because lately it seemed that if something bad happened, it happened to her. Or around her…

"She has to be okay…" he muttered. Because if she wasn't, he wasn't sure that he would be okay.

His dad barely braked the truck when Mack threw open the passenger's door and jumped out. His heart hammered in his chest as he ran toward the paramedic rig parked near Trick's truck. People were crowded around the back of it, and he shoved through them to see inside where he expected to find Wynona. But the woman sitting on the stretcher was blonde, her hair so dark with sweat that it took him a moment to realize she was his sister. "Sam?"

Then a cry filled the air, and he noticed the blanket-wrapped bundle in the arms of the man kneeling next to the stretcher. It wasn't Owen or Dalton, who were the paramedics, it was Braden.

"Sam!" Mack exclaimed now. She'd done it, his sister had become a mother.

"Sam!" Their dad echoed his shout, his voice cracking with emotion.

"Dad, you made it!" she said.

"Just a few minutes late, it looks like," the older Mack murmured, his eyes glistening.

"We were late, too," Trick said, his voice gruff. He was one of the hotshots standing around the open doors at the back of the rig.

"What do you mean?" Mack asked. And he looked at the bundle in Braden's arms. His brother-in-law's eyes were damp, too. "Who was late? What happened?"

"Your girlfriend delivered our nephew," Trick said.

"What?" He glanced around, looking for Wynona again.

"Thank God she was here," Sam said. And his sister, who was always so tough, started crying now. "I was so damn scared."

"Wynona called you a beast," Trick said, his voice warm as he spoke of the trooper. "That you were tough as hell."

"You both did well," Owen said. "But we still need to go to the hospital and get you and the baby checked out." He waved everyone back and began to shut the doors on them.

But Mack caught the edge of one of them. "They're really okay?" he asked through the emotion clogging his throat.

Owen grinned. "Yeah. I think your girlfriend might be more shook up than they were."

"Where is she?" Mack asked.

"She already headed to the hospital," Trick said.

"Why? Was she hurt again or did she reinjure herself?" he asked. "Her wrist is already sprained and she also has a concussion from when she and Owen crashed last night."

"She's a beast, too," Trick said with respect. "We all really misjudged her. She's super tough and super determined. That's why she went to the hospital, to talk to the wounded hotshots. We should have brought her into the investigation sooner. She probably would have already caught the saboteur."

Or the saboteur would have killed her by now. While he might have started out just trying to scare her off the investigation, once the perp realized that wasn't going to happen he would try harder to get rid of her.

That was why Mack had been so determined to get to her as soon as possible. He had to make sure that she stayed safe. And even though she was suspended from duty, she was obviously still working this case.

Like Trick said, she was determined to catch the saboteur. But once she did, the man wasn't going to go down without a fight and maybe not without taking her down, too. Mack had to make damn sure that didn't happen. Because if he lost her…

He wasn't sure what he would do.

WYNONA COULDN'T STOP SHAKING. She had helped deliver a baby before, during a ride-along while she was in the police academy. She'd helped then, but she hadn't been the only person responsible for the well-being of the mother and baby. And because of who this mother and baby were, Wynona had felt extra pressure.

She hadn't wanted anything to go wrong with Mack's sister and new nephew. Tears stung her eyes, but she blinked them back as she pulled into the parking lot of the hospital. That baby made her even more determined to catch the saboteur. That child was too young, too innocent, to lose any of his family now. He deserved to have his mother, father and uncles around to watch him grow up, and to support and guide him. Like her parents had supported and guided her.

Maybe too much since she'd felt so lost without them. She knew now what she had to do, though. She had to catch a very dangerous man.

Because with the saboteur on the loose, the Zimmers and McRooneys were all in danger, probably even the baby. As well as the rest of the hotshots and even townspeople. So screw her suspension, Wynona wasn't going to sit around and do nothing. Not when she knew she was capable. She'd saved Mack McRooney more than once, and she'd just delivered a baby. She was stronger than she'd realized she was, and she was smarter. She could take care of herself and this town. And she intended to stay...even if Mack left. But she wanted him to have the choice to leave or to stay. She didn't want that choice and his life taken from him. She cared too much.

Once she parked in the lot at the hospital she made a call on the cell phone she'd bought to replace the one she'd lost in the ravine.

"Sergeant Hughes," her boss answered.

"This is Wells."

"Not sure why you're calling me, Wells, you're suspended right now."

"If that's the case, then you'll be hearing from my lawyer," she said. "And I have a very good one who will make a case for discrimination and lack of support and resources, and you damn well know I have a case and I have the documentation to win that case."

She could hear the breath the man sucked in then released in a ragged sigh. "What do you want?" he asked.

"I want to know if any blood was recovered from the scene where the shells were found outside my house," she said.

"That's—how do you—why do you want to know?"

"Just tell me."

"Yes, is that all you want?"

"Of course not. This has been my case, and I want to close it," she said.

"You're too involved."

"And that's why I'm the only one who can close it." She suspected Mack could as well, but he wasn't a cop. She was, and she wanted to prove to everyone, including herself, that she was a good one. And she was beginning to believe that she was. She just had to finish this now. She had to put the saboteur away, so he couldn't hurt anyone else.

"You're hurt, and you don't even have a weapon."

"Who do you have stationed at the hospital for the hotshots who've been shot?"

"Ford."

"Tell him he's working with me," she said. "But I want the arrest."

"It's going to take a while before the DNA comes back on that blood, and we have to get samples to match it to—"

"I'll get a confession," she said.

"What? Do you think you're Columbo now? Or what was that TV show with Kyra Sedgwick? *The Closer*?"

Wynona smiled. "Yes." She wanted to be a badass like that. "I'll get a confession."

The sergeant chuckled now. "I was wrong about you, Wells, and so was Gingrich. You just might make it yet."

She felt a rush of pride.

But then he added, "If you don't get yourself killed first."

"I just want to interview the hotshots who are in the hospital right now," she said.

"I already did that last night," he said. "Nobody saw anything."

"Somebody did," she said.

The saboteur.

And she was going to let him know that it was over, that the DNA would prove what he'd done and that an arrest was imminent. Whichever one of the wounded hotshots it was...

But she wasn't sure when she talked to them. She talked to the younger guys first before the older ones. Their reactions ranged from amused to annoyed.

But as she spoke to them, Ford was listening to something on his radio. When they stepped into the hall, he shared what Sergeant Hughes had just told him. "The casings and bullets from the first scene, the one at the cabin McRooney is renting, came back from ballistics with a match."

"Who?" she asked.

"Donovan Cunningham."

Armed with that knowledge, she went back to the hotshots, but one of them was already gone. It didn't matter that he'd run, the saboteur wasn't getting away.

He wasn't going to stay on the loose and harm other people. Not anymore.

He'd already hurt too many.

BRADEN HAD NEVER felt such happiness and such fear in the same moment as he had when he'd showed up at Wynona Wells's house to find that his wife had delivered their son all on her own. Well, just her and the trooper.

He was so happy and so relieved that they were okay. A doctor just confirmed it. But after that confirmation he had to step outside the door where his father-in-law and brothers-in-law were waiting in the hall. He told Sam he was going to update her family, but he really just needed a moment to himself, a moment to regroup.

"Is something wrong?" Mack Senior asked with alarm. "Is Sam and the little guy all right?"

Braden nodded. "Yeah, they're both doing great."

Sam needed some stitches and would need some iron for the blood she'd lost at the scene. Remembering that had Braden feeling queasy again.

"Sam is so damn tough," he said with pride and awe in his wife. "And our son is strong and healthy, too."

"Of course he is," Mack Senior said. "He's a McRooney and a Zimmer."

"You're going to have to wait a few years to get him into hotshot training, old man," Trick said to his father with a teasing grin.

"I got the cigars!" Cody Mallehan announced as he came down the hall, leading a group of other hotshots.

At least the ones who weren't injured. They were still here, still in the hospital. And the thought of that made Braden feel sick all over again.

Hands slapped his back and shoulders while Hank gave him a big hug. And Cody gave him a bigger hug then handed him a cigar. "Congratulations, Daddy!"

Hank studied his face and cocked her head, making her braid swing over her shoulder. "What's wrong, boss? Is everything okay?"

Braden nodded. "I just…it's hard to be as happy as I should be without feeling guilty that some of the team is here, is hurt."

Cody cursed. "I know. This is crazy. Worse than the arsonist. Matt Hamilton just picked a few of us to go after. Now it feels like nobody is safe."

"What?" Younger Mack asked the question. "Why just a few of you?"

"Well, four of us," Cody said. "He went after Wyatt because Wyatt had been his mentor but didn't help him get on the team. And then Dawson for getting attention for saving some of those boy scouts. And me because I took the last open spot on the team. I got hired right after Bruce and Howie."

"You were supposed to stay with my team," Mack Senior grumbled. "Be a smoke jumper."

"You wanted me to have more experience as a hotshot first before you took me on as a smoke jumper," Cody reminded him.

"Yeah, you weren't supposed to stay."

"This town makes a person want to stick around," Cody said with a grin at Trick and a speculative glance at Mack Junior.

The younger Mack ignored the comment, and asked, "Who was the fourth? Who else did the arsonist go after?"

"Me, for not hiring him," Braden said. And he could just about see the gears turning in Mack's head. "What?"

"So Cody took the guy's spot. Have you taken something from someone, Braden?" Mack asked.

Braden tried to think, but Sam hadn't been involved with anyone when they met. She'd been like Trick and like he suspected the younger Mack was, unwilling to risk any relationship after their mother's desertion. He shook his head.

"What about your job?" Mack Junior asked him.

Older Mack chuckled. "You're one of the youngest hotshot superintendents."

"Gingrich said something about that," younger Mack said. "Like you just got the job because of that sixth sense thing of yours about fires…"

"Bullshit," Cody said. "He's good. That's why he got the job."

And lately that sixth sense hadn't been very reliable.

"Who else was trying for it?" Mack Junior asked. "Who else applied? There had to be someone else on the team who would have wanted to take it over and might have thought, because they were older and had more experience, that they were entitled to it."

Braden's head pounded as hard as his heart was suddenly pounding. "No…"

It couldn't be this simple. This basic. Because if it was, he'd been a fool not to realize sooner what the motive was for trying to hurt the team. To hurt him…

"Who?" Mack asked.

Braden swallowed hard, feeling like he was betraying them for even saying their names. But this had been his problem all along; he was too close to every team member to suspect any of them of being the saboteur.

"Who?" Mack prodded again.

"Donovan Cunningham, Ed Ward and Carl Kozak."

"And all three of them have gunshot wounds," Mack remarked. He was already walking away from them, already going off to talk to them.

"No," Braden murmured. He couldn't believe that it was one of them. Not guys he'd worked with for as long as he had. But part of him wished that it was one of them and that it could be proved because he wanted this all to be over. He wanted his family to be safe.

But that wouldn't be possible until the saboteur was caught.

Chapter Twenty-Four

Wynona was supposed to be here. That was what the others had said, that she was heading to the hospital. Apparently, it didn't matter to her that she was suspended, she still intended to investigate.

Mack should have looked for her the minute he got to the hospital, but he'd wanted to make sure that his sister and nephew were all right. He'd wanted to be there for his family like he hadn't been in the past.

But if something happened to Wynona...

He would never forgive himself for not being there for *her*. Where could she have gone?

He got the room numbers for the three guys who'd wanted Braden's job, who might have started the sabotage to get Braden fired or at least to prove that they would have been the better choice for superintendent of the Huron Hotshot team.

He headed to Donovan Cunningham's room first. Wynona had made her opinion of the guy clear after the way she'd seen him disrespect Michaela Momber. He figured if she wanted to break anyone it would be Cunningham. But she wasn't in his room. Mack wondered if she was even in the hospital.

"Hey, how are you doing?" Mack asked.

Donovan flinched as he sat up. "I'll be better when I get the hell out of here."

"Any news on when that will be?" Mack asked.

Donovan shrugged then flinched. His wound was to his left shoulder. "Why? Are you missing me?"

"It's just been chaos over the past several days," Mack said.

"Yeah, ever since you showed up in town."

"This has nothing to do with me," Mack said. "Bad things were happening long before I came to town."

"Like some crooked FBI agent going after Rory Van-Dam," Donovan said. "You showed up then. What's your deal, McRooney? What do you really want?"

"What we should all want," Mack said. "The saboteur stopped."

Donovan flinched again, but he didn't move otherwise. "It's not me. I don't give a damn what she said about that ballistics report. She knows that I was framed."

"What?" Mack asked, his heart pounding heart. "What ballistics report?"

"The one that said my gun was used to shoot at you," Donovan said. "Anybody could have grabbed it out of my truck. I leave it in there all the time."

"But you didn't use it to shoot at me? At us?" Mack asked, fury building inside him. "Why the hell should I believe you?"

"Your girlfriend figured it out," Donovan said. "Didn't she tell you?"

"What?"

"Trooper Wells was already in here, grilling me, grilling all of us, and even after that report, she didn't arrest me. She knows it's not me."

Mack narrowed his eyes and studied his face, skeptical. But he couldn't imagine her not arresting him unless she'd figured out who it really was.

"You doubt her?" Donovan asked, and he almost sounded hopeful.

Mack felt sick. "No. She's smart." She would have arrested Donovan if she'd really thought he was guilty.

"She had some bullshit story about finding blood at her house, swore it would get matched to whoever it was, the shooter that went after you and her…" Donovan shrugged again and flinched. "I told her it wasn't mine."

"And?"

"I think she went from room to room and then she came flying back in here. And it wasn't just about that report."

"Why?"

"Because Carl's gone. And she knows that he would have known about my gun. Hell, he might have been the only one who knew about it."

"Kozak?" Mack shook his head. "All he talks about is retiring."

"His wife talks about it," Donovan said. "It's why they split up. He's been staying at his pop's cabin out in the woods. I don't think it's far from your place."

Mack's stomach dropped. "Damn it." That was why Wynona wasn't here. "Did you tell Trooper Wells that?"

Donovan nodded.

"Where is it?" Because Mack had no doubt that was where he would find Wynona even though she had been suspended.

Donovan gave him directions, and Mack started for the door. "Wait," the older hotshot called him back.

Mack thought about ignoring him.

"You have to know something," he said. "Kozak's kind of a prepper. Guns. Rations. He's into the militia and protecting his place from trespassers or anyone else might try to tell him what to do."

Dread gripped Mack. "Protecting it how?"

"He's got stuff set up. Stuff that will go off if someone trespasses."

Mack cursed. "Did you tell the trooper that?"

Donovan closed his eyes and shook his head.

Mack cursed him. "You better hope like hell nothing's happened to her." He ran out then, and he hoped like hell that he got to her before something did.

IT WASN'T A CONFESSION. Wynona knew that. But Carl running after she'd told him about the blood at the scene was the same as an admission of guilt to her. And that ballistics report had made him look guiltier to her than it had made Donovan Cunningham look.

Sergeant Hughes was taking a bit more convincing. She was on the radio with him while Trooper Ford followed the directions that Donovan Cunningham had reluctantly given her. Obviously, he didn't want to believe that his buddy could have shot him or the other hotshots.

Carl hadn't reacted when she'd told him about the blood at her house. He'd just grinned and shrugged…while the others had actually been offended. And when she'd returned to his room, it was obvious he'd left in a hurry, slipping past Trooper Ford, who should have stopped him.

She glanced over the console at the trooper before speaking into the radio again. "We're going to need backup, Sergeant."

"The guy is wounded," Hughes replied.

"And he still shot other hotshots," she said.

Ford glanced nervously at her.

"We're going to talk to him," she said. "We'll get him to turn himself in. He obviously knows it's over, or he wouldn't have run."

Ford let out a breath. "He probably headed to the airport then."

She nodded. "Yeah, he might not even be here." But she had a feeling that Kozak had no place else to go. Cunningham admitted that the guy's wife had thrown him out because he wouldn't retire. Being a hotshot was everything to him. It was who he was.

And without it…

He had nothing left to lose.

Maybe that was why Mack had taken so many chances since his retirement. Because he had nothing left to lose… but he had everything she wanted. Family. Friends. A home here in Northern Lakes, and if he wanted her, he had her, too.

"I'm concerned, sir," she spoke into the radio, "that he's going to take his own life."

"So you're calling this a welfare check?" Hughes asked. "Because you don't have a warrant yet."

"You need to get one," she said. "You need to compel him to give his DNA so we can check it against the blood found at my house."

The sergeant hesitated for a long moment then he released a shaky sigh. "You're right. I'll call the county prosecutor. I'll get that going. But you need to be careful, Wells."

"We'll just check, make sure he's okay," she said. "He left the hospital against medical advice as well. He hadn't been released. The doctor said she wanted to watch him especially for infection."

"Why him especially?"

"She couldn't officially give me his medical information, but I was able to get a look at the chart on his door. His wound looked just a little bit older than the wounds of the other hotshots, and she had some concerns that it was already getting infected."

Sergeant Hughes let out a soft whistle. "He's your guy. How did he get past Ford?"

"I'm sorry, sir," Ford said.

"I mean, really, the guy was shot and has an infection," Hughes said. "He can't be that strong right now. He can't be that dangerous."

Wynona closed her eyes and wished he'd never said that because even though she normally wasn't a suspicious person, she felt like the sergeant had jinxed them somehow. That saying it wasn't that dangerous was going to make it especially so.

Ford, however, looked a lot less tense than he'd been. But he didn't know everything that the saboteur, that Carl Kozak, had already pulled off.

How many people he'd already hurt…

How long he'd terrorized and betrayed his own team.

Wynona didn't trust him. And she really wished she'd waited for Mack. But Mack wasn't a police officer. Despite all his clearances, he had no authority here.

And his family needed him. He had people who cared about him.

She had nobody.

But him…

But she really didn't even have him. According to his sister, his old life was calling him back, and she doubted that he would be able to ignore them, that he would be able to stay retired any more than Carl Kozak had wanted to retire.

His determination to stay working as a hotshot had ruined Carl's marriage and now his life. He hadn't just wanted to be a hotshot, though—he'd wanted to be in charge of the hotshots. That was probably why Carl had done what he had, to prove that Braden wasn't up to the challenges of the job and to gain the respect of his team.

Carl might have begrudgingly gained that respect because he'd hurt them without them ever realizing it was him this entire time. She could talk to him about that, about needing respect and use that as a way to relate to him, to talk him down. Because, after what he'd done, he must have lost the kind of respect that mattered most: self-respect. She understood that all too well, but she was getting hers back. She felt capable and competent in a way she hadn't felt before. She knew what she was doing. She was protecting as many people as she could, even Carl Kozak if he'd let her.

"This must be the driveway," Ford said as he stopped at the end of it. There was just enough space to turn off before a gate stopped any further access to the property that lay beyond it, to that cabin in the woods.

Again, Wynona had an uneasy feeling rush over her, that uneasiness that Sergeant Hughes had jinxed them.

"Stop here," Wynona said. "Out on the road, and let's make sure we're ready for this…"

"For what?" Ford asked. "We're just going to make sure that he's okay. That he hasn't killed himself or passed out from an infection, right?"

"Right," she said. That was her intention, but she had no idea what Carl Kozak's intentions were. But she was glad that she'd taken a few precautions moments later when she buzzed the intercom at the gate and a shot rang out, dropping her to the ground.

More bullets pinged off the car, striking the metal, shattering the glass.

Now she knew what Carl's intentions were. He wasn't going down without a fight. And he was going to hurt as many people as he could before he was done. Probably even himself...

TROOPER WYNONA WELLS had played him at the hospital. Carl knew that now. The sneaky bitch had wanted him to react, to run, just like he had. But the thing was, she probably hadn't been lying to him. There had to have been blood left near her house. His blood.

The blood that was seeping out of the wound he'd reopened when he'd run. He had more bandages on the kitchen table, but he ignored them to study the video playing out live on his laptop screen. Except nothing was moving. And she had to be bleeding now, too. Or maybe she was dead.

It wasn't going to end with her death, though. Others would come for him. Cops and undoubtedly hotshots, too. Especially one of them: Mack McRooney.

McRooney was more than a little attached to the state trooper, and he was going to be pissed that she was gone. That he hadn't been able to rush to her rescue this time like he had every time before.

He was too late to help her. And he would be too late to save himself from Carl's final acts of sabotage.

Carl was ready for Mack McRooney. He was ready for all of them. Just like he'd been ready for Trooper Wells.

She hadn't been ready for him, though. And she might have paid the ultimate price for her stupidity—her life.

Chapter Twenty-Five

Mack drove as fast as he could to where Donovan had sent Wynona. Had the guy realized what he was doing? That he could have been sending her to her death?

Braden needed to overhaul his whole team because there was more than one person on it that couldn't be trusted. But Carl Kozak wasn't going to have to be fired. While Donovan had called him a prepper, Mack knew that it wasn't for the end of days.

It was for this. For his end...

For the moment that he was finally revealed as the saboteur. He wasn't going to surrender or risk being arrested. And he was going to take out as many people as he could on his own way out.

And Wynona, as the one who'd figured it out first, would be the first Kozak would try to take out. Just as the saboteur had been the most focused on her recently, trying to get her out of his way. Because he knew that she would be the one who would want to bring him to justice, to arrest him.

Mack pressed his foot down harder on the accelerator and gripped the steering wheel for the curve in the road. But as he rounded that curve, he nearly passed it...

The police SUV parked in front of a gate at the end of a

gravel driveway. If not for that gate, the driveway wouldn't even be noticeable. It would have looked like any other two-track or off-road vehicle trail winding through all the forests in the Northern Lakes area. But that gate gave it away, that there was someone here who didn't want other people getting to him. Hopefully that had been enough of a signal to tip off Wynona to the danger.

Mack slammed on his brakes and pulled off to the shoulder of the road near that SUV, and that was when he noticed the holes in it and the shattered glass.

Pain gripped his heart, squeezing it.

"No, no…"

He was already too late. She'd already come under attack. She had to be okay. She had to be…

Mack reached under his seat and grabbed his weapon. Where the hell had those shots come from? Then he saw it, the barrel sticking out of one of the posts for the gate, the one across from the intercom. Keeping low and to the side of the road, Mack moved from the side of his truck to the back of the police SUV. He rounded it carefully until he got to the lowered driver's side window.

And a gun stuck out the side window toward him. "Don't—oh, McRooney…"

Mack recognized the trooper who'd helped out from time to time at the scene of every bad experience he and Wynona had had, every brush with death. "Where is she?"

"Wells? She's on the ground," Ford said, his voice cracking with fear. "I didn't know if I should try to get to her. Or just wait for help…"

That pain squeezed Mack's heart harder. "What about you? Are you hit?"

The young man shook his head. "She told me to take the shield."

Donovan Cunningham hadn't warned her like he had Mack, but Wynona was so smart she'd figured out the threat. And she'd protected her co-worker.

But not herself?

That woman cared more about everyone else than she cared about herself. She was so damn incredible. And she could not be gone.

She had to be okay. He would not be if she wasn't. But the panic gripping him paralyzed him for a moment, and he could only stare at her body lying on the ground, not moving. She lay near the gatepost that had an intercom on it. An intercom that had probably activated that gun. Another trap, another act of sabotage, from the saboteur.

"I called for help," Ford said. "Officer down. They're on their way."

Mack could hear the high-pitched wail of sirens in the distance, approaching quickly. But not fast enough for him…

Or for Wynona.

He dropped down and crawled across to where she lay on her stomach. That gun would have shot her right in the back when she pressed the intercom. But he didn't see any blood on her back.

"Wynona," he said. "Wynona…" And he rolled her over to find her staring up at him.

"Stay down," she whispered back at him furiously.

"Are you okay?"

She nodded. "Yeah, but I know he's watching…"

So she'd played dead. She was so damn smart.

Relief overwhelmed him, and Mack leaned down and

pressed a kiss against her lips, as he felt something stinging his eyes. Like tears.

"You're really all right?" he asked, his voice cracking with the emotions overwhelming him.

"Yeah, I'm wearing a vest," she said matter-of-factly.

"And you gave Ford the shield." She'd also been the one who had stepped out to do the intercom that couldn't be reached from inside a vehicle. Carl had set up quite a trap. And Mack suspected this wasn't the only one. "This is going to be too dangerous for anyone to go in there to try to get him."

"Sergeant Hughes can bring in SWAT," she said.

"Or me."

"What?" she gasped.

And he was worried that she was hurt. Even with the vest on, she could still have a broken rib. The force of the bullets could have caused internal injuries.

"I can get him," Mack said. After what the guy had done to her, how he'd hurt her again and again, Mack really needed to be the one to bring him in.

"I'm sure he has stuff set up to shoot or explode all over his property," she said.

"I know he does," Mack said. "Donovan Cunningham warned me."

She gasped. "But not me…"

"He's a son of a bitch, too," Mack said. "Braden's going to lose more than Carl from the team before this is all over." Those young guys had always been with Carl and Donovan, and Mack wondered how much they knew and how bad their attitudes were as well.

"He'll lose you, too," she said. "You can't go in there. You have no authority."

"I can get the authority," he said. He had no doubt about that, though he just might have to un-retire to do it. But he couldn't risk anyone else getting hurt when this was something he had experience doing, an experience that very few others had ever survived enough times to gain. "And I know about setups like this," he said. "I've maneuvered them before to get hostages out."

"I'm going with you," she said.

"You're suspended," he reminded her.

"Not anymore. Hughes reinstated me."

He could imagine how hard she'd had to fight for that. But he wasn't surprised she'd won. She was fierce.

"You have a sprained wrist," he said. He shouldn't have had to remind her of that. It should still be hurting like hell. But she didn't appear to be in pain, or maybe she couldn't feel it because she was so damn mad. Her face was flushed with anger. He felt that rage, too.

For months Carl had been putting the lives of people Mack cared about in danger. His brother Trick. Rory. Braden. And now Wynona...

And he was beginning to suspect he cared about her most of all. But the thought of that, of loving someone and losing them, scared him more than any trap the saboteur might have set for them.

"My wrist isn't sprained on my shooting hand," she said.

He smiled at her determination even while he worried that it was going to get her killed. It nearly had.

"And if you go in there without me, I'm going to follow you in anyway," she said. "I'll be safer with you than trying to maneuver my way on my own."

He cursed. "Wynona, it's too dangerous." And he'd lost

too many people who hadn't listened to him. Who'd tried to follow him…

"We can get him—together," she said. "It's when we try to go after him on our own that we get hurt."

She was right about that. Or at least she was right about those times in the past. But he couldn't help but worry she was wrong this time. And that it might be more dangerous with them together.

"You would have to listen to me," he said, "and do everything I tell you to do."

She nodded. Then she called out to Ford. "Back the SUV up and block the road. Don't let anyone through and don't let anyone follow us inside."

"Wells—"

"I don't want anyone else getting hurt," she said.

And Mack knew why. She hadn't been able to save her parents from that horrible illness, so she was determined to save as many other people as she possibly could.

Even him…

That was why she was so determined to go with him. Mack wanted to believe that it was as personal to her as it was to him, that she cared about him, too. But he knew she had such a big heart, with so much love to give, that she cared about everyone, no matter how crappy they'd treated her.

She was an amazing person, a person that the world needed. That Northern Lakes needed. That he needed.

But if he didn't let her go inside with him, she would try to follow him. And he would lose her for certain. So he had to let her join him and make sure that Carl didn't succeed the next time he tried to take her out.

Because he was definitely going to try to take them both out.

For good.

WYNONA TRUSTED MACK knew what he was doing, that he'd done it before. So she followed him, stepping where he told her to, ducking when he told her to...

As they crept around the property, more shots rang out and the ground dropped away in places, and things swung out of trees and seemingly out of nowhere. But Mack anticipated every single one, like it was some live-action video game he'd played so many times that he knew exactly what was going to happen next.

He was keeping them both alive. But she couldn't believe how dangerous it was and how many brushes with death he must have had in the past to know what to look for, what not to trust, what area to avoid.

Part of Wynona wished she'd avoided the whole thing. But she hadn't been about to let him go in alone. And he'd known that, known that she would follow him regardless of the threat. Did he know how she felt about him?

How hard she'd fallen for him?

She wanted to tell him, but she didn't want to distract him. He was too focused. And his focus was the only thing probably keeping them alive at the moment.

She wouldn't have noticed many of the things that he had. While some traps had been obvious, there had been others that she wouldn't have guessed.

But Mack knew because he'd encountered them before. But what if Carl had concocted something the former special forces agent hadn't seen before?

Mack was in the lead. Whatever it was would hit him first. And she would be helpless to stop it, to protect him…

Her heart pounded furiously as they continued moving slowly through the trees. And finally, she could see the glimmer of the metal roof of a building poking out through moss and tree brush.

They'd found Carl's cabin. And then he stepped out onto the front porch. "I knew it would be you," he yelled. "I knew you would be the one who finally caught me! But it's too late now…too late for all of us!"

And then he touched something in his hand and the whole world exploded.

LEAVING HIS WIFE and baby in the hospital had been hard, but Braden was glad now that he had. He needed to be here with the rest of the hotshot crew even though they hadn't been allowed very close to the scene. He needed to know how this ended and make sure that it did end.

He also needed to be here for his oldest brother-in-law because Mack had taken it upon himself to personally go after and try to apprehend the saboteur.

Before they'd left the hospital, Donovan had warned the hotshots that it wasn't safe for anyone to go after Carl, that he'd set up his place to withstand whoever came after him.

But if anyone could maneuver his way around whatever obstacles Carl had set up, it was Mack. Or so Braden hoped because his wife couldn't lose her older brother. They'd already been apart too long.

"Mack is really good at this kind of thing," Trick said as he paced the road where troopers had set up a barricade. "Or there wouldn't be people trying to get him to un-retire."

While Trick paced, Braden stood next to that barricade,

trying to listen to the troopers' radios as they communicated with each other. The troopers wouldn't allow the hotshots through to the scene because it was too dangerous. Too dangerous even for the police to try to get inside, but Wynona Wells had gone with Mack.

"He knows what he's doing," Trick said, but he sounded more like he was trying to convince himself than Braden. "He'll make it out of there…"

But then a sudden blast shook the ground underneath all of them and thick smoke rolled out from between the trees. Then flames licked up, springing up all around the trees. And more explosions went off.

"We have to get back!" one of the troopers yelled.

But at that moment Braden wasn't worried about himself. He was worried about Mack and Wynona Wells. Had they survived? Had anyone?

Chapter Twenty-Six

Wynona awoke with a start. But she had no idea where she was, if she was even still alive. That explosion…

And Carl Kozak. There was no way he had survived that. What about Mack?

He'd been ahead of her. He'd been closer to the cabin than she'd been when it had exploded. And she was hurt…

Her body felt bruised all over as her muscles throbbed and her bones ached. If she'd been hurt that badly, Mack had to have been hurt worse. She opened her mouth to speak, but no words came out. Her throat was so dry.

Had she survived?

Or was this some kind of hell?

"You're awake," someone said. The voice was female, so it was probably the ER doctor, Smits, or a nurse. But when Wynona turned her head, she found a familiar woman standing beside her bed.

"Sam…" she rasped. She tried to sit up, but the pain in her head intensified for a moment. "Mack…?"

Sam nodded. "He's okay. He never lost consciousness like you did. Something must have hit you…" Sam shuddered for a moment as if she could imagine how dangerous it had been and the things that had flown around in that explosion.

Wynona closed her eyes, but then she could see it, too. What had happened to Carl. That cabin must have been full of explosives. And unable to bear that image, she jerked her lids open again. "He's not hurt?"

"Carl's dead," Sam said. "But Mack is good."

Then why wasn't he here?

Didn't he care about her at all? And why was his sister here?

"Mack warned the others," Sam said with obvious pride in her big brother. "He wouldn't let anyone else onto that property. And he carried you out…"

"Is he really okay?" Wynona asked. Because she couldn't imagine how he had survived… "Are you telling me the truth?"

Sam nodded. "Do you think you would be here in the hospital if he hadn't gotten you out of there? It was crazy for you to go in there with him. And he's blaming himself for letting you go and for you getting hurt…" Tears sprang to Sam's blue eyes then.

"It was my fault," Wynona said. "I was determined. He knew that I would follow him if he didn't let me go inside with him." She'd intended to keep him safe, and he was the one who'd saved her life.

"That's what I like about you," Sam said. "You're tough. You're brave."

"I could have gotten killed and gotten Mack killed, too," Wynona admitted. "You should be mad at me for putting your brother in danger."

Sam chuckled. "I don't think my brother has ever not been in danger. It's what he does. And I could never be mad at you, not after you helped me deliver my son."

"That was all you," Wynona said.

"I would have lost it without you there," Sam said. "You kept me sane. I want you to be his godmother."

"What?"

"My son," Sam said. "I want you to be his godmother."

"But Henrietta Rowlins…she's going to be your sister-in-law." Wynona knew that the female hotshot and Sam's brother Trick were engaged.

Sam nodded. "Yes. But even Hank admits that she wouldn't have handled that like you did. My son's name is Mackenzie Wells Zimmer."

Tears sprang to Wynona's eyes now. She'd felt so alone for so long, so unconnected to anyone. But Sam McRooney-Zimmer was the last person she'd expected to form such a connection to. "That's…that's not necessary," she said but then admitted, "I love it, though." And she would love that child. From the moment she'd helped him out into the world, she'd felt a connection to him, too.

But neither of those connections was as strong as the one she felt to Mack McRooney. But he must not have felt the same way because he wasn't even here. "He's gone, isn't he?" she asked his sister.

Sam didn't ask her who she was talking about, she just nodded. And those tears pooled in her eyes again.

MACK HAD HAD no choice. He'd had to go back. When he'd called in a favor so that he could go in with Wynona to apprehend Carl Kozak, he'd had to commit to doing a favor in return. But he hadn't been about to let her go in without him. And really, calling in a favor with Homeland Security had been the right call.

Carl Kozak had been a domestic terrorist. The worst kind.

He'd terrorized the people who were supposed to be his friends, his teammates.

He was the worst kind of traitor in Mack's opinion. He'd turned on those he was supposed to protect, and he'd tried to hurt them.

Kozak had hurt Wynona. And even though the man was dead, Mack wasn't about to forgive Carl Kozak for doing that. He wasn't sure he could forgive himself if he'd hurt her when he'd taken off. Leaving her had been so damn tough because she hadn't regained consciousness before the helicopter had come for him.

But this was seriously the last time. His very last mission. And he thought his superiors, his former superiors, finally understood. Because once he'd wrapped it up, he'd headed right back to Northern Lakes.

No. That little job he'd had to do, that hadn't been his last mission. This was...

And it might be his most dangerous yet. For more than one reason.

"Put your hands up and turn around slowly," a female voice ordered him. "Who the hell are you?"

His arms high above his head, he slowly turned toward her, and he saw the recognition on her face, the way her green eyes widened. But she didn't lower her weapon yet. "Are you going to shoot me?" he asked.

She quickly pulled back the gun as if she hadn't realized she was holding it. Then she slipped on the safety and holstered it. "What are you doing here?"

"I'm back."

"What are you doing sneaking around my yard in the dark?" she asked. "Are you trying to get shot?"

"I didn't think you would be so edgy now that it's over,"

he said. Or he might have come up with a better plan. As it was, he hadn't even made it into her backyard yet. She'd caught him in the side yard.

She sighed, but it sounded a little shaky. "It is over…"

And for the first time he felt a pang of concern. Was she talking about them? Now that the saboteur was caught, did she think they had nothing else in common? No reason to be together.

"No," he said with a bit of panic. Just because he'd figured out that he belonged here didn't mean that she felt the same way about that or about him. "It's not over, Wynona."

"You and I both saw what happened to Carl," she said. "The only problems the hotshots will have to deal with from now on are fires."

"I know that's over," he said. His family would be as safe as they would ever be, as anyone could ever be. "But us… I don't want us to be over, Wynona."

"Us?" she asked.

"You and me, we're a great team," he said. "We work well together."

"Are you trying to recruit me for your next mission?" she asked, and there was a trace of humor in her voice now. And her hand wasn't anywhere near her weapon now.

"No. You are my next mission," he said.

Her brow furrowed. "What are you talking about?"

"You," he said. "I just want to be with you, Wynona."

"That's why you left when I was in the hospital?" she asked, and there was an edge back in her voice again. Anger. Pain.

He had hurt her.

"I didn't have a choice," he said. "I had to pay back a favor. I never would have left you if it was up to me."

She wrapped her arms around herself now as if she was cold. He would have asked her to go inside the house with him, but he had a feeling she wasn't going to welcome him back. "I've heard that's what you do, Mack. You take off when people need you…"

He flinched. "I was worried that that's what I do. That I'm like my mother. That I'm selfish and don't care about other people's feelings. But I'm not like her." He was more like his dad than he'd realized.

"You took off," she said.

"Not because I wanted to," he said. "And I came back as quickly as possible."

"Why?" she asked, and that suspicion was still there.

"Because I love you."

She gasped.

"And I never intend to leave you again."

She snorted. "Until the next mission."

"No. I mean it, this is my last one," he said. "You. Us."

She shook her head as if she couldn't accept what he had to say or his love. "You're going to miss the adventure. The danger. You're not going to stay."

"I don't know, this town has been pretty dangerous for me," he said. "And I need to stick around and look out for my nephew."

"My godson," she said. "I just got back from babysitting him for Braden and Sam." And now there was a softness and affection in her voice. She was already falling for the little boy.

"He's my godson, too." He'd already talked to Sam and Braden and Trick. He and Trick were good, really good now. Mack had apologized to him and promised to make up for letting him down when they were kids. But Trick had already forgiven him.

Mack had saved her for last. For always…

Her brow furrowed as she stared at him in the faint moonlight. "I guess I can share him with you."

He smiled at how possessive she sounded over his nephew. But if he had his way, little Mack would be her nephew, too. "He's not all I want to share with you, Wynona." He held out his hand to her.

She stared at it for a long moment.

"You don't trust me," he said.

"I don't trust me," she said.

"You should, Wynona. You're smart and strong and so damn beautiful…" His chest ached with the love he felt for her. "I missed you so much."

She blinked, as if she was fighting tears. And he knew she'd missed him, too. "I didn't think you were coming back…"

"It wasn't a dangerous job," he said. "Nothing like what Carl put us through…"

"I didn't think you were coming back," she repeated.

"I wish I just told you how I felt, how I was falling for you," he said. "But I was so scared."

She cocked her head and eyed him with skepticism. "You were scared?"

He nodded. "You scare the hell out of me. What I feel for you…"

"You love me?" She still sounded skeptical.

"With all my heart," he said. "Will you take a chance on me, Wynona? Will you trust me to stick around?"

She shrugged and sighed. "I don't know…"

And he wondered if he'd been the only one who'd fallen.

Maybe she really didn't care about him at all. He sucked in a breath. "I guess you and my brother Trick are right about me. I am too cocky. Too sure of myself. I'm sorry. I thought you cared about me, too."

He started to walk past her, back to his truck, but she reached out and caught his hand, stopping him.

"Don't run off now," she said.

"No more running," he said. "I'm too old and I'm retired. No wonder you're not interested in me."

She laughed. "I am more than interested in you, and you know it. I love you but…"

"But?"

She drew in a deep breath. "I'm afraid to lose anyone else."

"You're not going to lose me," he said. "I'm staying. You're going to get sick of me I'll be around so much."

"I will never get sick of you."

"And I will never get sick of you," he said. "But I felt sick when you got hurt, when I had to leave you. I'm so sorry, Wynona. I will never do that again."

"You might," she said.

He shook his head.

"If you have to rush off to save the world, I'll be okay with that," she said. "As long as you always come back."

He closed his arms around her then. "I will always come back to you." He leaned down and kissed her, deeply, passionately, with all the love he felt for her.

And she kissed him back for a long moment before she pulled away. Then she asked, "Where were you going? Why didn't you come up to my front door?"

He entwined his fingers with hers and led her around to the back patio which was aglow with lights and people. And as they rounded the corner, everyone applauded. All of the hotshots were there and some of the townspeople and her co-workers.

"What's going on?" she asked.

"It's a welcome home party," he said.

"For you?" she asked, and she laughed.

"For you, Wynona," he said. "I know you felt like you lost your home when your parents passed away. I know how alone you felt, so I wanted to make sure that you knew that you were home now. That Northern Lakes is your home."

She wrapped her arms around him and hugged him tightly. "No. You're my home, Mack. I love you."

BRADEN HAD WANTED to step down as the hotshot superintendent, but his team had refused to let him. They'd insisted that he needed to stay on as their leader. But he knew who the true leader was.

The heart.

In the end they'd all followed it. His hotshots were all in love and happy. And with his wife and his son, he was happier than he'd ever been.

And he could see that it was the same for his brothers-in-law. Trick and Hank had finally set a date for their wedding now that the saboteur was gone. And he could see from the way that Mack and Wynona Wells clung to each other, that they would be getting married soon, too.

And he suspected there would be more kids coming along to grow up with little Mack. Little kids of his and Sam's as well as cousins and friends.

His team was a family. And now they were finally all safe and happy.

* * * * *

COMING SOON!

We really hope you enjoyed reading this book.
If you're looking for more romance
be sure to head to the shops when
new books are available on

Thursday 26th September

To see which titles are coming soon, please visit

millsandboon.co.uk/nextmonth

MILLS & BOON

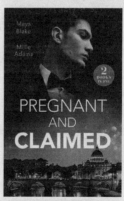

LET'S TALK

Romance

For exclusive extracts, competitions and special offers, find us online:

- **f** MillsandBoon
- **𝕏** @MillsandBoon
- **◎** @MillsandBoonUK
- **♪** @MillsandBoonUK

Get in touch on 01413 063 232